Defy the
DARK

For my friend Steve

Contents

To you, my dear friend:

Since my very first library card, I've loved nothing more than books. Through them, a kid who lived in government housing could also live in a windswept house by the sea (thanks, Lois Duncan!), in a secret-filled hacienda (thank you, Isabel Allende!), and even in the Metropolitan Museum of Art (love to you always, E. L. Konigsburg!).

Long Saturdays at the Warren Library supported my habit. I burned through novels and anthologies, bereft when I had to wait for new ones to arrive. In the meantime, I fantasized about meeting my favorite authors: we would be great friends!

We'd have tons in common, and we'd do cool stuff together, and oh yeah, they'd love to write a new story just for me. Anytime, about anything I wanted! I got older, but I never gave up the fantasy of getting my favorite authors to tell me new tales. We were friends, after all.

I loved Stephen King's anthologies especially because

they were frequent and fat, and in them, he wrote letters. (To *me*!) In *Skeleton Crew*, he said a short story is like "a kiss in the dark from a stranger."

That thought stayed with me. It rose to the surface when I wrote my first novel, my second, my third. Every time I put words down, I thought about a stranger's kiss in the dark. Anticipation and tension, romance and fear, places where bad things happen, places where wonderful things happen unexpectedly—the dark! Of course!

So I asked some of my favorite authors if they wanted to write about things that only happen in the dark—and they said yes.

From a wrong number that might be right to the blue-and-white pill that makes everything bearable, from the backseat of the Night Trolley to the smoky corners of Club Rose, this anthology contains seventeen kisses in the dark, from strangers.

They might scare you, or haunt you, or show you something you've never seen before. But these authors are trustworthy, I swear. It's safe to go into the dark with them, and this is why:

They're your friends now. They wrote these stories for *you*.

—SAUNDRA MITCHELL
INDIANAPOLIS, INDIANA

Defy the
DARK

Courtney Summers
Sleepstalk

Jed Miller is a sleepwalker.

I found out the first night I went to his house. I wanted to break his bedroom window into a million pieces. I had a rock and it felt good and heavy in my hand at first but the closer I got to his place, the lighter it became until finally, I was standing on his front lawn and I wasn't holding anything anymore. It probably would have looked bad to anyone who walked by: me, standing outside Jed Miller's house, staring at his bedroom window with no rock in my hand to break it. But no one walked by. That's how late it was.

It was also cold. Fall was giving itself over to winter and I could see my breath on the air. I wouldn't have known I was alive, otherwise. Ever since my accident, I'd been so empty. I couldn't feel anything. My parents kept telling me it could change if I just started making the effort, but they were wrong. I think they were wrong. The emptiness had to change on its own, and that night it did. It became an itch.

The itch made me pace for hours. It made me shove my knuckles into my mouth. It made my teeth bite down.

It made me crawl out of my bedroom window.

I had edged over the sill and jumped to the ground without hurting myself. I could have crept down the hall and left through the front door—I had the house key in my pocket for when I got back—but the window seemed right because it was the kind of thing I had done before, and I was trying to remember what that felt like. It was hard. I had to rewind past the Jed parts to do it except when I got past the soundless, fast reverse of him in my head, the tape would stop and if I tried to go back any farther, it was blank.

Once my feet were on the ground, I picked up a rock from our flower bed. I walked the streets with it, trying to make sense of this new feeling invading my bones, disturbing my cells. After months of nothing, it was this scream inside me begging to get out and I had to swallow to keep it down. I didn't run into anyone else. The whole world seemed dead, and for a moment I really thought it was. I tossed the rock onto the road just to hear something. The clatter of it was too loud and it made me wince.

I should tell the truth; no one will believe me, but I didn't know I was heading to Jed Miller's house, not that first time. I was told to stay away from him and I did. And if I didn't know I was heading to Jed's house that means I didn't set out to break his window, either.

It's just when I got there, I wished I had. Broken his window, that is.

Because I wanted him to see me.

I wanted to see him.

I wasn't wearing a jacket that first night. I crossed my arms and watched wisps of clouds drift across the sky. They were so faint, the stars shone through them. The moon was close to full and for as late as it was, I could see everything. It was that kind of night. Clear.

Nothing happened until something did.

The front door opened. The subtle *click* of a lock releasing interrupted the quiet all around me, and the Millers' front door swung out. I was already still but I made myself go even stiller than that. I stopped breathing.

A boy stepped outside.

It could've been anyone. It could've been Mr. Miller. It could've been Jed's brother, Erik, but it wasn't. It was Jed. He stood there and turned his face to me, and it was like a thousand knives carved themselves into my skin. I worried I'd bleed out right there, while we stared at each other, and that would be the end of me.

My lungs hurt. I never thought I'd see him again, face-to-face, even though we lived in the same town, even though the only distance between us was mere streets. I worried he wasn't happy I was there, that he'd want me to explain myself. I didn't want to explain. I wanted to ask if he thought about me to see what, if any, emotion flickered across his face when I did.

But before I could, he walked down the stone path leading to the street. He passed me and he kept walking. The shock of it froze me into place. He saw me, but it was like I was so much a part of the landscape, it didn't matter that I was there. It should have mattered.

Nothing should have mattered more.

I opened my mouth to call out to him when it hit me: he was sleepwalking.

I'd never seen anyone sleepwalk before, but some things you just know. His outfit: low-riding pajama pants, a rumpled T-shirt, mussed hair, slippered feet. Glazed eyes. He was there but he wasn't, which meant that I could be there even though I wasn't supposed to be, and with that realization, the clear night became clearer. I could breathe again.

I followed him.

I chose the opposite side of the street to do it. Each of us claimed our own sidewalk. I wanted space between us because I was still overcome with the fragility of our closeness. I didn't want to ruin it in case that night was all I had.

As we walked, I studied him. My mother deleted and burned all of my photos. I had memories, of course, but months without him faded them out so I wanted to imprint this new visual on my soul. Jed Miller is beautiful and to describe him as anything less is less than he deserves. He's a sturdy twenty-year-old with blond hair and blue eyes, the kind of eyes that make you melt. My mother said I needed to teach myself to see beyond them but I wasn't sure how I could do that when they were just as amazing as I remembered them, if not more.

Jed kept walking. I wondered where he was headed, when he'd wake up, or if he'd make it back to his room before then. I remembered hearing somewhere that waking a sleepwalker can kill them, can shock their body dead. That scared me. What if I killed Jed Miller? What if I made a noise and accidentally startled him to death?

I'd never hurt Jed unless I had to.

I turned away and left him, and yes, it was the hardest thing I'd ever done even if it wasn't the first time I'd ever done it. I took a shortcut through the Donnellys' front yard, crossing lawns until I wound up back at my house where I went inside and crawled into bed. The itch was there until the sun came up and then it turned back into the emptiness because I knew Jed was waking up at that moment and he was waking up thinking of her, maybe, and waking up without me, definitely. In spite of it, I hoped he got home safe.

Since my accident, everything is different. I don't go to school. I don't see Jed. There are no more days.

No one would believe me, but I tried hard to reconcile with what happened that first night.

I tried hard to let it go.

I wasn't supposed to be near Jed Miller, so I decided maybe it was the universe's way of helping me make peace with everything that happened and then I'd move on. Because what were the odds after months of not feeling anything, I'd get that itch that told me to leave the house the same night he just so happened to be sleepwalking?

I also tried to convince myself the itch that displaced my emptiness was a fluke, that it *wasn't* the universe, that I should take what I got and not get too greedy.

But I couldn't help myself.

In the end, I went to Jed's house a second night. Everyone would've gotten so upset if they'd known. I dressed for it. I put on a jacket and I stood outside waiting but he didn't come out so I went home. I read online you can't kill a sleepwalker just by waking them; you have to kill a sleepwalker like you'd kill anyone else.

It was a relief because I didn't want to kill Jed Miller by accident.

I also read sleepwalking is sometimes exacerbated by

stress, and then I started to hope maybe he was worried about me, he was thinking about me. The last time we saw each other was not good, so I could understand how it would torment him, and Jed's life was stressful, anyway, what with the pressure of having a father in politics and the entire family constantly in the spotlight—maybe that added to it, too. But mostly, I bet it was me.

I decided I had to be sure.

So the third night, I went to his place again. He still didn't come out. I thought I'd lose it. It was something to be there—the itch lessened, a little—but it was better when I saw him.

I sat on the curb across from his house and waited.

I went to the Millers' place sometimes. Before. But I had to. I did work on Mr. Miller's last campaign. The local TV station interviewed me and I told them I'd vote Miller if I was old enough to vote, and after that, I was occasionally asked to introduce the man himself at his rallies and talk about how much my generation believed in everything he said, like it was God's honest truth. The only thing I really believed in was Jed. I don't like politics. Politics is all strategy and secret keeping and climbing ladders and tearing people apart. But I got involved for Jed, so I had to come over. I *had* to. But it was usually Erik or Mr. or Mrs. Miller at the door—never *him*, no matter how much I hoped.

Until the day it was.

We'd talked before but only in public, at the kinds of events where everyone is on their best behavior and no meaningful words could be exchanged so nothing we said meant anything. But even when we had nothing meaningful to say, he knew I loved him. I know he did because the day he answered the door, he got right to the point. He invited me inside and told me he'd been watching me, too, and I stuttered over words that were so far removed from the normal formalities. He whispered things in my ear.

I have this way with the people I love. I always make sure they feel important around me and when you make people feel important, they want to be around you all the time.

For a while.

So that day he answered the door—Friday, June 10th, at 3:05 p.m.—was the beginning of everything. Each day after, I'd sit outside his house on the curb with my feet pressed flat against the pavement and my palms pressed flat against my knees, hoping he'd see me and invite me in and whisper those things to me all over again.

Sometimes he did. First, he'd open the door wide, gesture me over, and ask, *What are you doing here?* I never answered because there was only ever one reason I was there, and there was only ever one reason he'd open the door. Neither of us had to say it. It was our secret. He'd grin, and we'd go to his room. His hands would be on me, and I felt like I was made of electricity.

All through Jed's father's campaign it was like that. He would steal me into his room and run his hands over my skin, through my hair, and tell me how beautiful he thought I was and I loved it but I hated it, too, because as soon as those moments were over and I had to go home again, I'd feel the absence of that spark, a taste of existing without him.

I don't exist without him.

The fourth night, he finally came out again.

I was so relieved. Being close to him was terrifying but also made me feel powerful because he wasn't awake and I was and no one could stop us from happening. It was so nice. It was just like the first night; he stayed to his sidewalk and I stayed to mine. I tucked my hands in my pockets and matched his pace perfectly because I thought it would give me an idea of the kind of sleep he was having. It was unhurried and calm.

Jed. I whispered it so I wouldn't wake him. *Jed, do you think of me?*

He didn't answer.

Jed, do you think of me?

His mouth stayed closed.

I think of you all the time. Do you think of me?

He was supposed to say *yes*. Yes, he thought of me all the time. And he missed me. There was a second where it was like something stirred inside him, pulling him from sleep, and I was so sure he'd say what I needed him to say, but Roy Turner's porch light went on before it could happen and I couldn't afford to be seen by anyone, so I ran home.

The fifth night, he came out again and I followed him longer. It made me nervous. I worried he would wake up. I also worried he'd hurt himself and never make it back to his house so he could sleepwalk again and our nights together would end. That worry kept me awake.

The fifth night, no lights came on and I kept whispering that same question over and over because I needed to know.

Jed, do you think of me?

And then the most incredible thing happened: he answered my question.

But not in the way I guessed he would. When we reached the corner, he turned right. I had a feeling where he was going but I wasn't prepared for it. He took another turn, left, and it made me feel cold in a way that had nothing to do with the weather. He was going to the river. I had to stop following him. I didn't like the river. The river is where everything ended.

My parents wanted to move to a new town to get the ugliness behind us.

They meant well, but they didn't understand. I couldn't imagine giving up all these nights with Jed for days that would be hollow nothings.

I took a rock again, the sixth time out.

I wasn't sure why, but the itch made me feel like I should.

I held on to it, and he didn't show.

The seventh night was the same thing. The eighth night, I was so frustrated I decided to break his window after all. Even if it ruined everything, at least he would have to wake up and see me on his lawn. Maybe that was what was supposed to happen. He'd see me on his lawn and realize his family didn't matter; that girl he was with now, she didn't matter. What happened at the river didn't matter. I raised my arm and steadied myself. I'd never broken a window with a rock in my life—but before I could, the front door opened. He came out.

I love him.

People are funny when you talk to them about love. I don't think most people have the kind of heart I do. I've always been the kind of person who listens to my heart and follows it. When I say I listen to my heart, I mean I *have* to listen to it. It shouts at me. Sometimes it beats so loud, I can't think. When it does that, I have to pay attention, no matter what. It wasn't like the itch, it was different. It didn't tell me *what* to do, it just guided me to the people I needed in my life and then it made me wide open for them. It made me love them so much, it was hard to take.

With Jed, my heart beat louder than it ever had before.

He was the one.

One of the last times we spoke, Jed told me I needed to get him out of my head. I tried to explain to him in a letter he wasn't in my head, he was in my heart. But I didn't explain it well so I had to write another one but that one didn't do the job either, because he just didn't understand, but now I think he might have understood more than I realized.

I don't regret writing the letters, ever, but I wish Jed hadn't showed them to our parents after my accident. It made things far more complicated than they had to be.

But what's done is done.

It's not like there was anything in them he could doubt.

I couldn't follow him to the river that night, either.

Even though I wasn't ready for the river, I was ready to get closer to him.

The ninth night, I crossed the middle of the road and raised my voice above a whisper, but the words that came out of my mouth weren't the ones I meant to say.

Imagine you can't breathe. Imagine you're trying so hard to breathe, but every time you open your mouth, it's full of water and dirt you can't breathe.

As much as I loved him, I was angry with him, too.

That's how you can tell you *really* love someone. It's just, we had something good and he ruined it and now we were here and I couldn't touch him, I couldn't have a conversation with him, and my skin was burning with how much I wanted both.

I wanted to ask him how he could plan the rest of his life with her when she wasn't the kind of girl who would die for anyone. I'd give up everything for him, and now here we were, trapped in an endless cycle of nights. I needed to know what the itch driving me meant. It felt like there was something I had to do but I didn't know what and that made me angrier. I wanted him to taste the ground, but if I pushed him and pressed his face against it, he'd wake up.

Still. I bridged the distance between us and circled in front of him and then we were facing each other and seeing his half-open eyes staring right at me, I still wanted to make him eat the earth. That's the thing that worries me sometimes. I feel everything so much, it makes me say or do the wrong things. I don't think. And the things I do— from the outside they might look like the opposite of love, but they're really just actions inspired by it.

How do you think of me, Jed? I asked. I knew he thought of me, but I had to know how. *Do you think of me the way I think of you?*

I walked backward as slowly as he walked forward, and I wished again I had the rock. When they pulled me out of the river, my teeth scraped against the dirt, the stony embankment. I wanted him to know what that was like. If I had my rock, I would aim it at his mouth and he'd stay asleep while I tore up his lips and forced it against his tongue.

But then he said my name.

My name.

His voice.

I stumbled a little. He said it again but there was no flicker in his eyes so I knew he was still asleep. To hear him say it made me feel so alive and disappeared every bad thought from my head. He kept coming at me. I wanted to reach for him but instead I sidestepped and backed onto the curb. I watched him make his way to the river and wondered if, when he woke up in his bed that morning, I would just be a dream he'd had. A good dream.

The second-to-last time I saw Jed was before my accident.

It was the night the votes came in. His father won them all, won by a landslide but neither of us was concerned because we all knew Mr. Miller would win. Jed drove me home before the party was over. We sat side by side in his car and there was a nice buzz in the air but there was also a familiarity in it, too, the kind of familiarity that comes with sharing someone's soul, like you've been married for years and years.

Jed and I had that.

He pulled over an entire street away from my house and reached for my hand and then I was awkwardly underneath him and when we were finished, he said he was so glad we had time together, that I kept his head above the water, that he'd miss me. I put the first two compliments away for safekeeping, but the other I echoed back at him stupidly, not understanding. Still not understanding.

Miss me?

It was the first taste I had of drowning. The water was all around me, in my lungs, in my nose. Everywhere. I couldn't breathe and Jed had to hold me until I calmed down and even then, I only calmed down enough to ask what he was talking about.

This was nice, he said, *but now it has to stop.*

It seemed to take forever for him to understand my lack of understanding and then all of these horrible words were coming out of his mouth about this other girl and how could I not know about her, it wasn't like it was a secret. Her family was in politics, too. They'd been matched. They were in press photos together, it was broadly hinted at, well—everywhere.

You had to have known.

But love is exclusion. How was I supposed to see her in a picture of him? I said it before, but I don't really like politics. It's all strategy and secret keeping and tearing people apart. Selling your son off to another girl from a family even higher up the ladder because that's what it was, they were selling Jed, they sold him.

I screamed when he told me they were engaged and I couldn't stop screaming and in that moment, when I was screaming, I could see in his eyes how trapped he felt, stuck with her, a lifetime of her when it was supposed to be us. I kicked my legs, my arms out because I knew he didn't want her, couldn't want her.

Love is about expression.

You have to express it. You can't just let it sit inside you. You have to tell people how you feel. You have to show them or they will never know. So I called him. He didn't answer, but it was just enough to call him so he knew I cared. There were the letters, I wrote the letters, actually sat down and wrote them—no emails, no texts—and I sent them. My fevered handwriting had to make him realize how important he was to me. I did everything.

I sat outside his house and waited for him to be nostalgic about us, to invite me in. Nothing worked. He could never let on that we meant something to him, ever. I understood he was in a tighter spot than I was. He felt like he had a lot to lose, him and his family. He loved me but he was afraid he'd cost them everything. It's a terrible thing when fear overpowers love and the only way you can reverse it is by shaking a person to their core so that the fog inside their head lifts and the only thing they're thinking with is their heart.

I should stop calling what happened at the river an accident.

Jed's sleepwalking is an expression of love.

That's how I know what I'm going to do is right. I decide

to go to the river with him the tenth night, the coldest night. I have no more time to waste. I know, after it, Jed won't sleepwalk anymore. There is no way he will open the door and not feel the cold. This is our last chance. I put on my jacket and I put on my gloves. I grab a hefty rock from the garden. I finally understand the itch. I know what I'm supposed to do.

I stand outside his house, whispering.

Please come out, Jed. Come out. Please.

After an hour, my voice reaches his ears. He comes out, walking the stone path to the sidewalk and I walk next to him, dangerously close next to him, and he doesn't wake up and to anyone who sees us, I bet we look like we belong. We belong.

He turns two corners. Left, right.

You do think of me, I tell him.

I trudge after him. I am as ready for this as I was the last time we went to the river, even if it didn't end the way I wanted it to, then. It would this time.

The houses on either side of us gradually thin out and become less immaculately cared for. Jed's family avoids this side of town even though every single house was a vote for his father. I glance into the windows. There are no witnesses.

That night, that last night we saw each other at the river, went so wrong for something that started out so right. What happened was I called him and called him and promised I would stop if he agreed to meet me and talk. He agreed but said we'd have to meet somewhere private.

I was the one who chose the river.

Eventually, Jed and I cross the street and reach the brush, the brush you have to go through to get to the green bridge. His slippers crunch over the dead leaves. He doesn't wake himself but his sounds scratch my insides. When we finally step through the clearing, the roar of the water is in our ears. He pauses.

We have to go the rest of the way, I whisper.

He hears me. We move. The green bridge is what it sounds like. The metal is painted a washed-out green, always has been. It overlooks the dam and it's a walker's bridge. The wooden planks can't support cars but they hold us. My stomach twists. I step onto it with him.

He makes his way to the middle of it. He stops in front of the rail.

The last time we were here, it was like this. I was here first, waited for him, and by the time he arrived, I was crying because he looked so unhappy to be there. That was how much his fear twisted him. It brought down the corners of his mouth, made his face empty. He didn't want to be with her, but he didn't know how to be released. Even though he didn't say that, I could tell. I could tell because I know him better than anyone else.

You love me, I said, and he told me to stop it. He asked me if I wanted money. He thought I was there for money, to keep quiet about what happened and I just repeated myself over and over: *You love me.*

You love me, I said, and he shook his head. *You'll prove it to me.*

And then I stood on the rail.

Things I remember: the shock of the fall, the shock of the water, the water in my mouth, my nose, the nothingness, and then the dirt against my lips as I somehow made my way out of it alive and my family knew and his family knew and that's the only thing I like about politics now that I think about it—the secrets you're forced to keep. It was all so hush-hush. Jed's fiancée and her family could never know about us. My parents promised I'd stay away.

I remember the emptiness after. Because even though Jed was clearly bound to a life he didn't want, his heart was supposed to kick in and give him the strength to save me from falling and the act of saving me was supposed to make him realize it was me all along, I was the one. I thought because he didn't, it meant he didn't love me but it turns out I was just mixed up. He wasn't supposed to save me from drowning. We were supposed to drown together.

It's a good thing I didn't break his window that first night, now that I think of it. If I had—if I'd broken his window and he'd caught me outside his house—I wouldn't have discovered he was a sleepwalker. I wouldn't have heard the things he could never tell me in the day. I wouldn't have gotten this chance to rewrite our history in the dark, the way it was supposed to be.

My fingers curl around the rock. It feels good and heavy in my hand.

Aprilynne Pike
Nature

In the end, it's because of my hips.

The nurse doing my physical looks up from the icy calipers pressing against the skin fold at my waist. "When did you eat last?"

Caught.

"Monday," I mumble. When scores were released. There's no reason to lie; it's too late to change anything.

"I want you to go right to the cafeteria after this, do you understand? Eat something soft—yogurt, soup— otherwise you'll have a terrible bellyache."

"Yes, ma'am," I whisper.

She's still for a few moments before she loops a cold, plastic tape measure around me, pulling it firm but not tight across my navel. "You know," she says without looking me in the eye, "it's not about fat; it's your pelvic bones. They're perfect for a Nature." Her hands find my pelvic ridges and grip them almost possessively. I suppress the urge to pull away, to get her hands off me. "Good oblong girdle, wide, but with a generous depth—we'll have to do some measurements via ultrasound to be sure, but I predict a perfect-sized outlet."

"My scores are high," I blurt, not wanting my fate to be fixed yet.

"Not sure it matters," the nurse says, and marks down numbers for my waist, my bust, my hips. "These hips are going to subtract a lot of points."

"They're *very* high," I insist. It's a lie.

She laughs. "Please. Can't be all that high if you starved yourself to get your measurements down, can they?"

My face burns red and I want this physical over. I just want to leave.

And my stomach is growling.

Traitor.

Three and a half more minutes drag by before the nurse smiles. "You can go now," she chirrups in a tone that makes me want to strike her.

I grit my teeth, hating that I've succumbed to these violent feelings again. I've had a lot of them lately—it wasn't something I ever struggled with before.

Before the scores.

"I don't know how you did on your exams, of course," the nurse says, distracted as she writes more numbers on my chart. "But I suspect we'll see you tomorrow for that ultrasound. Don't fill up your schedule, just in case." Her busybody hands sweep me out the office door, quickly but not unkindly, and I shift to the side as another girl from my class gives me a nervous smile and takes my place in the examination room.

The door closes and I'm alone in the foyer. "They're quite high," I whisper to no one.

But the nurse is right—they're not high enough.

Last year I was fifteen, top quarter of my class, headed straight for the life of a Nurture. I had just finished a growth spurt that stretched me tall—five nine, with a slim, boyish figure I expected to keep. Everything was perfect.

But evidently my growth spurt was just the beginning, and I learned firsthand the definition of "late bloomer." In the last six months I'd gone from flat and skinny to curvy. I didn't think much about it until I couldn't zip up my jeans and had to go to the clothing emporium for new pants for the second time in three months. I had to fill out a special form and get my nutrition and body fat analyzed. But my fat percentage had barely changed. I just had hips and breasts now.

With the new clothes came the realization that those

hips could ruin everything.

It's been almost a thousand years since the Bust, when birth rates in the more developed parts of the world dwindled to the point that societies could no longer support themselves and collapsed. The economic devastation that followed was nothing compared to the war for resources that wrecked the environment and ended with most of Africa turned into a nuclear wasteland. It was a whole new Dark Age, characterized by the rise—and subsequent fall—of several high-control autocracies, theocracies, plutocracies, and just plain crazies.

"Doomed to failure," our government books say. And they were right. Human beings are too free-spirited to thrive under so much control. It's a concept we learn from our youth. Besides, in such a government, the balance is so precarious, it only takes one strong rebel to topple everything.

That's how New Horizon came to be. Founded by Stewart Richardson—a runaway from a totalitarian dictatorship—our community rejects the idea that a governing body should control our lives. But Richardson also knew that we had to avoid another Great Collapse (the proper name for what most people just call the Baby Bust). So, as a society, we give up a small part of our freedom for the benefits of a well-ordered community. In return, we have strict laws protecting the freedoms we most value.

It always made sense to me. How could it not?

Until five days ago.

One hundred and eight. My test score.

It's black and white; one hundred and over become Nurture. Ninety and under become Labor.

Ninety-one to ninety-nine are Nature.

If my hips weren't so big, I would have been Nurture for sure. Every inch over thirty drags down your score if you're female. For males, it's about chest circumference.

I saw the number the nurse marked down for my hip measurement. It brings my final score down to ninety-nine.

I scoop up a large spoonful of pudding and stuff the whole thing into my mouth, feeling the tingle of butterscotch on my tongue. For a moment—only a moment—it is me and my butterscotch in a world of pleasure that nothing and no one can touch.

Until I realize tears are streaming down my cheeks.

Natures are exactly average. I don't want to be average. I understand why our society is built around the mathematical median. *Extremes cannot sustain themselves.* Everyone knows that. It's the most basic principle, taught by Richardson to my ancestors two hundred and fifty years ago, when New Horizon was established. New Horizon has lasted longer than any country since the Bust, because we know that the answer to the age-old question of Nature versus Nurture is . . . neither.

And both.

Halfway. A median point. Median intelligence, median

education. That's what produces the most perfect human beings. The most *balanced* human beings. Cutting out the extremes keeps things stable.

But Richardson also understood that even the median can be taken to an extreme. Those are the more complicated philosophies, the ones they teach you when you're a Nurture—the ways to maintain the balance that keeps our community alive. I was going to spend the rest of my life learning about those ways, but one of them I already know. Everyone knows; the physical markers of females who are likely to be healthy mothers and produce healthy babies.

Good hips.

Wide hips.

One inch. And my plans for the rest of my life are shattered.

There is no ceremony. No elaborate good-byes. No awards or medals of distinction. It's just life. In the year we turn sixteen, at the end of March, we separate and go on to our assigned roles. It's the one big freedom we've given up to our governors. For our own good.

It always made sense to me.

Until five days ago.

There are no tears or heartfelt partings; it's not like we won't see each other. Nature, Nurture, Labor, we all mingle freely—a freedom that's heavily protected—but like those proverbial birds of a feather, each classification tends to flock together.

To be honest, I've never before given it a second thought. We all have different kinds of jobs. What Laborer wants their work interrupted by a chatty Nurture, anyway? Learning doesn't come easily to them, and they're often relieved to give it up. They are the pillars of support in New Horizon, and Richardson taught that we are never to look down on them. Their life is far from grueling—no one works more than forty hours a week and *never* in unsafe conditions. We have thousands of years of terrible history to teach us that breaching either of those standards is a sure road to societal dissolution.

New Horizon is better than that.

The Nurtures will head off to university. They're the learned of our society, and their mission is twofold: to enhance our society for the next generation, and to raise the next generation to enhance society. Most will go on to teach, to nurture children into proper citizens. It's the path I should be headed down.

Instead I'm following two other teenagers, one girl and one boy, to the tall, broad building where the Natures live. It's their job—our job—*my* job—to simply produce the next generation.

Well, not *simply*. Natures are intelligent enough to work what I always called the "semiskilled" jobs, because, in my mind, those jobs weren't as important as the Nurture jobs.

The job someone else is going to do now.

I'll be given a career that won't break down my body—a body that is now excessively precious to New Horizon as a whole—but that will require more skill than many of the Laborers possess. It won't be something that requires sustained focus or consistent attendance; nothing will be allowed to interfere with the creation of a new generation. I won't be assigned; I'll rotate until I find something I like, and then I'll get to choose. It's not like we're brood mares with no liberties.

But right now it kind of feels that way.

It's early evening. Most of the day workers are home. Almost all of them are through with dinner at the cafeteria and are home with friends. It's a time for socializing and enjoying life, a life that's comfortable for everyone.

I had butterscotch pudding again—*just* butterscotch pudding.

The woman leading us is barely pregnant enough to show, but not enough that it slows her down. She gives us name tags and cards that will let us into the Nature Building. She pauses at an elegant set of double doors and asks in a gentle, quiet voice, "Do you have any questions?"

I can hear that she expects there to be none. We've studied Richardson. We know our roles. We've been learning them since the first grade. There are no secrets in New Horizon.

I want to ask her if she's happy.

But I don't.

When none of us speak, she smiles, swipes her card, and pushes both doors open. I've never been here before and don't know really what to expect.

But a party?

Maybe this is normal.

We're surrounded by surprisingly attractive people gathered around tall tables that are just the right height to lean on while standing. Munchies are set out, and I feel a little sick when I catch sight of a tray of cream puffs drizzled with chocolate. I should have eaten something decent at dinner.

There are a good number of pregnant women, many reclining in comfortable chairs set around the perimeter of the enormous room. I admit, not as many as I thought there would be. I guess I expected everyone to be waddling around with swollen bellies. But there are only a handful of those, maybe one in ten.

But they look good. Weirdly. They're swathed in colorful clothing that makes them look chic and sophisticated, smiling and chatting with one another—not merely fulfilling a biological process that any female could potentially do. Prior to being initiated as a Laborer or Nurturer, anyway. Only Natures have children.

I'm trying not to stare when a shout from the front of the room mercifully pulls my attention from the women. It takes me a few seconds to locate the source of the noise, and by the time I do, he's done talking and he's raising a glass high in the air. Higher than everyone else. I crane my neck as those around him raise their own glasses in response and realize he's sitting on one of the tall tables.

A grin full of straight white teeth fills much of his face, barely leaving room for his straight nose and pale blue eyes. Messy curls top off a look that could have come straight off the cover of a pamphlet about the Natures.

I admit, I take a moment to notice his long torso and broad chest.

Oh.

Broad chest. That's the big score adjuster for males. Not only because a broad chest is indicative of both strength and virility, but because the male Natures need to be attractive to the female Natures.

So it works. So what? It's built into millions of years of my DNA.

But that's as far as it goes. This virtual god is clearly happy to be here, *wants* to be here. Probably always wanted to be a Nature and was thrilled when his chest pulled him up from Laborer.

I turn away.

I don't like him.

I slap the dough down on the floury countertop to force the air bubbles from it. I'm making a yeast-based confection called *bienenstich* from a country that vanished in the

Bust. Allemagne, it was called in some places. Germany. Deutschland.

I admit, I was surprised when I saw baker's assistant on the list of job openings suitable for a Nature, but I soon discovered there's more to the position than making cakes and bread. You oversee the regular Laborers, create new recipes, file paperwork. Marie, the current head baker, needs someone to manage the bakery when she births and then spends six months focused on breast-feeding.

Seeing as how Marie has already birthed four times and is not yet thirty, I suspect it will happen somewhat often. I look at her wide hips and wonder if they were once the same measurement as mine.

The dough. I have to think about the dough.

I've only been doing it for three days, but I like this job. I do paperwork with Marie at night and I'm picking it up pretty quickly.

After all, I am one of the highest-scoring Natures. I won't forget that.

Sometimes Marie looks at me with a strange desperation in her eyes and asks how I like the work. I get the feeling she's had a lot of Natures rotate through here—clearly none of them chose to stay. New Horizon won't force us into a job. Another freedom.

I'm happy I can honestly assure her that I'm enjoying it. The yeasty scent on the air, the feel of dough in my hands, watching a simple lump turn into something beautiful and mouthwatering in the oven . . . and cooking is a lot like chemistry, which I was leaning toward when I thought I would be a Nurture. Baking's not exactly lab work, but it has a similar charm.

It's satisfying work that, surprisingly, helps me understand Laborers more than I ever thought I would. Do they feel the same satisfaction in creating something with their own hands? In putting forth physical effort—even to the point of making their muscles ache—to be rewarded by everything turning out just so? The Laborers I oversee seem to.

Except that when their shift is finished, they go home. I stay with Marie and learn the management of the bakery. I don't mind that, either. It adds variety.

Nonetheless, at the close of my third day I'm tired, and when the bones in my spine crack as I stand, Marie reminds me that I don't have to work so hard on the bakery floor— that I can leave the mixing and kneading to the others.

To the Laborers.

"It's important that you learn not to overtax yourself," she says. "When you're carrying a little one, you'll have to listen to your body and know when to stop." With a smile she adds, "Your role as a child-bearer is much more important than your career. Don't forget that."

Like I could. It's in my face every day.

Our government would never force anyone to have a child. Or to have sexual relations. But their *encouragement* is everywhere, reminding us not only about the biology but also that New Horizon is counting on us, that we are the guardians against another Great Collapse. Already my shock is fading and I'm growing numb to the encouragement of "coupling" in the Nature Building.

Nothing is segregated by gender, and while changing stalls are available—and you can practically gauge how long a new member has been living there by whether or not they still use them; I still do—you can't expect everyone *else* to use them. Each night and morning I am surrounded by beautiful, virile bodies in various stages of undress. There's nothing sexual about it, for the most part, but it's so *different*.

Just as the strength of males makes them ideal Laborers, resulting in more male Laborers than female, the birthing capability of females is needed among the Natures, so every year there are far more girls than guys. And because that ratio isn't conducive to strict pairings, promiscuity is also encouraged.

It's still hard to accept.

I wouldn't call myself a prude, but, if nothing else, finding that one perfect someone has always been a dream of mine—a dream much better suited to a Nurture, where the ratio of males to females is a nearly even split.

But even with their sometimes carnal encouragement, the governors have tried to be sympathetic to people like me, and there is a long wing full of more private rooms where . . . well, where anything can be done. I like to take some snacks from the large gathering room and get some quiet time.

Alone.

I'm balancing a bottle of apple juice and some soft snickerdoodles (the eggs are the secret to perfect cookies) on a plate when I reach the end of the hallway. Even in this quiet, private area, I try to get as far away as possible.

I reach out a pinkie and manage to push the door handle down and kick it open.

Too hard.

It hits the wall behind it and I bite off a shriek when someone stands up from a pile of pillows on the bed.

"I'm so sorry," I apologize, throwing my arm up over my eyes.

The arm holding the plate of cookies.

They hit the floor with dull thuds, crumbling to pieces around my feet.

"My fault," a deep voice says. "I guess I didn't throw the lock all the way."

I chance a peek and the first thing I see is a completely clothed torso.

Thank goodness.

I peer behind him and don't see anyone on the bed. There's a rather high pile of pillows, but not big enough to hide a tryst partner.

My breath escapes from my lungs in a loud sigh before

I realize it and I blush at the sensitivity that marks me a newbie.

I look up at him, daring to meet his eyes for the first time.

It's him—the guy from the first night—the one with his glass raised high as though he hadn't a care in the world. As if being a Nature was the most amazing thing that had ever happened to him. I look away as if his gaze might burn my eyes. Maybe it would. It practically shines with life and vitality.

Or it did—right now he looks almost as nervous as I do.

I drop to my knees and start picking up pieces of cookie. "I'm so sorry. I was just looking for a quiet room to read and . . . and the lock, well, obviously—" I'm rambling. "I'll get out of your way. Right now." I look at the floor, my long brown hair falling around my face as I try not to look at him, red heat creeping up my neck. Maybe I can get away before it reaches my face.

"It's okay."

His voice is butterscotch.

"I was doing the same thing."

I pause and look up at him skeptically. "Reading?" The adrenaline pumping through me makes the question pop out with more disbelief than I intended.

I hear him swallow hard, and he looks away toward the window, where I can see the inky black sky and pinpricks of starlight. "Don't sound so surprised," he says, and there's a quiver at the edge of his voice.

Guilt surges through me and I mutter what's supposed to be an apology but is really only a mishmash of random syllables. The pieces of snickerdoodles are back on my plate and there's nothing I can do about the crumbs, much less the oily butter stains. "I'll go now," I murmur, my head still down. At the last second I say again, "I'm so sorry."

"It's okay!" the boy snaps, then sighs and runs his fingers through his honey-colored curls, which bounce back like feather-soft springs. "*I'm* sorry," he says, the toe of one foot blocking the door. "You're new. I'm Jeremy."

He lets the introduction hang, an unspoken invitation.

My heart is beating wildly and I can't say exactly why. After a moment Jeremy reaches out his hand, palm down. I have to tuck my bottle of juice under my arm to free up my hand, but years of social niceties, honed to instinct, have me doing just that before I can even think. My cold hand slides into his warm one.

"Kylie," I whisper before I flee.

Jeremy is everywhere.

Raising his glass in toast after toast, walking trays of food around to all of the near-due mothers to make sure they're "getting enough for you both," flirting in the hallways.

Flirting in the bedrooms.

Flirting in the cafeteria, on the streets, in front of the Nature Building.

For two weeks I stand in the shadows and watch. Everyone knows him. Everyone likes him.

Everyone *wants* him.

Not me.

Not me.

I slap down the bread dough.

Not me. He disgusts me.

Slap.

The chime above the front door rings, and I lock gazes with a set of equally shocked blue eyes.

They remind me of a swimming pool. So light they're almost clear, but still with that aqua hue that makes them unmistakably blue. They're wide in surprise, mirroring my own but, unlike mine, are lined with light lashes—almost blond—that curl ever so slightly at the ends.

Something is warm on my feet, and every inch of my skin flushes red when I realize I've dropped an entire pile of half-kneaded dough onto my shoes. I crouch so quickly, I suspect it looks like I fell. Because the klutz who just dropped eight pounds of bread dough would, obviously, also trip on it.

"Marie!" My voice is shaking; I shouldn't be so embarrassed—it's just bread dough—but the moment feels oddly tragic.

Marie hurries forward, giving me a brief questioning

glance, but not stopping to speak to me. *Thank you, thank you, thank you.*

I slip out of my shoes and try to get as much of the dough off as possible. I don't think they're a completely lost cause. But I'm glad I'm due for a new pair next month.

"Kylie," Marie says, lowering her body so we're eye to eye. I want to look up and see if Jeremy is still there, but I don't dare. "This young man is here to speak to you. I'll take care of this."

Me?

Oh no.

Not only am I going to have to look at him, I'm going to have to try to create coherent sentences.

I pad over to the counter in my stocking feet. In his defense, Jeremy isn't smiling. Not that he's scowling. I guess there's a pleasant sort of turning up at the edges of his mouth, but he's not smiling in the way that really means laughing. At me.

I don't move. I don't look at him. I say nothing.

"Kylie?"

He says my name like a question; I have to look up at him. I would rather heft a full-stuffed sheet cake from the hot ovens than lift my chin three inches.

But I do. I have to.

"There you are." And now he smiles.

My face flushes even hotter and I try to look down again, but a finger on my chin stops me. "Don't—"

It seems like the move should be seductive, a calculated finger on my face meant to flutter and excite. But something about the way his voice cuts off makes me think, somehow, that he's feeling as awkward as I am. The curiosity of that thought makes my eyelids rise—my eyes peer up to meet his.

And I see fear.

Why fear? I'm not someone to be afraid of.

"I—I have to admit I didn't expect to find you here."

"I work here," I say flatly. He flinches as though I've struck him and I don't know why that was the wrong thing to say. But it was.

He laughs with a nervous, tinny tone and runs his fingers through his hair. He's had a trim since I last watched him do that, but the curls are still silky, and instead of frizzing like most people's curls, they simply fall back against his head, soft and bouncy. "Yes, but—I didn't know," he says as if that were some kind of an answer.

Silence.

It stretches between us like sticky taffy, equally fragile, and I wait for it to break.

"I came to buy you something."

"At my job?"

"I didn't *know*—" That snappy tone again. Like there's a hot temper always bubbling just beneath a thin glass exterior. "I didn't know it was your job. I wanted to get you some kind of dessert. Something special. Since I made you break your snickerdoodles," he says, and by the time he reaches the last word I can barely hear him, his voice has grown so soft.

The taffy silence again, and dimly I realize Marie has gone to the back room and Jeremy and I are alone.

My turn.

But my mouth refuses to speak. It's dry and crumbly, like the flour.

"Maybe this was a bad idea," Jeremy says, and glances at me.

It wasn't a statement, but a question. *Is this a bad idea?*

Is it? "Butterscotch," I blurt, way too loud. My voice fills the small space, echoing off the walls.

"Butterscotch?" he echoes.

"Butterscotch cookies. The ones with butterscotch chips, I mean—the big ones dipped halfway into white chocolate," I say, inclining my head to the case full of delicate pastries. "They're my favorite."

He drifts over to the case. As if in a mirror, I scoot as well, matching him on the other side of the counter.

"These ones?" He points.

I nod, my mouth too dry to speak.

"I'll take one," he says, digging into his pocket. "Gift-wrapped, please. With a ribbon, if I could."

"Of course," I say in my cheeriest we-have-a-customer voice. This is definitely the strangest thing I've ever done. When I'm finished wrapping the box with a ruby-red ribbon—also my favorite—I set it on the counter.

"How much?" he asks, digging into his pocket.

I'm not sure. He insinuated it was for me. Is he expecting it for free? I'm not allowed to do that. "Four credits," I whisper.

We're not a strictly socialistic society. Yes, the government provides for our needs—and then some. And no, we don't get paid for our jobs. But there are numerous ways to earn individual credits that you can spend on anything you want. All of them involve going above and beyond your everyday requirements.

I'm not sure I want to know what Jeremy did that was considered "above and beyond."

He hands me his card and I run it through my scanner, deducting the four credits. It doesn't tell me what the remaining balance is. I'm dying to know and I'm not even sure why.

The box sits there like a flashing light between us.

"Meet me tonight?" Jeremy asks, and for a few seconds he doesn't look at me. When he does, I almost take a step back.

He wants this.

So much.

Not *me*. *This*. Wants me to meet him.

I'm not sure I should do something Jeremy wants so badly.

He must see the hesitation in my face. He leans forward,

so close I imagine I can feel his breath on my face. "I heard you hoped to be a Nurture. That you almost were."

I say nothing but can feel the blood draining from my face.

"Meet me?" he asks again, his voice full of pressure. Temptation. "That same room. I'll make sure it's free."

The world stops. There is only me. There is only him. There is only now.

"Yes," I breathe.

Sound returns, the world presses PLAY. Did I win?

Jeremy wants to smile, to grin. Maybe to laugh. I can tell. But he simply reaches out and slides the box off the counter.

"I'll see you at nine," he says without looking back.

He is gone for at least a minute before I pull my aching fingers away from the smudged glass.

I don't know what to expect. Have I read him completely wrong? Did he say that Nurture thing just to get me to come? Bait to draw me in only to seduce me the way he probably has a dozen others?

But . . .

I can always leave if I don't like what I hear.

See.

With that thought running over and over in my mind, I step away from my assigned cubby—one with a lock only I have the key to (right to privacy)—without looking at the full-length mirror affixed to the door.

My heartbeat pounds in my ears as I put one foot in front of the other, traversing the long, romantically lit hall. Everything in this godforsaken building is romantic.

I pause in front of the last door, the door to the room where my snickerdoodles and I humiliated ourselves in front of Jeremy two weeks ago.

As opposed to the bakery, of course, where my bread dough and I humiliated ourselves just this afternoon. The lock says OCCUPIED, the red words shining out at me like a searchlight.

Knock?

Walk away?

He said he would make sure this room was available.

I lift my hand and stand like that for a long time, my fist shaking as my courage threatens to fail me. I don't so much knock as let my hand fall in such a way that my knuckles hit the door.

Whatever happens next is gravity's fault.

The sound seems to echo and I wonder if anyone is in there at all. Maybe the lock is just jammed. It would be my luck.

The door opens.

It's Jeremy, and he lets out a breath at the same time as I do. We are a mirror—the fear, the anxiety. It's strange to see it on Jeremy's face, Jeremy who's always so confident. Cocky, even.

Which one is the act? I wish I knew.

His eyes scan the hallway. "Come in," he says, stretching to let me duck under his arm, the door inches from my back as he almost sweeps me into the room with it.

He turns the lock back to OCCUPIED with a sound like the fall of a headsman's ax. It's too late to change my mind. Not too late to run away, but now it *will* be running away, not standing him up.

Jeremy attempts a smile, but it looks awkward. He reaches down and brings out a white box from under a pillow on the bed. A bed that seems to have grown threefold and is the only thing I can look at.

"For you," he says, handing me the white box with the red ribbon. "I'm sorry it's not a surprise."

I shrug with one shoulder as I take the box. "If it was a surprise, I probably wouldn't have gotten my favorite." I'm being nice to him now. Did I do that on purpose?

He stands with his fists on his hips, looking at my feet long enough that I start to squirm.

"My score was 107," he whispers. "But my chest is forty-eight inches."

I say nothing, but my hands start to tremble. I study him. His body. He's tall—at least six five. A paragon of virility. No wonder they want him to make strong, healthy babies. His chest is particularly wide, I realize. It tapers to a narrow waist slung with jeans that are tight and loose in all the right places. He's everything any female could want. A perfect Nature.

"I don't want to be here," he says as though reading my thoughts.

"But—"

"I *know* what it looks like," he interrupts, and there's a hint of that bubbling anger. I understand now; it's not directed at me. "It's how I hide. In plain sight, you know?" He forces a short bark of a laugh and then is silent again.

He walks over to the bed and reaches for the blanket and I get ready to bolt. He throws back the covers to reveal . . .

Textbooks?

I look at him, questions in my eyes.

"I study," he answers. "Every night. It's not technically against the rules. I—I have a friend who is a Nurture who gives me—anyway . . ." He waves at the books and stops rambling.

I look over at the books and my hands ache to go stroke their shiny covers. I didn't realize until now how much I miss my classes—crave them.

I don't belong here.

Apparently, neither does Jeremy.

"I hide them up in the box spring," he says, dropping to his knees and pointing to the hammock-like shelf he's rigged there. "They vacuum under here, but no one ever really looks." He peers up at me and appears strangely small on the floor before me. "They're always here. You can come study anytime you want. But . . ." He hesitates and the fear is back in his eyes. How does he mask it all the rest of the time? I've never seen even a hint before. "What I'd really like is if you come study with . . . *with* me."

He's looking down at the ground, and I stand wordless until he looks up and meets my eyes again.

It takes a long time.

"Why me?" I whisper.

"I—I don't know," he admits. "I haven't been interested in anyone—anyone—since I had to come here. I haven't . . . I never . . . never more than just what people see," he finishes, and I'm grateful he's looking elsewhere again when my face burns red.

"But you—after that night. You made me *want* something again. Not just, you know, but company. Friendship, Kylie." He's looking at me again; he wants me to know that he's telling the truth. As if I couldn't already tell with his transparent swimming-pool eyes that can't hide anything.

Not from me. How did I not see that before?

"When I came here, it was like I died inside. And these last couple weeks, watching you— learning you—it's like I might be alive again someday. Maybe."

His eyes plead with me to say something. Anything. Even rejection.

I don't know what to say. He's laid out all the feelings in *my* heart and they resonate within me like a violin string.

Then a sinking feeling comes over me. "This is how they do it, isn't it?" I choke.

"Do what?" Jeremy asks.

"Keep us happy," I whisper, admitting to myself that for the first time since I saw the measurement of my hips, I *am* happy. "Someone for everyone. Even us."

It takes a moment before Jeremy understands and I see the realization dawn in his eyes. He looks down again. "Does it matter?" he murmurs almost too quietly to hear.

"I don't know."

Silence stretches between us and I'm not sure what to do.

Maybe I should leave.

"Stay."

It isn't a command. It's a plea.

"Stay with me." His voice is stronger now.

To stay is to admit I belong. But it also means confessing that I don't.

Is it enough?

I sink to the floor—I'm not ready to share a bed with him, even if that bed is simply a space to sit—and pull the loose end of the deep-red ribbon. Inside the box is the oversized butterscotch chip cookie; the white chocolate is soft but not quite melty against my fingers. I break the cookie in half and hand a piece to Jeremy with a tentative smile.

His eyes sparkle and for a moment I wonder if I see a

mist of tears, but he turns away and clears his throat before biting into the sweet confection. He pauses midchew, sets his piece in the white box, and reaches for the ribbon.

"May I?" he asks, and his hands are reaching toward me before I can speak. His fingertips brush the sides of my neck and my breath catches in my throat. When he's done tying the ribbon around my ponytail, he pulls away and again those warm hands touch my skin. "Red looks good in your hair."

My turn to confess. "That's why I picked it."

His eyes sparkle and I realize I've given him a gift.

He turns and stretches his long, beautiful arm up to the bed and slides a book down. "Chemistry?" he asks, already leafing through the pages.

I smile and wonder if the innuendo was intended.

But I guess it doesn't matter.

As I sit, my shoulder brushing his, the bliss of butterscotch on my tongue, I know what will happen. I see it laid out before me like a film. Jeremy and me, hiding in plain sight, living our elaborate lie. I'll wear the red ribbon, and no one will even notice. Except Jeremy, who will say nothing. Not in front of anyone, anyway. Never together in the daylight, we will laugh, and drink, and flirt, sharing only the rarest of secret glances.

But at night, we will be here.

Perhaps there will be kisses one day. Perhaps we will be lovers.

But that doesn't matter. Because now I know.
When the sun goes down we will be
Together.
I will be
Myself.
And we will find
Truth.

Dia Reeves
The Dark Side of the Moon

When Cado snuck up on Patricia in her backyard, her first reaction was not to scream but to thwack him over the head with a silver watering can.

And that was what he loved about her.

"Oh my God, Cado!" She dropped the watering can and tried to break his fall as he wilted into the petunias. "I'm so sorry!"

"Not as sorry as me," said Cado, blinking away stars similar to the red, white, and blue ones he'd seen strung in the redbud trees along the block as he'd driven up.

Charter was less than an hour from Portero, both

towns hidden within the East Texas piney woods, but while Charter consisted of unlovely acres of livestock and hay farms, Portero could have been carved out of gingerbread. By pixies. Stars in the trees, cobblestones in the streets, flowers in all the gardens. A place that charmed and disarmed with its tweeness . . . and then thwacked you over the head.

After she'd checked to her satisfaction that she hadn't cracked his skull into a million pieces, Patricia threw herself into Cado's arms and rolled him around in the flowers like she thought she was a milkmaid. "You're not even supposed to be here until tomorrow!"

"I know, but I wanted to sleep over, and I figured your folks wouldn't've agreed if I had asked first."

"That's amazingly diabolical." Patricia's kiss was like a stamp of approval. "My influence is finally rubbing off on you."

But she didn't ask why he'd come early, probably assuming he wanted to catch her in the shower or something predictable like that. Patricia knew a lot, like what all the initials in the *Wall Street Journal* stood for and how to apply lipstick so that it never smeared no matter how hard Cado kissed her. But she didn't know him. Not as well as she thought she did.

He sat up and rescued the bouquet of daylilies from where he'd dropped them after getting clobbered. The petals matched the setting sun and blazed against the black of Patricia's dress as he presented them to her. "I brought this for you."

"Why?" Patricia asked, hip deep in flowers, yet staring at the daylilies as if they were alien babies.

"Because you like flowers. Duh."

"Not as a symbol of love. Those are going to wither and die in a week. Is that what you think about our relationship? That it's going to wither and die in a week?"

"No," he said after realizing the question wasn't rhetorical.

Patricia grabbed the bouquet that he had painstakingly selected and threw it so hard, it sailed over the wrought-iron fence and smacked a passing soccer dad in the face.

Patricia didn't understand him, but sometimes Cado didn't understand her, either.

After she helped him to his feet, he grabbed his duffel bag and flute case from the petunias and followed her through the back door into her home.

"Want a cool drink?"

"Maybe later," he said, distracted by her outfit, a black dress with no back and shoes that exposed her manicured toes—definitely not a milkmaid. She smelled cold and Parisian. "You look nice."

Patricia twirled for him, showering the floor with pink petunia petals. "My folks are at a canasta party, but after they've heard all the neighborhood gossip, they'll swing by to pick me up. They're treating me to a farewell dinner at

Gitano's before you steal me away. Wanna come?"

They hadn't seen each other since he'd gone to Castelaine to see her perform two months ago. They almost never saw each other except at recitals and band camps, like the one they were driving to tomorrow. Although they talked and texted all the time, the whole long-distance thing was beyond suck. "I'd rather stay here with you."

"They'll be home any minute," Patricia insisted, and before he could stop her, she popped the zit on his chin. She was always doing that to him. "I don't care if it scars you," she'd say whenever he complained. "I'd rather look at scars than pus."

"We only have enough time to change you into something less transy," she said, dabbing his chin with a kitchen towel.

Cado held her away and looked down at himself, his worn jeans and new, blue Fourth of July T-shirt. "Transy?"

"It's short for transient." She put her hand over her mouth briefly, as though she had been impolite. "It doesn't mean anything bad; it's just what we call people who obviously aren't from Portero. Usually Porterenes wear black in public."

"How can y'all stand it? Especially in the summer." It had to be close to one hundred degrees outside.

"We're used to it, though it helps not having anything to compare it to." She led him upstairs and into her room.

"I mean, it's not exactly a law, but it may as well be."

"Why?"

"Because people die all the time here," she said solemnly, taking his duffel bag and setting it on her bed. "Death surrounds us. Did you pack a suit?"

"Um . . ." He was inclined to take Patricia seriously when she spoke of death and monsters, now more than ever after what he had seen last month, but still, her mix of weirdness and practicality always mystified him.

"I have a black shirt and pants."

She rummaged through his poorly packed bag, but after finding the shirt and pants, the search continued. "Where're your ties?"

"Ties? I thought we were going to dinner, not Buckingham Palace."

"You can take the boy out of the country," she muttered, giving him a pitying look. "I'll get something of my dad's."

Cado changed clothes while she was gone, noting the real art on the walls, the violin from Austria gleaming in an open case on her desk, the blue silk covering her bed and pillows, and the fresh yellow daylilies ironically scenting the air. He tried his best not to smudge anything.

Patricia returned and gave him her dad's jacket and tie, which he struggled into while she dumped the contents of a red purse into a metal one that reminded him of an anorexic version of his mom's toaster.

Cado examined himself in Patricia's full-length mirror.

The jacket fit tightly on his arms; if he flexed, he would burst the seams like the Incredible Hulk.

"I look like a gorilla at the opera."

"You do not! Don't be so down on yourself. You're handsome and smart"—Patricia jabbed him with the metal purse after each point—"and a soon-to-be world-famous flutist."

"I guess. You smeared lipstick on your purse."

"That's not lipstick," she said, and then applied some to her mouth, as if he had reminded her. "That's blood. And what do you mean, 'you guess'?"

"Are you bleeding?" He grabbed her hand and she wound up with lipstick on her chin.

"That's not *my* blood, silly." She swatted him away and fixed her face while he examined the purse. "It's not even fresh; it just looks like it is."

And it did, dripping across one side of the metal like an open wound but not staining his hands.

"A couple years ago, there was a plague of blood grackles," Patricia explained through lips that matched the stain on her purse. "They looked just like regular grackles, except blood grackles liked to eat people instead of worms. Fortunately they couldn't abide metal, so for a while, it was all the thing to wear metal accessories as protection. Mama bought me that purse for my birthday, and wouldn't you know that very same night, I had to bash a couple of blood grackles out of the air when they dive-bombed me. On my birthday of all days!"

She finished doing her makeup and fluffed out the curly afro puff resting cloudlike atop her head, not even interested in his reaction to her story.

No one back home would have believed her, but Cado did. Patricia wasn't the type to bullshit anyone or mince words. "Are they still around?" he asked. "Those blood grackles?"

"They got wiped out last year. All the metal was too much for them." She nodded at the purse in his hands. "That stain is all that's left, as far as I know." Patricia unknotted the mess he'd made of her father's tie and redid it. "Some of the faculty from the Shepherd School are gonna be at the retreat."

Patricia's ability to flit nimbly from the bizarre to the mundane floored him yet again. "The Shepherd School at Rice? Why do you care? I thought you wanted to go to Oberlin?"

"Rice is closer. And cheaper." She smoothed her hand over his now-perfect tie. "Cheap enough even for gorillas who play the flute."

"It'd be better for my family if I went to A&M and studied farming or—"

"The hell with your family! Just man up and make a decision, Cado, and don't hide behind your family."

Definitely didn't mince words.

"That's why I came early," Cado told her. "To man up."

The car horn startled them both. Patricia peeped through the window blinds; the dying sunlight clawed her face.

"It's my folks." She took her purse from him and tucked it under her arm. "This conversation isn't over."

Cado didn't like when she got upset with him, but he didn't mind it—Patricia was cute when she got her back up. He grabbed her hand and held it all the way down the stairs. "Do you have any other magic weapons like that purse?"

"There's no such thing as magic. Otherwise I'd send a wise old elf to tell you to apply to Rice so that we can finally be together. Not a day here or two weeks there, but really together. For as long as we want."

"I might not get in. It's not a sure thing."

"You were on *From the Top*, for God's sake. You know how many classical musicians would kill to be on that show? Rice would slit its wrists to have you enroll."

"But it's so . . . high art. You know? Tuxedos and tea sandwiches." His hand sweated all over hers just thinking about it. "That's your world, not mine."

She didn't give Cado a pitying look this time; she looked into him, there on the bottom step, and she liked what she saw. "You're awesome enough to make it in any world."

And because it was Patricia who'd said it, he believed her.

✦ ✦ ✦

Cado wanted to stick a fork in his eye, but there were four to choose from, and the Markhams would sneer if he chose wrong.

"A salad fork?" they'd say. "In the eye? Everyone knows salad forks go in the ear."

At least Patricia's folks were devoted. Not just proud of their daughter but pleased with her. Cado, on the other hand, they seemed to find thoroughly and mouth-twistingly unpleasant.

"So," said Mr. Markham heavily, as Cado toyed with the overabundance of heirloom cutlery. "Why the flute? Were the ballet classes all filled that day?"

"Don't be tiresome, Daddy." Patricia rested her foot atop Cado's and sipped from her wineglass. Red wine that looked like blood and tasted like Mardi Gras.

"I don't mind," Cado told her. "I get it worse at home. You'd be surprised at the numerous and creative ways my dad finds to impugn my manhood."

His vocabulary impressed the Markhams against their will. Those soul-numbing SAT drills had been good for something at least.

"Have you been to Portero before?" Mrs. Markham asked, her polite tone at odds with her stony expression.

"No, ma'am."

Mrs. Markham touched her daughter's hand. "Be sure to show him the sights, darling: the Old Mission, Fountain

Square. The historic district is always nice." She gave Cado a tight smile. "You can look at the pretty houses."

Cado sipped from his own wine, resisting the urge to stick his pinkie out. "That sounds like fun, ma'am."

"Does it?" Mr. Markham said. "Would you also like to go antiquing with my grandmother this Saturday?"

"Maybe. Is your granny as cute as Patricia?"

Patricia laughed and clinked her glass against Cado's. "Excellent riposte, sir. But no one is as cute as me."

Cado was saved from Mr. Markham's retort by the arrival of their waiter. While Mr. Markham ordered for everyone, Patricia and Cado began texting each other.

Patricia: You're the cute one.
Cado: Not for much longer. Your dad hates my guts.
Patricia: Sure does.
Cado: Why? Cuz I haz white skin?
Patricia: No. Cuz you haz white penis.

"I wish the two of you would stop that," Mrs. Markham said as the table shook with the force of their laughter. "That's incredibly impolite."

"It is not," said Patricia, even as she put her phone away. "We're multitasking." She kissed Mrs. Markham's cheek. "Don't be so twentieth century, Mama."

Cado considered taking some of the bread that had been left with them—and that had been architecturally arranged with more thought than the Sydney Opera House—but lost his nerve at the last minute.

"Which college are you going to?" Mr. Markham asked him.

"Um . . ."

Patricia said, "He's trying to decide between Rice and A&M."

"It just depends on how things work out," Cado added when Mr. Markham kept staring at him.

"With the Young Artists' Retreat or with my daughter?"

"Neither. It all depends on the night trolley."

The Spanish guitarist seemed deafening in the intense silence that followed Cado's statement.

"What do you know about the"—Patricia lowered her voice—"night trolley?"

"About a month ago I was on a hunting trip with my uncles. We thought we were about to flush a wild hog from the bushes, but it wasn't a hog.

"At first I thought it was a naked man running wild in the woods, a maniac or something. But even as I thought it, I knew it wasn't a man. It wasn't human. It had sick white skin and needle-sharp teeth and a head three times as big as mine."

Patricia said, "Big as a pumpkin?"

"Yeah!" The recognition on their faces healed something in Cado he hadn't known was damaged. His family had half convinced him he'd been seeing things.

Even his uncles who had seen the same thing he had.

"A cackler?" Mrs. Markham said to her husband. "In Charter? I've never heard of such a thing."

"They get out, but they don't last long." Mr. Markham turned a sour eye on Cado. "Certain people aren't as tolerant as we are."

"That wasn't any sort of thing I was ready to tolerate," Cado said. "It was already dying when we flushed it out, but it was more than ready to take us all with it. I got in behind it with my hunting knife and put it down.

"My uncles buried it and said not to tell anybody. That even though it was a crazy mutant, we could all end up in jail."

"A mutant?" the Markhams exclaimed.

"Uncle Beau said that was the only logical explanation."

"That a man was bitten by a radioactive pumpkin and became a mutant?" said Mr. Markham. "That kind of logic?"

Patricia said, "What does any of that have to do with the night trolley?"

"Uncle Beau said that it came from here. That Portero was full of mutants. And he told this story about a friend of his who moved here. The locals started in on him, telling him he should move back where he came from, that he didn't have what it took to live in their town. So Uncle Beau's friend asked what was the bravest thing anybody could do. And they all said the same thing: ride the night trolley.

"They said it was a kind of ghost on wheels that only came in the dead of night, and people who rode it were never seen again. They told him that if he could survive a ride on the night trolley, every Porterene would worship him as the most hard-core badass in all creation. So Uncle Beau's friend agreed.

"They sat with him at the stop till three a.m., and after the trolley appeared out of thin air, they watched him climb aboard. They waited all night for him to come back, but he never did.

"You Porterenes have your cacklers and your blood grackles and no fear of anything. Except this one thing. That's the reason I came early, to do what Uncle Beau's friend couldn't— ride the night trolley and live to tell the tale. If I can be brave enough to do that, to experience something that even a Porterene thinks is scary, I can be brave enough to do anything. Even become a classical musician."

At the end of Cado's long, heartfelt recitation, Patricia and her parents laughed. They laughed until they couldn't breathe.

But Cado was a redneck who played the flute. People would probably still be laughing at him at his own funeral.

After dinner, Cado and Patricia escaped her parents and went to Fountain Square to watch the fireworks with her friends who were all band geeks and, like Cado, played uncool instruments: the oboe, the xylophone, the piccolo. Everyone wore black, just as Patricia had claimed, but they also managed to show their patriotism with Fourth of July buttons and hats. Several people had painted the American flag on their faces.

As they sat together in an amphitheater—with a huge fountain at its center spouting red, white, and blue water—Cado noticed that the Porterenes shared an odd resemblance; but not like relations, nothing that simple. More like they had once all been held hostage together and still bore the psychic scars.

After the fireworks show, Cado and Patricia left the square and strolled past businesses still open, past people chatting under awnings and on the cathedral steps and on benches, in no hurry to be anywhere.

The night was warm, but Patricia was cool on his arm. Cado had never seen her break a sweat. The knowledge that she'd never done a hard day's work—unlike the women in his family, who worked on a pig farm—secretly pleased him.

"Why didn't you want to hang out with my friends?" she asked, curious instead of upset.

"It's getting late."

"You wanna go home?"

"No." They went up a short flight of steps to a part of the street that held more homes than businesses and so was correspondingly quieter. "I wanna find that trolley stop."

"That joke stopped being funny two hours ago."

"It's not a joke."

Patricia stopped walking, and so Cado left her behind. He didn't have to search for long. The stop was just a few yards down the street, bathed in the warm glow from the windows of the skinny brick homes that stood in a row behind it.

Patricia ran after him and then blocked his way. "You are not getting on that trolley."

"Sure I am," said Cado, lifting her out of his path. "It'll be good for me. The kind of experience that'll put my whole life into perspective."

"Or kill you!"

"Either way." He sat on the blue bench next to the brown-and-white trolley stop sign. "Death is an answer."

"Death is a question. The ultimate question." Patricia tugged at him but didn't have the muscle to move him off the bench.

The more frantic she became, the calmer Cado felt, happy even. She wasn't laughing at or pitying him now.

Patricia gave up her attempts to haul him bodily from the trolley stop and instead sat beside him. She took his face in her hands, forcing him to look at her. "Only one person ever came back. One person. Who gave birth to many, many babies. With many, many legs."

"Obviously I'm not gonna give birth to anything," said Cado, amused.

"It was a guy who came back," Patricia said, stabbing Cado's amusement in the back. "And his babies ate him alive; he smiled the whole time." She didn't see what she wanted in his face, so she released him and stared out into the street. "They killed all the babies, of course, but there's one on display in the museum."

"Bullshit!" Cado said before he could stop himself. Before he remembered that Patricia wasn't a bullshitter.

"I'd show you if it wasn't closed. The trolley—the regular trolley—is part of the museum. A rolling exhibit. They started work on it in the 1800s, but they ran out of money. So it doesn't go anywhere. Tourists get on from the museum, and it takes them around the square and that's it. Except not really. Sometimes people travel a lot further than they ever intended.

"This town is full of doors. Crawl spaces. Jagged little holes that you never see until you step through them. That's why we have things like cacklers and blood grackles and the night trolley.

"The man who had the babies? He said the trolley took him to the dark side of the moon, only it wasn't dark at all, but filled with a light so pure and holy that he couldn't stop smiling. The things he gave birth to, though, were neither pure nor holy."

Cado saw it then, the gulf between them—he never had before. He stared at her the way she'd stared at his daylilies: like she was an alien. That inexplicable awareness screamed from her face, as loud as language.

"When you shine a light into the dark places," Patricia continued, "you see the world as it really is. The rats pee-ing on your toothbrush, the roaches laying eggs in your shoes, the bogeyman salivating as he watches you sleep. You don't want to see those things."

"Sure I do."

"You do not!" Her voice scared a pigeon into flight. "You don't even want to face the truth—that you'd rather die than be looked down on for being a candy-ass flutist!"

Cado knew that the truth hurt, but he'd never felt its jagged claws rip into him before.

He fished out his cell and pressed the number three nine times. When Patricia realized what he was doing, she tried to bat the phone out of his hands, shocked that he even knew what to dial.

"Wait!" She grabbed his wrist before he could press SEND. "This isn't a game, Cado. Why can't you understand that? Sometimes people prank call that number, just to see what will happen, and then they don't show up to take the ride. So the trolley pulls up in front of their homes and gets them."

Cado knew that Porterenes were scared of the night trolley, but seeing that fear on Patricia's face frightened him in a way all her talk had not.

"If you call," she said, her icy fingers digging into his flesh, "it will come for you."

"And take me to another world? You said I could make it in any world. I believe you. Even if you don't really believe in me."

He pressed SEND.

Patricia's hands flew to her mouth as if to stopper a scream.

"Night trolley." The bored, sexless voice was decidedly unfrightening.

"This is Cado McCoy." He took a deep breath. "I need a ride."

"It's a dollar, one way."

Cado said firmly, "This'll be round trip."

"This stop, three a.m.," said the voice. "Don't be late."

After he put his phone away, Patricia said, "Do you realize what you've done?" She couldn't look at him, her hands still covering the lower half of her face.

"I'm not afraid—"

"Because you're an idiot!"

"—of the trolley," Cado continued calmly. "But knowing you don't have any more faith in me than I do"—he touched Patricia's face—"now, that's scary."

Cado had meant to rest before his otherworldly appointment, but it was impossible. Mr. Markham kept coming in to check that he was still in the guest room and not lolling sexily in Patricia's bed. When the door opened for the fifth time, Cado threw his pillow at it.

"Dammit, Mr. Markham, I'm—"

But it wasn't him.

Patricia snuggled next to Cado, her gown soft, but not as soft as her body through the gown. Her feet curled around his ankles. She must tiptoe across the backs of geese and the tops of clouds to keep such velvet skin.

"If I were nicer," she whispered, "you wouldn't be doing this, would you?"

He brushed his thumb over the tip of her nose. "You're the nicest girl I know."

"I'm not nice! I wish I had a dungeon so that I could throw you into it and chain you up until this madness leaves you."

"Would it be weird if I said that sounds like fun?"

His alarm went off, and he had to leave Patricia's embrace to shut it off. He turned on the lamp and got dressed.

Patricia threw back the covers and held out her arms. "Come back to bed." Her nightie wasn't black, but sunset-colored, like the daylilies she hadn't wanted. Her toes sparkled at him.

"I refuse to be distracted by your body right now," Cado said, lacing his Chucks. "But feel free to distract me with it tomorrow."

"What tomorrow?" she said bitterly, and then with an equally bitter resolve climbed out of bed. "I'm coming with you."

"No way."

"Why not? We're the Bonnie and Clyde of the classical music world, and they died together in a car—we'll die together on a trolley. I'd prefer a private jet or a yacht, but I'll take what I can get."

"It doesn't count if I bring a brave kick-ass girl to hide behind. I have to do this on my own."

"You're taking your flute?" Patricia asked when he grabbed his case.

Cado stroked the cracked black leather. "Turns out I don't need your magic purse after all. I got my own right here."

"*A flute case?*" she said in a voice too shrill for two a.m. "You think you're one of the Hardy Boys or Harry Potter? That if you're clever and plucky, you can play a tune and save the day with the power of music?"

"I know what I'm doing," he reassured her. "And it doesn't involve pretending to be the Pied Piper."

"What does it involve?" she asked, not in the least reassured.

"What's going on?"

Mr. Markham's robed appearance in the doorway barely registered, Cado and Patricia too busy staring into each other's eyes as if for the last time.

"Nothing," said Cado, finally looking away. "I was just leaving."

"Where do you think you're going at this hour?"

"To learn about fear," he said, his mind already on the adventure ahead. "About real fear."

But instead of walking out the door, he looked back at Patricia and immediately wished he hadn't. She seemed bruised somehow, as if he had struck her. That's how she would look at his funeral. Of course she wouldn't stand over his grave and laugh at him. Cado was amazed he had ever thought such a thing.

"I wish I had kept those flowers," she said. "Looks like they were a good symbol after all." She put her hands on his shoulders. "At least kiss me good-bye?"

Cado kissed her between the eyes and once on each cheek.

Patricia made a tsk of impatience. "That's not good enough!"

"That's because it wasn't a good-bye kiss. Just, you know, a 'see you later' kiss. I'll kiss you for real when I get back."

"What is going on around here?" Mr. Markham asked as Cado escaped downstairs.

Patricia answered but her tears distorted the words. Her father's response, however, was as clear as arsenic:

"You should have kissed him good-bye."

St. Teresa Avenue was within walking distance of the Markhams' home, so it didn't take long to reach. Cado had the town all to himself, the shops now closed and the street empty. His steps echoed like a giant's. The purple-tinged fairy glow beneath the lampposts only illustrated the absence of light.

Cado went up the steps that beveled the sidewalk and stumbled over an indistinct lump. No. Not a lump. A person.

A bum?

A stroke victim?

"Hey, you okay?" Cado grabbed what felt like an arm and pulled the person beneath the lamppost a few feet away. The weak light illuminated a woman in black sweats with long, pale hair and no face. It had been peeled neatly off from hairline to chin like the skin from an apple.

Cado scrambled away and fetched up against the blue bench at the trolley stop. After winning the struggle to free his phone from his pocket, he sat and dialed the sheriff's office with fingers that had gone numb and spoke with a voice he hadn't used since he was thirteen.

"A woman without a face?" the deputy was saying, uninterested. "Another one? We'll get someone out there as soon as we can, miss."

Miss? Cado looked down at himself, then quickly away. If he looked too long, he might grow breasts. Or if he looked directly at the dead woman, his own face might peel off for no reason. The world felt dangerously malleable.

He called Patricia.

"Cado? Is it over already?" The hope in her voice was

painful to hear. "Cado?"

"Am I awake?"

A long pause. "You were when you left," she said, all hope gone. "You sound weird. I'd tell you to come back, but it's in God's hands now. God's or whoever's. Why aren't you saying anything? Cado!"

"There's a dead woman on the sidewalk," he whispered. "Her face—"

The line went dead.

Out of the corner of his eye, he watched the dead woman prop herself against the lamppost, giggling facelessly.

The phone cracked in his fist; otherwise Cado didn't react. If he ignored the dead woman, surely she would remember she was supposed to be dead and shut up.

A thick tearing split the air. Like whatever had stolen the dead woman's face had decided to rip it in half. Only nothing so small as a face—this was vast. Mountainous. The sound of the world clawing itself open so violently, the force of it snuffed out the scant halos of light beneath the lampposts.

The cathedral bells chimed but distantly, as if they were miles away instead of down the street. On the third chime, the trolley appeared.

Cado squinted against the sudden light it brought. The single burning headlight and the interior lights all cast a feverish glow. Even the trolley itself was the yellow of something spit up from a diseased lung.

The doors accordioned open when Cado stood. For several moments his legs refused to move forward, but once he took the first step, it became easier.

Cado noticed an animal stink as soon as he boarded, like the inside of an iguana cage. The odor emanated from the motorman crammed into the driver's seat, too tall for the space if the awkward jut of his knees was any indication. The motorman had no eyelashes, and his lids made a gummy smack when he blinked.

"One dollar." It was the same sexless voice Cado had heard earlier, but it didn't belong to the motorman. It came from a speaker on the control panel. A recording.

Cado put two Sacagawea coins into the cash box. "I told you," he said, proud that he no longer sounded like a girl. "Round trip."

He turned to take a seat, and a sharp pain stabbed through the base of his skull just before the doors banged shut.

Cado grabbed the back of his head and whipped around in time to see a stinger retreat into the motorman's palm as he grabbed the lever and set the trolley in motion.

"What did you do to me?"

The motorman punched a button on the control panel, and the voice hissed once again from the speaker. "Sit."

Cado realized, just as he had with the cackler, that he was in the presence of something inhuman. Not just smelly and misshapen, but inhuman. Something he might have been tempted on any other day to stomp beneath his shoe, but today he did as he was told. He went to the back of the trolley and sat on the hard wooden seat. The sting hadn't hurt him; it simply made everything floaty and pleasant.

Above the windows but below the arched roof were old-timey ads for stuff like Dictaphones and athletic trusses and nerve food, whatever that was. The ad didn't show what nerve food looked like, only a woman holding her head in agony, and a bunch of words he wasn't close enough to read. He wondered if nerve food was good for what ailed him.

Cado touched the sore spot on the back of his head, and his finger came away bloody. The motorman had stabbed him in the brain or maybe the spinal cord. Both? Either way, Cado should have been dead. Or paralyzed. Or at least worried. But the only thing he felt was the trolley propelling him through town. And then out of town.

Cado no longer recognized the landscape. East Texas was thick with piney forest, but the passing trees were massive, big enough to tunnel through, which the trolley frequently did. After a few moments, it began a steep ascent, and the giant trees fell away as a city rose before him.

It was what Cado imagined New York City must be like, only with buildings so tall they were wreathed in clouds. The tracks twined about the mile-high, artfully sculpted towers like ribbon unspooling from a beautifully wrapped gift.

At the height of the track, the trolley paused and Cado's window aligned with the top window of one of the skyscrapers. A woman sat inside at a vanity applying mascara to the third eye in her forehead. That third eye winked at Cado just before the trolley plunged into freefall. Into darkness.

The track leveled off seconds later, and after Cado's stomach had settled back into place, he realized the trolley lights had shorted out, maybe damaged by the rapid descent. Outside, however, glowing pink corkscrews of light spiraled down in the dark like fancy New Year's Eve confetti.

After a few moments, it began to get lighter inside the trolley, not the same feverlight as before, but bluish and intense. Cado could see again, the motorman hunched at the front, the hand straps hanging like nooses, the ads. The nerve-food woman was still holding her head, but now she was laughing. Even though her body was peppered with almost comically large bite marks.

Cado tittered nervously and turned away, but the strange light had destroyed the exterior view. He could only see his own reflection, half asleep like a boy daydreaming in class. Or nightmaring. Waiting for a rap on the knuckles to snap him out of it. But there was only the motorman who had stabbed his brain and robbed him of his fear, which was fortunate because Cado realized he could see inside his own head.

The blue light shone through him like radiation, his brain barely visible, obscured by a thick whitish soup. Like whatever the motorman had shot into his head had turned it into a giant zit. Without thinking, Cado put his hands over his ears and squeezed. Patricia would have done it if he had allowed her to come. He could no longer remember why he'd been so against it.

Fluid gushed out of the hole at the base of his skull and splatted against the back window. He could see his brain now, clean and clear. Everything was clear. And so bright. Not just in the trolley. He could see past his own reflection to a moon as big as the Himalayas crowding the horizon so closely, Cado could see its pockmarked texture. The light it cast fell on him like a weight and killed even the possibility of shadows.

The gleaming stretch of track skated over swirls of rock, valleys of ice, but his view of the terrain was eclipsed by a horde of creatures that mobbed the trolley, scuttling alongside like fans chasing a pop star's limo. But these fans, like the motorman, weren't human.

The creatures were small. Half Cado's size. Children, really, from the waist up, but from the waist down they had too many legs. Too many to count. So many they were able to easily keep up with the trolley, which had begun to slow down.

They peered at Cado, their gummy eyelids smack-smack-smacking at him. Interested in him. Waiting for him.

After the trolley came to a complete stop, the motorman unfolded from his seat and faced Cado. The sick moonlight shone through him, revealing an unfamiliar grouping of organs, a swish of pale blood, and the motorman's legs—his real ones—unfurling wetly up the walls to make room.

Cado, without realizing it, had begun whistling "Tango Etude No. 5" to give himself something nice to listen to instead of the motorman's scabrous approach. He wished the poison in his head was back. There had been no room for fear then—now fear was the only thing he had. That and his flute case.

He reached for it, careful not to look down and see his own quivering guts, his frozen blood. He still couldn't feel his fingers, but he saw them snatching open the latches, saw through them without meaning to, his own blood not frozen but red and frantic when he grabbed the hunting knife from the case, the one he'd killed the cackler with. It was a foot long at least, bone handled, and sharp enough to decapitate a wild hog.

Cado's arm whipped at the motorman, at those endless legs, at the chest, at the face with its gummy eyes shocked to see prey fighting back. Cado let his seemingly demonic arm do all the work as the rest of him screamed while blood splashed over the trolley walls like water.

When the spider children began to scream with him, an almost beautiful sound, like wolves howling, Cado's arm stopped swinging. Because the motorman was dead, just an untidy leggy heap.

Cado clambered over the motorman and settled into the driver's seat. He put the trolley into reverse and hid from the light as best he could.

The trolley pulled up in front of the St. Teresa stop and Cado exited, his eyes so traumatized by light that several seconds passed before they adjusted enough to see Patricia sitting on the blue bench. Her sunset gown covered with a black silk robe. Her feet bare.

Her toe polish chipped.

"You came back," she said wonderingly, staring at him like she'd never seen him before.

Cado grabbed her and lifted her off her feet. "Why are you running the streets barefoot like a country girl?"

"Never mind my feet!" She squeezed him even harder than he was squeezing her. "You sounded so weird on the phone. I just knew—"

Whatever she knew was drowned out by the cathedral bells striking four.

He'd only been gone an hour? It had felt like a million years. Yet there was the dead woman, as faceless as ever but no longer animated. The lampposts were on again. Maybe they'd never gone out—he had gone out.

Cado buried his face in her neck. "You smell good."

"Like Paris, still?" said Patricia, amused that he thought such things when he'd never been out of Texas. "Or maybe like Amsterdam?"

"Like life."

"You know now, don't you?" she said. "What I meant about reality?"

He nodded, then tried to speak, but it took a while. Patricia understood. She lived in a town where everyone understood such things. But only he had survived it.

He sat with her on the bench and told her what had happened.

"How strange," Patricia said when he was done, staring at the trolley and the spidery surprise inside. "But it'll make a nice addition to the museum exhibit, I'm sure. Can I see the knife you killed it with?"

"You can have it," said Cado, handing her the case. "That can be our symbol, since you hate flowers."

"Your flute can be our symbol?" said Patricia, confused.

"My flute's in the trunk of my car still," Cado explained, snapping the latches open. "I lost the sheath to my hunting knife, so I've been carrying it around in this old case ever since."

Patricia turned the knife, cloudy with alien blood, this way and that. "What's the symbol?"

"That our love can destroy anything." As soon as Cado said it, he regretted it, struck by a powerful image of Patricia and him rampaging like Godzilla, trampling whole cities into rubble.

"Cado"—Patricia clutched the knife to her chest—"that's so sweet!"

He took her in his arms, carefully, and then kissed her. "And just for the record," he said, "that wasn't a good-bye kiss, either."

Some time later, after Cado had insisted on dressing her feet in his Chucks, they began the walk back to Patricia's house.

"Are you brave enough to make a decision now?" she asked him.

"Rice," he said immediately. "If they'll have me."

Her squeal of joy echoed over the whole town.

"I feel stupid to have been so worried," he said, the bricks of the sidewalk cool beneath his socks. "Life's too short not to do what you want."

"Sorry I didn't believe in you," Patricia said as they stepped over the dead woman in unison. "I do now. You look like one of us—brave and confident. A touch insane."

His stomach growled.

"And hungry."

"I can't be hungry," said Cado, almost offended by his stomach's insistent rumbling. "I was nearly killed, like, ten minutes ago."

"Life doesn't stop just because a spider creature nearly lays eggs in you, Cado. Of course you're hungry. There's lobster salad left over from lunch." She smiled. "Or we could have tea sandwiches and caviar."

Cado sighed. "Do I have to wear a tie?"

"I'll make an exception," Patricia said generously, "just this once." Arm in arm, they disappeared blithely into the dark.

Malinda Lo
Ghost Town

1. October 31, 11:57 p.m.

cKenzie shows up at the Spruce Street Guest House a few minutes before midnight, dressed all in black as if she's some kind of ninja. She's even got a black stocking cap pulled over her blond hair, which is sticking out from the bottom in a luminous sheet and ruining the disguise. She's carrying a backpack, out of which she pulls a flashlight. "Ty?" she whispers.

She can't see me. I'm leaning against the back of the house, and the light of the half-moon doesn't reach that far into the covered porch. I step forward and she squeals in fright.

"Jesus! You scared the hell out of me."

"Sorry," I say. "You sure you want to do this?"

She huffs a little, as if I've offended her. "Whatever, you just startled me. I'm prepared for what's in *there*." She clicks on the flashlight and sets it on the top step while she opens her backpack to rummage through it. "I brought an audio recorder and a video recorder, although it probably won't pick up much in the dark." She pulls out a slim metallic device and hits the power button. A tiny red light glows at the tip. "Audio's on. I'm putting it in the outer pocket of my backpack so it'll be recording the whole time." She stuffs her video camera into her pocket and slings her backpack on again. "You ready?" she says, picking up the flashlight.

"I guess. I didn't bring any equipment."

McKenzie grins. "That's what I'm here for. This is your first ghost hunt; how would you know?"

"Uh . . . TV?"

McKenzie laughs and climbs the porch steps. "Don't believe everything you see on TV." The back door is locked, but McKenzie pulls a key out of her pocket.

"Where'd you get that?" I ask.

"Kelsey's mom's on the Pinnacle Ghost Tour staff. Kelsey swiped it and made a copy." She unlocks the door and pushes it open. The hinges whine, a thin, shrill noise as unpleasant as fingernails down a chalkboard. "You ready to see what Pinnacle's all about?" McKenzie asks.

There's a hint of a come-on in her voice and, despite

everything, it gets to me. I wish I could see her face, but it's too dark. "You bet," I say, and I follow her inside.

Pinnacle, Colorado, bills itself as the Salem of the Rockies—except there have never been any witches here, and it's not exactly in the mountains. But people love that slogan, even if it's a marvel of false advertising. Pinnacle is a dinky little town on the flat part of Colorado (people always seem to forget about the flat part), an hour and a half from the Rockies and a light-year from San Francisco, where I grew up. I moved here with my parents and little sister in August when my dad got a job at a technology company. They like to think of Colorado as a social experiment—a chance to see the middle of America—but I think of it as time in purgatory. I have one year left of high school, and then I'm heading back to Cali.

The only good part about being here, at least until tonight, has been McKenzie.

She enters the kitchen and shines the flashlight around. It's dirty and dilapidated and creepy: everything a haunted house is supposed to be. A bunch of the bottom cabinets have rotted, making the counters slope toward the floor. The upper cabinets have mostly lost their doors, turning them into yawning black boxes displaying a few pieces of chipped china. The ancient stove looks like it hasn't been operational in decades, and the once-white sink has reddish stains in the bottom. "Gross," McKenzie murmurs as she looks down into the sink.

The Spruce Street Guest House is on Old Main, which was the center of town during its heyday in the late 1800s. Back then, when coal mining was Pinnacle's chief industry, this place was the Wild West equivalent of a bustling metropolis, complete with eight saloons, a brothel or two behind the tracks, and plenty of gunslingers who went around shooting people whenever they had a bad day. When the coal mine dried up, so did Pinnacle, and for a long time it really was a ghost town. During the tech boom of the nineties, it came back from the dead. Now there's a brand-new "downtown," centered on a strip mall anchored by a Super Target. But the buildings on Old Main were abandoned, and they developed a reputation for being haunted by the ghosts of those gunslingers and their victims.

Personally, I think it's all a big gimmick, but the first thing I learned when I moved here was that the locals take their legends seriously. Every Halloween, Pinnacle dusts off Old Main to create a quote-unquote ghost town for the annual Pinnacle Spooktacular, a week of "family friendly" activities celebrating the ghostly remains of the town's outlaw past. It culminates in the Spooktacular Spectacle, a dance in the ramshackle theater on the eastern end.

The guesthouse is on the western end. We can't hear the music down here, though I know the party's still going on. By now all the little kids have gone home, and the few teens who remain are being edged out by adults in sexy zombie nurse costumes. I saw some of them lurching around half drunk on my way to the guesthouse.

McKenzie heads out of the kitchen and I follow. The only sounds are the whisper of our footsteps and the occasional groan of the floorboards. It's in pretty good shape for a building that's been abandoned, and I know it's because the Pinnacle Spooktacular has renovated it— discreetly, of course—to make sure that tourists don't accidentally fall through the floor on the ghost tour.

Still, it's definitely got a creepy vibe going on. We walk down the long hallway toward the front of the building, passing the door to the basement, a dining room with a crooked chandelier, the decrepit powder room, and finally the main parlor, where all the furniture is draped with yellowing sheets. In the foyer, a staircase that used to be grand sweeps down from the dark second floor, and McKenzie turns to face me.

"Have you heard the story about this place?" she asks.

I shrug. "Somebody died?"

Her lips curve up in a slight smile. "Yeah. Somebody died." She starts up the stairs. "This used to be a boardinghouse, and one of the people who stayed here was a woman named Ida Root. She was from the East Coast and came out here for a teaching job. She didn't have a lot of money, so she ended up sharing her room with another girl, Elsie Bates. Ida came back from school late one night, after dark. She was feeling sick and decided to go straight to bed."

McKenzie stops at the top of the stairs and waits for me, the flashlight beam pooling on the floor. The last step creaks under my feet. "What happened then?" I ask.

"In the morning, Ida woke up. Elsie was right there in the room with her . . . except she was dead."

McKenzie's a good storyteller, and a shiver runs down my spine.

"Somebody murdered her and wrote a message on the wall in her blood."

I step closer to McKenzie, so there's only a foot of space between us. She holds her ground, but the flashlight wavers in her hands. "What did it say?" I ask.

"That's the weird thing," McKenzie whispers. "There's no record of that. But there were plenty of rumors going around town about Ida and Elsie. Whether they were more than friends."

McKenzie's expression is unreadable, but warmth flushes across my own face, and it pisses me off. I've heard this story before, although it's usually set in a college dorm or at summer camp. I can hardly believe that McKenzie thinks I'm going to buy it.

"The room where Ida stayed is the third door down," McKenzie says. "Want to take a look?"

"You think her ghost is in there?"

"Maybe," she says coyly.

The door has an old-fashioned crystal handle, and

McKenzie fumbles with it for a few seconds before she gets it open. She goes inside, but stops abruptly.

"Oh my God," she says, her voice quivering. "Oh my God."

I follow her in. The moonlight shines through the window, which is hung with lace curtains. The room has a rusted metal bed frame in it, the mattress long gone. A chipped pitcher and basin rest on a bureau that's missing half its drawers. A rocking chair is pushed into the corner, the woven seat eaten through in the center. McKenzie trains her flashlight on the wall over the bed. A word is scrawled there, red letters dripping down the peeling wallpaper.

DYKE.

A shock jolts through me, hot and cold all at once. I become aware of a dim buzzing in my ears as I stare at the word. The whole effect is, I have to admit, very well done. The drips look just like blood, and it ties in perfectly with the story McKenzie just told me, although I know that the word isn't about Ida and her maybe-girlfriend Elsie.

It's for me.

I've been to the Dyke March in San Francisco and seen women with the word tattooed on their shoulders or written across their chests in lipstick. I've never used it to describe myself because it sounds so old. But it doesn't bother me, either. It stopped offending me a long time ago.

Seeing it like this, though, is a lot different from seeing

it tattooed on a girl's arm with a heart around it. I feel like I just got my breath knocked out of me. As if someone came over and shoved me, then spit in my face.

I hate Pinnacle.

All the frustrations I've felt since I moved here knot up inside me in a burst of hot anger. I want to punch the person who wrote that on the wall.

I know that McKenzie's watching me, trying to figure out why I didn't scream and run out of the room in terror. I'm not sure what to do. To buy time, I walk past her to the wall and reach out to touch the red letters. "What are you doing?" she cries.

The stuff that was used to write the word is still a little damp, and it rubs off on my fingers. I sniff it.

"What is it?" she asks.

It's sticky and has a chemical smell that I recognize. It's fake blood. They probably bought it at the Super Target in the Halloween aisle. "I don't know," I say impulsively. "It's kind of . . . warm."

"It's warm?" She sounds confused.

"Yeah," I lie. I rub the fake blood residue onto the wallpaper, leaving a streak next to the D. "I heard a different story about this house," I say as I turn to look at her.

She visibly stiffens. "You did?"

"I read it on the town blog."

"Oh?"

Her tone is skeptical, and I wonder if I'm pushing it too

far, but the anger inside me is developing a reckless edge. "Yeah," I say. I cross the room toward the window so that I can peek at the backyard. There's nobody there, or at least nobody I can see. "You want to hear it?"

McKenzie hesitates. Then she says, "Sure, why not." It's not a question. She's acting all cool, but I can tell she's trying to figure out if I know what she did, and if so, how.

It's so clear to me that the word on the wall isn't *real* to McKenzie. It's a four-letter word chosen for dramatic impact. She doesn't get that the word and her ghost story suggest that a woman was murdered in this room for being gay. She probably thinks it's funny. I almost choke on my disgust for McKenzie. But I force myself to swallow it, because now I know what I'm going to do.

"I read that back when this place was a boardinghouse, two chicks died," I say. "One was probably the girl you told me about—the one who died in this room. But another girl died here a couple of days later." I pause for dramatic effect. "She hanged herself in the basement."

McKenzie's breath hitches, and I know I've got her.

I walk over to her and take the flashlight out of her startled hands. "What do you say we go downstairs and check it out?"

"The basement? Are you crazy?"

I hold the flashlight up so that it illuminates our faces from below, classic ghost-story style. I give her a sardonic smile—one of my best, if I must say—and she blushes. "I thought you wanted to go ghost hunting with me," I say. "Are you scared?"

"Of course not," she snaps. She crosses her arms defensively and adds, "It's just not safe down there. Kelsey's mom says the tours can't go into the basement."

I cock my head at her. "I thought you liked to live dangerously."

Her gaze flickers briefly to the window, then back again. "Fine. Let's go." She holds out her hand. "Give me back the flashlight."

"Not yet," I say, and lead the way out of the room.

"Ty!" she objects, but I don't stop, and since she doesn't want to be left in the dark, she has no choice but to follow.

A latch holds the basement door shut, and when I lift it, the door pops open with a sigh. A scent of dampness and rot wafts up from the darkness below. A chill runs over my skin, and I wonder if this is a good idea.

"It smells down there."

There's something prissy about the way she says it, and it completely annoys me. My anger comes back, hard as armor, and I'm not scared anymore. I want to do this, even if it's stupid, because if there's anybody who deserves to have their safe little bubble popped, it's McKenzie. "Come on," I say, and I point the flashlight down the narrow wooden stairs.

The basement is really more of a cellar. The floor and walls are hard-packed dirt, and the ceiling is the bare rafters supporting the floor above. When I reach the bottom, I turn and shine the light up at McKenzie, who has paused halfway down.

"I don't think this is a good idea," she says.

I can practically feel the dark against my back, cool and slightly wet. But I see that she's on the verge of splitting, so I say, "There's nothing down here." To her credit, she descends the rest of the stairs, and when she steps onto the dirt floor, I offer her the flashlight. "You can be in charge now."

She takes it, and when our hands touch, I notice that her fingers are freezing. She sweeps the light around. There isn't much to see. The room is small and bare, except for a pile of broken wooden crates next to the stairs. The light skitters over a door on the far wall, and I reach out to grab McKenzie's hand.

"Jeez!" she shrieks.

"Door," I say calmly, and guide the flashlight beam across the room. I start walking.

"Where are you going?"

"I want to see what's on the other side." Adrenaline is racing through me now, electric and insistent.

"You're crazy," McKenzie says, but she scurries after me, keeping the beam leveled at the door.

This one has an old metal knob, spotted with rust. I turn it and push and, at first, the door sticks as if there's something behind it. McKenzie's so close I can hear her breathing, quick and fast. Suddenly the door gives way, and the air that whooshes out is even more musty than the stuff we're breathing already.

"Ugh," McKenzie groans as she shines the flashlight inside the space.

There's something hanging from the rafters.

It moves in the light before darting back into the dark. McKenzie's hand clamps down onto my arm, her nails digging through the material of my jacket and into my skin. She's mumbling *oh my God* over and over again, pulling me away from the door.

Someone else is breathing down here.

It's not McKenzie's panicked hyperventilating, and it's not my own breath, which isn't exactly steady, either. It's slower, raspier, as if it's coming from an ancient pair of lungs.

"Oh my God, did you touch my back?" McKenzie whispers.

"You're holding my arm," I point out.

She shrieks and spins around, the flashlight beam jerking around the cellar. The thing hanging from the rafters moves again, and McKenzie screams and runs, dragging me with her, her fingers so tight around mine, it feels like she might crush them.

Upstairs McKenzie sprints for the exit, but I pull away from her.

"Ty! What are you doing?"

"Closing the door."

She doesn't wait for me. I'm alone in the hallway at the top of the basement stairs. I look back down, hesitating. And then I push the door shut and drop the latch in place.

"Thanks," I whisper.

2. October 31, 10:49 p.m.

The Spruce Street Guest House's backyard is full of shadows. Spruce trees are clumped together in one area, and a dilapidated shed leans to one side near the brick wall at the back of the property. It's cold tonight, but at least it's not snowing. From what people have told me, it almost always snows on Halloween. I huddle in the dark corner between the shed and the wall, squatting in my increasingly frigid jeans so I don't have to sit on the even colder ground.

It's not long before the girls come through the broken section of the wooden fence along the right side of the yard. I hear their giggling before I see them, and I wonder if they realize how loud they are. I recognize Kelsey Fisher's voice as she says, "Watch out! Shh!"

Lauren Meier gasps a little, as if she's trying to stop herself from laughing. "Did your mom notice you taking the key?" She seems to be trying to whisper, but the question carries all the way across the yard.

"No," Kelsey answers. "She's so busy this time of year, she barely pays attention."

"You guys are being too loud," says a third girl, and my stomach lurches when I recognize the voice. It's McKenzie. I'm not entirely surprised—she and Lauren and Kelsey are best friends, and they seem to do everything together— but I am disappointed. More than disappointed. A sharp pang goes through me, and I get mad at myself. I don't know why they're here yet. Maybe it's not what I think it is.

They run across the yard, crunching over the fallen leaves so loudly, it doesn't matter that they manage not to say a word. I hear them climb the steps of the back porch, and then more furious whispering as Kelsey unlocks the door. It creaks as they push it open, and one of the girls— probably Lauren—squeals in fright.

"Shh!" McKenzie hushes them. "Let's go."

I wait till they're inside and then I follow as silently as I can. I'm a lot quieter than they are. They've left the door partly open, and I slide inside by pushing it just a little. It gives a barely noticeable groan.

I look around the kitchen. Luckily there's a half-moon shining through the windows tonight, because I can't turn on a flashlight and expose myself. I don't want them to see me. At first I don't know where they went, but then I hear them going up the stairs, and I pad softly into the hallway after them.

"Did you bring the camera?" McKenzie asks as she climbs the stairs.

"Yeah," Lauren says. "My brother showed me how to set the timer and everything."

"Cool," McKenzie says.

Once they reach the second floor, they disappear into one of the bedrooms, and I tiptoe after them, flattening myself against the wall outside the room they've entered. Something thumps onto the floor, and a bag unzips.

"Give me that," McKenzie says.

"Jeez, I'm just trying to help," Lauren says.

"I want to make sure this goes off without a hitch," McKenzie says. She's definitely in charge, and the disappointment I felt earlier turns toward myself. I should've known better.

The first time I saw McKenzie was on my first day at Coal Creek High. I was walking down the hall outside the school office, reading my class schedule and trying to figure out where homeroom was, and I bumped right into her as she came out of the girls' bathroom.

"Sorry," I said. "I didn't see you."

She was wearing jeans and a white Oxford shirt, unbuttoned just enough to show a hint of cleavage. Her honey-blond hair hung in loose waves over her shoulder, and her makeup was flawless: not too much, not too little. She was as preppy as it got here in Pinnacle, and I bet she had a closet full of plaid skirts.

"It's okay," she said, and then looked at me more closely. "You're new."

"Yeah."

"I'm McKenzie Wells," she said, and smiled.

"Tyler White," I said, "but people call me Ty."

It took her a minute to figure out that I'm a girl. I knew when it happened, because this tremor went over her face, as if she was buzzed by static electricity. After that, she excused herself, clearly rattled by making such a basic mistake, and I was left standing there in the hallway as she practically fled toward the lockers and her friends.

It bugged me, sure. I'm not the butchest chick on the planet, and in San Francisco, enough people look like me that I'm not an anomaly. But in Pinnacle, girls don't wear boys' clothes and have short hair. I think it's my walk that confuses them the most, though. Girls usually have this swaying motion when they move, so that even from far away, it's obvious they're girls. But I've never walked like that. I walk like my dad.

I think she would have just avoided me from then on, but her last name is Wells and mine is White, so we were assigned seats next to each other in physics and study hall. She was nice enough to me in class, but it wasn't like we were friends. And her friends didn't talk to me. Only she did—usually when they weren't around. She had this way of looking at me, though—kind of under her eyelashes when she thought I wouldn't notice—that made me think she thought I was cute.

I should've known better.

I hear McKenzie and Lauren arguing over where to place the camera. "We can attach it to the ledge here," Lauren says.

"It's just going to poke out if we put it there," McKenzie objects.

They decide to stick it on the top of the window. "The tape will hold it," Lauren says. "We have to point the lens down. Nobody's going to be able to see it in the dark."

Their lights bob inside the room as they rig the camera over the window. And then Kelsey says, "Look what I got to write on the wall."

Lauren and McKenzie make appreciative sounds. Kelsey wants to do it, but ultimately McKenzie prevails. "I'll use my own hands. It'll look awesome."

"Ty's gonna freak," Kelsey says gleefully.

"Do you think it's too much?" Lauren asks, sounding hesitant.

"Nah," McKenzie says dismissively. "It's a joke. Wait'll we post the video. Everybody's gonna love it. We have to do a Halloween prank—we live in Pinnacle."

A Halloween prank. I feel sick to my stomach. This is why McKenzie asked me to meet her here: to play a joke on me. I suspected something like this—that's why I got here so early—but the confirmation sinks inside me like lead weights.

I could go home right now. Stand her up. Never speak to her again. But even though the idea of running is extremely tempting, I'm also pissed. McKenzie Wells might rule the school, but she doesn't rule me.

When I hear them finishing up, I slide farther down the hall, edging into the room next door. It's empty, but out of the corner of my eye I see something move. I almost jump out of my skin before I realize it's a mirror: one of those old-fashioned ones on a wooden stand. Somebody left a damn mirror behind. I let out my breath slowly, hoping the girls can't hear me.

After they leave, I walk down the dark hall, back to the room they outfitted with the camera. I want to check it out, but then I realize I'll be caught on tape. Crap. Something in the house creaks, and the hairs on the back of my neck stand straight up.

I decide to head outside to wait for my date with McKenzie, and I book it down the stairs in my haste to leave.

3. October 31, 9:02 p.m.

The tour guide gathers us on the sidewalk outside the guesthouse. This is the second-to-last stop on the tour; after this he'll lead everybody back to the Pinnacle Theater for the Spooktacular Spectacle. I stand on the edge of the group, the hood of my new winter jacket pulled up. The crowd is mostly adults, but there are three boys about my age nearby.

"This is the Spruce Street Guest House," the tour guide

says, "which operated from 1886 to 1923 and then was briefly turned into a sanatorium before it shut down in 1929. While it was a guesthouse, it was operated by Maud Collins, a woman who married a much older man who had made it rich in the gold rush. When he died, she took her inheritance and bought this place, intending to turn it into a high-class hotel. Unfortunately for Maud, Pinnacle was never quite as sophisticated as she hoped."

The tour guide laughs dryly, but the crowd is getting restless. The boys whisper to each other behind cupped hands. I don't recognize them from school, but lots of people from the neighboring towns come to Pinnacle on Halloween night.

The guide clears his throat. "The Spruce Street Guest House is home to at least one ghost, which was documented three years ago on camera by a ghost-hunting team from the cable TV show *Ghost Seekers*." The boys shut up, and I shift a little closer to the front. "Before I tell you more about the ghost, let's go on inside and take a peek, shall we?"

An excited murmur goes through the crowd. So far we've only been inside two other buildings—both of them saloons—and this house is way bigger. The tour guide leads us up the path to the front door, which he unlocks and pushes open with a dramatic creak. I wonder if that was staged. The guide switches on an electric lantern and ushers us inside. A few of the tourists pull out their own flashlights, and we crowd into the foyer.

The guide starts up the staircase and tells us to gather around. I stand in the doorway to the front parlor, eyeing the slipcovered furniture uneasily. In the pale light of the lantern, the armchairs look like monsters. The guide begins to tell us about the history of the guesthouse and how Maud Collins was picky about the boarders she allowed to stay here, how she had rules about how late the women could stay out and whether they could be seated next to the men during meals. The boys are clumped together a few feet away from me, talking in low voices and not paying attention.

I don't blame them. Everybody wants to hear about the ghost, but the tour guide wants to set the scene. I zone out because I already read about the history of this place last week, after McKenzie asked me if I wanted to meet her here on Halloween night. Her invitation, during study hall, was delivered so casually that at first I didn't get it, and she had to ask again.

"It's a Pinnacle tradition," she said with a flirty smile as she tossed her ponytail. "Every newbie has to go ghost hunting on Halloween night."

"Really?" I said, not sure if I should believe her.

"Yeah. It's really fun."

"Have you ever done it before?"

She shrugged. "It's not my first time." She gave me a conspiratorial grin and leaned across the library table toward me. "I'll bring some of my mom's secret stash of vodka and we'll make screwdrivers and stuff."

I wondered if she understood what this sounded like. Me and her, in an abandoned house on Halloween night, drinking vodka. "You aren't worried about your reputation?" I said, a slight smile on my face.

She rolled her eyes. "Oh, come on. You can tell me all about your life in California and I can introduce you to Pinnacle's finest ghosts."

I studied her face for a minute. She was all shiny-eyed confidence, and warmth spread through me as I thought about it. Yeah, I wanted to spend Halloween night with McKenzie Wells in an abandoned house drinking vodka. I definitely wanted to do that. "Okay," I said, and something like triumph flashed over her face before she gave me a dazzling smile.

"Awesome."

But that brief flash of triumph I saw stuck with me, chipping into my anticipation over spending Halloween night alone with McKenzie. The only time we'd gotten together outside of school was to work on a physics report at the library. This was totally different. As much as I wanted to believe McKenzie wasn't entirely straight, I didn't think I should count on it. So I did some research on the guesthouse, just in case. I might be new to Pinnacle, but I wasn't born yesterday.

That's why I decided to go on the ghost tour. I figured

I'd get a sneak peek at the place before McKenzie showed up. I like to be prepared.

The guide finally finishes his boring recital of the guesthouse's history and says, "Let's head upstairs and I'll tell you all about the ghost, all right?" We follow him down the hallway and crowd into a room overlooking the street. There's nothing in the room but an ancient armchair that nobody moves to sit in. "I've brought you in here because we can't all fit into room number three down the hall, which is the site of one of the two deaths that this guesthouse is known for."

He tells us that in the fall of 1897, two young women boarded here, one of them a teacher, the other a seamstress. They shared a room because neither of them could afford her own, and because back then it was safer for two women to board together than alone. One night, the teacher came back from work to discover that the seamstress was dead—shot by a gunslinger who mistook her for a prostitute who had turned him down. A few days later, the teacher herself died.

"She took her own life," the tour guide says, and the whole group is silent. "We'll never know why she decided to do it. Perhaps her delicate feminine sensibilities were too upset by the untimely death of her roommate. Just before Halloween, she hanged herself in the cellar."

A noticeable shiver ripples through the crowd, and I wrap my arms around myself.

"Now, who's up for checking out the deceased's room?" the tour guide says cheerfully. Nervous laughter titters through the group. "It's pretty small, so you'll need to take it in groups of four or five."

Everybody starts moving toward the hallway, and since I'm on the edge of the group, I get pushed out of the room first, bumping into one of the boys standing just outside the door. They're all wearing puffy down jackets and ski hats, and I separate them out as Tall, Medium, and Short.

"Dude, watch out," Tall says.

"Sorry."

"Hey, do you go to Westfield?" he asks. "I don't recognize you."

"I go to Coal Creek," I say, pitching my voice lower. I know he doesn't realize I'm not a guy, and I don't think I want to deal with him figuring it out. A thick rush of homesickness fills me. I'm so sick of being new all the time. I miss my friend Jada with her blue hair, and Kendall who's obsessed with anime. I miss the warm weather and I miss—God, I miss Angie. Even if she never really liked me that way, at least she didn't think it was crazy that I liked her.

The shortest of the three guys comes back from looking over the railing at the foyer and says, "Hey, do you remember seeing that door down there? I bet it leads to the basement. Wanna go check it out?"

"That's where the tour guide said that chick killed herself," Tall says.

"Duh," says Short. "That's why we should go down there."

"Yeah, let's go," says Medium enthusiastically. "This tour is boring."

Tall gestures at me. "Hey, dude, wanna come?"

I glance over my shoulder at the tour guide, but he's busy corralling the crowd in small groups into the bedroom. "Yeah, okay." The guys are right. This tour is boring, and I want to check out the rest of the house before McKenzie shows up.

We go back down the stairs as quietly as possible.

"What's your name?" Tall asks.

"Ty."

"Hey. I'm Brian. This is Chad and that's Jason."

"Hi," I say, nodding to them.

"What are you doing on this tour?" Brian asks.

"Just moved here. Wanted to see what it was about."

Jason's already at the door they spotted. It has a latch holding it shut, and when he lifts it, the door springs open. "Whoa," he says, and shines his flashlight down the stairs. I see dirt at the bottom; the basement's not finished.

"That's creepy, man," Brian says.

Chad is apparently the one with the most need to prove himself, because he shoves his way to the front and says, "Whatever. Don't be a chicken." He heads down the stairs, and Brian and Jason chuckle nervously before following.

I trail them down the steps into the cellar, the smell of damp dirt surrounding me. The space is pretty small, but as they shine their flashlights around the room, I spot a door on the far wall.

"Check that out," Chad says. "That is awesome."

I try to suppress the shiver that runs over me, but I can't. I'm not cold, exactly, but there's definitely something eerie about the air down here. It feels thick against my face, as if I'm walking through fog.

Even Jason seems a little freaked out. "Dude, do you really—"

But by then Chad has already crossed the basement and opened the door in the wall, and the scent that spills out is foul.

"Something must've died in there," Brian says.

We all go stiff with silence, until Chad says, "Yeah, dude, like a rat."

Jason gives a nervous laugh and joins Chad at the threshold. They sweep their lights through the space. I'm standing behind them, beside Brian, but I can see a little. It's a big room; I think it goes underneath the whole house. There are several piles of furniture in it, chairs and tables and an old tufted armchair that must have once been pretty nice but is now clearly a nest for whatever died.

Something flutters at the edge of the flashlight, and Chad curses out loud, bumping into Jason. "Dude, get away from me," Jason growls.

"Shut up—check that out." Chad shines the light up, and for one terrifying second I think there's a body hanging from the rafters. "It's a sheet," Chad says triumphantly. "Somebody tied a freaking sheet to the ceiling."

The boys start laughing, and I join in—I can't help it—it's just a sheet nailed to the rafters. It's not a ghost at all; it just looks like one.

Something touches my back, and I glance over at Brian, who's closest to me, but he's at least three or four feet away.

I freeze.

There's something behind me. I want to turn around but I'm paralyzed. The boys are joking about how someone got that sheet up there in the first place. They don't notice that I've stopped laughing. The impression of five fingers on my skin—even though I'm wearing my own puffy jacket—is unmistakable. And then I feel someone lean over my shoulder, an unseen weight bending toward my head. I feel breath against my ear. Even though I want to scream, I don't, because of that *hand* pressing against me as if to say, *Don't say a word*.

Suddenly the door slams shut, and Chad and Jason and Brian shriek and leap back. One of them trips on something and falls onto his butt, his hands scrabbling in the dirt, and *still* I'm unable to move. I'm stuck in place as if roots have grown out of my feet and dug into the ground.

"Move, move, move!" Brian shouts as they race toward the stairs.

Their feet pound up the steps, and I'm alone in the dark with this thing.

The breath on my ear is like a kiss: cold lips against my warm skin. I know I should be scared. I should be pissing my pants with terror. But the feeling that sweeps through me isn't fear; it's awe. There's something *real* down here in the cellar. Something that upends everything I've ever believed about life and what comes after.

As if this entity, whatever or whoever it is, can sense my wonder, the fingertips slide over the small of my back in a cool caress. It's almost inviting. And for some reason I remember that day in the library with McKenzie and our physics homework. It was just the two of us, with nobody there to see the way she looked at me. Her flirty grin, her body angled toward me, leaning into the possibility.

I don't want to leave.

Something on the other side of the door in the wall thumps, like someone's knocking. *Get. Out.*

Cold ripples across my skin as I realize there isn't only one entity in this cellar. There are two. And one of them does not want me here.

The hand on my back shoves me toward the stairs, unsticking me from the ground.

I run.

Rachel Hawkins
Eyes in the Dark

As soon as I see the truck parked behind the Smart-N-Sav, I know I'm in trouble.

Lindsey knows it, too.

"Nooooo!" she groans as I freeze in the doorway. My heart races and I have enough self-respect to remind myself that it's kind of pathetic to get all flustered just from seeing some guy's *car*.

But he's parked right under one of the few streetlights that hasn't blown out, and now I can see him, sitting in the front seat of the truck, his long fingers tapping out a rhythm on the steering wheel.

And just like that, I go from flustered to straight up twitterpated.

"He's waiting for me, right?" I ask Linds. "I mean, he knows I work here—why else would he be waiting in the Smart-N-Sav parking lot at night?"

"We *are* having a sale on sliced ham tomorrow," Lindsey says, squinting out into the darkness. "Maybe he's trying to get a jump on that."

Scowling, I start tugging on the strings of my apron. "Linds, there is a chance *Kelley Hamilton* has come to get me from work for the express purpose of making out with me. I'm gonna need you to get real serious *real* fast."

Linds gives the huffy sigh that always accompanies an eye roll, but I'm still watching Kelley. So far, he hasn't noticed me and Linds in the doorway, which I am very grateful for. No girl looks her best in a bright red apron with SAV SMART! ASK ME ABOUT OUR FRESH MEAT! scrawled across the front.

"Sam, we have been over this," Linds says as I stuff the apron in my purse. "That way?" She nods to the truck. "Lies madness. Sexy, sexy madness with really nice hair, but madness nonetheless."

She is right. There are three major reasons—all with their own subset of accompanying reasons—I should not walk out to that truck. I know this because last week during Government and Economics, I made a list. I used highlighters and different colored pens and everything.

But then Kelley sees us. The corner of his mouth lifts, and even though it's not a full-blown smile, it does all those clichéd things. It turns my knees to jelly. It gives me a sudden case of stomach butterflies. It makes my blood feel hotter and thicker.

It also blows my organized, reasonable, extremely colorful list to pieces.

"Okay," I say, turning to Linds. "So I'm supposed to be sleeping over at your place tonight, anyway."

"And you are." She crosses her arms over her chest. "I'm serious, Sam—you are not spending the entire night with that guy."

"Duh," I tell her, fishing my phone out of my pocket. "I'm not that kind of girl. I promise, I'll be at your place by"—I check the time—"midnight. Maybe half past. How much trouble can I get into in two hours?"

Linds glances toward Kelley. "With him? Probably too much."

"Eleven thirty, then," I tell her, and when she keeps frowning, I tug on her sleeve and widen my eyes. "Pleeeeease?"

Finally, she laughs. "Oh, God, not the anime eyes. Fine. Eleven thirty. But after that, I'm calling a SWAT team. Or worse—your parents."

There's someone else she could've mentioned calling. That she didn't is yet another reason Linds is my best friend. "Thank you," I tell her, giving her a quick hug.

"You're welcome. And understand that I expect payment in the form of a thoroughly detailed account of what making out with Kelley Hamilton is like."

"Done."

I turn and start walking to the truck, wishing I'd thought to put on some lip gloss while I was arguing with Linds.

As I approach, Kelley gets out, coming around to lean against the passenger door. He stands there, legs crossed at the ankle, and grins at me. "Samantha Porter. Fancy meeting you here."

My brain races for some witty retort, but he's *smiling* and *leaning* and his dark hair is falling in his face, and it's a wonder I can think to breathe, much less banter. Still, I manage a weak "Are you stalking me?"

His grin deepens. "No, I'm stalking the Smart-N-Sav. Last week, she sold me canned peaches for fifty cents, so I'm pretty sure she likes me."

"Hate to tell you, but she actually sold everyone her peaches for fifty cents." By now, I'm standing right in front of him, close enough to breathe in the clean, soapy smell of his skin. I lean closer, dropping my voice to a conspiratorial whisper. "And today? They went down to just a *quarter*."

"That skank," he says, and I laugh.

In a series of easy, graceful moves, Kelley reaches behind him, opens the passenger door, and bows. "Since Lady Smart-N-Sav has broken my heart, may I at least escort her handmaiden home?"

"You may," I tell him as he helps me up into the truck. Inside, it's shockingly clean and smells like Kelley. The leather seat is cold through my jeans, and I wonder how long he's been waiting for me.

Kelley cranks the engine, and stale warm air rushes out of the vents. The radio blares to life, some pounding rock song, and Kelley and I both jump, laughing nervously when he turns the music off.

"I have to say," I tell him, "you don't seem like a Truck Dude."

He shrugs, looking over his shoulder as he backs up. "My dad got it for me. Figured since I was moving back to Alabama, I ought to try and fit in with the locals."

"Are you glad? To be back in Hellburg?"

Kelley snorts at the nickname. We live in Haleburg, but in a deep Southern accent, it sounds like Hellburg. And, to be honest, that name feels more fitting sometimes.

"I'm not *not* glad, how about that?" he says. He pulls out of the parking lot and onto the two-lane highway. "It's not the worst place I've ever lived, that's for sure."

Ah. And there we have it. Coming in at the bottom of the list: Reason Number Three I Should Stay Away from Kelley Hamilton: his super-weird past. I wrote that in green highlighter.

Until we were in the sixth grade, Kelley lived in Haleburg with both his parents. His dad was a doctor in Dothan, the nearest big town, and his mom taught at the high school. Even back then, I'd had a crush on him. I mean, I still had a drugstore valentine he gave me in kindergarten.

But when we were twelve, Kelley's parents got divorced. His dad moved to Dothan, and Kelley's mom took him back to her hometown, somewhere in Georgia.

But Haleburg is a small town, and people still talked. When I was in eighth grade, my mom heard from a nurse who used to work with Kelley's dad that Kelley was having . . . issues. And then the next year, that same lady said that Kelley'd had to go to Atlanta and live either in a hospital or reform school. No one was ever really sure.

And then of course there were rumors that he was messed up on drugs, and someone else said they'd heard he was homeless in Nashville. But just as many people said that it was nothing like that, that yes, he'd a rough time with the divorce, but nothing out of the ordinary.

And then, a few months ago, at the beginning of our junior year, Kelley suddenly reappeared. He sure as heck didn't *look* like someone who'd been a junkie and/or homeless. And there was his easy grin, his quick laugh. If he were all psychologically damaged, he wouldn't be so *nice*, right?

I mentioned that to my mom just the other night, but she got a funny look on her face. "Maybe, but I still don't want you hanging around him. Just to be on the safe side." (That, by the way, was Reason Number Two I Should Stay

Away from Kelley Hamilton.)

We come to a four-way stop, and Kelley glances at me. "Since I'm not stalking you, I actually don't know where you live. Which way?"

"I'm staying with Lindsey tonight." Now he's looking at me, and the next words come out in a rush. "She's not expecting me for a few hours, so we can hang out or . . . whatever."

Oh, God. *Or whatever?* I'm so glad it's dark in the truck so he can't see the blood rushing to my face.

Or whatever. I hate myself so hard right now.

But Kelley nods. "Excellent. You, uh, wanna drive around then?"

I'm not sure if that's universal code for "go kiss each other's faces off," or if it's just a Southern Guy Thing. I do know that I've never just "driven around" with any boy.

So even though my voice is light when I reply, "Yeah, sure," my hands are twisting in my lap, pulling at the hem of my sweater.

Kelley makes a right, and soon, we're leaving Haleburg behind, the truck speeding down the dark road, nothing on either side but peanut fields. Overhead, there's a crescent moon, and the stars look bright and cold against the dark blue sky.

Kelley opens his window, and I roll down mine, too. Even though it's a chilly November night, I have to fight the urge to stick my head out like a dog. I settle for dangling my hand in the air, my skin quickly going numb. Ever since Kelley strolled into homeroom in August, I've felt like we were circling each other, heading for this night, this moment. And now—

A chime rings from my purse. I fish out my phone, expecting a text from Linds. But the name flashing on the screen is JUSTIN, and the text reads HEY, U AT LINDSEY'S? MISS U!

I hold the phone for a second, debating whether or not to answer. Because this? This is the Number One Reason I Should Stay Away from Kelley Hamilton: I have a boyfriend.

Or I kind of do. I mean, Justin and I have never had a conversation that involved words like *boyfriend* or *girlfriend*, or *exclusive*. There's been no, like, *jewelry* exchanged or anything. So I have no reason to feel guilty, really.

But thinking that doesn't stop my stomach from clenching as I slide the phone back into my bag.

"Anything important?" Kelley asks over the rush of the wind. By now, we've passed the peanut fields and are driving through the woods that encircle Haleburg. Thick copses of evergreens block the moon.

I smile back at him. "Just Linds, checking on me. So are we driving anywhere specific, or . . ."

He grins, and I catch my breath, hoping he doesn't notice. "I thought we might go check out the covered bridge."

"Cater Creek Bridge? We can't."

Something crosses Kelley's face, and for a second, I think it's annoyance. But it's gone as soon as it appears, and he shrugs. "I know we're not supposed to, but—"

"No, I mean we actually *can't*. They blocked the road."

The covered bridge used to be kind of famous in Haleburg. My parents had taken me there a lot when I was little. Sometimes we'd had picnics under its broad red roof, sometimes I'd played in the icy-cold creek running under it. It had been a pretty spot.

But over the years, fewer families came to the bridge for picnics, and more teenagers went there to get high or have sex. The bridge, which had been so picturesque and quaint, had started to feel seedy and sinister.

I couldn't remember if Kelley had been here when Cater Creek Bridge started going downhill, but then he says, "So did the county finally get sick of picking up joints and condoms?"

I laugh nervously, even though him saying the word *condoms* brings another rush of heat to my face. "No, um, it's actually kind of weird. There was a couple from Dothan about three years ago who went down there. Never came back."

"This is the part where I start humming *The Twilight Zone* music, right?"

"Well, it's not that mysterious. I mean, they found their car but none of their stuff. Everybody thought they just ran away together. But it was still enough of a big deal that the county decided to close off access to the bridge."

Kelley slows as we reach the little dirt road that winds through the woods. There's still a sign that reads, CATER CREEK BRIDGE: ALABAMA'S LARGEST COVERED BRIDGE with a fluorescent-white arrow pointing into the trees. Under that, block letters scream, ACCESS FORBIDDEN. TRESPASSERS WILL BE PROSECUTED.

"Why not just take down the sign?" Kelley mutters.

Branches scrape against the roof of the truck, and I bite my lip. PROSECUTED blares in my brain. All the happy, euphoric feelings rush out of me, replaced by that awful twisting sensation that's your stomach's way of saying THIS IS A BAD IDEA.

But it's not like we can even get to the bridge. They brought in mounds of dirt and clay and piled them into hills about halfway down this road. We'll get to those, Kelley will see that the whole bridge idea is impossible, and then we'll leave. And maybe go somewhere else to make out, although, I have to admit, I'm not much in the kissing mood anymore. There's even a small part of me wishing I'd just gone home with Linds tonight.

But then Kelley takes my hand. It's the first time we've touched (if you don't count a round of duck, duck, goose in second grade), and it sends a pulse through me. Keeping his eyes on the road, Kelley rubs his thumb in little circles on my palm. "You're awfully quiet over there."

My mouth is dry as I say, "Signs that say 'forbidden'

and 'prosecuted' tend to freak me out a little, that's all."

I want him to say something like "Okay, we'll leave then." Instead, he says, "Where's your sense of adventure?"

But as we pull up to the hills of dirt blocking the road, his grin fades a little. "Whoa."

I'd expected pretty big piles. Tall enough to discourage people from trying to climb them in trucks or ATVs, but not so high as to make it impossible. But these hills tower over the truck, nearly eight feet high, and steep. Not only that, there are branches, pine straw, and all shapes and sizes of rocks mixed with the dirt, making the mounds seem dangerously unstable.

"Oh, bummer," I say, hoping I sound legitimately regretful. "Those are way higher than I thought they'd be."

It's 10:32, and I'm suddenly annoyed. It'll take us another twenty minutes to get out of here, then who knows how long to find somewhere else to go? And Linds's house is on the other side of town, so that's ten more. . . . At this rate, Kelley and I will have time to maybe shake hands.

"Oh ye of little faith," Kelley says, waggling his eyebrows.

By now, all I want to do is get the heck out of this spooky forest and go somewhere normal to make out. Like a parking lot or a cul-de-sac. Any place that doesn't give me a major case of the creepies. And if he thinks I'm *climbing* up giant mounds of packed clay and dirt . . .

"There's no way we can get over these things," I tell

him, hoping that whatever his plan is, he'll drop it.

Kelley grabs the gearshift, and I expect him to put it in reverse. Instead, he pulls the handle all the way down. The truck makes a grinding sound as it starts up one of the dirt hills, the cab rocking alarmingly from side to side. I grip the door handle. "What are you doing?"

"Four-wheel drive," he tells me. "One of the few awesome things about driving this redneckmobile."

The tires spin. For one brief, sickening moment, I feel them lose contact, and all I can see is the truck rolling down the hill, crushing me and Kelley in the wreckage. And they won't find our bodies for *forever* because no one knows where we are, and when they do find us, everyone will know that I was cheating on Justin with Kelley Hamilton, even though I haven't even *gotten* to the cheating part yet.

I look over at Kelley. He's gritting his teeth, hands tight on the steering wheel.

But then the tires touch the dirt again, and suddenly, we're cresting the top of the hill. Juddering and bouncing, the truck makes its way down the other side, and when we finally come to a rest at the bottom, Kelley kills the engine.

The lights are still on, illuminating an overgrown road that should really be called a path. It winds its way through the trees, disappearing around a bend a few yards in. I'm shaking, with both fear at nearly getting killed and the elation of *not* getting killed.

Next to me, Kelley starts to laugh, a relieved and kind

of breathless sound. And then I start giggling, too. Our eyes meet, his reflecting the blue lights of the dash. He reaches out, cups my cheek in one palm, and then I'm unbuckling my seat belt and sliding across the bench seat and into his arms.

Once his lips are on mine, I'm not scared anymore. I can't feel anything but *want* and *heat*. Kissing Kelley Hamilton is better than I'd thought it would be, and trust me, I'd thought it would be pretty amazing. But my daydreams didn't capture how soft his hair is, or the low sound he makes in his throat as he holds me tighter. When we break apart for air, he presses his forehead against mine.

"I've wanted to do that for a really long time," he breathes.

"Me too," I confess, just as shakily.

Kelley kisses me again, softer this time, his hands cold on my lower back. He pulls away, fingers still sliding over my spine, making me shiver. "You know, we don't *have* to go down to the bridge. I feel pretty good about staying right here."

My face is pressed against his neck, so I know he can feel me smile. "I'm actually good with that."

I lift my head and he sinks one hand into my hair as we move toward each other. But before we kiss, Kelley freezes, his head jerking to one side as he stares out the windshield. "What was that?"

Irritated, I slide back. "Don't do that."

His eyes flick to my face for a second before turning back to the woods. "No, I'm not being a dick. I saw something. Like, for real. Lights or something."

Kelley turns the key, and with a click, the headlights go out, plunging us into darkness. "Just watch," he tells me. "Over there, to the right."

I cross my arms as I settle back into the passenger seat, squinting out into the darkness. "I don't—" I say, but then, suddenly, I *do*.

They're dim, but several yards away, twin orbs of red light are glowing faintly. They're maybe the size of quarters, and as I watch, they disappear for a second, only to then reappear in exactly the same place.

"They look like—"

"Eyes," Kelley finishes. "They look like *eyes*."

Goose bumps prickle my arms. "Shut up," I tell him, but I'm still staring out in the darkness. God, he's right, they do look like eyes. They vanish again for a second, but just like before, they come back almost immediately.

"See?" Kelley points at the lights. "They're blinking. What the hell has eyes like *that*?"

There are all kinds of creatures in these woods. Possums, raccoons . . . my mom even thought she saw a mountain lion out here when she was a teenager. So my brain races, trying to match those glowing circles to one of those animals. But none of them seem to fit. These eyes are too big to belong to a possum or a raccoon; they're too *red*.

Still, I tell Kelley, "Probably just a trick of the light."

I wait for him to let it go and to pull me back to him. Instead, he leans over the steering wheel, peering out. "But seriously, Sam, what is that thing? I mean, what has *eyes* like that?"

The mood is now sufficiently broken, and I can't keep the poutiness out of my voice as I say, "Who cares? Let's just get out of here. I promised Linds I'd be back by eleven thirty."

This time, there's no mistaking the annoyance on Kelley's face. "Sam—" he starts, but before he can say anything else, this . . . *sound* fills the air. Part howl, part shriek, it's like nothing I've ever heard before. Now the goose bumps aren't just on my arms, they're everywhere. The howl fades away, dissolving into a kind of chittering. I push the LOCK button on my door even though it's already locked.

It's just an animal. Some weird kind of animal that makes a weird, awful sound. My mind balks at calling it anything else. Still, I fasten my seat belt and tell Kelley, "I want to go. *Now.*"

But instead of starting the engine, Kelley grabs the door handle.

I grab *him.* "What are you doing?"

Still watching the darkness, he shakes off my grip. "I just want to get a closer look."

All I can do is stare at him. "What?"

"Whatever it is, it's weird, okay? So I want to see it."

"You know what else is weird?" I say, already reaching down for my phone. "Getting your face eaten off by some *chupacabra* in the woods. Woods we are *not even supposed to be in.* Now let's just forget it and *go.*"

My fingers close around my phone. If he won't take me out of here, I'll call someone. Linds. Heck, even my parents. Getting in trouble with them seems way less scary than getting mauled by a monster.

Kelley laughs. "A *chupacabra?*"

"You know, those monsters people see in Mexico, Texas, places like that," I say, suddenly self-conscious. "They kill goats and cows."

"Well, since we're not in Mexico or Texas, and neither of us is livestock, I think we'll be okay," he says, opening his door. "Give me two minutes, okay? I just wanna check it out."

He's out of the truck, closing the door with a quiet *thunk* before I can even reply. I don't know if it's fear or anger making me shake, but I suspect it's a decent mix of both.

Kelley walks in front of the truck. He moves slowly, his hands held out slightly in front of him. For a second, I think about leaning over and hitting the horn. It would serve the dual purpose of scaring the crap out of Kelley and running that thing off. And it would probably piss Kelley off, ensuring that our first kiss was also our last. But do I really care anymore?

Justin's face pops into my mind. He never would have taken me out here. And if he had, he would have taken me home when I said I wanted to leave. Guilt floods me, washing away all the anger and a fair amount of the fear. I read his text again. He misses me. Sweet Justin misses me while I'm out here fooling around with Kelley Hamilton, who may be hot, and may not be a junkie or a psychopath, but *is* something of a jackass.

I hit REPLY, and a message flashes on the screen: BATTERY POWER TOO LOW FOR RADIO RANGE. What?

But there, in the top left-hand corner, my battery bar has one little sliver of red. It's almost the same color as the thing's eyes. Which reminds me that I've been so busy futzing with my phone and being self-loathing that I haven't been watching Kelley.

Heart pounding, I look up, and the sound that comes out of my mouth is half groan, half whimper.

Kelley isn't there.

"No, no, no, no," I mutter, the sound of my own voice too loud, too harsh in the quiet truck. Leaning forward, I squint out at the trees, trying to spot Kelley's white T-shirt. But there's nothing. Just trees, trees, and more trees. I don't even see the red glow anymore.

Turning back to my phone, I speed-dial Linds, but that stupid low battery message comes back again. I toss the phone to the floorboard.

I could go out there, but the thought of doing that

makes me shudder. At least in the truck, I have doors that lock. Speaking of . . .

I lean over to the driver's seat. Distracted, I realize Kelley left the keys in the ignition, but how the hell am I supposed to get back over those hills? I remember the strain on his face as we climbed. Hadn't his left hand been doing something? Was there a button to press? How did four-wheel drive even *work*, and damn it, why had I never *learned*?

I am nearly sobbing with frustration when there's a thump under the truck. A small, stifled scream bursts from my throat, and I freeze.

The thump comes again, harder this time. The sound of my own blood rushing in my ears is almost painful. It's like every piece of me, every last molecule, is straining to hear. Another thump. And then another.

The truck shimmies, and there's a scrabbling that sounds like it's right in front of me. The cab shakes again and I lower my face to the leather, trembling. I lie there for what feels like years as the truck rocks, and the harsh sound of something scraping against the plastic bed (claws, claws, oh, God, its *claws*) fills the air. But I can see my phone—my stupid, useless phone—from where I'm lying, and I know that only three minutes go by before the sounds and the rocking stop.

Three more minutes go by before I find the courage to lift my head. I make myself look out the windshield first.

Still no sign of Kelley, no sign of anything. And then I turn to the back.

It's dark. No red orbs. Holding so still that my muscles shiver and ache, I keep watching. I know this moment. This is the part in scary movies where the girl relaxes, only to have the creature or killer or alien fling itself out of the darkness. I brace myself, thinking that if it does happen, my mind will shatter into a thousand tiny shards. Because really, once a monster has jumped out of the woods at you, how can you ever go back to being okay?

But that doesn't happen. I stay still and watch and breathe, but nothing jumps at me. Nothing growls. And the silence goes on just long enough to make me think that I imagined it. Somehow, that's worse.

I'm still staring into the bed of the truck when the driver's side door flies open.

I do scream then, but it doesn't sound anything like those girls in movies. It sounds high and breathless and crazy, and I can't seem to stop it, even when Kelley slides into the seat.

"Sam," he says once the door is slammed behind him. He grabs my shoulders. "Sam. SAM. It's okay—it's just me."

He's breathing like he just ran a marathon, and even though his face is sickly pale, his eyes are bright.

"You said two minutes!" is all I can think to yell once I can finally form words again. "You said two minutes, and my phone doesn't work, and there were things in the back, and—"

"Shh, shh," Kelley murmurs, but he's already letting go of me and starting the truck. The relief I feel is so intense, I sag against the seat, running trembling hands over my face. I don't even care where Kelley was, or why he was running, or why two minutes turned into an eternity.

I want to go home. I want to see Linds. I want to text Justin and tell him that sure, he might be a little boring, but at least he's never gotten me nearly killed.

I never want to see Kelley Hamilton again, no matter how good his hair is.

The truck lurches forward, and I wait for it to turn around, to make the climb back up the hill. Did I really think that was terrifying just a few minutes ago? Did it take less than half an hour to radically alter my definition of "scary"?

There is a crunch as we run over what sounds like a bunch of sticks, and the truck picks up speed.

It does *not* turn around.

I open my eyes and watch trees race past. We're not heading back. We're going deeper into the woods.

"What are you doing?" I shriek.

Kelley swerves around a pile of sticks and pine straw, speeding down the road. "I saw it, Sam," he says. "I saw it, and it was *not* a possum with mange, or a bobcat, or a mutated raccoon, or anything." His words come tumbling out in a rush, and I realize with dawning horror that he's *smiling.*

"We are talking some kind of brand-new species, Sam. I mean, the kind of crap that makes people famous. We'll probably get our own show on the Discovery Channel."

"I don't want a show on the Discovery Channel!" I reach out and punch him in the upper arm, hard enough to make him wince. "I want to go *home*, you douchebag! That thing could *kill us.*"

Kelley shakes his head. "No way. It was pretty small, like one of those miniature collies."

"But there's more than just one of them," I say, remembering the rocking of the truck, the scraping of claws. How many "miniature collies" would it take to make a truck this big sway like that?

It's like he doesn't even hear me. "It ran this way, but if I can corner it . . ."

I lift my hands, wanting to wrench the steering wheel out of his hands. But as fast as we're going, that would probably crash us into a tree. Instead, I tuck my legs underneath me, rising on my knees to face him. "Kelley, listen to me. There are lots of these things. And I think they have claws, and it doesn't matter that they're small if there're hundreds of them."

"There aren't hundreds, Sam. People would've seen them. And besides—HA! Got you, you little bastard!"

Something bounds into the headlights. Kelley's right—it's not very big. Maybe four feet long, and I can't tell how tall because it sort of leaps as it runs, almost like a deer. As it flees, it glances over its shoulder with a quick flare of red eyes. I catch sight of its long muzzle, and the briefest hint of teeth.

Lots of teeth.

Branches slap the windshield, the roof, the windows, as the truck flies over roots and rocks. I hang on to the strap by the door, but all that accomplishes is pulling a muscle in my shoulder. We're rocking back and forth, and my stomach is somewhere in my mouth, so even though my brain screams, *Stop stop STOP*, no words come out. There's a high-pitched whimpering coming from somewhere, and I suddenly realize it's *me.*

Beside me, Kelley grips the wheel, his jaw set, his eyes focused right between the headlights. The thing's powerful hind legs flex as it bounds in front of us, moving in and out of the lights.

"Come on, come on, come on," Kelley mutters under his breath, and I wonder if he's talking to the truck or to the thing.

The tree is there so suddenly that I don't have time to scream. I barely get out a gasp, and then we're slamming against the trunk of a towering oak. There's a crunch of metal, and the surprisingly loud *pop* of the airbags, but even over that, I hear that shriek/howl again. It's louder this time, and it rises in a cry of pain before trailing off. And then everything is quiet except for the tick of the engine, the creaking of the tree, and my own chattering teeth.

Kelley flings open the door and leaps out while I sit, shaking and staring at the thing pinned between the tree and the truck. Lying against the hood, mouth open, its long tongue is very pink against the dull silver paint. Its eyes are still open, and, the red slowly fades into nothingness.

Kelley leans over it, shaking his head as if he can't believe it. He meets my eyes through the windshield. "Holy crap, right?"

My legs are shaking. Getting out of the truck is hard for me, but I manage it. I walk across the back of the truck and come around to stand next to Kelley. He's still smiling when I reach out and punch him as hard as I can.

As his breath whooshes out and he doubles over, I stare at the ruined truck. There's no doubt that it's totaled, that it'll never get us out of here. And I focus on that, because it's a lot easier than wrapping my brain around the fact that monsters are real, and that Kelley has just killed one.

"Sam," Kelley wheezes, "I'm sorry about this—"

"About what exactly? The leaving me alone part? Or ignoring when I said I wanted to leave? About *ramming your truck into a tree like a lunatic?*"

"All of it," he replies, and he does look sorry. Then that grin again. "But come on. You have to admit this is pretty badass."

"I want to go home," I say for what feels like the thousandth time. I think about my phone, probably dead by now, somewhere in the truck. I wonder what time it is. I wonder if it's past 11:30, and if Linds is worried about me.

Kelley heaves a sigh. "We will. Let me just call . . . I don't know, my dad, I guess."

While Kelley reaches into his pocket for his phone, I slump to the ground, leaning against one of the tires. It's hot against my back. Kelley is lit up in the glow of his phone as he turns it on, so I can see the panic that darts across his face. "Shit."

"What?"

"I don't have a signal."

I laugh. The noise startles Kelley and he glares as giggles pour out of me. "Of course," I gasp. "Of course you don't have a signal! And mine is dead! *Of course* that happens when we're trapped in a monster-filled forest!"

"Jesus, Sam, calm down. You sound crazy."

That just makes me laugh harder. "Oh, right, I'm crazy. You just totaled your car chasing down a freaking *chupacabra*, and *I'm* crazy."

Kelley scowls. "You know—" he starts, and then whatever he was going to say trails off as he stares into the trees. I follow his gaze.

Monsters are real, so maybe that means other bizarre stuff is real, too. Stuff like time travel. Or wishes.

I wish now. I wish to go back to the Sam I was just a few

hours ago, the Sam leaving stupid Smart-N-Sav with her best friend. I wish Kelley Hamilton hadn't come to get me tonight. I wish that I had gone home with Linds, and texted my boyfriend, and never known how truly terrifying the world could be.

I wish, and I watch as two, then four, then dozens of red eyes start to glow in the darkness.

Valerie Kemp
Stillwater

Nothing ever changes in Stillwater. Nothing. I get up every morning at the crack of dawn, in the blazing heat, and drive our pickup all over, delivering eggs and milk and whatever else my daddy feels like selling, to the good people of Stillwater, population 319.

I work my way in a circle from the edge of town, where we live, to the center. I endure all the little old ladies who like to pinch my cheek when they tell me, "Why, Pruitt Reese, you are becoming more like your daddy every day!" Like that's a good thing.

Then I stop over at Henderson's, top off the gas tank,

and wash the sweat off my face before heading to the Stillwater Café, and Delilah. Not that she cares. The way her nose wrinkles up whenever she opens the back door for me, you'd think I'd rolled myself in manure.

To understand Delilah and me, you have to understand the Reese family—both halves. And to understand that, you have to go way back. I'm not gonna lie, it ain't pretty. Although if you ask my folks, they'll say they don't know what you're talking about. Our ancestors weren't bad people. They didn't break the law or nothing.

"Times was different," my granddaddy would tell you. I s'pose he's right, but that don't really make it better.

Anyhow, once upon a time, a man named Jedediah Reese found himself a nice piece of land, high up on a hill overlooking a little creek, and started a farm. He had a lot of land and only a couple sons, so he did what most folks did back then. He bought himself some slaves and set to work building his fortune. And he was so successful that he founded the town of Stillwater.

Then the Civil War came. Jed was already dead by then, his land split between his two sons, Ezekiel and Thomas. They both fought for the right to feel superior and died trying. Zeke had a son, so his half of the land went to him, but Thom didn't have any kids that outlived him. And his wife, displaying a kindness unknown to the men in my family, left it all to her housekeeper, Elisabeth Reese, outing a long-kept family secret—that Elisabeth came by the name Reese honestly. Jed was *her* daddy, too.

And there you have it. The saga of the Reese families. One black, one white. Neighbors and sworn enemies. At least, that's how my folks see it. If you ask me, they spend too much time focusing on what we used to have instead of making something of ourselves now.

Delilah, Elisabeth's six times great-granddaughter, is the brightest thing in this whole town. And even though I'm supposed to hate her, I can't help but notice. Even when she turns her nose up and walks right past me like I'm not her seventh half-cousin once removed or whatever. Like I'm nothing at all.

Today's no different. She pulls the door open and steps back, her pretty brown eyes all scrunched up like just the sight of me is painful. I find myself fumbling for the right words and staring at her shoes, like always.

Delilah sighs. "Just put it in the back," she says as she leaves me to haul in my stuff, and she opens the walk-in refrigerator.

She's wearing a red Stillwater High T-shirt under her apron today. It brings out the little bits of auburn in her long, dark curls. Most people probably think her hair is plain black, but that's 'cause they don't pay attention. When the light catches it just right, you can see a whole rainbow's worth of colors in it.

The way she handles the deliveries like she owns the diner and not like she's just working there for her folks makes me feel like a sorry excuse. We're both seventeen, but she runs circles around me.

"Delilah," her dad shouts. "Did that boy deliver those supplies yet?"

"He's here now, Daddy," Delilah calls from the doorway.

"Tell him I'm tired of his father sending us the crap no one else wants. Needing money is no excuse for being a cheat."

I can feel the heat rushing up my face. I got my back to Delilah, but I know she can see how red my ears must be. My daddy ain't no cheat, just stubborn and proud. He overcharges Delilah's daddy because he knows they can afford it. Delilah's daddy pays because they pity us. Least that's what my daddy thinks. Which just makes him madder and more inclined to give Delilah's daddy less.

If you ask me, Delilah's daddy is just as stubborn and proud, and he overpays to prove how much better his business is doing. Of the two Reese families, Delilah's is for sure the more successful. But they're equal when it comes to foolish pride. Only in Stillwater would folks *choose* to do business with each other out of spite.

I busy myself with clearing a space for the last crate until I figure he's gone. It ain't like I haven't heard it before, but I feel like a fool all the same. I keep my eyes straight ahead on my way out, and when I pass Delilah, she turns away.

Me and Delilah ain't never gonna happen. I don't know why I can't get that through my head.

After I finish the deliveries, I drop the truck off and get on my bike before anyone decides they got something else for me to do. Once I get down the hill and through the town, there ain't nothing but empty roads and clumps of trees and fields as far as the eye can see. I keep on going, anyways, just looking for some kind of sign that there's a world out there worth escaping to.

There's got to be more to life than Stillwater.

The air is so thick, I can't hardly feel a breeze as I'm riding. It's so humid, my wheels don't even kick up any dust on the dirt road. Sweat runs down my face in little rivers.

Days like this, when I'm hating everything about my life and wishing the summer would end already, I like to push myself.

I focus on the sound of my tires on the dirt, my heavy breaths. I pretend I can pedal myself into a new life—I just have to keep going, ignore the heat, ignore the pain. Ride just a little bit further.

I ain't stopping this time till I collapse. They'll have to scrape me up off the ground. I grit my teeth and pedal harder, right down the middle of the road. All of a sudden, my bike slams into something and I'm flying. Not over the handlebars, but back, like someone snatched me up and threw me. I have just enough time to give the bike a shove away from my body before I hit the ground. My back slams down first and then my head. It don't hurt as much as I expect. Just one bright white flash of pain and then the dark.

A hand grabs me by the jaw and gives my head a shake. "Holy crap, Pruitt! You all right?"

I open my eyes and see a face so much like my own that for a minute I think I'm hallucinating. Same slightly crooked nose, same dirty-blond hair, but shorter than I like to keep mine. He looks about my age, but his eyes are tired and older—an "old soul" my granny would call it— than mine could ever be.

He slaps my cheek and starts looking worried. "Pruitt, can you hear me?"

Matt. The name comes to me from the back of my mind. How could I forget my own brother? "Yeah," I say, pushing his hand away. "What happened?"

He sits back, relief all over his face. "It's what I wanted to show you."

"What?" I'm lying in the middle of the road. Other than my bike and his, there's nothing out here to see but trees.

Matt throws out his arms like he's presenting something. "The Stillwater town limit."

I start to lift myself up onto my elbows, but a sharp pain in my arm stops me. I suck air in through my teeth to keep from crying out. My right forearm is shredded. It's gonna be one hell of a scar.

Matt's eyes are all lit up and I can't figure why he's so excited. He's not talking a lick of sense. "Why'd you have to knock me off my bike for that?"

"I didn't," he says, frowning at me. "Something ain't right about this town. Can't you feel it?"

"The only thing I feel is a knot coming up on the back of my head."

Matt smacks my good arm and stands. "Jeez, Pruitt, why do you have to be such a kid sometimes?" He holds a hand out to me. "Get up."

My head aches. I lie back down on the ground and shut my eyes against it. "Just gimme a minute."

Matt ain't having it. "Pruitt. Get up."

I sigh real heavy so he knows I'm irritated before I open my eyes and sit up. "Fine," I say, but I'm talking to the air. There ain't no one out here but me. It takes a minute before I realize that's how it should be. I came out here alone, and I don't have a brother. I must've been dreaming, but it felt more like a memory. Like that déjà vu stuff people talk about. I guess that's what I get for riding like a maniac. Crazy dreams about brothers I never had.

My hands and legs are all scratched up and bleeding, but when I lift my right arm to check the damage, there is none. Instead, I see the jagged scar I've had for as long as I can remember. That fall must've really done a number on me. I'm woozy but I manage to make it to standing. It's gonna be a long walk home. Mama's gonna love it when she sees me crawling in all scraped up and bloody, tracking in dirt on her kitchen floor. If I'm lucky, I can slip past her and say I'm taking a nap before she gets a good look at me. That's all I want anyhow, to sleep this day away like none of it ever happened.

When I wake it's dark out, and I got pieces of a dream clinging to me. Not enough to make any kind of sense, though. Just me and Matt again, feeling so much like he's my big brother, out on the ridge at the edge of our land. I keep hearing his voice telling me: *Something ain't right about this town*. And my gut keeps saying he's right.

The clock says it's after ten, which means my folks are out cold for the night. I'm wide-awake with nothing but time and a jumble of thoughts in my head. Might as well see if I can puzzle this thing out.

I climb out my window onto the porch roof and jump down to the grass. The sun might've gone down, but it's still too hot to be decent. I miss the fan in my room already.

In the northeast corner of our property, where it meets Delilah's, the land rises then drops off. We don't farm that area, so it's mostly still full of trees, but there's a clearing where the ridge juts out over the dry creek bed, and that's where I'm headed.

If the moon ain't full, it's as close as it can get and I'm glad for the light. I haven't been out to the ridge at night since I was a kid. I'm not supposed to go out there alone on account of it's dangerous, but I've never thought much of rules. Folks have been saying the ridge is cursed ever since the creek dried up forever ago. Seems like my whole life is cursed. I can't see how going out to the ridge makes any difference.

The night air is sticky and heavy with the scent of pine, just like in my dream. The closer I get to the ridge, the more them pieces of my dream start making a whole picture.

I was following Matt down this same path. He made his way through the tangle of branches like he'd done it a hundred times before, and I was just trying to keep up. He'd woke me out of a dead sleep and all I wanted was to go back.

"Can't this wait till morning?" I asked. I was cranky, and the mosquitoes were biting.

"No," Matt said without looking back. "It has to be now, so you'll remember it."

"I remember things much better on a full night's sleep."

Matt just shook his head. "A full night's sleep won't do nothing but make you forget. Trust me."

And I did. Even when he was talking crazy and marching me out to the ridge in the middle of the night. So I kept on following him, right up to the edge of the ridge.

"Look," he said, and pointed out into the dark.

All I saw was black. "I don't see anything."

"Exactly," he said. "There's nothing out there. Nothing at all."

"You woke me up to show me nothing?"

"Think about it, Pruitt, shouldn't you be able to see the fields out there? The stars? Clouds? Something?" He turned and pointed at the sky behind us.

I looked up, and sure enough, there were stars, and even a cloud in the night sky behind us, but in front of us, over the cliff, there was nothing. Just black. "What the . . ."

"Hold on, it's almost midnight," Matt said.

And this is how I know I was a dreaming and not remembering, because right then, the black in front of us wavered. Specks of light popped up, one by one at first, and then a whole world appeared. Headlights and taillights, streetlights and porch lights, and way in the distance, tiny skyscrapers all lit up and clustered together like a city.

"Do you see it?" Matt asked. It was the first time I'd ever heard him sound unsure about something.

My heart pounded in my chest. This had to be some kind of a trick. There's nothing outside of Stillwater for miles and miles. Too far to see, even at night. "What is that?"

Matt blew out a long breath and then squared his shoulders. "That's where I'm going."

A rustle in the trees startles me, and I'm surprised to find myself standing right at the edge of the ridge. Just like in my dream, there's nothing out there but darkness. No stars or signs of life. The crack of a branch breaking comes from my right, followed by footsteps, each one closer than the last.

I'm man enough to admit that whatever's coming has got me scared. I don't know if them rumors about this place being cursed are true. And this dream, or whatever it is in my head, has got me all shook up. The rustle of leaves on leaves gets louder, and I crouch next to a cluster of big rocks.

For one crazy second I think maybe that dream was real and it's my brother, come to take me away to the city. "Matt?" I mean to shout it, but it comes out all weak like I don't want to be heard.

Delilah steps out from the trees. "Who's there?"

My heart keeps right on stuttering in my chest at the sight of her. In the moonlight her skin could be any color: blue, silver, white. She stands still as a statue, frowning, fists clenched up like she's fixing to fight. Her eyes catch on mine and I can't look away, even though I want to.

She lets her fists come loose but holds on to her frown. "Pruitt?"

I stand and brush the dirt off my knees like it's the most natural thing to be hiding in a bunch of rocks in the middle of the night. I try to smile but my mouth won't cooperate. "Hey, Delilah. What're you doing out here?"

She crosses her arms and lifts her chin. "It's my land, too."

One sentence in and I've already stepped in it. "I know. I just meant, uh, what brings you?"

"Oh." She shrugs and drops her arms to her sides.

"Same as you, I expect."

"Yeah?" My voice is too high, but I can't control it. "What's that?"

Her lips curve up a little in an almost-smile. "Trying to escape."

"You know about the ridge?" The hairs on my arms stand at attention.

Delilah's almost-smile disappears as quick as it came. She rolls her eyes and walks past me to stare out. I can't tell if I'm relieved that she don't seem to think the ridge is magic.

Delilah slips her hands underneath her long hair and lifts it up. My eyes fall to the spot where her neck curves to meet her left shoulder and I get lost in the thought of running my fingers along it.

"I come out here to think sometimes," she says, and then she turns and catches me looking. Her mouth falls open in surprise.

There I go again, making a mess of things. She probably thinks I'm a pervert now. "Well." I take a step back so she don't get the wrong idea. "I'll leave you to it." My face is so hot, sweat's beading up at my temples.

"You can stay, Pruitt." She moves away from the edge and sits down on the ground with a shrug. "I mean, I can't kick you off your own property."

It sounds crazy, but the way her eyes hold on to mine for a second, it almost seems like she wants me to stay. She lies back in the grass and looks up at the stars. I feel like I might fall over just trying to get down there next to her. Maybe this whole night is a dream.

When I've finally settled into a spot that's close but not too close, Delilah asks, "Aren't you tired of it?"

"Of what?" She smells like lilacs, and I take a long, deep breath of it.

"Being a Reese, and all the mess that comes with it." She rips up pieces of grass and tosses them as she talks. "Being locked up tight in someone else's idea of who you're supposed to be."

"Hell, yes." Every single day. But I'd have never thought Delilah felt like that, too.

"I swear it feels like I'm never getting out of here. Like I'm never gonna turn eighteen and go away to college. It's like time keeps on passing, but everything stays the same."

I don't know why I'm surprised. If anyone from Stillwater was gonna go to college, it'd be Delilah. It's just, far as I know, no one's ever left. But I keep that thought to myself and tell her, "I keep waiting for summer to end and school to start, but it never does."

Delilah tilts her head to me and looks me in my eyes. She takes a deep breath, like what she's got to say is important. "Sometimes I dream we're all trapped—the whole town—inside a snow globe. And I just have to find the hole they used to fill it to get out. But I always forget what I'm looking for before I find it."

Her eyes stay locked on mine while she waits for me to say something. I want to reach over and hold her hand, but my palms are sweaty and I don't think she'd appreciate it anyhow. It's nice to know I'm not the only one who dreams of escaping this place. "You ever feel like something's not right about this town?"

"Yeah," she sighs, and turns her eyes back to the sky. "All the time."

We're both quiet for a while, and then, out of nowhere, Delilah laughs. It's the kind of laugh that gets right under your skin and spreads.

"What?" I ask, a grin already fixing itself on my face.

"My daddy would kill me if he knew I was out here talking to you." It's a fact that should have me running for the house, but her smile is brighter than the moonlight and I know I could never leave as long as she's aiming it at me.

"Mine too." I picture my daddy's face so twisted up with rage, he looks like a cartoon character—and that's all it takes. We laugh until we can't breathe.

Seems like she's done talking, but I'm all right with that. I've never been too good at it, anyways. 'Sides, just being with her, the stars look a hundred times brighter. I've thought about kissing Delilah more times than I can count, but somehow just lying here next to her, knowing that she understands me, feels better than kissing ever could.

I think this might be the best moment of my whole life.

I don't know how long we watch the sky before Delilah sits up.

"I gotta get back to the house. My daddy always checks in on me at midnight."

I sit up, too, and fight the urge to grab her hand and beg her to stay when she stands. "I should get back. Early start tomorrow."

"Yeah." She cocks her head and smiles at me. "You're all right, Pruitt. You know, for a *Reese*."

I feel myself grinning like a fool. "You ain't so bad yourself."

She laughs as she backs toward the trees, and it makes me brave. "Maybe I'll see you out here tomorrow night?"

"Maybe," she calls over her shoulder, just before she gets out of sight.

I stay right in that spot, my face aching with the smile I can't wipe off, till Delilah's been gone long enough to reach her house. Then I let out a shout.

She doesn't hate me.

I know I should get on home, but I don't want the night to end yet. I'm afraid if I go to sleep, I'll wake up and find that none of this ever happened.

Knowing that Delilah hates living in Stillwater as much as I do has got me wired, so wired that it takes me a moment to realize that things have gone quiet. Too quiet. My mind flashes back to my dream. I remember how, just before the lights showed up, it was dead silent then, too.

Almost like the whole world went to sleep, and only me and Matt were awake to see.

I look over to the ridge and everything beyond it is dark. Above it the sky's split in two. Stars—not stars. Like one of them black holes they have in space just sucked up part of the world. I walk to the edge of the ridge and wait.

It starts with a sound. A faint *whoosh*, and then another, and then the black in front of me flickers in and out. Behind it are tiny points of light all red and white and orange. I can hear cars driving, and the hum of streetlights, and underneath it all, the faint sound of water, lapping at a shore.

It takes every bit of strength I have to keep standing. I pinch my arm hard, but nothing changes. There's a whole world out there. So close I can almost touch it. I can *smell* it—exhaust fumes and smoke and this metallic scent that must come from the city. Moonlight glints off something below me and I look down. In the place where the dried-out creek bed should be there's a pool of water.

I follow the faint ripples to the shore. And what I see there knocks my legs out from under me. A great big rock sits close to the edge of the water. Painted on it in big, white letters is a message. For me.

PRUITT
JUMP!
—MATT

On my hands and knees, I read that rock over and over. It wasn't a dream. Matt's real. He got out.

All of a sudden, a heavy wind starts blowing. It pushes me back, away from the edge of the cliff. I press my back against a boulder and watch as my view of the outside world gets smaller and smaller. The black closes in around Matt's message until there's nothing left but darkness. Then the wind settles down and just like that, I'm alone, wondering if I lost my mind.

I'm shaking something fierce. My heart's fixing to beat right out of my chest. I don't know what I'm more afraid of, the idea that I'm crazy or the idea that this might be real.

But it ain't till I stand up and turn around that I realize I didn't know the meaning of the word *scared*. 'Cause scratched into the rock I've just been leaning on is another message:

DON'T FALL ASLEEP

But that ain't even the craziest part. The craziest part is that I recognize the handwriting.

It's mine.

My message said not to fall asleep and I'm taking it to heart. I'm on my third pot of coffee when the sun starts to rise. My thoughts have been running around in my head all night, but there's only one that's dug its heels in and stuck—I ain't leaving without Delilah.

Far as I can figure, last night wasn't the first time I saw that hole open up in the sky. What I don't get is why I don't remember. And how I could forget my own brother. But I got all day to work that out. First, I need to see Delilah.

"Pruitt? Did you make the coffee?" Mama stands in the kitchen doorway looking perplexed. She usually has to drag me out of bed in the morning.

"I thought I'd get an early start for a change," I tell her.

"Well, isn't that nice." She gets herself a mug from the cabinet and ruffles my hair on the way to the coffeepot. "Your father will be impressed."

She smiles at me and I smile back, but we both know that ain't true. Nothing I do will ever impress him. "I best get going, then."

I make sure to kiss her cheek on my way out of the house. Seeing my mama makes me realize I've been considering running off and leaving without so much as a good-bye. My daddy will probably say "good riddance" when I'm gone, but Mama, well, that just seems cruel.

I skip my usual deliveries and go straight to the Stillwater Café. Delilah is just tying on her apron when I burst through the door.

"Delilah," I practically shout. "You won't believe what happened last night!"

Delilah just stares at me with her eyes all wide. "What?"

"Last night after you left, it was—" The words dry up in my mouth. Delilah's looking at me like I'm spouting nonsense.

"What are you talking about?"

My heart's racing and I can't tell if it's from the coffee or something else. "Last night, up at the ridge?" If she don't remember, I don't know what I'm gonna do.

She shakes her head back and forth real slow.

I want to take her by the arms and shake her or something, but I just stand there with my hands out like I'm begging. "We saw each other, remember?"

"I was nowhere near the ridge last night."

She's looking me dead in the eye, so I know she ain't lying. The way she's standing there with her arms crossed and frowning at me, it's like the whole night never even happened for her.

Then I notice she's wearing her red Stillwater High T-shirt, just like yesterday, and it all makes sense—what Matt meant about a full night's sleep making you forget, why I left that message for myself, why Delilah keeps having that dream.

"All right, I know this is gonna sound crazy, but you know that dream you have about us all being stuck inside a snow globe?"

Her mouth drops open. "How do you know about that?"

The coffee's got my mouth sped up and my words tumble out all over each other. "You don't remember, but you told me. And it's true, I can prove it. I found the opening last night, and I think you've seen it, too." I reach for her without thinking, and my hands are on her shoulders before I can stop myself. "Meet me up at the ridge tonight, a little before midnight, and I'll show you."

Delilah stares up at me like she's trying to figure me out, and my heart kicks up just from having her eyes on me so long. I know I should let her go, but all I can think is how I'm close enough to kiss her. And how even though I've never touched her before, it feels *right*.

Delilah's still got her eyes locked on mine. She leans toward me, just a tiny bit, but I could swear she feels it, too. "I can't," she says, but doesn't move away.

She bites down on her bottom lip and that settles it—if she won't come with me, I'm just gonna lie down and die.

"Please." I'm so desperate, my voice is practically a whisper. "Something ain't right about this town, Delilah. Even if you don't believe me about last night, I know you believe that."

My breath is coming up short, like I've been running. Delilah presses her hand to my chest and suddenly our heads are a whole lot closer together. And then I know, sure as the sun comes up every morning, I'm gonna kiss her and she's gonna kiss me back.

"What in the hell?" Delilah's daddy shouts so loud it echoes off the pots and pans.

I jump back from Delilah but it don't even matter, her daddy's already got me by the collar.

"Daddy, don't!" Delilah reaches out for us, but we're halfway to the door.

I raise my hands up high. "I'm sorry, sir."

Mr. Reese unloads a stream of curses while he drags me out, and I hold my tongue. Even when he calls my whole family hillbilly white trash. I don't know if it's just 'cause I'm wired on caffeine, but I can see it real clear now. Delilah's daddy, our family feud, this whole town, they ain't nothing but background noise. The only thing that matters is Delilah.

She follows us out, screaming for her daddy to stop.

When he slams me against the cab of my truck, I twist my head till I can see her, and when we meet eyes, I do my best to smile. I got the wind knocked out of me but I mouth the words, "We can get out."

"Okay," she says, real quiet, just to me. The tears in her eyes catch the light as she nods her head. "Just let him go, Daddy. He didn't do anything."

Delilah's daddy shoves my head against the door and holds it there. I'm sure it's gonna ache something fierce later, but right now I don't feel a thing. He presses my temple into the metal and leans in close. "You touch my daughter again, I'll shoot you. You hear?"

"Yes, sir." It's amazing how stuff ain't scary once you know you're never gonna see it again.

Mama's unloading groceries in the kitchen when I get home. For once, I didn't mind doing the rest of the deliveries. It helped pass the time and kept me awake.

Mama's on me as soon as I set foot in the room. "What were you thinking?"

I guess she heard. Figures. Nothing in Stillwater stays quiet for long. "It wasn't nothing, Mama. Delilah's daddy overreacted."

Mama grabs a dish towel and starts wringing the life out of it. Her knuckles go white with the effort. "Are you messing around with that girl?"

I don't have the energy for this. "Can we save this for when Dad gets home?"

Mama purses her lips like she's upset at the suggestion, but I know she prefers for Daddy to do the yelling. "Fine. But don't you come out of that room until then."

"Fine," I say, and head for the stairs. If I know my daddy, he'll be too pissed to deal with me till morning. He'll make me sit up in my room all night without supper and "think on what I done." I ain't feeling so guilty for leaving anymore.

Now all I got to do is stay awake.

Nothing ever changes in Stillwater. Nothing. Every day in this town is exactly the same—hotter than all get-out, and just as boring. I'm up with the sun, but I'm exhausted, and my head hurts, like I hardly got any sleep at all.

I'm craving coffee, even though I can't stand the taste. That's different, but not so much as to be exciting. Mama and Daddy are at the breakfast table when I stumble into the kitchen.

"Morning, Pruitt," Mama says all chipper like. Daddy just grunts.

"Morning." I can feel their eyes on me while I fix myself a thermos of coffee. I load up the truck and make my deliveries same as always. And like always, Mrs. Pearson pinches my cheek too hard when she tells me, "Why, Pruitt Reese, you are becoming more like your daddy every day." I never can figure why everybody in town thinks that's such a good thing.

At least by the time I get to the Stillwater Café, I'm feeling more like myself.

Delilah's at the back door before I'm even halfway out of the truck. "Pruitt?" There's something different about the way she says my name. Like it matters to her whether or not I say something back. If I didn't know better, I'd get my hopes up.

"Hey, Delilah," I say as I put the gate down on the truck. "Just gimme a second to get unloaded."

She puts her hand on my arm, giving me a start. "How are you feeling, Pruitt?"

I'm having a hard time breathing right now with her touching me, but I don't think that's what she's asking. I can't think straight enough to come up with anything else, so I tell her the truth. "I'm fine. Just a little tired, is all."

She nods like I just said something real important. "Me too."

Delilah will always be beautiful, but she does look a bit tired around the eyes.

"How's your head?" She reaches up and brushes the hair at my temple aside like she's looking for something. I flinch both 'cause I'm surprised and 'cause it stings there like I got punched.

I've imagined this more than once—her coming out to meet my truck, reaching for me, but this is real life and I don't know what to do. She smells like lilacs.

"Pruitt, I need you to do something for me."

Right now, with her hands on me, standing this close, she could ask me anything and I know I'd do it. "Okay."

She's got her eyes on mine, and part of me keeps waiting to wake up. She only looks at me like that in my dreams.

Delilah gives my shoulder a squeeze like she knows what I'm thinking. "Meet me out at the ridge at eleven forty-five tonight."

"Okay." My voice cracks on the word, but I'm way past caring.

She looks at me like she's looking *into* me. "You really will, won't you? Without even knowing why?"

I can't breathe let alone remember how to say yes. I nod my head and hope she can tell how much I mean it. And then it hits me. "Wait, is this . . ." I take a step back, out of her grasp. "Are you messing with me?" It's the only thing that makes sense, but I never figured Delilah for being mean-spirited.

She smiles when she shakes her head, but it's sad somehow. "I would never do that." Delilah closes the distance between us. She puts her hand on my chest and I realize my heart is racing. When she lifts her pretty brown eyes to mine, I can feel her breath on my face.

Somewhere nearby a car backfires, and I remember we're right outside the back door of the diner. As much as I don't want this to end, I don't want to get caught, either. Her daddy scares the hell out of me. "Is your daddy around?"

Delilah grins and my heart damn near stops. "We don't have to worry about Daddy."

Before I can ask why not, she slides her hand to the back of my neck and kisses me. Soft at first, but then she pulls me close and my arms find their way around her waist. It's like our bodies already know how we fit together, and we kiss like it's the one thing that's been missing in our lives.

"Delilah," her daddy shouts from inside the kitchen. "Did that boy deliver the supplies yet?"

We fly apart, breathless, and Delilah backs toward the door to shout, "He's here now, Daddy."

I start unloading the truck. Delilah's dad is still talking but I can't hear a thing over the pounding in my chest.

Delilah turns to me. Her cheeks are flushed and I have to grip the handles of the crate to keep from grabbing her and kissing her again. "Promise me something."

I set my crate down on the dolly and grin at her. "Anything."

She looks me dead in the eye, as serious as I've ever seen her. "Don't go to sleep today. Not even a nap. Just don't sleep. Okay?"

I can't imagine ever sleeping again. "Okay."

She grabs my face with her hands. "Promise."

I put my hands over hers. "I promise."

She studies my face like she's trying to memorize it and then lets me go. "Good. Remember, eleven forty-five tonight."

How could I ever forget?

When I walk into the clearing, Delilah is there waiting. Her face lights up when she sees me, and I want to pinch myself to make sure this ain't just another one of my dreams.

She runs over to me. "You came!"

After this morning, I can't figure how she'd think I'd be anywhere else. "Of course I did."

"I've got something to show you." She takes my hand and leads me over to a cluster of rocks out on the ridge. "Yesterday you asked me to meet you out here. You said something isn't right about Stillwater. That the reason we felt so trapped here is because we were. You said there was a way out."

"I said that? To you?" The only thing I remember about yesterday is that it was just like today—minus the kissing. I got up. I made my deliveries. I was bored as hell.

Delilah laughs. "I know. Yesterday you sounded as

crazy to me as I sound to you right now—until you told me something I've never told anyone. And then I saw this."

She points at the biggest boulder, and on it I see my own handwriting.

DON'T FALL ASLEEP

If this is some kind of trick, it's a damn good one.

"You must've fallen asleep yesterday and slept till morning. That's why you don't remember, I think." Her eyes are shiny in the moonlight. "You could've left, but you waited—" Her voice hitches. "For me."

There's something familiar about what she's saying; it's right there at the edge of my mind. "I don't—"

"You'll see." She squeezes my hand and pulls me up to the cliff's edge. "It's starting."

At first all I notice is the quiet, like somebody turned off the night. Then the black sky beyond the ridge fades away and there's cars and houses and skyscrapers where there should be nothing but empty land. It calls to mind a dream I once had.

"This can't be real," I say, but somehow, in my gut, I know it is.

"Look." Delilah points down below us, at a pool of water, and then across it to the shore. "Out there."

The letters on the rock are faded, but they're still clear enough to read in the moonlight.

PRUITT
JUMP!
—MATT

"Holy . . ." *Matt.* All them little memory pieces floating around in my mind pull themselves together and I remember. I have a brother. It feels as real as Delilah's hand in mine.

"We have to jump," she says.

My brain keeps trying to tell me this is crazy, but in my gut it just feels *right*. Me and Delilah, too. It's like we've always been right, we just forgot.

Delilah's grip on my hand tightens. "We don't have much time."

Even as she says it, the wind kicks up and darkness spills back in, blocking out the lights.

A heavy gust pushes us back from the edge. I wrap my arms around Delilah and hold her tight against my chest until it stops. I could stay standing like this forever but I know that won't get us nowhere but stuck. We have to jump.

Over the ridge, there ain't nothing but empty black space again. "Think it's still out there?"

Delilah laces her fingers through mine. "It has to be."

I step up to the edge.

"Wait." Delilah reaches up and kisses me fierce, and I know whatever happens, we can handle it together.

I take a deep breath, and she gives my hand one last squeeze, and then we jump into the dark.

I think maybe I'm supposed to feel scared, but all I feel is free.

Sarah Rees Brennan
I Gave You My Love by the Light of the Moon

There was a creepy guy staring at her in the coffee shop.

Berthe, sitting up at the high table by the window with her two best friends, became aware of it in a gradual, nasty way, like when Berthe had gone camping for the first time, years ago, and only realized the ground was damp when the wet had already seeped into her clothes. As soon as she was aware of his stare, she knew it had been going on too long.

She even got up from the table to fetch herself a tiny

packet of sugar that she didn't want. She was hoping that he would look at Natalie or Leela, that the stare was just the unpleasant one some guys would give any girl, not personal but something they apparently felt you had brought on yourself by having boobs.

It wasn't. His eyes followed her path to the unwanted sugar and then back. Berthe perched on the edge of her stool, self-conscious and furious, too, that some idiot just looking at her was enough to spoil her fun with her friends.

Being almost six feet tall and a sixteen-year-old girl made you self-conscious enough most days, and today Berthe had the worst cramps she'd ever had in her life.

So someone giving her the stalker eyeballs was the outside of enough. He looked like a college guy, or maybe he was a bit too young, maybe he was one of those high school boys who couldn't wait to get into college where everyone could appreciate his tortured soul. He was wearing a tweedy hipster scarf and black rectangular-framed hipster-boy glasses. His eyes gleamed behind them, pale and intent. In fact, he was pretty pale all over, that particular shade of pale that suggested he was waiting for someone to invent technology that would allow him to get a tan from the light of his laptop screen alone.

Not at all the sort of boy Berthe would have anything in common with, even if he hadn't decided to stare at her like a creeper when she already felt like crap.

Another cramp made Berthe hunch forward, almost

tilting off the stool. Her face must have shown some of what she was feeling, because Leela reached over the table and touched her arm.

"Are you all right? You feel hot."

Natalie, the vivacious creature of the group, all laughs and curls, and the one who usually drew boys' eyes, raised her eyebrows at that and said, "I bet she does. Rawr."

Leela was too concerned and Berthe was frankly too freaked out to laugh. Berthe didn't feel hot. In fact, the skin at the back of her neck was prickling with cold sweat. She touched her fingertips to her cheek and felt them slide on the clammy surface.

"I just have, you know"—Berthe waved her hand at her midsection even as she lied—"a headache."

As though it were punishment for her lie, Berthe actually felt a twinge start in her head, a jagged line of pain that went from skull to spine. She put her elbow on the table and put her head down, brow pressed against her palm, until the sharp pain and the slow grind of agony in her stomach eased.

She looked up. Natalie looked serious now, and almost as concerned as Leela. Berthe really didn't like being the center of attention; eyes on her made her feel as if she should be doing something and was too inadequate to know what. Unless she was playing lacrosse.

"I'm just going to go home," she said abruptly—she didn't want any more fussing, she didn't want to spoil their day—and she got up, holding on to the edge of the table as she did, so that she would look steady. "I just need an Advil and a nap. Call you guys later."

She left precipitately; if she didn't want one of them coming with her, haste was essential. They would be held up paying for their coffees and discussing whether to go after her, and she'd be long gone.

When Berthe found herself staggering down the steps of the exit and almost reeling into the alleyway beside it, pressing the clammy-cold, prickling-hot skin of her face against the brick wall, she began to rethink her amazing strategy. No matter how awkward she felt about being fussed over, it beat not getting home at all. It was pitch-black outside, the night sky pressing down on her, dense and dark, and she did not think she could walk.

Pain crumpled her insides like tissue and she made a sound horrifyingly like a whine, like the sound of that animal at the campsite weeks ago, the wild snarling thing Berthe had barely seen but whose teeth she could sometimes still feel, as sharp in her memory as they had been in her skin. Berthe wanted to touch the bandage on her arm, but she gritted her teeth and kept her hands flat against the wall, braced. She wasn't going to fall down.

"You can't stay here," said a voice behind her.

Berthe wanted to spin around, but the voice barely cut through the waves of pain. The most she could do was force her eyes slightly open.

The boy from the coffee shop swam in her vision, his pale face blurring into moonlight and then coalescing into features behind spectacles again. Sweat stung Berthe's eyes. A stalker had her cornered in an alleyway at night, and she could hardly bring herself to mind.

"Oh, give it up," she said, always bad at being tactful and now not even able to be polite. "Do you have some sort of fetish for girls getting sick on your feet?"

"I implore you not to give me the chance to develop one," he said. "But you need help."

His face kept disintegrating with each new wave of pain, nothing but glittering shards of moonlight in her vision. Berthe put her hands to her stomach, clutching at it, and realized her mistake when she almost toppled over sideways.

The boy had hold of her arm suddenly, grip cold and firm and inexorable, like being held up by a piece of machinery. Berthe was vaguely startled that he could hold her up at all, since they were the same height, and he was so skinny.

Berthe was starting to think she did need help. But that didn't mean she had to accept it from him.

"So g-get my friends," she said, her teeth chattering so hard that she was afraid they would smash like porcelain. "They're in the—you know who I mean, you were staring like a—you're creepy."

He seemed entirely unaffected by this assessment.

Possibly it was not news to him.

He said, as if she had not spoken at all and in relation to nothing, as if he was just plucking random words out of the air: "You don't want to hurt anyone, do you?"

It was strange enough that Berthe opened her eyes all the way, even as another snake of pain uncoiled and struck in her belly. He looked at her, eyes unblinking behind his silly glasses, everything she saw about him at odds with his stone-fast grip.

She saw he was perfectly serious.

"Of c-course I don't want to hurt anyone," she gasped out.

"Come with me," the creepy boy from the coffee shop said. "Or you'll kill someone."

Come with me if you want someone else to live, Berthe thought, her mind so muddled she could not even remember what movie she was mangling a quote from.

She wouldn't have responded to a threat to herself; she would have screamed and hit out at him, not because she was brave but because that was something life prepared you for, creepy guys threatening you in darkened alleyways. She was not prepared for someone to say that she could be dangerous. She had never hurt anyone in her life and never wanted to. It was not a warning she could ignore.

Berthe staggered, a violent enough lurch so she was almost jarred out of even this boy's grasp. "All right," she got out, between stiff lips and chattering teeth.

The creep from the coffee shop wasn't just strong, he was fast. Berthe stumbled in the boy's speeding wake, and after a few streets, tilting into swathes of moonlight and then back to shadowy road, he stopped at a door. Berthe leaned her face against it, forehead pressed to peeling gray paint, and the boy fished out a key from the pocket of his skinny jeans and opened the door.

She went sprawling into a tiny coffin of a hall.

"Come on, come on," the boy muttered, his keys falling to the floor with a clatter and a thud. He hauled her up again, arm an iron bar across her midsection, and pushed her up stairs covered in brown carpeting, worn white with the constant passage of feet. Even the white traces of age on the carpet shimmered in Berthe's eyes like moonlight.

They got up the narrow little stairs and into another tiny hall, then through a door that looked out of place, heavy and dark in the midst of all this cheap flimsiness. The boy towed Berthe inside the door.

There were shutters on the windows, heavy and dark like the doors. There was a single bed in the corner, neatly made.

Sick and staggering, Berthe still felt a panicked fist clutch at the inside of her throat. She remembered what she had allowed herself to forget amid all the pain—that what she was doing was crazy.

"Oh no," she said weakly, and backed right into the boy. She spun to face him, even though the sudden movement made her stagger and sway. "No—" she repeated, raining down blows on his narrow chest. They landed like kittens on lily pads.

He caught her wrists in that stone grip of his, pushing her firmly into the room and stepping backward over the threshold as he did so.

"Trust me," he said. "You couldn't pay me to stay in this room with you."

He slammed the door shut. Berthe did not even feel afraid that she was now trapped in a stranger's bedroom. She was just relieved to be alone with her miserable sickness, not to have to split her focus between current agony and present danger.

She sank down onto the carpet on her hands and knees and arched her back; she felt as if her spine were made of metal and somehow turning molten inside her skin, dissolving and burning at once. She gagged, wrenching pain all the way through her, as if her insides were being torn out. The bite on her arm where the creature from the campsite had sunk its teeth in throbbed as if it might start bleeding again.

Berthe sobbed. She was scared that she would choke up her internal organs, have them laid out ruby red on the carpet before her, her heart bitter in her mouth.

Her fingers clawed on the carpet, tearing it into ragged shreds. Berthe howled her agony and her vision whited out, all moonlight, moonlight, moonlight in the dark.

✦ ✦ ✦

Berthe woke up aching in a nest of chaos. She lifted her head, her hair a snarled blond veil between her and the world. When she reached her hand to brush it back, her whole body shuddered in protest.

The room she had seen last night was destroyed. The bed was a metal skeleton, scraps of cloth that had been sheets and a mattress hanging on it like mournful ghosts. There was a wardrobe at the other end of the room that she had not even noticed: its door was torn off its hinges. The walls had been beige: now they were carved with deep, gray lines. The boards beneath the torn carpet were savagely scored as well, the floor a mess of splinters and nails.

Berthe was naked. She very urgently did not want to stay naked, curled up and whimpering like an animal.

She climbed gingerly to her feet and went over to the wardrobe with its door ripped off. There were clothes inside, boys' clothes, and weird boys' clothes at that, but beggars couldn't be choosers, and naked people couldn't be fussy about fashion.

There were a lot of button-down shirts that did not fit across her boobs, but she got into a T-shirt that said ORGAN DONOR, INQUIRE WITHIN. The fit made it embarrassingly obvious she wasn't wearing a bra.

She went down the stairs barefoot.

It was silent in the house, so silent she thought that

perhaps she was alone here, that she could just open the door and go home now without having to face anything.

She pushed open the other door in the little hall, just the same.

Inside was a kitchen-cum-living room, all the blinds drawn. In the dimness she could see clean countertops, a battered sofa, and on a low table, a cup of tea with a cookie lying beside it.

In the darkest corner of the room stood the creep from the coffee shop.

He was still wearing his jacket and his dumb scarf, and he had his hands in his pockets. He looked up as she came in.

"I suppose you have a lot of questions," he said. He sounded patient, like someone talking to a small child who could not possibly understand anything on her own.

"No," said Berthe. She was grateful, suddenly, that he put her back up. It pulled her away from the edge of screaming, senseless terror. "I went out camping in the woods, and I was bitten by something that I thought was a wild dog. Last night was the full moon. And I've seen horror movies before. I think I know what's going on."

She did not know until he just kept looking at her, gaze level and undisturbed, that she had wanted him to come up with another explanation. She'd wanted him to tell her she was crazy.

"What I don't know," she said, hearing her voice go

high and unpleasant, "is how you knew."

He didn't say a word.

She plunged on. "I mean, do you make a habit of staring like a freak at girls and then, if they seem ill, dragging them into your bedroom on the off chance they're . . ."

"I can tell," he said. "I could smell you."

She felt a flash of shame stronger than terror, so ferocious and so unreasonable—that she could care how she smelled, with all this—it made her furious with herself and him.

"And how could you—what were you—" Embarrassment as well as rage throttled her. She could not believe she could not even ask him something important about her own body.

"You'll be able to do it as well," he said. "Smell things other people can't smell. See things other people can't see. Do things other people can't do."

"Will I be able to leap tall buildings in a single bound?" asked Berthe. Her mouth tasted sour, and her words were all coming out sour, too. She could not seem to care.

She went over to the window and began to fiddle with the pull on the blind so she wouldn't have to keep looking at him.

"Medium-sized buildings," he said. "Crouch first. Don't go for a skyscraper. I'd describe that as o'erarching ambition."

Berthe twisted the pull around her wrist, plastic beads

digging into her flesh hard. She could not believe he was trying to make a joke.

"So you're—" she said, and could not find the words in her sour, dust-dry mouth. She tugged hard at the blind. "You're like me?"

The blind tumbled down with a rattle and a bang, the plastic cord suddenly slack around her wrist and sudden sunlight flooding in, making her blink.

Her ears filled with the sound of the boy hissing, a cat's noise from a boy's throat. She saw him move fast, backing away from the sudden sunlight and into a different dark corner.

There was a hand held up, protecting his face, but she could still see his bared inhuman teeth.

"No," he whispered. "I'm not like you."

This last revelation was too much, the world of strangeness expanding too far. Berthe could not bear another second in this little house.

She turned and ran, as she'd wanted to before, out into the sunlight where he could not follow her, and she told herself that it would not happen again.

She kept telling herself that. She sneaked in through her bedroom window and pretended she had got in late and slept in her own bed that night, tucked in innocent and harmless under her sheets.

She told herself that when she lied to her friends that

she was all better now, she told herself that when she refused to go on the next camping trip, even though she had always signed up to go on every trip before. She told herself that, lying in her safe bed, under her safe sheets, with the windows open so she could see the moon had not become bright and dangerous yet.

She could hear her parents having whispered fights all the way across the house, and even though they were ordinary fights that left no trace of bitterness behind, she had never known they had those fights before. She didn't want to know now. She could hear Natalie and Leela murmuring secrets meant to exclude her, and even though she knew she'd done the same thing with both of them, that every pair of friends had secrets between just the two of them, actually hearing it hurt.

That she was able to hear all these things hurt worse. The scar on the inside of her elbow was a silver crescent moon, shining and smooth on her skin, but the moon was long past crescent.

She could not get away from the world or herself. The night and her body lay in wait to betray her.

She stopped telling herself that it would not happen again, because she could not bear to think about it at all.

But she remembered, as well as the fear and pain, what the boy at the coffee shop had said.

You don't want to hurt anyone, do you?

She walked across town as the sun died, on the night of

the next full moon, and knocked on a gray door.

The boy from the coffee shop let her in.

It happened again.

Berthe came downstairs in another pair of sweatpants and a T-shirt that read BEING PESSIMISTIC WOULDN'T WORK ANYWAY. She was not tempted to run out the door this time. She had spent a month running already.

The boy was standing in the same shadowed corner he had stood in the last time. Berthe noticed he had fixed the blind.

He had loomed large in her mind, the moment of hissing and teeth overwriting everything else, but he looked very much like he had in the coffee shop, dark hair swept back in a particular, deliberate way, wearing fingerless gloves of all things. The room looked exactly the same as well, down to the cup of tea and the cookie on the table.

"Thank you," said Berthe. She felt she had to, even though she didn't know how to mean it.

"You're welcome," he said quietly. He gestured toward the table. "Do you want a cup of tea?"

"Yes," Berthe said. "All right."

She walked toward the table and sat down in the chair. "Can I—"

"I do not drink . . . tea," said the boy, and smirked to himself before his face smoothed out, serious and pale. "I don't eat. It's for you."

It made her feel strange, to realize that he had gone out and bought tea and cookies for her last month, laid them out thinking she might be hungry.

She took a sip of the tea. It was cooling, but she saw the strips of sunlight on the kitchen counter and knew he could not have made it later. The whole room had sneaky pieces of sunlight in it.

The heavy shutters and door upstairs clearly formed his refuge, and she had exiled him from it.

"Thanks," she said again, and meant it a little this time. "The tea's good. Is there a cure?"

"It isn't a sickness," said the boy. "It's who you are now."

"So that would be a no."

He was silent, though his attention stayed fixed on her. Now that Berthe was looking back at him, she saw why he might wear glasses: they helped hide his eyes' strange brightness and the way they tracked movement, more alert than a human's would.

Or maybe he needed glasses. Could a creature like him need glasses?

"You knew what I was," Berthe said, utterly unable to talk about him smelling her. "You recognized it. So you must have met other people like me."

"I knew one. She was kind to me," said the boy. "But she can't help you. I'm sorry. She's dead now."

"What did she die of?" Berthe heard her voice shake, felt her lips tremble, and put the cookie to her lips to hide it.

"She killed herself," said the boy softly. He added, "I'm sorry," again.

"I'm the one who should be sorry," Berthe said, swallowing desolation and a mouthful of cookie so dry it scraped her throat. "She was your friend."

Killed herself, Berthe thought despairingly. Because she hurt somebody, or because she could not live being like Berthe was now a moment longer? She didn't know, and the woman could not tell her now. She could not tell Berthe anything.

"What about the—the person who bit me in the woods?" Berthe asked desperately. "They must be like me. Couldn't we find them? Couldn't you smell them?"

The boy's eyebrows rose. "I'm not a sniffer dog," he said mildly. "Even when you were human, I'm sure you could smell a pie. I don't imagine you could wander the city streets and track a pie down by scent."

"Isn't there some way?" Berthe said. She put down the cookie and the tea and put her face in her hands, too wretched to be embarrassed. "Isn't there any way?"

The boy cleared his throat, a soft apologetic sound, after she had sat with her head in her hands for some time. She looked up and saw him looking at the floor, at one of the strips of sunlight.

"They might still be in the woods," he said. "If they are, I don't think they'll be able to help you. But if you want, I'll go with you to look."

"Yes," Berthe said. Any relief at this point felt like overwhelming joy. "Yes, please. Thank you. Can we go now?"

"Well," the boy said, "no. I fear that if I burst into flames and died in agony, it might hamper the expedition somewhat."

"Oh." Berthe felt like an idiot and also just felt lost. She had seen him leap away from the fallen blind, seen his teeth, but every moment in his company it seemed more unreal. She could run around the room pulling up blinds, and though he seemed solid and real, he would turn to ash. A shudder rang through her, all the way to her aching bones. "Can we go tonight?"

The boy said, "Of course."

"Thank you," Berthe said again. Every one of her thanks had become more real, by degrees. She turned away from her tea and the crumbs on the table, tilted her head so she was looking at him, at the strange eyes glittering behind his glasses. "I'm Berthe."

"Berthe," he said, pronouncing it correctly right off. "That's French, isn't it?"

"Yeah."

Berthe always felt a bit awkward about her name. She didn't look elegant and French, dainty and well dressed like her mother, who she'd once heard described as everything a woman should be. Berthe was tall and blond with strong shoulders, like her dad. But they hadn't known what she would be like when she grew up.

The creepy guy from the coffee shop, the creature with the teeth who had saved her, said, "I'm Stephen."

It was such an ordinary name, it made Berthe almost smile, and then bite on her lower lip in case that offended him.

He didn't look offended.

"I can't say it's nice to meet you, under the circumstances," said Berthe at last. "But . . ."

He smiled, mouth closed and teeth hidden. It was, under the circumstances, quite a nice smile.

"Likewise."

The woods near her town were not full of gnarled oaks and whispered legends of a curse. The trees were all pine trees, grown for lumber, with a lot of handy campsites. Berthe had gone hiking through these woods a hundred times and never felt the least alarm. She had been so absolutely sure that when it came right down to it, she was safe.

The woods at night, nobody but her and a relative stranger, were very quiet. It was also very bright, even considering that the moon was one night past full, a shining coin in the sky. Berthe could see the silver stir of pine needles as a tiny animal ran through them, yards and yards away. Every tree branch was a clear silver line struck against the sky.

When she looked at Stephen, he had his glasses off.

She'd been right, she thought: he didn't need them for anything but concealment. His eyes looked silver, too, his pupils subtly wrong, darting after every movement in the wood.

Just like her eyes were. Berthe wondered what her eyes looked like to him.

"Which of us can see better?" she asked.

"I don't know," Stephen answered. "Does it matter? We can both see very well. We are predators. But you're stronger and faster. My kind are built for a more cunning type of hunt."

Predators. Hunt. The words danced grotesquely in Berthe's mind.

Stephen blinked. "Sorry. That came out a great deal more disturbing than it sounded in my head. I'm afraid I'm out of practice with conversation."

"You don't talk to people?" Berthe asked blankly.

"Not really," said Stephen. "Not in depth. The less contact with other people, the less chance they'll notice I'm not aging. I can stay in one place longer."

"You don't," Berthe said. "You don't age. Right, obviously. Because that's how you work, with the no sunlight and the—not aging. And you talk like an old person. How old are you?"

You talk like an old person, Berthe repeated to herself silently. She never had known how to talk to boys.

"Sixty-two," Stephen answered.

Berthe stared.

"I know," said Stephen. "It seems glamorous and otherworldly for someone like me to be a hundred years old, or two hundred. But there is the problem of getting there."

It was a real age, an age that a person could be, the age for women with blue hair and blouses, for men with canes and tweed caps, for grandparents. That made it much harder to assign to the boy in front of her, his face smooth and his eyes faintly glowing.

"You wait until I'm a hundred years old," Stephen said, mouth quirking. "The ladies will love it."

"I'll be fifty-four by then," Berthe told him.

There was a brief awkward pause.

"I meant the ladies in general," Stephen said. "They will be lining up. I will have to carry extra dance cards, on account of how my dance card will be entirely full."

There was another silence, broken by a rustle far away that made Stephen's head turn, chin lifting, scenting the air. Berthe turned with him, trying to make out whatever he did, and caught something: wild and strange, musk and fur. She wondered if that was how she smelled to him, and then she did not have time to wonder further: Stephen was running, fleet and sure, faster than any boy who looked like he did should have been able to. Faster than anyone should have been able to.

Berthe was fast. She didn't run track or anything, but

she played lacrosse and in gym she tended to win races. She wasn't fast enough to keep up with Stephen, she knew, but she tried, anyway, and it was shockingly easy. Her feet found every place, tree roots and leaf drifts where she might have tripped or slipped, seeming not even there. It was like running over smooth ground, and she was past Stephen, toward the wild scent, with the wild wind in her hair.

There was a dark shape at the foot of a tree, and it twisted away from her and almost ran into Stephen, who hissed at it, teeth gleaming. For a moment Berthe felt a tremor run through her, a chill of profound unfamiliarity: that Stephen was not like her, and the shape between them was.

Except Stephen was here to help her, and this was the creature that had attacked her.

"Why," Berthe said, voice tearing in the wind, "why is he still a wolf? It's not the full moon—he shouldn't be—"

"Some of you turn wild." Stephen's voice was calm because it was always calm, but there was a slight strain to the calm now. "And you don't turn back."

Berthe's heart banged in her ears like many doors slamming all at once: no answers, no hope, no help to be had, just a dumb thing with eyes shining up at her, green like her own but split with lines of yellow like lightning.

It was moving, low on the ground but with intent, toward Stephen.

The hair on the back of Berthe's neck stood up, but for once she didn't feel afraid. She felt—it was more like outrage, and she moved in her new smooth way and was standing between them, making a sound that was mangled by her human throat.

I won't let you: challenge: mine, said the sound, and the animal backed away. It understood her.

It understood her because she was halfway to being an animal herself, because there were no answers but only this horror beyond words in the woods.

The wolf backed away on its belly, and Berthe sat down among the pine needles.

"Sometimes they still turn back," Stephen said. "I thought perhaps—I wanted there to be something here for you."

"A look into the future?"

"No," said Stephen. "They make a choice—they turn toward the wild—"

"And what other choice is there to make?" Berthe demanded. "The one your friend did?"

Berthe had to look up from the pine needle floor because she could not hear Stephen. He did not breathe and his heart did not beat; when he was still he was a creature of perfect silence and she could not tell if he was there. She was suddenly afraid that he had left, suddenly aware that things could get worse.

Stephen had not left. He was looking down at her, eyes

moonlight-eerie in his thin, serious face, and then he knelt down so they were on a level.

"She was very lonely," he said. "She didn't know what was happening to her at first. She hurt people. She hurt her family. You haven't done that. You're not alone."

"No," said Berthe, and thought painfully of her parents, and of Leela and Natalie. They all seemed so far away in a world she did not know how to scramble back to. "But I could hurt them," she said. "And I can't tell them. And I'm alone with this."

"You're not," said Stephen.

"You're not like me," Berthe told him, her voice low.

She did not just mean what they were, or the feeling of being on different sides in a dark wood. He was in control as she was not: he was not tearing rooms into shreds.

"I only wanted . . . ," Berthe tried to clarify, "I wanted someone who could explain this to me, from the inside out."

Stephen looked off into the trees, after the fleeing wolf, and then knelt down on the ground among the needles with her.

"I'm not telling you this to trump what you're feeling," he said, "or to try and win the argument. I was made by a man who had a whole bevy of us—teenage minions, old enough to be useful, but not old enough to survive on our own with ease. He told us what was happening to us, and what to do, how to feed, how to serve him and recruit for him. We were dependent on him, because of what we were."

Feed, Berthe thought, and whispered, "Did you kill someone?"

"I killed three people," Stephen answered, without hesitating. "The last one was the worst, though I doubt the first two would agree with me. I had a family, once. I waited for my chance to get back to them. When it came, I didn't get away clean—someone was watching me. A window broke, and I was cut, and one of the others had her teeth in my wrist to the bone. I had to tear free. They were hunting me through the streets, and I did not know what to do. I knocked on doors and a woman let me in, a teenage boy covered in blood. In return for her kindness, I knocked her to the floor, ripped her throat out, and gulped down her heart's blood. I stayed in her house all that night and the next day with her body. Without her, I don't think I would have escaped.

"I wanted to get away from the man who made me and taught me. I wish I had not asked for that woman's help. Being able to depend on nobody but yourself isn't so bad."

"If you can depend on yourself," Berthe said shakily.

"You can," Stephen said, and sounded sure, calm again, the alien creature, the murderer who had saved her from hurting anyone. "And you're not alone."

The night was crystal clear and terrifying, the wolf running through the woods, and when she closed her eyes she could not hear anyone's breathing or heartbeat but her own.

But when she looked up, she wasn't alone, after all, and when she got home from the dark woods, her mother made her hot chocolate, popping in a marshmallow. Berthe looked at the tiny treat in the cup and thought about all the little sweetnesses love slipped into your daily life, almost unnoticed except that when they were added up, they meant you could bear anything.

At her next lacrosse game she was running, running across the field with her stick in hand, her parents and friends cheering as they watched. Another girl ran at her full tilt, body-checking her.

Berthe barely paused, but she bumped the girl's shoulder—carefully, careful, she had to be so careful, you don't want to hurt anyone, do you?—and the girl fell back, and Berthe ran ahead with the ball and her victory.

It was a bright sunlit moment, but the girl had a bruise on her shoulder afterward. She said in the locker room, with a little admiration but mostly spite, "You're an animal, Lindstrom."

The other girl was the one who had not been playing fair. If Berthe was playing fair by playing at all, considering what she was.

Berthe went and took a hot shower, scrubbing hard at her unmarked body. She came out of it and looked in the fogged mirror set over the sink, misted glass reflecting back pieces of her grotesquely: blond hair dark-stringy with water, pale blur of flesh and eyes cut with lightning, like the eyes of the wolf in the woods. She pressed her face against the wet glass and took deep shuddering breaths, and outside the building she heard Natalie and Leela whispering secrets Berthe was not supposed to know.

When she was done taking breaths, she leaned back from the mirror, wiped it with her shaking hand, and looked at herself whole and clear.

"**H**ow do you," Berthe said, on the third morning after a full moon, sitting with her cookie half-eaten in her hand. "How do you feed now?"

Stephen sat in the corner away from the sunlight. He did not, as she had feared, look offended by the question.

"Not well," he answered. "There is no way to do it that's right. People who are sleeping on the street. People who are passed out drunk at parties in a garden. Stealing from a blood donation clinic, or a blood bank. I feed in small, dark ways, but I don't kill."

It was a horrible picture, the monster preying on unsuspecting people. The savagery that ripped through Stephen's bedroom every full moon, that would rip through people, was horrible as well.

And there was something else besides horror in it: the thought of kind Stephen spending half his life desperately scavenging for sustenance.

"You must be hungry a lot," she said quietly.

He was silent.

"If you want," she began. She had brought her own clothes this time, and she fiddled with the sleeve of her warm, comforting sweater, pulling it up to expose the veins on her wrist.

It could not be anything like as bad as the liquefying pain she had suffered last night and would suffer, again and again, as long as she lived. And she would get to do something for Stephen: something that might make him happy.

"I wouldn't mind," she told him.

"My kind can't feed on your kind," Stephen said, and after a pause, very politely: "But thank you very much. I mean it. Nobody's ever offered me that before."

It hurt for a moment that her body was disqualified to do something for him. She felt monstrous for not being prey for him, and how stupid was that?

"When I'm—like I am, upstairs, can you hear me?" she asked. "Is it awful?"

"No," said Stephen.

"How can it not be?"

"How can you stand to look at me," Stephen said, "when you know what I am? Once you change things from the general to the personal, what does 'monstrous' even mean? It's not awful. I hear you and it's Berthe, upstairs."

It didn't seem like her, and she was scared of thinking of it as her, but she gave some thought to trying to remember next time.

Berthe tucked her feet up under her. "How'd you get so smart?"

"Well, I've been around awhile," Stephen said. "Gives you time to think things through, even if our minds don't mature like yours will."

"How do you know your mind isn't mature?"

"I'm speculating," said Stephen. "Of course, it's quite probable that being scared and uncertain and stupid is something you never grow out of, and I just want to think there's some way for other people to do it."

Berthe blinked at him, startled into speechlessness by the idea of Stephen being scared or uncertain.

He looked the same as ever, inhuman-bright eyes steady behind his glasses, wearing a T-shirt that seemed to be about robots, his face pale and thin and thoughtful.

"I'm glad I can't drink from you," Stephen told her. "I don't want to be a monster with you."

"You're not," said Berthe. She didn't like words as much as Stephen did, couldn't frame the right things to say the way he could, but she smiled at him and said awkwardly, "It's personal for me, too."

Stephen smiled back. She thought he might cross

the room to her, but of course he could not get past the sunlight, the rays between them like iron bars.

It was three weeks more until Leela told Berthe what she had already told Natalie: that she was gay. After Berthe told Leela that she loved her, was glad to know anything about her friend that Leela had to tell because she loved her, and nothing would change that love, Leela let her know when she was planning to tell her parents, and that she wanted a sleepover at Natalie's house afterward. On the night of the full moon.

Berthe had to say no and hurt Leela with awkward lies. Berthe knew that in the human world, there was no excuse for what she was doing.

"You did get back to your family," she said to Stephen as the sun was sinking behind his blinds, and her whole body wavered on the edge of the abyss. "Didn't you?"

"I did," said Stephen. "I got back to them, and I got to stay with them for two years. But after that—it was beginning to be obvious I wasn't aging, and hunting was so hard to hide. I couldn't stay with them."

Berthe could not talk to him any longer. She had to run up the stairs, lock the door behind her, and feel pain twist her body into a whole new shape, casting her humanity far, far away. She lifted her face to the shut-out moon and howled because it would not stay.

The next day she did not stop for tea or Stephen, just

threw on the clothes she had left outside the door and pushed her battered body, used all of her inhuman speed, for the task of getting coffee and pastries from Leela's favorite place. She ran all the way to Natalie's house and rang the bell with the sun still tentative and new in the sky.

Leela opened the door and looked at her, and for a moment there was a silence of hurt and hesitance, a possibility that the door would be shut in her face, but instead Leela reached out and drew her inside.

The three of them spent the day together, talking about how it had gone and what Leela was thinking and feeling, and planning out things they might want to do next, discussing movies and sports and coming back around to Leela because this was her day.

They walked around town until evening came and they got to a certain coffee shop and went in to find crowded tables and people who looked like they were in for the long haul, student types with their laptops.

Stephen, with a book and a coffee cup he had not touched, wanting to be with people even though he didn't speak to them. Stephen, who had made his house something like a home for her—somewhere he had chosen to always let her in, whenever she came—but who had been too scared to stay in his own home, had told her that he felt eternally young and scared, so scared that the only thing he could think of to do was spend all his life in hiding.

"I see a table," she said to Leela and Natalie, and

marched up—the idea of it, of her marching up to a table where a boy was. "Hey," she said as Stephen blinked inhuman-brilliant eyes behind his glasses and let his book fall onto his saucer. "Can we join you? This is Leela and Natalie. Girls, this is my friend Stephen."

Leela turned out to have read Stephen's book and discussing it with him made them both smile. Natalie drew Leela to the register, on the blatant pretext of wanting another cookie, to discuss Stephen and Berthe with her, and Berthe stayed behind to discuss them with him.

"Won't they wonder about—where I go to school?" Stephen asked, apparently nonplussed and pleased enough to come close to Berthe's level of conversational flailing.

"Tell them you're homeschooled," said Berthe, tactfully not adding that the way Stephen talked, they might be assuming this already—though either she didn't notice how he talked was strange anymore or he was talking a bit more normally. "Or maybe a college guy taking a year out. Very glamorous."

"Do you really think I look old enough?" Stephen asked, sounding almost shy.

"Definitely," said Berthe.

"**D**ad," Berthe said a couple of weeks later. "Next time you have a little space between jobs, I was wondering if you could help out a friend of mine."

"Space between jobs, what are you talking about? I work my fingers to the bone keeping you in designer clothing and handbags," her dad told her, pulling on the hood of her sweatshirt. "Is it Natalie or Leela? Leela needs a bookcase set in her wall—I've been saying it for years."

"It's another friend," Berthe said. "Um. A boy. Stephen. Is his name. He has porphyria." And here she turned her face away, because she'd never lied to her dad before. "He's sensitive to sunlight. And he works at a call center—he doesn't have a whole lot of money. I thought if we could put shutters on his windows downstairs . . ."

Her dad was quiet for a little while. "Is that where you've been, some nights you've been home pretty late? Or rather, pretty early in the morning?"

"If the boy can't go out during the day, it's different," her mother said, as quick to sympathy as she was quick to anger, and her dad looked at her and then pulled Berthe into a hug.

"I'll see what I can do," he said.

"You should bring this Stephen around for dinner," said her mother. "What does he like to eat?"

Berthe could not tell her mother that Stephen liked to eat people. She could not tell the people who loved her best in the world what she had become.

But she wasn't like Stephen. She was going to grow up, and maybe that meant becoming a little less scared. Maybe by the time she was ready to go to college, she could tell them. Maybe she could think about telling her friends.

Leela and Natalie assumed Stephen was Berthe's boyfriend, that he was a little weird but nice, that he and Berthe fit, though being at opposite ends of some spectrum. Her parents clearly thought so as well. They all thought they knew what was going on.

They knew nothing about his weird staring and wonderful rescue in the coffee shop, or his silent presence in the woods. And Berthe knew nothing about romance.

He liked her, she thought. But he never did or said anything like that: he was the boy who had quietly left his home to spare his family, who did not talk to other people at all, who kept hidden.

Berthe rather self-consciously wore a T-shirt that said TOO LONG, DIDN'T READ she'd bought, because it made her think of Stephen and also said something about herself, on the night of the next full moon.

It made Stephen smile his small, crooked smile as he opened the door, but he didn't comment on it. She didn't know what she was supposed to do if he didn't say anything: Stephen always knew the right thing to say.

"See you in the morning," she told him, for want of anything better, and smiled back.

She took off her shirt in his hall, folding it neatly, took off the rest of her clothes as well and realized for the first time that he could probably hear her getting undressed. She went into his bedroom with her cheeks burning.

Stephen always made the bed, even though he knew she was going to wreck it. Berthe went and lay down on it, felt the cool material of his pillow against her face, and concentrated on that scrap of comfort through the pain.

When she woke up, there were more scars on the walls, but she had not ripped the mattress apart this time. It still looked as if there had been a beast inside the room, but just a little more controlled this time.

She dressed slowly, getting comfortable with being back in her own skin, went downstairs, and opened the door to find her tea on the table beside her cookie, her Stephen in the corner shutting his book as soon as he saw her.

He had reached out when they met, she thought, taken steps with her she could not have taken alone. She could do that now, when he might be paralyzed from being in hiding, from years and years in the dark.

Berthe crossed the floor, and the sunlight was no bar to her. She approached Stephen and he rose politely to meet her approach, and she did not try to say the right thing.

She took his face in her hands and kissed him. He moved in toward her at once, a little awkward and seeming so glad, and she was so glad, too. It felt like a different kind of moonlight moving through her and changing her.

He was a little shorter than she was now, and he hadn't been a few months ago. She was growing up, and he was not. This moment, his narrow chest against hers, could not be kept. She smiled against his mouth: a little sweetness in the cup of her life and his, having this moment and the next, and being unafraid of change.

"I was wondering," Berthe said, soft as her own breath. "What are you doing tonight?"

Beth Revis
Night Swimming

We don't have "night" on a generational spaceship. The solar lamp in the roof of the Feeder Level goes dark, but it's no more night than the clouds painted on the metal ceiling are sky.

Nevertheless, everything important that has ever happened to me has happened at "night."

For once, Harley isn't painting. I lean over his shoulder—he's doing some sort of math, never my strong point. Never Harley's, either.

"What are you doing?"

"Shut up," he says genially.

"What is he doing?" I ask Kayleigh. She shrugs and returns to the digital membrane screen she's reading. Math *is* her specialty, but she's reading scientific articles on physics and propulsion. Probably something to do with whatever crazy invention she's going to work on next.

I resign myself to silence, staring out the window. No one else is in the common room of the Ward. The others have long since gone to their rooms. The solar lamp will be covered soon, washing the Feeder Level of the ship *Godspeed* in darkness for exactly eight hours, the precise amount of time we are allotted to sleep. My mind plays with words—*darkness, sleep, night-that's-not-night*—maybe I can form them into a poem or some song lyrics later. It has been a while since I've written anything new, and the urge to create itches me from the inside.

But I can't think of anything now.

Instead, my mind is filled with the words Doc gave us when it was time for our meds. The blue-and-white pill stuck in my throat as Doc entered the common room. Even the nurses stiffened. We never know what to expect from Doc, but none of us thought that his announcement would be that the Elder of the ship, the boy who will one day grow up to become the leader of us all, was moving into the Ward.

We all know what Elder looks like: thirteen years old, scrawny, with a hollow expression in his eyes and sickening devotion to Eldest, the current leader. Eldest is a kind, old man . . . on the outside. We here at the Ward are loons, marked crazy almost since birth, as far away from normal people as possible. Eldest mostly ignores us, letting us fill up the Recorder Hall with art that no one cares about and spending our days being the only inefficient crew members as the ship crosses the universe.

But sometimes Eldest doesn't ignore us.

Only last year, Selene, a girl who sang beautifully, was sent away from the Ward. Doc was the one who led her out to the farms. He left her there to spend the rest of her life in dull labor, working on food production for the ship's crew. But I don't think any of us doubts that the order really came from Eldest. Selene had been determined a threat to productivity, someone whose art was deemed less valuable than manual work.

I swallow the lump in my throat. Selene wasn't a friend of mine, not exactly, but we spoke together. I miss her. I miss the sound of her, the way her voice could change the way I saw things.

It's not right, how Eldest silenced her.

The way he could silence any of us.

"Twenty-four thousand," Harley says triumphantly, breaking my concentration, "and three hundred eighty-seven frexing days."

"What's that?" Kayleigh asks without taking her eyes off the screen she's reading from.

"That is exactly how long it'll be before the ship lands."

She looks up now. We both stare at Harley, gaping.

"Twenty-four *thousand* days?"

Harley repeats the whole number.

"We'll be so . . . *old*," Kayleigh mutters.

"Just over eighty," Harley replies. He sounds almost cheerful about it, but the days feel like stones in my stomach, weighing me down.

"Twenty-four thousand three hundred and eighty-seven days," I repeat, unable to comprehend a number so large.

"Isn't it great?" Harley asks, jumping up and tossing the screen he's been working on to the chair.

"Great? That's forever away!" I snap back.

Harley shrugs.

I'm in the mood to pick a fight, but Kayleigh laughs, stopping me and my argumentative words. "He has a point. It's a long time from now—but it's not forever."

Harley whistles as he meanders away, the sound drifting from the hall and wrapping around the common room for several moments before I hear his door close.

Aroo! Aroo! The sirens blare from the ceiling: the solar lamp is going dark in a matter of minutes.

I stand up. "Come on," I say to Kayleigh.

"Nah," she answers, rolling her shoulders and letting the screen she's been reading drop down on the table beside her chair.

"Time for bed," I say again, confused at her response.

Kayleigh stands languidly. "No it's not," she says.

"But—" My eyes drift to the big windows that line one wall of the common room. There is light now, but once the shade descends, the entire level will be far darker.

"Just because it's 'night' doesn't mean I have to go to bed," Kayleigh says. She strolls over to the elevator.

"Where are you—"

"You can come," she offers, pushing the button. "I don't care. I just don't want to be bossed around by some siren."

By the time the elevator doors open, it's dark. Kayleigh walks out of the lobby of the Hospital with confidence though, not even slowing as she bounds down the steps and veers toward the path that leads to the garden.

"Where are we going?" I ask. It feels dangerous to be out here, even though there's no express rule against it. But often, on *Godspeed*, the most important rules are the unspoken ones.

"I am going to the pond," Kayleigh says. "You can go wherever you like."

She doesn't say this in a mean way: she means simply that she intends to spend this night on her own terms, and she won't stand in the way of me doing the same.

I follow her anyway. I would follow Kayleigh anywhere.

The path meanders through the garden, twisting chaotically around hydrangea bushes, hulking flowers, and a statue of the first Eldest. Kayleigh doesn't slow at all, but I start to feel my way around the path, hesitating before each footfall. I wonder how many times Kayleigh has left the Hospital at night, how often she has performed this one tiny form of rebellion against the darkness, against Eldest. Did she reveal her plans to me tonight because I happened to be there when she was ready to go, or had she wanted me to follow her into the dark?

By the time I reach the pond, Kayleigh's already in the water. Her pants and tunic lie in a heap on the soft ground—I can't see her clearly from here, but she must only be wearing her tank top and panties. My stomach twists at the thought. We have been living together since we were children; we've seen each other naked.

But Kayleigh's not a child anymore.

And neither am I.

I kick my moccasins off and roll up the cuffs of my trousers, but I don't dive into the water.

"Come on in!" Kayleigh calls. The water moves around her as she sweeps her arms through it, the sound almost musical.

I shake my head.

"Don't be a chutz!" she says, laughing self-consciously. She's more nervous to speak a dirty word than she is to defy the implied curfew and swim at night.

"I'm fine here," I call back. I stand very still—so still that the koi fish nibble at my toes, their mouths tickling the edges of my feet. I try to stare through the water at their white and orange and gold and red bodies flitting between the roots of the lotus flowers, but my eyes drift up and out.

To Kayleigh.

She's ignoring me now, caught up in the act of swimming. She's always loved the water; Harley's nickname for her is Fish. She glides smoothly, her body lithe and filled with a grace that isn't present when she's dry. Her hair swirls around her. The koi, apparently accustomed to her presence, dare to dart close to her, their bright scales flashing next to her dark skin. She takes a deep breath and bends in half, kicking and swimming for the floor of the pond.

I count the seconds, waiting for her to resurface.

I'm about ready to dive in after her and drag her back up when her head bursts from the surface, water arching over her and splashing down. She's laughing gleefully, excited to be here, now.

And she is beautiful in this moment.

Her skin hidden in shadows, her body highlighted by the white tank top. She swims closer to me, still laughing at her own joke, and I notice the way her top moves with the motion of the water, pulling up and down, giving me tantalizing hints of what the cloth hides. When Kayleigh stands, the fabric sticks to her body, showing me every curve, filling my fantasy with details I'd not dared to think of.

"This," she says, stepping past me and reaching for her tunic, "is why I swim at night. Because it's only here, now, that I can be free on this frexing ship."

She dances away from me then, heading back to the Hospital or somewhere else, I don't know. I'm left with my feet in the water and fish nibbling my toes and the first important realization of my life:

I am in love with Kayleigh.

The next day, Elder comes.

Doc introduces him at med time, as the blue-and-white pills that are supposed to keep us sane are distributed by the nurses. Elder is tall—already taller than me—and lanky. He looks underfed and scared.

Doc pulls Elder aside and whispers to him privately, then hands him something small. I crane my head around the nurse in front of me, trying to see what it is.

A blue-and-white pill.

My eyes narrow. Interesting. So our future leader is just as crazy as we are. No wonder Eldest had him sent to the Ward.

I swallow my pill dry.

Elder stands near the elevator, watching as people drift past him toward their rooms. Doc's given him a room near his office—no doubt to keep an eye on him—but Elder doesn't make a move to go to bed. His big eyes watch us, drinking in everything. It makes me uneasy. I can see how one day this boy will grow into his long arms and legs. I can see Eldest in him.

Eventually the room clears to just us—me and Kayleigh and Harley—and him.

"Right," Kayleigh announces, cutting through the awkward silence. "Let's go."

She jumps up and heads to the elevator.

"Where?" I ask. My eyes shoot to Harley, who's already following Kayleigh. I don't want to share night swimming with him, even though I have no claim to it. Or her.

Kayleigh shrugs. "Somewhere."

The elevator doors slide open, and I bound across the common room to get to them in time. Elder watches me, motionless.

The elevator doors start to shut, but Kayleigh sticks her hand out to stop them. Harley leans forward. "Coming?" he asks Elder.

The kid's whole face lights up, and he rushes inside.

He's practically vibrating with joy as the elevator descends. I glower at him. When the doors open, he jumps out, skids to a halt, and waits for Kayleigh to step forward and show him where to go.

We all follow her—Elder bouncing beside her, Harley right beside him, and me in the back.

This was *our* time.

Something Kayleigh says makes the others laugh. I pick up my pace, eager to hear whatever it is she said. Harley grins back at me.

I shake my head, making the negative thoughts dispel.

This was never *our* time. It was always *her* time, and she's free to include whoever she wants.

Kayleigh takes us down the path behind the Hospital and my heart sinks; despite my resolve to not be a chutz over this, I want to keep the water to just us. But instead of veering toward the pond, Kayleigh takes us to the Recorder Hall.

The Recorder Hall is a big brick building, one of the few buildings besides the Hospital and a few remote farmhouses on this side of the ship. Despite its size, only one person lives inside the Hall—Orion, the Recorder, who maintains all the records we have from Sol-Earth, and all the research we've done as we—and the generations before us—travel to the new Earth.

Aroo! Aroo! The sirens startle us, making us all jump and then laugh at ourselves.

Elder pauses as Kayleigh strides forward.

"What?" she asks him. There is a challenge in her grin, and I can tell that Elder knows what her smile means: you can defy the dark, defy Eldest, and go with her through the night, or you can run back to the Hospital and never be invited out again.

"Nothing," Elder says, running to catch up to her.

The solar lamp darkens just as Kayleigh puts her foot on the first step of the Recorder Hall.

Elder pauses again, though no one notices but me.

"Come on," I say in an undertone. "What's the big deal?

We're not forbidden to go outside in the dark."

I can see the whites of Elder's eyes, huge and staring at me. We're not forbidden—but we're not allowed, either. An unspoken rule is still a rule, and Eldest would still look at us as if we had broken it. He would still punish us.

Elder's jaw sets, and he nods once. He turns on his heel and jumps up the stairs.

Kayleigh has already slipped into the entryway, a vast area at the front of the Hall lined with huge, wall-sized digital membrane screens. She slides her hand across one, bringing it to life. The light from the screen casts shadows behind her, barely illuminating the giant clay sculptures that hang from the ceiling: two globes to represent the two Earths, and a model spaceship flying between them.

Elder's eyes are on the ship: his future kingdom.

Mine are on the planet.

The planet is the only thing that gives us any hope. It's the only goal. All of this: Doc's rules, living in the Ward, hoping to slip past Eldest's notice for one more day so we can continue living as we like and not be forced to be productive members of the ship. . . . The only hope we have is to one day land on the new Earth.

"Twenty-four thousand three hundred and eighty-six," Harley whispers in my ear, grinning, and I finally understand that the number is a promise, not a sentence.

"Look at that," Kayleigh crows triumphantly. Harley shushes her.

"That's the ship's diagram," Elder says, his eyes growing round. "You're not supposed to be looking at that."

"Are you going to stop me, little leader?" Kayleigh asks. She bends down, and although there's a smile twitching up the corners of her lips, her question is serious.

Elder shakes his head no.

"I just wanted to look is all," Kayleigh says, her eyes scanning the complicated diagram. I can barely make heads or tails of it: there are lines and numbers everywhere. Kayleigh, though, is the inventor: she must know what it means.

The entryway grows silent. Kayleigh reads the diagram with a sort of desperate fierceness. Harley stares at her, wonder in his eyes. I glance at Elder; we're the outsiders here, watching something neither of us understands.

"What are you *doing*?" The voice bellows so loudly that I feel as if the giant globes should fall from the ceiling and shatter at our feet.

Orion, the Recorder, strides toward us. Elder takes one look at him and scampers, his feet skidding across the smooth floor. The heavy door slams behind him.

Harley laughs at Elder's childish flight, but a part of me wants to chase after him. I've never seen Orion look so furious before. He's wearing nothing but trousers and his hair is a mess; clearly he was already in bed. There's a hardness to his jaw, and I can see the muscles on his chest tightening.

"You frexing idiots! Do you know what you've done?"

Even Harley looks cowed now, but Kayleigh dances up to Orion, still laughing. "I was only *looking*," she says.

Orion grabs her by the shoulders and shakes her until the smile slips from her face. "There are people in the fields right now who are there for 'only looking,'" he sneers. "You want to be one of them?"

"Let him try to send me to the fields," Kayleigh says. No laughter now. Just determination. My heart swells. She's like a flame burning brightly—a flame almost out of control.

"He can do worse than send you to the fields." Orion's voice is low. He means these words to cut down Kayleigh's challenging posture, but it doesn't work. On her, anyway. The thought of Kayleigh being punished by Eldest instills within me a heart-thudding sort of terror I've never felt for anyone else, even myself.

Harley catches my eye and jerks his head to the door. This is something that Kayleigh has planned, something that Orion's caught her doing before. We are just witnesses. With enough time and rage, maybe Orion can make her finally see how dangerous her whims can be.

I take the stairs two at a time, already on the path before I notice Harley's sitting on the steps. "Go without me," he says. "I'm going to wait on Kayleigh."

I stop.

I know the way Harley's been watching Kayleigh—for

years now. She's been just a friend to both of us, never quite willing to take it further. There was a time when I thought they were growing more serious, but that was just before Selene was banished. Once Eldest sent her to the fields, Kayleigh withdrew. She was quicker to smile, but it took longer for the smile to reach her eyes. She was more daring, though, and I worried about that, about what that would mean for her. For us. For them.

"Go on," Harley says again. His voice is dismissive. He doesn't even think that I might want to stay behind, that I might want to be the one to comfort Kayleigh after Orion's chewed her out. He just assumes that it's him she wants to see.

And, probably, it is.

Acid roils in my stomach.

Who am I kidding?

One night swimming with her in the pond, and I expect her to turn to me? One night realizing that she fills my mind and heart in ways I never thought possible, and suddenly she's mine?

I plod down the path, away from the Recorder Hall. Away from Kayleigh.

But not all the way. As soon as the garden starts up, I veer left. I don't stop at the pond. Its still surface mocks me. I keep going, even though there's nothing out here. Nothing but the wall.

I sit down. Underneath me is dirt and grass. But behind

me, pressing against my back, is the curving steel wall of the ship. I let my head fall back, a dull thud of my skull against metal. I'm such a frexing chutz.

I don't know how long I stay there, staring at nothing but darkness. It gets cooler—the allotted ten degrees cooler dictated by the ship's program—and I think about going back to my room in the Ward. Before I can move, though, I hear voices.

Kayleigh.

And Harley.

And a splash.

He's calling to her—he jumped in first. Kayleigh squeals with delight and I see the outline of her body diving into the pond.

She comes up for air, gasping and laughing.

And then there's no sound. I see his arms around her body and her arms around his and they're swimming and not swimming and the water slips over their bodies and I hear the flutter of a gasp and I see, I see, I see.

And I know.

This is the second thing I learned in the nighttime:

I may love Kayleigh, but she will never ever love me.

Harley counts the days until the ship will land, one by one.

24,385 . . . 24,384 . . . 24,383 . . .

✦ ✦ ✦

I count the nights.

On the 24,302nd night, Kayleigh purposefully waited until I (and Elder and everyone else) was gone before she and Harley snuck out. I know. I waited in the corner of the hallway, and I saw them go.

On the 24,287th night, Kayleigh and Harley went outside and didn't come back until the morning.

On the 24,245th night, Kayleigh didn't bother going out at all: she stayed in. In Harley's room.

On the 24,238th day, Harley quits counting down the days. He and Kayleigh quit pretending that there is nothing going on between them.

"Gross," Elder complains as Kayleigh leans over the couch and gives Harley an upside-down kiss.

I agree but keep my mouth shut.

I'm writing again, and that's good, at least. Long, rambling, angry poems that amount to nothing, but they're words. I hunch over my little book—I don't like writing on the membrane screens, I prefer paper—and scrawl out my latest poems.

I tried not caring. I gave up somewhere around the 24,290th night.

"What's wrong?" Kayleigh asks.

I immediately smooth down my face: I had not realized that I was scowling at her. At the two of them. She slips down beside me on the couch and wraps her arms around mine. "What is it?" she asks again, so much concern in her voice that I know she's sincere.

I shake my head.

Kayleigh stares at me a moment longer, then shoots Harley a look. There is a message in her eyes, though, a message that Harley must be able to read, because he jumps up from his seat. "Come on, Elder," he says. "I'll show you the art gallery in the Recorder Hall."

Elder—eager to be included—follows immediately. I wait until the elevator doors close behind him before I dare to look at Kayleigh.

Her eyes are kind, and sad, and knowing.

"You wouldn't understand," I say immediately, hoping to stave off her pity. I want nothing of her pity.

"Maybe not," she concedes. "But you look sad; I don't want you to be sad."

She brushes a lock of hair out of my face. Her fingertips barely touch my skin, but I feel as if there's a trail of fire following her touch.

I don't mean to, but I find myself staring into her eyes. I can see it then: she loves me. But her love for me is nothing like my love for her. My love eats away at me until I'm hollow inside, filling me with bitterness at every moment she spends with Harley. But her love is kind and good. She loves me as a friend, a true friend, and the purity of her emotion leaves me breathless. In this moment, she wants nothing but to make me happy again. For the past 149 days, I have wanted nothing but for Harley to disappear—and I would have reveled in Kayleigh's misery.

The selfishness of my feelings makes me ashamed. I swallow hard, and with that, I resign myself to this simple fact: I can love her, and she can never love me back. But what I feel for her is real, even if she doesn't feel it. And what I feel for her is good, as long as I remember that I care more about keeping the love and light in her eyes, even if it isn't for me.

"Nothing's wrong," I tell her, and I mean it.

She squeezes my arm and smiles. "Good."

A shadow passes over her face.

"Now it's my turn to ask," I say. "What's wrong?"

Kayleigh bites her lip. "The way you've been sad and grumpy lately—Doc's noticed."

This is beyond anything I expected to hear. I don't try to deny my negative attitude, even though I hadn't realized she'd been aware of it for so long. What really surprises me is the way she brings up Doc. I swallow again, this time remembering the way the blue-and-white pill I take every day tastes.

"I've been thinking a lot about Selene," Kayleigh says. "Before she was sent back to the fields, she was sad, remember?"

"She had every reason to be." Selene's story was a miserable one, but it was her story nevertheless.

Kayleigh nods again. "But the thing is . . . do you

remember the way Doc switched her meds when she was sad?"

I shake my head.

"He did," Kayleigh continues. "She showed them to me. And the longer she was on those pills, the more she seemed . . . different."

"Different?"

"Come on," Kayleigh says, standing. "I'll show you."

We ignore the siren, and neither of us pauses when the solar lamp blinks out. This trek seems different from our other outings. Kayleigh is on a mission here, with a clear goal.

She leads me away from the Hospital, toward the fields. The Feeder Level is ten square acres, most of it taken up with farmlands. Corn and wheat grow closest to the Hospital, but Kayleigh strides down the path between the two with confidence. I wonder how many times she's visited Selene.

"It was after she was . . . you know, and Eldest decided not to punish her attacker," Kayleigh says. "That's when Selene started being depressed. And soon after that, Doc changed her meds."

"So?"

"When he changed her meds, he changed her."

"Obviously," I said. "We're loons. Without meds, we'd be crazier."

Kayleigh stops dead. "No. I don't think that's true. I

think the mental meds are what keep us sane. I think—it's the others who are different."

I shake my head. This is crazy, even for Kayleigh.

She doesn't waste time arguing with me. She grabs my hand—my heart can't help but race at her touch—and pulls me toward the rabbit farm. She bends the thin wire fence down to climb over it. The rabbits look up, their ears pointed toward us and their noses twitching. A few hop languidly away as we steal across the field to the small house lined with rabbit hutches.

Kayleigh doesn't bother knocking or announcing her presence. She pokes her head into the door and whispers loudly, "Selene!"

I hear murmuring inside. Kayleigh jerks her head, and I follow her into the little house.

Selene is sitting up in bed. Her quilt pools at her lap. It's obvious that she just sat up as soon as Kayleigh called for her.

"Selene," Kayleigh says again.

Selene turns her head to Kayleigh, and in that simple motion, I'm reminded of the girl I used to know. Vivacious but reserved, usually quiet, but when she opened her mouth, music came out.

"Yes?" she says in a dead voice. "I am Selene."

Air leaves my lungs.

"Selene, are you happy?"

"I am here."

"But are you happy?"

"It is darktime. Night. I should be sleeping."

"Selene, do you feel anything at all?" Kayleigh is insistent, her voice rising with each question.

"I feel sleepy. It is time for sleeping."

"Do you know who I am?" Kayleigh asks.

"You are residents of the Ward. You should be in the Hospital."

"Yes. We are. And we used to be your friends."

Selene frowns—the first time she's shown any emotion at all. Kayleigh seizes on it, leaning forward, her eyes sparkling. "Do you remember us? Do you remember what it was like before? What happened to you? What did Doc do to you to make you like this?"

Selene blinks.

"Doc did nothing," she says in a hollow voice. "I am sleepy because it is night."

She leans back down into her pillow. She doesn't adjust her body or pull the covers up. She just closes her eyes. A moment later, I can see by the even rhythmic rise and fall of her chest that she's asleep.

I start to leave, but Kayleigh pauses to tuck the quilt over Selene's shoulders.

We don't talk until we're back on the path away from the fields.

"See?" Kayleigh rages. "That is *nothing* like the way Selene once was."

"Maybe she's still depressed."

"No!" Kayleigh stops. The Recorder Hall is a dark outline to our left, the Hospital to our right. Maybe, if someone squinted and knew where to look, we'd be noticed despite the darkness.

"Don't you understand?" she asks. "Those blue-and-white pills we take every day. They don't keep us from being crazy. They keep us *sane*. There must be some reason Eldest needs at least some of the people on the ship *normal*, and he uses the label 'crazy' to keep us separated. It's them—the workers—they're the ones not normal. They don't feel anything, they don't think anything. I bet they're easier to control; that must be why Eldest does it."

"Does it?" I ask. "Does what?"

"Drugs them! Something! I don't know, but he's done something to make the people not be—not be *themselves*. Even when she was sad and depressed, Selene was never like *that*." She spits out the word. "When Eldest had Doc send her away, he made sure there was something else done to her, another drug or something, to make her be like that. Empty. Dead inside."

Kayleigh words are loons, but . . . I saw Selene with my own eyes. I know the way that pill sticks in my throat, the way Doc and the nurses watch us each swallow one every day. Even Elder, the future leader of the ship. They wouldn't have Elder be heir to the ship if he was crazy. But if that blue-and-white pill actually kept him sane . . . then of course they'd give it to him.

Kayleigh must see the understanding dawning on my face because she grabs both my hands and leans forward, excited.

"There's more. Remember the ship diagrams? Orion's been giving me access—he was mad at first, but he realized that I understood them, understood the schematics. He's shown me things, things Eldest doesn't know we know. And I think—"

"Kayleigh!" The voice cuts through the night, and I could curse. Instead, I force a smile on my face.

"Oh! There you are!" Harley strolls up and wraps his arms around Kayleigh. In that simple motion, he claims her.

I step back.

"I've been looking for you. Where did you go?"

Earlier, Kayleigh shot Harley a look, and he understood her silently. Now she shoots me one. And I understand. These ideas, these suspicions and accusations—they're not for Harley. Harley, who counts down the days until he lands, who sees only the happy end result and none of the horror behind dead eyes, the fear of Eldest. Harley, who latched onto Elder as just another kid and never saw him as his future dictator.

Kayleigh saw something dark in me and realized she could share a dark secret. With me. Not him.

As Harley pulls Kayleigh into a kiss, I duck back into the shadows, making my way to my room in the Hospital.

It's twisted, I know, but it fills me with a sort of satisfaction to know that Kayleigh shared something with me that she hasn't with Harley.

Everything important that has ever happened to me happened at "night."

But they didn't find Kayleigh's body until the next morning.

On the 24,237th day before the ship was scheduled to land, Harley and Elder find Kayleigh in the pond.

Her body is covered in med patches. Doc says she must have plastered them on herself and let the drugs in them lull her into a sleep so deep, she didn't feel the water fill her lungs as she drowned. Sometime in the night, after I left her, after Harley left her, she went to the pond and killed herself.

Only she didn't.

Because I know—I know and no one else knows—that Kayleigh's death was no suicide. She thought of twenty-four thousand days as a promise, just like Harley. And she was piecing together the lies Eldest wove, discovering the truth behind Selene's dead eyes and forbidden blueprints.

This was no suicide.

And it was no accident.

I watch silently as Doc examines Kayleigh's body, then orders her to be sent to the stars.

I say nothing as Harley descends into his own spiral of depression. Doc gives him new meds—and I wait for the emptiness I saw in Selene to hollow out Harley, but it seems as if Doc has decided this is a pain Harley must live with.

I avoid Elder. He might be a kid, but he's the future Eldest.

And whatever Kayleigh died for, it was for a truth that Eldest didn't want her to find.

I will find that truth. It may take the rest my life to understand what Kayleigh saw in the tangle of lines on the ship's blueprints, to dredge up some sort of meaning from Selene's dead eyes, but I will find it.

I don't care about the truth. I only cared about her. But I will use that truth to destroy Eldest.

I cannot sink into depression like Harley. I've seen people look at me—they offer me sympathy for the loss of a friend. None of them know that Kayleigh was more than a friend, at least to me. I cannot mourn her like Harley does. I cannot mourn the love that never was.

I can only scribble in my notebook.

Not poems or lyrics.

Plans.

Revenge.

Kate Espey
The Sunflower Murders

I got to second base with Zachary Feldman the night Tasha disappeared.

Not that *disappeared* is the right word to describe what happened to her. The newspapers always used words like *abduction* and *murder*, but that's probably because *cut up into tiny pieces and scattered across a sunflower field* wouldn't fit on the page.

Anyway, it was pretty awkward explaining it to the police when they questioned us. No, officer. I don't know where Natasha was at twelve thirty. I was a little preoccupied with Zach's tongue.

Wow. I'm sorry. I don't know why I just told you that. It's not like you don't already know what happened. Well, not the kissing Zachary Feldman part, but the other one. The Tasha part. The Sunflower Murders.

I remember the first time I heard that name. I was channel surfing maybe a week after they found the third body, and I paused on a late-night news broadcast from Kansas City. Before, they'd called it a double murder, but I guess three's a crowd so they decided to tack a name onto it.

It still sounds ridiculous to me. Like a bunch of yellow-rimmed flowers finally drew their seeded heads away from the sun and started killing each other.

Honestly, I think the reason they decided to call them the Sunflower Murders had more to do with Tasha than it did with the six teenage bodies strewn across various sunflower fields in the state of Kansas.

Because, I mean, have you *seen* Tasha? Not the headline, poor-girl-who-got-murdered-by-a-serial-killer-that's-still-at-large Natasha Robeck. The real deal—sparkly, green-eyed Tasha with freckles sprinkled across her nose and ginger hair falling into her face. She was like a sunflower personified.

Maybe that's why the guy chose her. I mean, there were other variables, like how she was alone late at night and there weren't any houses nearby, and the closest streetlamp hadn't worked properly in three years so she was shrouded in darkness. But the way I figure it is that he saw her, thought she was beautiful like a flower, tried to pick her, and when she withered and died, he returned her to a field of her sisters.

If Tasha were here, she would say it was *so* like me to try and poetically rationalize murder. Then she'd raise her eyebrows and widen her eyes while she smiled, just like she did in the empty parking lot of the Kroger back when she was two hours premortem.

"Are you having fun?" she yelled.

"No," I deadpanned, examining my nails. I'd broken one on a bowling ball earlier, and every time I caught sight of it, my stomach twinged with annoyance.

I could hardly see her in the pale glow of the randomly placed streetlights. I sat underneath one, and occasionally Tasha would push the shopping cart she was riding close enough that it would gleam through the darkness. Otherwise, she was all shadows and hints of red hair.

"You know, I bet it's still going on," I said, referencing the dance our high school was having. I looked up in time to see Tasha skid her navy blue Converse across the cracked asphalt. She let go of the shopping cart, and it rolled to a stop a few feet away from us. "If we go now, we could probably make it in time for the last song."

"Ugh, gross." Tasha groaned. She stepped halfway into the light, and everything but her face was illuminated. "Why would you want to do something so boring?"

"We've been standing in this parking lot for the past hour."

"Yeah," Tasha admitted. "But that's because we've been trying to think of a good place to put our ball."

She pointed at my feet, where a neon-green bowling ball was nestled against our bags. We'd stolen it from the Country Lanes bowling center along with four others and placed them at various locations throughout the night. It was our tradition: a sort of delinquent version of a game that started when Tasha and I went through a rebellious phase in seventh grade. Think regular bowling, only outside with fewer lanes and more thievery. Tasha wanted to make the last one count. I wanted to go to the dance and run into Zach.

It's hard for me to describe what I found so appealing about Zachary Feldman. There wasn't anything extraordinary about him—he was average looking and a mildly terrible conversationalist. But he appeared to want me, and when you live in a small town, you lower your standards and take what you can get.

There was always that part of my brain that wondered if he was lowering his standards for me, too—if we were caught in some sort of limbo made up of ignored aspirations. But that part of my brain was easy to overlook when I was too worried about how many winky faces I could send in one text message before it became overkill.

"We could leave it here," I suggested, casually checking my phone for a text from Zach. Nothing. "In penance for the hour of our lives wasted in this godforsaken parking lot."

"How can you call it godforsaken?" Tasha exclaimed. "This place is magical! It's full of so much opportunity. We could meet time travelers or find a cursed necklace."

"Why would we want to find a *cursed* necklace? Wouldn't it kill us?"

"I can't believe you want to leave," she said, not acknowledging my comment.

I sighed loud enough for words to be unnecessary. My broken nail found its way to my mouth and I bit it, fighting the urge to check my phone for a text I knew wasn't there.

Tasha shrugged and mounted a new shopping cart. She twirled out of the light and around the parking lot like no one was watching, and no one was. Not even me, which I regret, because it was one of the last times I got to see Tasha as Tasha and not as a poster child for homicide.

When I imagine it, her red hair is fanned around her head like a halo, and her eyes are closed in a kind of bliss that I'd resent. There was something about Tasha that always made me inherently angry, because I knew I would never get to be her, and it wasn't fair.

I told that to a police detective once. He asked if Tasha had any enemies. As if Tasha could ever alienate someone enough to make them want to kill her. At that point I was an emotional mess, and I just wanted to help, so I mentioned the natural jealousy that she caused. He looked at me like I'd just confessed.

"I am ninety percent convinced that if we stay here,

something brilliant will happen," Tasha called across the parking lot. She gripped the handle of the shopping cart and leaned back. Even in the dark I saw how close her head was to the ground, and it made me wince. It was a wonder she didn't fall off and split her skull on the pavement.

It probably would've been better if she had.

I abandoned my place under the dingy light and followed her into the dark.

"There's so much potential in the air," she whispered, excited. "Can't you feel it?"

"I can feel my patience wearing thin," I snapped, but regretted it once I saw the disheartened look on her face. "Come on. It's time to go."

"One more ride," Tasha insisted. She pushed herself toward me. "It's your turn."

"I don't want to ride the stupid shopping cart," I muttered, annoyed.

"Okay," she said shakily, biting her lip to hide a frown. "Then I'll ride. All night if I have to. Until the time travelers come."

"It's time to *go*," I said, emphasizing the last word. I was so sick of humoring her pointless fantasies.

"How can you know that? Did the weatherman forecast our destinies this morning?"

She was about to smirk. I saw the early formation of it before the streetlights cut out and we were engulfed by darkness. And then I couldn't see anything at all.

"Looks like the Fates have decided for us," I said as I pulled my phone out of my pocket. The screen lit up, its weak glow barely cutting through the night. Shadow covered Tasha's face, but I could still make out her green eyes, wide with anticipation.

"See?" Tasha beamed. "This is something."

"This is electricity," I retorted. "Come on, Tasha. Even the streetlights are going to bed. Time to go home."

"Carmen," she whined, "quit being such a grouchy face."

"I am *not* being a—" I started to object, but I cut myself off when I noticed the headlights. I squinted, and through my eyelashes I surveyed a truck idling toward us. At first I didn't recognize it and my heart skipped a beat. I fumbled for Tasha's hand in an attempt to sedate my fear, but she was still annoyed with me and slipped her hand from my grasp. The truck came to a stop and the driver stuck his head out of the window.

It was Zach.

"Hey," he said, smiling. "I thought that was you. What are you doing?"

"Just hanging out," I said. I tucked a lock of hair behind my ear in an effort to feel less flustered.

"In a parking lot?" Zach questioned. "It's, like, almost midnight."

"*Someone* felt potential in the air," I told him. Tasha casually shifted her foot so that it rested on top of mine. She proceeded to put all of her weight on it to let me know that she was pissed. This wasn't the adventure she'd imagined. "But it is clearly and tragically absent. Can you give us a ride?"

"Hop in," he said. I walked over to our stuff and picked up my bag. I didn't touch the bowling ball; I didn't care what happened to it. I tried to brush past Tasha, but she shot me a look.

"What?" I asked sharply. "It's late and it's cold and I want to go home."

"Whatever," she sighed. She grabbed the ball and hugged it to her stomach while I got into Zach's truck. It was a bench seat, so I awkwardly scooted toward the center when Tasha shoved her way in.

He didn't have to ask where we lived. Our town was too small to even bother. There were about four neighborhoods, and they were all pretty close together. He'd get there eventually through trial and error.

"So," I said meekly, trying to make the situation feel less awkward. "What were you up to tonight?"

"I went to the dance," he replied.

Tasha snorted. "How cool."

"Would you lay off?" I demanded, and turned to look at her. "What more were you expecting, huh? We went bowling. I listened to you ramble about potential in a parking lot for an hour while you waited for *something* to happen."

Tasha's eyes widened in shock. I never attacked her like this. Quietly, she protested, "Nothing was going to happen if we just sat at home or went to a stupid dance."

"For all you know it could have happened *there,*" I said.

"That doesn't mean it would," she mumbled.

I heard Zach cough and I blushed, embarrassed that I was arguing in front of him. Sighing, I looked away from Tasha and stared straight ahead.

That's the thing about Tasha that I keep forgetting: she always wanted *something* to happen. She never said what. It was like she expected life to hand her an adventure and she'd just go on her merry way with no consequences. She grew up thinking she lived in a fairy tale. No one knew it was actually a horror movie.

We drove in silence until Zach pulled up to a stop sign. Before I could comprehend what was going on, Tasha had unbuckled her seat belt and ducked out of the truck.

"What are you doing?" I asked, exasperated.

Tasha stepped up to the window, a grim look on her face. "Carmen," she said slowly, urgently, "this is important. This is our chance to live and breathe and *do* something."

"Do you even know what you want?"

"No." Tasha stared at me with a glint in her eyes that said she didn't like what she saw. "But I'm not going to find it here."

Then she walked into the darkness, away from me. I knew that I was supposed to go after her. That was what best friends did. And we were, I reminded myself. Best friends.

But I hesitated.

Something was ending. Like a story coming to a close and there would be no epilogue, no To Be Continued.

I thought that it was the end of our friendship. I didn't know it was the end of her life.

Anyway, my hand hovered over the door handle and I was going over the pros and cons of following her when Zach put his hand on my leg. Well, not really my leg. More like my thigh. My *really* upper thigh, which, now that I think about it, might've made it third base instead of second. But whatever. I was still staring out the window, unable to shake that sense of foreboding.

Then Zach pressed his lips to my neck.

Suddenly, trailing after Tasha yet again didn't seem so appealing. I tilted my head back and let him do his thing, trying to relinquish the knowledge that this would be awkward and involve an unsexy amount of spit.

I caught one last glimpse of Tasha's fiery red hair before I closed my eyes. She looked so small, all alone in the dark.

The sheriff found us, parked at a stop sign. He knocked on the window and we broke away, mortified. I never made out with Zach again after that. We didn't even kiss. I mean, nothing kills the mood quite like getting busted. But when it's by the police, and it's because your best friend is missing, not even the strongest of hormones can prevail. I stopped talking to him.

And then they found her body. Then I didn't talk to anyone.

There were five other girls besides Tasha. At first they thought it was a one-time deal, that Tasha was horribly unlucky and nothing like this would ever happen again. But then they started finding more girls, all in sunflower fields, all chopped up into itty-bitty pieces. Then it was a serial killer. Then it was worthy of national news coverage and the FBI.

Then it was the Sunflower Murders.

I went out to Tasha's field last week. You know, where they found her. It's bare now. The guy who owned the land got sick of the media coverage and mowed the flowers down. When I found out they were gone, I was angry. Everyone in town seemed so relieved, but I was livid.

Tasha was dead. I understood that. But she was still there, in that sunflower field. If she was going to be dead, then she should at least be somewhere beautiful. Not in an empty field.

So I went.

It was two in the morning, and there was no moon and everything was bathed in black. I thought I'd feel closer to her there, but I was as empty as the field. I tried lying down; the earth was dry and scratched my face. There were no sunflowers. There was no sun.

There was no Tasha.

I stared at the stars and waited for the tears to come. They never did, and when the sun came up, I went home. It was like I hadn't even gone. So I thought that if I wrote it down, it would help. But it hasn't. Nothing's changed.

My best friend was murdered, and I made out with a boy in his truck. My best friend was all alone when someone grabbed her from behind, and I worried about what to do with my hands.

She had unspeakable things done to her that everyone spoke about anyway, on national news, with official-sounding words meant to mask the unpleasantness of it all, and I let Zachary Feldman do things to me that would've been whispered about in locker rooms and hallways if everyone weren't already talking about poor Natasha Robeck. The lost little girl. The angel in heaven.

The first of the six Sunflower Murders.

I'm sorry, Tasha. I'm so, so sorry.

Carrie Ryan
Almost Normal

t was stupid of us and we knew it. The news said we had a few more days before the dead made their way this far south, and Wylie was the one to suggest we have one last blowout. The roads were too clogged to leave town and everyone's parents were freaking out about how to secure their houses, so it wasn't hard to sneak away once night fell.

All the restaurants were closed and everywhere else was packed with panic. It was Sarah who saw the lights down the hill and made the decision for us. "The coasters are still running," she said. And sure enough, when I squinted my eyes up tight, I could see the streaks of cars sailing over the humps and ridges of the monstrous metal serpents writhing along the horizon.

The amusement park was still charging admission, which we all agreed was pretty stupid, but what else would we spend our money on, anyway? Almost overnight, currency became useless as, before the military hit town, people just broke into stores and took what they wanted. Apparently no one thought about breaking into the amusement park. That was one of the strangest aspects of the whole thing: the rules that persisted and the ones that were quickly lost.

My family was no exception to jettisoning inexpeditious rules, even though I know it bothered my mom an awful lot. I remember that first morning hearing my parents arguing about how they'd get enough food to stock up the pantry, and my father was telling my mom they had to get to Costco with the minivan and fight their way inside.

There were bodies piled up outside the store, she'd told him. They'd been shot by packs of soccer moms who'd taken control of the place and were only doling out food to people they knew.

"It's a good thing Connor was an all-state keeper this year," my father told her, and that was that. We got a full car of food because in the semifinal games of the state championship, I'd guessed their star forward would fake left and shoot high center. I'd been right and blocked it.

And here I was, no one caring about trivialities like high school soccer anymore because everything in our world was falling apart except for these roller coasters. As kids, this place had been our Mecca. During the summer, Sarah, Bart, Wylie, and me would spend every waking moment trying to convince our parents to drive us out here, swearing we'd take on any chore imaginable just for the chance to spend a day sticky with sweat and cotton candy, standing in line for the moment when our hearts would race loud and hard.

It was our own kind of rapture, the rides so fast they'd strip away all layers and leave us bare until the car came skidding back into the wheelhouse for the next group of kids to worship.

Though none of us said it, that's what we were looking for: we thought we wanted to forget the crushing imminence of the end of our world, the dead walking toward us with a slow and steady determination.

But really we wanted to recognize the end of the mundane: unreciprocated crushes, failed tests, blank college applications sitting in a drawer waiting. These things that had once been so all-encompassing but were now rendered moot.

The park was emptier than we'd ever seen it before, which made sense with everything going on in the world. People were out looting stores for food and weapons, but there was nothing to take from this place. Besides, I think most people liked the idea that something could still be going on as it had before. You could see the lights of the coasters from nearly anywhere in town, and staring at the spinning and whirling of them almost made us forget about the truth of our new reality.

Our little group wasn't the only one that had been drawn to the park that night. We stood in line for the Tower of Doom behind a slew of kids from the class below us, and we saw a few graduates attempting to bribe one of the Western bar slingers to tap a keg for them.

Beyond that there were several families trying to pretend that spending the night in an amusement park before the end of everything familiar made the most sense in the world. I had a hard time watching them all, kids' eyes so bright with excitement over the heady combination of missing bedtime and getting access to the rides after hours, and the parents trying not to shatter under the strain.

"How many of them know they're not going to make it?" Wylie asked, nodding his chin toward a family hovering by one of the maps to choose their next ride.

Sarah slipped her hand into mine. But it was too late. Already Bart and Wylie were turning it into a game, muttering "lunch" every time they collectively voted that a pack of strangers would soon become food for the dead.

Except we weren't in the amusement park that night to remember that everything was falling apart, we were there trying to remember that once it had all been held together by something indefinable. Maybe we wanted to prove we weren't friends just because we shared a second-period class or sat at the same table together at lunch but that there was something deeper bonding us and we wanted to hold on to that until the very end.

It was Sarah's idea to ride the Screaming TerrorCoaster, and we joked about the name of it while we stood in line. Behind us, Bart and Wylie played their game of picking winners and losers in the impending apocalypse, but that didn't matter as much to me because Sarah still had her hand in mine.

I began to wonder when she'd have to let go and if she could feel the sweat I was sure was gathering in my palms and slicking the webbing between my fingers. If she noticed, she didn't seem to mind as the cars rumbled into the platform, disgorging their contents and sitting empty for more.

When we got to the front of the short line, it ended up perfectly with Sarah and me in the front car and Bart and Wylie behind us. As the operator locked the safety bar into place, I put my hand on Sarah's knee.

She didn't even glance at me, but she also didn't make me move it.

That first trip down the rails was wind and rush, screaming and adrenaline, and the entire time my fingers gripped the contours of Sarah's leg as the edge of her skirt fluttered up in the night air.

It was almost more than my body could handle, and when the car slid back into the wheelhouse, I found myself shaking as if I might crack apart. I wanted to rip Sarah free and run with her down the stairs into a dark corner and push her against the wall.

When the ride jerked to a stop, she turned to me with her hair wild around her face and her eyes glistening. This is how I wanted my world to end: here with her and the night sky and the sounds of the park roaring loud.

I didn't want to go home to where my parents had boarded up every window and cut away the stairs to the second floor. Since I'm an only child, it would just be the three of us and the dwindling days and a slowly emptying pantry.

"Let's go again," Sarah whispered, and she might as well have told me she loved me because that's what it felt like as she took my hand and pulled me back around to the line.

Behind us Wylie and Bart hooted and giggled, but that didn't matter anymore.

On the second ride Sarah let me kiss her. On the third she slid my hand under the edge of her shirt. On the fourth we refused to leave the car, and the operator threw up his hands and let us stay.

And then on the sixth or eighth trip around, the coaster ground to a halt at the top of the highest ridge. So enraptured was I in Sarah at the time that I wouldn't have noticed if Bart hadn't thumped me on the back of the head.

"Wakey, wakey, lovebirds," he giggled.

I expected Sarah to blush and pull away. That's what the awkward neighbor I'd grown up with would have done, but something about this night made her different, and she laid her cheek against my shoulder as she twisted toward the car behind us to face Bart and Wylie.

I'd never been on the coasters at night, and for a moment I was almost dizzy with the scope of Vista spread beyond the gates of the park. To one side lay the darkness of the national park edged by a long strip of abandoned condos. All along the coast road I could see the flickering of headlights as a military convoy threaded into town.

But the other side was empty, a pure darkness that stretched unbroken. The ocean roared out black and severe, no indication of where it met the sky out on the horizon, so the entire expanse seemed to be nothing but a void.

Staring at it for too long summoned feelings of dread, and for that moment I understood how we'd underestimated what we were about to face. I looked into the emptiness and I grasped that this was what awaited us all: an eternal oblivion that would never end with death.

Bart began making all kinds of sly jokes about the state of Sarah's clothes, but his words hardly pierced the abyss that was pouring into my head until Sarah pressed her lips against my neck and said, "Hey, you," so softly that I couldn't help but be reminded of warmth.

I smiled down at her, the girl who could tether me against the emptiness, and just when I was starting to feel a sort of hope again, Wylie cut off whatever Bart was saying with a slice of his hand through the air.

"Something's wrong," he said.

Bart laughed. "Of course something's wrong—the coaster broke down."

Already Wylie was shaking his head. "More than that."

Bart opened his mouth to say something dumb, and Wylie silenced him with a hissing command. "Listen."

At first there was the usual bustle of the park that sounded distant and faded up here so high: the *plink* of carnival games, the roar of machines, and the shouting of kids as the Tower of Doom dropped them toward the ground.

Nothing seemed out of place until Wylie said it. "The screaming."

"It's just from the other rides," I said, already feeling uneasy knowing it couldn't be true. There were too many voices, too much urgency.

"Oh, God." Sarah's voice shook, and when I glanced at her face it was pale and beaded with a sheen of dawning terror.

I didn't want to see what she saw. I didn't want to look. I watched her face instead, as her lips drew thin over her teeth and her breath came faster and her eyes widened, welling with tears. She never blinked, not once.

Behind us Bart started to buck against the safety bar, trying to pull himself free as if he'd forgotten we were trapped so far up in the air. Wylie threw his arm across him to physically hold him back and started screaming in his face to calm down.

I couldn't resist any longer. With the people running and screaming below, all I had to do was trace back to what they were fleeing from.

Once, a few years ago when Halloween fell on a crisp Saturday afternoon, Wylie convinced us to dress up and come out here together. We'd taken several cars, and almost all of our friends came out for it: Micah, Guy, Leroy, and Omar dressed as Charlie's Angels, Calvin carting along a stuffed tiger as he did every year because it was the cheapest costume he could think of, Danny done up as a bookie, and his sister, Sally, tagging along wearing a miner costume with a sign that read UNACCOMPANIED taped to her chest.

As part of the festivities, the park held a Dreadful Dead Walk and that's what Wylie, Bart, and I had dressed up as. We'd spent the morning perfecting the look of our fake blood and determining what kinds of wounds we'd sport and how we'd been killed. I fashioned a noose that rose up from my neck, Wylie went with scores of scorch marks as though he'd been electrocuted, and Bart chose the execution route with a row of bullet wounds to the gut.

My mom even put a picture of the three of us up on the fridge.

For a moment, sitting there on top of the roller coaster, I tried to believe that this was like that autumn afternoon and everything happening was just another display by the park's entertainers. That the people straining against the fence and lumbering into the park weren't real.

I wanted to convince myself that they had better access to special effects and that a flotilla of makeup artists had encamped in the parking lot to stage this entire event.

But then Wylie started to sob and I realized I'd never seen him cry before. He'd always been the one of us in perfect control of himself, the center around which we all revolved. Watching him break apart shattered the delicate layer of denial I'd built up.

I lost the ability to inhale.

Without anyone holding Bart back, he slithered from the restraints and climbed through the empty cars to the end of our little train.

I still couldn't move, terror shutting me down, but Sarah had forced her way out of frozen fear and she went after him. "Bart! Wait!" she cried.

Bart perched on the edge of the last car, straining his feet toward the slick rail of the tracks and the wooden trellis underneath. "We can still make it," he called out to her. "If we climb down now, we can get out to the car and make it home."

I glanced to the ground, wondering if he was right. Already the dead had made their way deep into the park, lunging from shadows as the living raced toward the entrance. There was a surge of people at the gates, a purposeful choke point for crowd control, and the dead were there, picking off the stragglers like it was some kind of carnival game.

Some people were fighting back, but it seemed useless from this far away.

"We won't make it." Wylie wasn't crying anymore, and though his eyes were red and puffy and his upper lip glistened, his voice was calm and under control. He'd taken charge again, and before the words even sank in, I knew he was right.

Wylie was the one to talk Bart back into the cars while I sat staring at the gates and trying to avoid being drawn to the yawning darkness of the ocean beyond. Sarah slipped in next to me, almost silently, and this time when she took my hand there was nothing sexy about it. Her grip was pure need born of the simmering realization that we were stuck.

Below us the dead flowed in like the tide and we were creatures who could no longer swim.

"What are we supposed to do now?" The words choked in my mouth and I couldn't force them out. I wasn't sure I wanted the answer. Because from up here I couldn't see any options, and the longer I sat paralyzed, the more dead came.

They commanded my attention; I could look nowhere

else. Some of their wounds were garish and disgusting, limbs torn almost free, cheeks ripped from skulls, mouths torn open. But with others it was almost impossible to see the bite; there was no evidence of blood and struggle. Their clothes were still freshly pressed, some with their shirts tucked in and shoes neatly tied.

They looked normal. As if this was some sort of game they'd stumbled upon and decided to join. But then they'd open their mouths and the moaning would spill forth and it became clear they were just as dead as the others.

Sarah pressed her face into the crook of my shoulder, shuddering. "They're everywhere."

That's when the lights in the amusement park blew. One moment everything was alive with brightness of various colors and the next it was absolute darkness. I couldn't see the ground, I couldn't see the front of the coaster car. I couldn't even see Sarah sitting right next to me.

And all I could think about were the dead bodies stumbling around below, seeping around the base of the coaster, turning their gaping mouths toward us and stretching their arms high.

"Can they climb?" Bart whispered from a few cars back.

The horror of that question drilled into me. Suddenly I knew—just *knew*—that the dead were already scaling their way toward us. Their moans turning to grunts as they wrapped their arms around the trellis and found footholds to push higher.

We had no escape. We had no weapons.

Sarah's response was strangled. The tips of her fingers dug against my skin, one hand clawing at my ribs and the other at the side of my neck as she buried herself deeper against me as if I could be some sort of protection for her.

I wanted to be strong. I wanted to fold my arms around her and let her believe my strength could keep us safe, but even I didn't believe that.

"No," Wylie finally said. "I don't think so. The news reports didn't say anything about them climbing. Otherwise they wouldn't be building those big fences at the forest."

For a moment none of us said anything. We were surrounded by the noise of panic: the living crying out for help, kids calling for their mommies and daddies, people screaming with pain as they were overtaken, and woven through it all was the sound of the dead: a moaning so visceral it invaded my skull, making me want to claw at my ears as if that could make it stop.

With the darkness there was no way we could attempt escape. Climbing from the coaster would be suicide either in a misplaced step or making it to the ground only to be taken by the dead.

We were trapped.

"Maybe in the morning, when it's light, we can figure

out what to do next," Wylie said, confirming that he'd come to the same conclusion.

"I'm telling you, it'll be too late then." Bart's voice sounded agitated and sharp. "They're just going to keep coming through the night. In the morning there'll be too many to fight our way out."

Wylie lost the edge of control he'd been holding on to. "Then what do you propose we do, Bart? What other option do we have?"

"We climb back to the wheelhouse," Bart shouted back. "There's bound to be something we can use as a weapon in the control room. Wrenches or broomsticks—things we can use to fight our way out."

"You're being stupid." Wylie was the sound of frustrated ire. "They're probably already swarming the tracks down there. And seriously? A wrench? You think that would be enough?"

The car began to shift then as one of them threw himself at the other, fists hitting against flesh. It felt like at any moment we could go careening off the rails, and Sarah gasped, slamming her hands against the safety bar.

"Stop it, guys!" I shouted, but they were beyond caring. I fought my way free of the tiny car and started making my way back toward them. Already my eyes were adjusting to the darkness, but depth was still impossible to judge and my progress was slow as I felt my way from bucket seat to bucket seat, holding my breath every time my foot slipped along the plastic noses of the cars.

As I got closer I saw the dark forms of Bart and Wylie tussling, and then I was there between them, barely able to fit my body into the tiny space only meant for two. I shoved them away from each other. "This isn't helping," I said, trying to keep my voice calm.

They were both panting and Bart's teeth glistened with something dark that I assumed was blood. He swiped it away and then looked back down the tracks. "We can't just sit here."

"Yes, we can," I answered before Wylie could. "What we're not going to be is stupid."

"How long do you think we can stay up here?" Bart responded. "The dead aren't just going to go away. They're not going to disappear no matter how much we want it."

"It's the rule of threes," Wylie answered. "The human body can survive three minutes without air, three days without water, and three weeks without food. We have time to figure out a next step."

Bart shook his head. In the black night, the whites of his eyes shone like stars. "Those rules are worthless. Those things on the ground—they don't need any of that stuff."

Neither Wylie nor I had a response to that. Instead I said I'd better be getting back to Sarah, and I made my way along the cars, leaving the silence of my two best friends behind.

✦ ✦ ✦

At that point it just became about waiting for the dawn. The screams of our fellow park-goers had dwindled, so now we were left with moans.

Wylie settled into the car behind us but Bart was more restless, moving about and even venturing onto the tracks, though he never went very far.

Sarah leaned against me, her breath alternating between the hiccuping aftereffects of sobs and the regular rhythm of sleep. I thought about the rides we'd taken just hours ago. How it'd been the most alive I'd ever felt.

"If you had to go now—if this was it—would you have any regrets?" I found myself asking.

"Virginity," Wylie said almost immediately, and I started to laugh, even as I became hyperaware of exactly how Sarah draped herself over me, her head cradled in my lap. His response made her grin, her nose crinkling up just a bit like it always did when she was truly happy.

"Does coming here tonight count?" Bart shouted from a few cars back, and then he was laughing as well. For a moment it drowned out the sounds of moans.

Sarah blew out a short breath. "I wish I'd studied less and snuck out more, but then again, who could have figured a four point oh GPA would become so worthless so quickly?" She shifted her focus to me, asking, "What about you?"

Everyone else's answers had been flippant and light, but I felt a different kind of pressure building in my chest, and I knew that if I didn't say it now it would become the thing I'd regret most.

I brushed the backs of my knuckles along Sarah's cheek, twisting a stray strand of hair around my thumb. "I wish I'd told the girl next door that I'd fallen in love with her."

At the end of the train of cars Bart snickered and Wylie just grunted before heaving himself free and going back to join him, leaving Sarah and me alone. Her lips were parted and I could just catch the hint of the edge of her teeth.

"Really?" It was a question voiced along an exhale.

I nodded. "Years ago. Maybe even forever."

She maneuvered around the safety bar until she was straddling my lap, her knees pushed into the depths of the bucket seats. "You should have said something before." She placed her hands on my shoulders and then slid them down my back.

"I was too afraid."

Her lips covered mine but this time there wasn't the thrill of racing along the roller coaster, wind whipping her hair around us. Now there was a desperation, a longing deeper than I'd ever felt.

I took her hips, my fingers pressing against the curve of flesh, and wished I could forget about Bart and Wylie only a few yards behind us. Wished I could forget the dead scattered below.

Wished we could have been, even if for just a few heartbeats, the last people on Earth.

She said something in my ear I couldn't understand and I traced my fingers up her spine, under her shirt, reveling in the feel of her flesh.

And then there was a scream, one of agony and pain, followed by Wylie shouting Bart's name. Sarah froze, as if she'd known this was our last chance together and it was over too soon.

The cars shuddered as Wylie scampered over them wildly and then he grabbed my arm. "You gotta help," he said in a panic, and I let him pull me away from Sarah, her eyes glistening with tears.

The night must have been damp, because my feet kept slipping as we raced toward the back of the train. Bart's screams were horrid and piercing, like no noise I'd ever heard.

Wylie kept trying to explain. "He was crawling along the tracks. I don't know what happened." He sounded close to panic. "He must have slipped through."

"He fell?" I asked as we made it to the last car and leaned over the edge.

"Not all the way." Wylie's face was ghostly pale and I realized that the moon had begun to rise on the horizon, laying down a dull sheen that reflected off the coaster rails.

It was just enough light to find Bart. He'd fallen maybe twenty feet and gotten caught in a tangle of wooden supports. His body seemed twisted wrong, as if he were hanging by his knees, but the proportions were all off and then I saw the gleam of white through his jeans.

Both of his legs were broken, almost in half, right in the middle of his shins, and the bones had pierced through skin and fabric. Bart hung upside down, his arms flailing as he tried to relieve the pressure on his legs.

Through all of it he kept wailing, but now he was forming words, begging for help. Everything about him screamed agony.

"Whatdowedo?" Wylie's question came out as one word.

As a keeper on the soccer field I'd learned to take all the angles, all the approaches, and calculate them instantaneously and then make a decision and commit without question. I looked for any way to scale down to Bart, but every path was too convoluted, too dangerous.

I was already shaking my head when Wylie grabbed my arm. "What are you saying?"

I opened my mouth, but I couldn't find the words to put to the truth that there was no way we'd make it to Bart without getting hurt ourselves and, even then, I didn't know what we could do for him.

"You're a shitty friend," Wylie said, banging his hand against the edge of the car. But he didn't go out after Bart, either.

Bart's screams were becoming more desperate and I wanted to push my hands against my ears, but that didn't seem fair. Wylie started calling back to him, telling him it would be okay and I echoed him, hating the lie of it. Bart kept struggling for a handhold to pull himself free, and after a few tries he succeeded in getting one of his legs loose.

For a moment it looked like he'd be able to untangle himself and I wondered if we should go down for him after all. He got his body bent over one of the wide wooden supports and started to yank on his other broken leg when something went wrong.

He wavered, his hand gripping at the empty air, and then he fell. Just like that. His body slid through a gap and the darkness swallowed him whole.

I heard him hit the ground. Wylie clutched at my arm, and from the front of the car Sarah kept shouting, "What happened? What just happened?" But all I could hear was the sound of Bart choking as though every molecule of air had been forced from his body on impact.

And maybe it had. I pictured his ribs snapping, his lungs collapsing in on themselves. He was too far away and the night was too dark to see, but we could still hear him as he tried to wheeze and grunt.

"We should have climbed to help him." Wylie wrapped his arms around his chest and began to rock.

Bart's voice drifted weakly from below. "Please."

I pressed my hands against my face.

Sarah kept shouting, asking what happened.

"We should climb down," Wylie continued, urgent. "There could still be time to save him."

Bart repeated the word *please* like a prayer.

It wouldn't take long for the dead to find him.

I didn't know how long it would take for him to become one of them.

Wylie flung a leg over the edge of the car, reaching toward the slick railing and wooden tracks. I grabbed him around the chest and hauled him back to safety. "Not you too," I shouted in his face, and then he started hitting me, but I still wouldn't let him go.

Below us Bart begged and I wished for the dead to find him faster, just to make it all stop. Instead his death came slow. At first I was glad for the darkness so I didn't have to see it, but the sounds didn't stop my imagination from visualizing every detail. The dead moaned, different timbres of need radiating off each other, and then I heard their teeth ripping into flesh.

Bart's whimpers sounded wet and he kept choking without ever once inhaling.

Wylie curled himself into the corner of the car, arms wrapped around his ears and rocking. I rested one hand on the back of his neck as I listened to my friend die. Eventually the only sound remaining was a new moan added to the mix, and I shoved the palm of my hand into my mouth and tried to swallow my screams.

When I made it back to the front car, Sarah sat straight and still. I reached for her but she shook her head. What she was staring at, I never knew.

✦ ✦ ✦

Here's how we escaped: dawn came oozing in and that's when the gunfire started. Military men dressed in black from helmet to boots swept through the park shooting at anything that moved.

Wylie was the one to suggest we duck into the cars. Sarah wanted to scream for help, but there was something about the calculating coldness of those men that made me hesitate. In the end I sided with Wylie.

The shooting lasted for a good hour as the sun gained strength. After that was silence. It was probably noon by the time we started making our way down. It was impossible to scale the wooden supports of the coaster without thinking about how Bart had fallen.

I hit the ground first, and as I turned back to help the others I felt something tug at the cuff of my jeans. A hand tried to twist around my ankle and I kicked myself free.

Bart dragged himself from the shadow of the coaster, his fingers scraping raw against the concrete. His legs twisted at wrong angles and the teeth in his gaping mouth were broken and sharp. His moans sounded sickly and desperate.

I didn't hear Sarah come up behind me. One minute I was facing my former friend alone and the next she was there, a metal stanchion gripped in her hands and the sound of rage on her lips. She swung it at Bart, slamming it against him with a sickening crunch.

It was so unexpected I didn't know what to say. She brought the stanchion down again and again, screaming as the heavy bottom of it cut into Bart's head.

Wylie leapt next to her and pulled her away but she fought against him. Ultimately she ended up kneeling on the ground, panting and heaving, with Wylie towering behind her, holding her arms behind her back.

She looked up at me and I couldn't hide my horror. Bart had been our friend. Not too long ago he'd told us lewd jokes and thwapped me on the back of the head when I got distracted.

Now he was nothing. In the span of darkness everything had changed.

Wylie dragged Sarah back to standing and as a group we ran for the gates. It was easy to find his car in the lot, and the first thing Sarah did was lock the doors once we huddled inside. When the engine turned over, the radio began blasting music and that was the hardest part, remembering that things had been normal once and never would be again.

Wylie reached to mute the volume and Sarah snaked her hand behind the seat, looking for mine. We drove for Vista, each of us trapped in our own mind, wondering what we could cling to and what we'd have to jettison in this new and terrible world.

And then Sarah began to laugh. I don't know what prompted it, but it was perhaps the most beautiful sound I could have imagined. I joined in and so did Wylie, and we drove down the road, all of us practically crying from the force of our laughter.

We almost felt free.

Jon Skovron
There's Nowhere Else

Monday, February 1, 8:15 p.m.

Usually I get the dreams when Mom's working the night shift at the hospital and Bill's between demolition jobs and has been drinking a lot. He passes out on the couch and starts to snore. God, he snores so loud. I can hear it all the way up in my room with the door closed. The only way I get any sleep is by putting on my headphones and turning up my music. I don't know why it's easier to fall asleep to loud music than Bill's snoring, but it is.

Those are the nights I have the dreams. They feel

different from regular dreams. Mostly because I'm never *me*; I'm always someone else. Well, not even that really, because I don't do anything. I just watch through someone else's eyes while they live their regular lives. Sometimes it's someone cool, like a cop busting a drug dealer or a NASCAR driver in a race. And sometimes it's someone boring, like a guy sitting in an office, typing numbers into a spreadsheet all day.

When I first started to get the dreams, I didn't think about it much. Everybody has weird dreams. They don't mean anything. But last night, I was an old lady in a hospital bed. The smell was disgusting, all chemicals and BO. I couldn't get up because I could hardly breathe. My hands were twisted so bad I couldn't even lift a book. I had a tube attached to my wrinkly old stomach and piss was draining into a bag at the other end. My whole dream was just sitting there for hours watching game shows.

This morning when I woke up, I had this feeling that something about these dreams wasn't normal. I started to get worried. Like maybe something was wrong with my brain.

I decided to ask Ms. Randall, my English teacher, about it. She's my favorite teacher, and not just because she's hot. She knows I read a lot, so she lets me borrow books from her personal collection. But she doesn't make a big deal about it in front of the other students. I appreciate that. She also has a nice voice, especially when she's reading plays in class. Like for instance, we were reading *The Importance of Being Earnest,* and when she read Cecily, she did the English accent, and I closed my eyes and it was like I was right there in the story.

Anyway, I had her for the last class of the day and she was packing up to go home, putting papers into her laptop bag, getting her coat on, all that.

"Ms. Randall," I said, "can I ask you a kinda personal question?"

"That depends on if it's polite or not, Sebastian," she said. She's from Cleveland and she has this funny way of saying words with long As in them. All up in her nose. Makes her sound real sharp.

"It's polite," I said. "At least, I think it is. I wanted to ask, do you ever have dreams where you're somebody else?"

"Sebastian, I think we *all* sometimes dream of being someone better. Or maybe somewhere better."

"No, I mean, like real dreams," I said. "And not necessarily about being someone better. Just somebody else."

She looked at me for a moment and pursed her lips, like she had to think carefully about what she wanted to say next. Finally, she said, "You enjoy those fantasy books I lend you, don't you?"

"Sure," I said. "I know it's not great literature or anything. It's just escapism."

"You say it like it's a bad thing. Like that makes it

less important, less useful. But sometimes, it's the only thing that can keep you sane. There's nothing wrong with dreaming of another life. Especially if things aren't so great at home."

"Right . . ." I was getting the feeling like we weren't exactly talking about the same thing.

"If you need anything," she said, "someone to talk to about . . . things at home, my door is always open."

"Okay, Ms. Randall. Thanks. I really appreciate that."

As I walked out of the classroom, I wondered if maybe I didn't explain myself right. Or maybe I had just asked the wrong person.

Max is one of those big, red-faced guys who get pissed off real easy. But at least he hangs out with me. I can't be real picky. I'm not the most popular kid in school. Anyway, we were shooting some hoops in his driveway after school, and I asked him if he'd ever had dreams about being other people.

"Sabe," he said and shook his head. "You're the weirdest guy I know."

"Yeah," I said. I couldn't really argue. I was the weirdest guy I knew, too. "So I guess that's a no, then?"

"Damn right I ain't never had no dream about being an old lady," Max said. Then he punched me in the shoulder. "Now take your shot."

I shot the ball and bricked it.

"You suck," he said as we watched the ball go rolling

into his patchy crabgrass yard. "Now, go get it."

So tonight is one of those nights. Mom is working late, something that seems to happen more and more these days. And Bill is downstairs with the TV so loud it almost drowns out his snoring. Almost. I went down there to turn the TV off, and he woke up and yelled at me to turn it back on. So I did. But about a minute after I was back upstairs I could hear him snoring again.

I probably should have been doing my homework, but I couldn't really concentrate, so I ended up just putting on my headphones and picking up the paperback Ms. Randall gave me a few days ago. It's one of those thousand-page monsters with lots of warriors hacking each other to pieces and hooking up with babes in chain-mail bikinis. I never get tired of those kinds of stories.

I wonder if I'll have the dreams. And if I do, will it be someone cool? I hope so. Something to look forward to, anyway.

Tuesday, February 2, 2 p.m.

Something different happened last night. I had the dreams. And like I'd hoped, it *was* someone cool. A basketball player for the Cavs. A big Hawaiian guy who moved so fast and so strong, for the first time I understood why some people actually like to play sports. He was pounding down the court, slamming that ball to the floor over and over again, not missing a single dribble, not even thinking that there was a possibility he could. And that was all really great and I was having a lot of fun. Maybe too much fun. Because toward the end of the game, I had this crazy impulse to shoot the ball from half-court, just sling it, one armed. And I did it. I mean, *he* did it. The guy I was being in the dream threw it. And of course he missed and everybody on the team got mad and started yelling at me. I mean, *him.* "What's wrong with you, Kapono?!" and "What's your problem? You on drugs again, man?" and "What kind of juvenile stunt was that, you moron!" I wanted to run away and hide.

I started to wake up, but right before my eyes opened, I heard his voice in my head say:

"What the hell did I do *that* for?"

And then I was awake in my bedroom, sweating so bad my sheets were sticking to me. It was only about four in the morning, so it was still dark out. I turned on the ceiling fan and lay there and tried to fall asleep as the fan dried my sheets, turning them cool and stiff against my skin. I kept remembering how it felt to be that basketball player. The power, the freedom. I wanted so bad to fall asleep and go back there and be that guy again, and this time I wouldn't screw it up. But I couldn't fall back asleep.

About two hours later, right around sunrise, I heard the front door slam and I winced. Mom was home from work and she must have been pretty tired, since she forgot how much Bill hates it when people slam the door. A minute later I could hear him yelling and her yelling back and then some things breaking.

One time, about six months ago, I tried to step in when they fought. I thought I could stop him from hurting her. But I ended up in the hospital, which was worse than she usually got. After that, she made me promise not to get in the way. She could take a lot of things, she said, but not me getting hurt on her account.

So now I just try not to listen, wishing I was anywhere else. Yeah, maybe I did want to escape from my life sometimes. I wouldn't mind being a big warrior guy with a chain-mail babe. But then I thought about these dreams I've been having and I wondered if Ms. Randall was wrong. Maybe instead of keeping me sane, all this escapism was making me crazier.

Mom was hiding in her room when I got out of bed, which meant he'd probably left a mark on her face. It made me mad, but not in that way you see in the movies where the hero gets this tough look in his eye, makes a fist, and punches out the bad guy with some amazing strength. It just made me feel like I was going to throw up. And that's more or less how I felt all through my morning classes.

But if I thought *I* was in a bad mood, Max was even worse. All through lunch he just sat there, looking at his roast beef sandwich like he wanted it to turn back into a cow just so he could kill it again. I knew better than to ask him what was wrong, so I just kept my head down and ate my lunch.

"You see the game last night?" he asked after a while.

"No," I said. "Who won?"

"Damn Heat, man!" he said, and slammed his fist on the table. "Because of goddamn Kapono!"

"What?" I said.

"Yeah, I know, right?" said Max. "The Cavs were in the lead just about the whole game. Then in the last minute, Kapono was heading for the hoop and he got this crazy look in his eye, then just chucked the ball from half-court. It bounced off the backboard, the Heat got the rebound, ran it back, and hit a three-pointer before the clock ran out and won the damn game."

I stared at him for a couple seconds before I realized he was expecting me to say something.

"Wow," I said.

"Yeah!" he said. "They should fire his ass, don't you think?"

"Um," I said. Because I was pretty sure the poor guy shouldn't be fired for something that was my fault.

So now I'm sitting here in study hall, not sure if I'm going crazy or if I'm some damn Harry Potter wizard. And I don't even know who to ask about this. Not Ms. Randall, and definitely not Max. Especially if it's true I made his team lose.

Maybe there's nobody I can talk to.

Tuesday, February 2, 7:05 p.m.

You know, I'm never going to ask anyone about anything ever again. Well, okay, maybe not never. But I'm going to really think about it before I ask other people about weird stuff that happens to me.

When I got home from school, Mom was sitting at the kitchen table, staring at a nice bouquet of flowers in front of her. Our kitchen is small and it's all different shades of brown, so flowers always really stand out in there.

"Hey, Mom," I said.

"Hi, Sebastian," she said. She had a bruise on her left cheek, and her eye was a little swollen. It looked like it hurt pretty bad. I guess that was why she was drinking wine coolers at four o'clock. Even Bill usually waited until dinnertime to start drinking.

"How was school?" she asked.

"Okay," I said as I grabbed a bag of pretzels from the pantry.

"Yeah? Then why did Ms. Randall just call me to tell me she's concerned about you? She asked how things are at home. Why'd she ask that?"

"I don't know." I stuffed a handful of pretzels in my mouth. "I didn't tell her nothing."

"Sebastian Younger, don't you talk with your mouth full."

I swallowed real quick even though I hadn't finished chewing. It hurt a little.

"Sorry," I said.

"So, Ms. Randall, she says you're having trouble sleeping? A lot of bad dreams or something?"

"I didn't tell her anything about bad dreams," I said. I started to head for the stairs and the safety of my room.

"Stop," she said.

I stopped.

"Sit," she said.

I sat down at the kitchen table across from her.

"So," she said, leaning in, still clutching her wine cooler, which made it tip a little. But it was mostly empty so it didn't spill. "What *did* you tell her?"

I thought about lying, honestly. But I just wanted to talk to someone about the crazy thoughts I was thinking right now, and if you can't talk to your mom, who can you talk to, right?

"Okay," I said. "Now, I know how this sounds, but hear me out. I been having these . . . well, I thought they were dreams. I thought I was dreaming I was other people or something. And I thought that was kinda weird so I asked Ms. Randall about it."

"Why Ms. Randall?"

I shrugged. "She was just the person who was there when I thought to ask someone, I guess." I didn't want to hurt Mom's feelings that I would choose Ms. Randall over her. "So that's what I thought it was. Dreams. Then last night I was a basketball player for the Cavs and I accidentally made him mess up a shot. But today I found out that the *real* basketball player, the same guy, messed up in real life in the same way that I messed him up in my dream!"

She stared at me, and I could tell she wasn't getting it at all.

"Mom," I said. "Somehow, while I'm sleeping, I'm, like, possessing other people's bodies or something! It's like . . . I don't know what. *Magic*, I guess."

She was still looking at me and I couldn't really tell what she was thinking, partly because of the bruise on her face. But then she took a last swig of her wine cooler and put the bottle down. She rubbed her good eye with the heel of her hand. Then she looked at me again.

"Sabe, honey, I know things are hard right now," she said. "And I promise things are going to get better someday."

"Mom, I don't think you're really getting what I'm talking about. Maybe if—"

"No, Sabe. I get it. I'm not dumb. You wish you were somewhere else. Someone else. Can't say I blame you. But come on, it's time to grow up. It's time to—"

"It really happened. You have to believe me! I—"

"Now, Sabe—"

"You think I'm some stupid, crazy kid, lying to get attention—"

"You better quiet yourself down—"

"You have to listen to me! I'm not making it up—"

"Sebastian! Enough!"

"No, Mom! You're never here and when you are, you never listen!!"

"SHUT UP!" And she threw her wine cooler on the floor. It smashed into tiny, sharp pieces that slid all over the place. Then she reached out and grabbed my chin with her thumb and forefinger. "You listen to me," she said, a snarl on her face. "There's no such thing as wizards or dragons or magic lands or any of that shit. There's nowhere else out there. This is all there is. Do you hear me?"

She still had my chin and she pinched it hard.

"Do. You. Hear. Me," she said through clenched teeth.

"Yes, ma'am."

She let go and leaned back in her seat. "Now, go up to your room and do your homework. And mind the broken glass. I don't want you cutting yourself."

I nodded and walked across the kitchen, trying to tiptoe around the glittering shards. I climbed the stairs two at a time, that feeling of needing to be alone in my room like a craving in my gut. I closed the door and dropped down on my bed. I felt so stupid, so embarrassed. I curled up in a ball so hard I felt like I'd turn myself inside out. Of course I wasn't magically possessing other people's bodies. That was just idiotic.

I wanted to pull the covers over my head and sleep until the sun was up. Maybe tomorrow I wouldn't feel like the stupidest person in the world anymore. Maybe. But I couldn't even keep my eyes closed, much less go to sleep. I picked up my book and almost started reading. But then I thought, *What if these books are the problem?* Filling my head with wishes that couldn't come true. I threw it across the room.

It lay there on the carpet, the sword on the cover glinting in the light. Maybe that was too harsh. Maybe I didn't mean it. . . .

To distract myself, I decided to write in this journal. I thought maybe it would clear my head. Help me see what's really going on. But it still doesn't make sense, and now I want to pick up my book again.

Screw it. I'm going to go read. At least it'll stop me thinking about what a jackass I am.

Wednesday, February 3, Butt-Ass Early

I think I really messed up. I don't know how, exactly, but here's what happened.

Last night I read so late that I fell asleep on top of my covers with my clothes still on. Then I had one of my dreams. If that's even still what I'm calling them. And this one was the weirdest yet. I was inside this old black guy. He was dressed all in white and had lots of jewelry. Like necklaces, bracelets, and rings. Except it wasn't jewels and gold. It was all made of bones and fabric and a few weird crystals here and there. He was sitting in a chair in a motel room. You know, the kind that all look the same. He was reading some book, but it was in another language. French, I think. But I don't read French so I couldn't say for sure.

I watched the foreign words in the book as his rough, dry hands turned pages. And I got that crazy impulse again. To assert myself. What did it matter, anyway, since none of this was real? So I grabbed the book and tossed it across the room just like I'd thrown my own book earlier in my room.

"Interesting . . . ," said the man. He had a French accent, but not a heavy one.

He stood up slowly. I expected him to walk over and pick up the book, but he went the opposite way to the dresser. There was a mirror above the dresser, and he looked at himself in it. He had long gray dreadlocks and his face was wrinkly and scarred. But his expression was curious. Playful, almost. He touched the mirror and whispered something quietly in French. The mirror shimmered. Then, instead of looking at his reflection, I was looking at my own.

"Hello, little nightwalker," he said. "You should be more careful where you go. No telling what sort of attention you'll get."

I snapped awake in my own room, on my bed. But I was breathing hard like I'd just been running, and in my ears I could still hear his quiet, dry chuckle.

I didn't sleep the rest of the night. I didn't want to,

because I was afraid I'd go back to that guy. But even if I wanted to sleep, I couldn't because my mind was racing. Nothing but questions without answers and no one to ask. All I've got is this stupid journal that just stares back at me with my own thoughts.

Wednesday or Thursday, Hell If I Know What Time It Is
It was hard to get through school that next day after only three hours of sleep. I kept nodding off in class and then jerking back awake, afraid I'd slip off to somewhere else. Or I guess, someone else. I never did, though. Not sure why. The old guy had called me "nightwalker," so maybe it's something I can only do at night.

Max wasn't at school. And neither was Ms. Randall. I heard they were both in the hospital, Max with appendicitis. They didn't say what Ms. Randall had, only that she'd be out at least a few days. Did the old guy do this to them? Curse them or something? He hadn't seemed evil, exactly. But he had jewelry made from bones. That was like witch-doctor stuff. I thought about going to check in on Max at the hospital, but then I thought if the old guy did it, maybe that was exactly what he wanted me to do. No, if I did that, I might be putting Max and Ms. Randall in more danger. Not to mention myself.

After school, I tried to do some homework. It was kind of nice to do math, something that was predictable. But eventually Bill came home and he turned the TV up extra loud again and it was getting late and I was so tired by then that I started to nod off over my homework. And if I was right that I could only go places at night, I definitely didn't want to fall asleep right then. I thought about reading for a while to keep myself awake. But I was still half convinced that all this was some crazy paranoia from reading too much of that crap. So instead I did something drastic. I went downstairs and watched TV with Bill.

"Well, goddamn, if it ain't Sabe," he said as I walked into the den. He was sprawled out on the plaid wool couch, his big belly sticking up, a can of Natty Light in his hand. "Didn't even know you still lived here."

"Hey, Bill," I said, and sat down in the easy chair across from him.

"Get too sore to jerk off anymore?" he said, then laughed. But the laugh turned into a nasty, hacking cough that went on for about a minute and ended with him spitting some big glob of something into his handkerchief.

"What are you watching?" I asked.

"One of those reality shows," he said, his eyes still watery from coughing so much. "'Bout this guy who makes stuff out of junk." He took a gulp of beer. "I shoulda done somethin' like that. Makin' stuff, instead of destroyin' stuff for a living." He chugged the rest of his beer. "Well, too late now." He put the empty can with the rest of the empties on the coffee table, then picked a fresh one from the case on the floor next to him.

The guy on the show wandered around a junkyard, picking up stuff that you would have thought would be totally useless. Then he put all these useless things together and came up with this cool tractor-car thing. But even though the show was kind of interesting, my eyes started to get heavy, and before I'd realized what was happening, I fell asleep.

When I woke up a little later, I was looking at myself. It took me a second to figure that out because it was hard to think for some reason. First I stared stupidly at myself snoring in the easy chair. Then I noticed I had a beer can in my hand. Well, that explained why I was having trouble thinking. I was drunk. I looked down at myself and I was sprawled out on the plaid couch with my big belly sticking up in the air. I was inside Bill.

I was thinking to myself that this was about the worst thing that could happen, when my mom came home. She walked in without looking at us and slowly put her bag on the kitchen counter. Bill stood up, stumbling a little. I'd had a few beers here and there with Max, but I'd never felt drunk like this. It was weird how slow his body was. It felt kind of numb, too. As he walked over to the kitchen, he banged his shin on the coffee table and it barely felt like anything.

"What you doin' home so early?" he said. He didn't sound happy about it.

"They sent me home because of my face," she said.

Then she turned toward us. Toward *him* I mean. And what had been a small bruise before now covered half her face. It had a weird purple shine to it, except around the eye, which was leaking some kind of fluid.

"What the hell happened to you?!" he said, stepping back.

"*You* happened, Bill," she said quietly.

"Bullshit. I didn't do that. Yesterday, that was an accident. I said I was sorry. But this? No way in hell I did this."

"I'm telling you," she said. "Nothing else happened. It just keeps getting worse and worse. It's what *you* did."

"You better shut the hell up, woman, or I *will* make it worse."

"Not with Sabe over there sleeping!"

"Who gives a rat's ass about that whiny little bitch?"

"Don't you talk like that about my son!"

"Or what?"

"Or . . . ," she said, her one good eye wide, angry, and desperate. "Or I'll leave you."

"That's it," Bill said. I could feel the blood pounding through his drunk brain, feel him make a fist, feel his shoulder tense as he hauled off to hit her. For a split second I felt and watched it all start to happen, and I was so scared I wanted to scream.

Then I thought, *I can stop this.*

His fist was halfway to the good side of her face when I stopped it in midair. Mom stared at me. I mean *him.* Us.

Stared at us, looking scared and surprised. I wasn't sure if I could talk to her, or what I'd say. *Hey, Mom, don't worry. It's just me, Sabe, possessing Bill's body.* Yeah, I knew that probably wouldn't work, so I just didn't say anything.

I made him walk to the front door. It wasn't easy. Controlling someone else's body was already pretty awkward, and being drunk made it even harder. After stumbling back and forth a little, I made it to the door. It was hard to turn the knob and open the door, too. Finally we made it out onto our rickety old front porch. Thankfully, Mom didn't follow.

I wasn't sure what I was going to do with him at first. I just knew I had to get him away from Mom before I lost control of him. But once I got outside into the cold night air, I started to think maybe I could solve this problem forever. We lived real close to the freeway. Everybody in the neighborhood knew Bill was a useless drunk, and it wouldn't surprise any of them to find out tomorrow that he'd walked out in front of a semi truck going seventy miles an hour.

It took a little while to stumble up the steep grassy hill to the short metal guardrail that ran along the side of the freeway. But finally we were there, right on the shoulder. It was still way before midnight, so there was plenty of traffic zipping by. The wind hit our face every time a car or truck blew past. If I stepped us out now, it would happen in seconds.

But I hesitated. Because now that I was here, now that I was feeling less drunk and a little more calm, this looked a lot like murder.

"Do it," said a voice like rock scraping tar.

I turned toward the voice. It looked like a man, big and muscular, with gold armor that shone in the fluorescent freeway lights. He sat on a white horse with a sword sheathed at his side and a long wooden spear in his hand. But even weirder than all that, he had a lion head. His mouth was open slightly and I could see his big canines. His cat eyes flashed as he stared down at me.

"What the hell . . . ," I whispered with Bill's voice.

"An amusing choice of words," he said. "I am Sabnack, and I am here to take you away from this banal and tedious existence to a place better suited for you. But first, destroy this useless meat sack. I want to make sure you can follow orders."

"I don't think he's going to do that," said another voice. That one I recognized. I turned to my other side and saw the old black guy with the gray dreadlocks.

"You!" I said.

"Hello, little nightwalker," he said with a tired smile. "It looks like you've picked up some unwanted company."

"*You* are the unwanted company, *bokur*!" said the lion-headed guy on the horse. "I have been watching this one for weeks, working in the background, waiting until his abilities had acceptably matured. Your sudden appearance has forced my hand." Then he turned to me. "This old fool is weak and poor. What can he possibly give you? I am strong. I am powerful. I have lived for five centuries and have forgotten more than he will ever know."

"You said you'll take me away from here?" I asked. "What, like some magic land?"

"More strange and magical than you can imagine," he said. "A world of heroes and beasts, beautiful maidens and cruel, villainous foes. Kill this mortal whom you hate so much and prove your loyalty to me. Then I will take you there."

"It's true," said the old man. "I'm old and weak. Sabnack is far more powerful than me. He can take you to a world so unlike this one, you'd scarcely believe your own eyes. A world that contains both breathtaking beauty and horrifying destruction. But think about what he asks of you. To kill, even a man as wretched as this one?"

"I deal out life and death without hesitation," said Sabnack. "And if I tell him to kill this mortal, that is the only justification he needs."

The old man's eyes narrowed. "It's true you deal in death. I've heard that the sword and spear you carry are only symbols. That your real weapon is sickness and decay." He turned to me then. To Bill and me. "How's your friend? Your teacher? Sick, aren't they? Very suddenly?"

"Mortals are weak," said Sabnack. "They get sick constantly."

"What about your mother?" the old man said to me.

"And even the body you occupy now is in the grip of a cancer. You can feel it yourself, can't you? Try and look— you'll see."

I *could* feel something dark and heavy at the bottom of Bill's lungs.

"This is what he is: disease and decay," said the old man. He turned back to Sabnack. "Will you deny your nature, demon?"

"Why would I deny it?" asked Sabnack. "Disease strikes down the weak. Decay repurposes them so that the strong may thrive. This is a fundamental law of the universe."

I noticed that what Sabnack was sitting on wasn't really a horse. It was a white, horse-shaped creature. But its eyes were red, its teeth were sharp, and it had claws instead of hooves.

"You're making everybody around here sick?" I asked Sabnack. "On purpose?"

"I cannot be bothered to concern myself with the effects I have on regular mortals. And neither should you," Sabnack said. "You have been granted a gift from the gods. The ability to transfer your soul to another and dominate it. You don't belong here. You deserve more. I can give you more."

"But I have to kill somebody first."

"You'll have to do more than that," said the old man. "You will have to swear fealty to him and to Lamia, the Grand Duchess of the East, whom he serves."

"The east of what?" I asked.

"Hell," said the old man.

"What?" I said. "You're kidding!"

"I'm not," he said. "It's actually not all bad. Hell isn't quite what most people think it is."

"And you are not quite as good as you pretend," said Sabnack. "Tell him what *you* are, and we will see if he still trusts your word over mine."

The old man nodded. "My name is Poujean and I am a *bokur*, or what you might call a voodoo priest or witch doctor. And I make no claims of being good. I commune with powerful spirits, called *loa*, who grant me certain abilities. Some of these *loa* can be just as cruel as Sabnack. But ultimately, I am, like you, a mortal, often forced to make hard choices like the one you must make now."

"So what's my choice?" I asked. "Get out of this place and have everything I've ever wanted but become a killer who gets bossed around by demons? What's the other option? Stick around here and watch my mom get beat by her boyfriend until he dies of lung cancer?"

"That's not the only other option," said Poujean. "If you want, you may come with me on my travels. I can't show you magical lands, but I can show you the magic of your own land. Not a luxurious life, but a vibrant one. Perhaps together we can help you learn to master your own special abilities. And though my means are humble, I still have my humanity. I will never ask you to do something you feel is wrong."

"Well," I said, "that's good enough for me."

Poujean held out his hand and I shook it. It felt dry and warm and strong. Handshakes are important to me, and his felt good.

"Stupid mortals, both of you," said Sabnack, his lion face curling into a snarl. "Her Grace told me to bring him back alive if I could, but dead was an acceptable alternative." Then he drew his sword.

But Poujean smiled and drew a small glass bottle from beneath his robes. "We have never met before, Sabnack, so you do not know that before I became a *bokur*, I was a priest. I still remember all the rites of exorcism, and it just so happens that I learned them from the best." He popped the lid off the bottle with his thumb and flicked it so that water splashed on Sabnack. "In the name of Jesus, Moses, and Abraham, I command you to return from where you came!"

Sabnack hissed and his horse creature screamed. They stumbled backward, then the creature threw him. He landed in a clatter of metal. He stabbed his spear into the ground and pulled himself up with it. His legs looked too skinny and weak to hold him up by themselves.

"Shall we continue or was there somewhere else you had to be?" asked Poujean as he pulled a silver crucifix and rosary beads from his bag.

Sabnack roared at him; then both he and his hellsteed

disappeared in a smelly, brown gas cloud. The spear he had buried in the ground remained, sticking up from the grass like a little tree without branches.

"Could you have really destroyed him?" I asked.

"I'm not sure. I've seen my friend Paul do it, but I've never had an occasion to try it myself before."

"What if he'd called your bluff?"

Poujean shrugged. "Then we would have found out if I could really destroy a demon." Then he put his hand on my shoulder. "Do you still want to come with me? It won't always be an easy life. Or a safe one."

"I've always felt like this wasn't quite right for me. I want to go with you."

"But?"

"My mom. This guy." I touched Bill's big belly. "He's gonna hurt her again if I'm not around to stop him."

"Ah, well, if that's all," he said, and smiled. "Stopping a man from beating his wife or girlfriend is something I am *very* good at. Come, I will need to gather a few ingredients. Then before you release his body, we will give him a potion that will make him violently ill whenever he tries to harm your mother."

"You can do that?"

His smile grew mischievous. "That and many other things, little nightwalker. Watch and learn."

"What about that?" I asked, pointing to the spear sticking out of the ground.

"See if you can take it," he said.

I walked over and tried to pull it out of the ground.

"It won't budge," I said.

"It must be for someone else then," he said. "Come—let's take care of this man and his violence problem before the sun rises and you lose control of him."

Are You Kidding? I Don't Even Know What Day It Is Anymore

We were at a rest stop outside Chicago. I think a few days after I left home, or maybe a week. I'd left a note for my mom, but Poujean said it might make her feel better if I called. I wasn't looking forward to her freaking out on me on the phone, but I figured he was probably right.

Luck was on my side, though. Or maybe Poujean's *loa*. Because she didn't pick up her cell. I just leaned back against the side of the pay phone and talked into her voice mail. And I have to say, it felt really good.

"Hey, Mom, it's Sebastian. Just wanted to let you know that I'm doing great. Eating healthy, taking care of myself, getting sleep, all that stuff you're always fussing about. So don't worry about that. I hope your face is healing. Keep putting that cream on that I left for you. I know it smells a little funky, but my friend tells me it'll do the trick. Also, I don't think Bill will be beating on you anymore, so you don't have to worry about that, either. I'll try to make it home at some point, but it probably won't be for a while. I've got some stuff I have to learn, places I want to visit. That kind of thing.

"One thing I want you to know, Mom. You were wrong about there not being anywhere else. There are other places. Amazing places. And amazing people, too. There's a lot more to the world than you think. I'm seeing it now. I hope maybe someday I can show it to you."

Myra McEntire
Naughty or Nice

When I was seven and he was eight, I broke all of the crayons in Henry Bishop's supply box. He didn't tell on me.

When I was eleven and he was twelve, he tried to give me my first kiss. I laughed so hard I peed in my pants, which would've killed the moment had it not already been really, really dead.

When I was seventeen and he was eighteen, we went on a school trip to Bavaria. I learned to believe in monsters, and in Henry.

✦ ✦ ✦

After thirty hours of traveling and a scant amount of sleep, we finally circle W. A. Mozart airport.

"Get off me." I push Henry's head off my shoulder. "You're drooling."

Semi–sleep state or not, my best friend is ready with a comeback. As always. "No, honey, that's you. Tell me what did it. Was it the smell of my shampoo or my close proximity?"

I groan and return my seat to its upright position. Ignoring Henry, I lean my forehead against the cold window and look down.

Nature has spilled a sugar bowl over a gathering of Baroque gingerbread castles, the snow so white it's blue. Purple mountaintops are haloed by clouds, and the hills that remain green year-round seem too lush for the cold temperatures.

I've waited for this since I was a freshman—the annual and legendary senior winter trip our private school takes. It was also known as everyone's early Christmas present, like when Lucy Price got knocked up, or when Jerry Maner got suspended for skiing naked.

After the chaos of claiming our baggage, an hour-long train ride, and twenty minutes in a van that smells like diesel fuel and dead fish, we pull up to the hotel.

Six buildings make up the Edelweiss. The wood juts out at odd but pleasing angles, complemented by curves. When I look up, snow-covered mountains fill most of the sky. I have to lean my head all the way back to see the sun or a tiny slice of blue, and my eyes are watering from the cold. I'm grateful for my faux fur–lined boots, coat and matching gloves, and the resulting toasty toes and fingers, even if it does scream tourist. Still, I head inside before my eyeballs freeze.

The lobby is warm and cheery, and now crowded to all four walls with tired, stinky students. Our teachers corral us into lines so we can check in.

"Willkommen!" The girl behind the desk offers us a bright smile. Her dress—*dirndl*—is a Swiss Miss fantasy come true, pushing her boobs so high I half expect them to fall out and land on the desk. The bodice is tight, the skirt is short, and the apron seems like an afterthought. Her name tag reads ELKE.

I check in first, and the smile never leaves her face. I think it's just excellent customer service until Henry steps up to the counter beside me, and I figure out she hasn't been smiling at me. She's been smiling *past* me.

"Welcome." She takes his parents' credit card and enters the information into the computer. It takes twice as long as it should because she keeps stopping to look at him.

My chest tightens, a relatively new but altogether stressful response to the way girls react to Henry. It's not his fault he's grown five inches taller and his skin cleared up and he finally got his braces off. He's still my Henry.

Just . . . hotter.

When she hands the card back, she sounds decidedly less local. "My friends and I are having drinks later at Sterndlbar. It's down in the market. You should come."

"Are both of us invited?" he asks.

Oh yay. He remembers I'm here.

"You want to bring your sister?" Such a subtle insult. The girl's a pro.

"Oh, no," he says, winking at her. "She's not my sister."

Elke's face falls a country mile. "Well then. You're both welcome. I guess."

Henry leans closer to the counter. "She's just *like* a sister."

Her smile is big again, and I swear she pushes her boobs together with her arms, creating an endless chasm of cleavage. "I'll see you tonight."

"Looking forward to it."

"Our concierge is just over there." Back to business, and the accent, Elke points to a man in *lederhosen* that were probably too short when he was twelve. "He'll assign a bellboy to help you with your bags."

"Thanks." Henry hooks his arm around my neck and pulls me away from the desk.

I jerk free the second we're out of Elke's range of vision. We've always horsed around, but his touch feels different now, and not just because I stopped winning the fights.

"You're such a douche." I busy myself by straightening my scarf with my free hand. Henry takes my bag from my other.

"Proven, scientific fact. Women find men they believe to be attached more attractive."

I take my bag back. "Are you using your mom's *Cosmo*s for bathroom reading again?"

"It has really good articles." He shrugs. "Lobby in an hour?"

I stare.

"Come on, Bex, you have to go with me. You were invited. You can't be rude. International relations and whatnot." He shakes his hair out of his eyes, and I can't help thinking of how soft it felt when he was asleep on my shoulder.

"Fine. I'll see you in an hour."

The walk to the market takes forever. I have my faux-fur ensemble, and Henry wears one of those ridiculous fleece hats with the wool-lined side flaps. For some reason, on him, it works. His dark hair is contained, and I can actually see his eyes. I forgot how green they are.

The amber circles of the town market lights shine on the snow as we reach the pub. The bar sign swings merrily above the door, inviting us to come into the warmth and cast off our worries.

Or our inhibitions, as the case may be.

Henry scans the room, and his focus lands on Elke in a booth in the back corner. She has on a berry-red scarf and a matching beret.

"She's got on so much lip gloss that if you try to kiss her, you'll slide off her face like a penguin off an ice cap."

Henry grins, like he could be down for that.

"She's so obvious." I scoff, removing my coat and hanging it on a moose-antler rack by the door.

"I'm on vacation. Who needs complications?"

"Right."

I take off my hat and he reaches out to smooth down my hair after a stealth attack of static electricity. "Your hairdo looks as uptight as you are."

"I'm not uptight. I'm just . . . selective." I smack his hand away with more force than necessary.

"It's a joke." He waves his fingers in mock pain and then holds them close to his chest, like I've injured him. "You can laugh."

"Oh, I am. On the inside."

Henry tucks a strand of hair behind my ear. It's a sweet gesture, but his words don't go with it. "Come be my wingman?"

I sigh. "You can get off the ground all by yourself."

"Bex—"

"I'm tired of being a means to an end for you." I pull away from him. "How come you aren't ever my wingman?"

"Do you need one?" He honestly looks confused.

This is part of the problem of having a dude for a best friend. They get so used to looking at you, they never see you.

"I'm not asexual, Henry, in case you haven't noticed."

He frowns and takes a step back to check me out, starting at my feet and making his way to my face. His gaze stops a couple of times before ending at my lips.

"Henry?"

"Nope." He shakes his head. "Definitely not asexual."

He sees me now.

A movement in the corner of the pub catches his eye. I don't bother looking over my shoulder. Elke and her friend. "Go. No complications, remember?"

I walk away first.

The pub smells like beer and Christmas. Voices are cheery. Holiday music plays in the background, and a fire burns in the hearth. Kids of all ages sit with their parents, and a few even have glasses of cider. European sensibilities.

A guy slings drinks behind the counter. Young, with wild hair and fast hands. Cute. Smiling at me.

No complications.

Sadly, mine will be going home with me, assuming Henry doesn't get lost in Elke's cleavage.

I hide behind a gaggle of French tourists for a while to work up my nerve, then make my way to the bar to order a Coke. "And can you put some ice in that?"

The bartender grins. In spite of the goatee, he's even better looking up close. "Not enough of the cold stuff outside for you?"

"I'd rather have it in my soda." I watch him for a minute

while trying to pragmatically figure out how to do this. Henry's the flirt. I'm the sarcastic sidekick. How would he handle the situation if he were in my shoes?

He'd start by hitting on a girl.

"You're Australian?" I ask after I clear my throat.

"British. But I'll forgive you."

I know Henry's staring at me from the way the bartender keeps looking toward the corner. I'm guessing it's an evil death glare. I have no idea if it's protective or jealous.

Not my problem.

I screw up my courage and take another stab at it. "So, where are the best places to ski?"

"Do you really want to know, or are you trying to flirt with me?"

I am so not cut out for this. "I'm trying, and failing, to flirt with you."

"Give me ten seconds so I can bribe a replacement." The grin becomes a full-blown smile. "I'll flirt back."

I blush, regretting that I'm too far away from the fire to blame it on the heat. I didn't expect success. Not so quickly.

The bartender's smile is still in place as he comes out from behind the bar and hands me a glass of Coke. "I'm Kit."

"Bex." I take the glass and we do an awkward sort of handshake thing. "Short for Rebecca."

"I like it."

"Thanks." I sip my drink. It's full to the brim, and loaded with ice.

"Come sit with my friends," Kit says. "They're with that guy you walked in with."

I can't respond. I'm too stuck between having to sit with Henry and Elke and some random girl, and Kit noticing I came into the pub with Henry. Maybe it's a bartender thing. Totaling numbers in their head to make sure they're within fire code or something.

We jostle our way through the crowd. Languages twist together in an exotic chorus, and the sound is pleasant, if surreal.

"Kit!" Elke's smile flashes a lot of white, but she doesn't have a good teeth-to-gums ratio, and for some reason this boosts my confidence.

Neither of them introduces their friend.

"Thought we'd join you." Kit pulls up a wide stool and nods like I'm supposed to sit down. When I do, he bumps my hip with his and then crowds in to share. We're close. Really close.

I stare at the floor, hoping he won't notice my grin. When I look up, I see that Henry did. His eyes are narrowed. I stick out my tongue at him and they go wide.

"Are you here from the States, then?" Kit asks, pouring beer from a pitcher into an empty glass on the table. He offers it to me, but I hold up my Coke.

Henry answers in some kind of weird, deep Man Voice.

"Virginia, near Charlottesville." The voice gives out on the last syllable and he coughs.

"We're here on a school trip," I add over Henry's coughing. Elke hands him her glass of beer. He takes several deep swigs and slumps back in his seat, staring at Kit's hand, which has landed on my knee.

"A school trip?" The other girl has an expensive button nose with nostrils so tiny that snot blockage from a simple cold could suffocate her. I think her accent is British, too, but it's a little too nasally to be certain. "You mean you're not here for the Krampus walk?"

"What's that?" Henry's back to his normal voice, and he's eyeing the beer pitcher.

A look passes between Kit and the two girls. I speak before they can.

"The Krampus walk," I say, happy to have a chance to show off my geek research side, "is a tourist thing, a festival to get people to come into town and spend money. I read it in my brochures."

Henry laughs. "Brochure my ass. You have a stack of travel books bigger than you are."

"Some people read other things besides *Cosmo* and *X-Men* comics."

A shout goes up from the game of darts being played beside us. A guy takes a wide step back and bumps into me. Kit's fingers slide up, gripping my thigh to keep me steady. It has the opposite effect.

My voice is a little wobbly. "People dress up, buy masks to hide behind so they can run wild, get drunk in the street, hook up with strangers."

"Sounds like a good time to me," Henry says, his arm lowering from the back of the booth to Elke's shoulders.

"Sounds stupid to me," I return. But I put my hand on top of Kit's.

No one at the table knows where to look, and the room goes quiet, like the universe put Henry and me in time-out.

"Anyway," I continue when the bar noise returns to its previous volume, "it sounds like the Krampus is a cheap knockoff of Santa."

Henry is the only one at the table who doesn't look at me like I've slapped his grandma.

"What did I say?"

"Krampus isn't anything like Santa. He's the anti-Santa," Elke says, her local accent completely gone. Definitely British. "Santa gives out toys, but Krampus gives out punishment."

"For being naughty?" Henry asks, his fingertips sliding down over Elke's collarbone. Lower.

She laughs. "Trust me, you wouldn't want to end up on his list."

Henry picks up Elke's beer glass and takes a long drink. "Maybe it wouldn't matter. Depending on what got me on it."

"I wouldn't let anyone hear you say that." Button Nose tilts her chin up. I'm momentarily entranced by her perfectly symmetrical nose holes. "It could be bad news."

"Um . . . why?" Derision saturates my voice. "I've seen his picture in the freaking travel brochures. A cute comic of a red, furry monster with horns, shaming the naughty kids. Like Elmo on speed."

"The Krampus isn't for kids." Kit sounds more like a nanny than a bartender.

"Grown-ups only, huh?" Henry's grin goes wicked, and his fingertips go lower over Elke's sweater.

"If he comes looking for you, you might end up stuffed in his sack," Button Nose says. "So he can take you home and have you for dinner."

"Unless you grab his sack," I say.

Henry grins. "That's what she said."

Henry is three shades of buzzed, and these people are either total nutters or they've breathed the mountain air too long.

Or they're messing with us.

I try to meet Henry's eyes for affirmation, but he's busy staring into the bottom of his empty beer glass. He's drinking like a dehydrated fish.

Elke takes Henry's glass and refills it. "The tourist industry plays it off as fun in those brochures on purpose. They want to encourage people to show up and participate."

"It's better for the locals if tourists are available.

Better chance for survival." Kit's voice is exaggerated and dramatic, and the tense moment passes as we all laugh.

Definitely messing with us.

A murmur starts at the front of the bar.

It's minimal at first, just voices, but it grows louder and louder, morphing into screaming laughter and drunken shouting. Kit stands and grabs my hand.

"What are you doing?" I clamber off the stool.

"Krampus is walking. Come on!"

Henry and the girls follow us out of the bar. Henry's unsteady—he's not a drinker at all—and he puts his arms around the necks of both girls to stand up straight.

The cold air stings as Kit pulls me into the crowd. I follow him, crunching through the snow, laughing at the prospect of adventure. We make our way to the front. Monsters are everywhere.

Kind of like *Sesame Street Gone Wild.*

There are red fluffy ones, blue scraggly ones. There are some who remind me of the beasts from *Where the Wild Things Are,* and others that look like something my cat might throw up.

None of them are scary, and none of them are carrying sacks.

They mostly just dance around and play hide-and-seek and chase with the children on the street.

"Perfectly harmless, right?" Kit asks, pulling me against

his chest. He leans down, and I'm certain he's going to kiss me.

Henry shouts my name from across the street. I smile regretfully and pull away from Kit. He looks disappointed.

I make my way through the crowd to Henry and the girls. Kit is behind me, his hands on my waist, like we're doing the bunny hop. He's been touching me since he came from behind the bar. I thought the British were supposed to be standoffish.

Henry's mouth is set in a thin line of determination, and he has beads of sweat over his upper lip.

"What's wrong?" I ask. "Sick?"

"Drunk. And real sad about it." I look in the direction he's pointing.

It's Ms. Belcher, our toughest chaperone, and she's fifteen feet away. "We need to get back to the hotel," I say.

Kit overhears. "You can't leave. We barely got to talk at all."

The way he's staring at my lips suggests that wasn't all we didn't get to do.

"We're here for a week." Henry is green. Lost opportunity or not, if Henry blows groceries in front of Belcher, we'll be on the first plane back home.

"Promise you'll come back tomorrow night." Kit won't let my hand go. The touching thing feels weird all of a sudden. "You'll have to get masks so you can run with us."

"We'll be back. We'll find masks." Desperation makes

me blurt out the promise. Belcher is getting closer and closer, and now Coach Smith is with her. I pull away from Kit and push past Elke and Button Nose. "We have to go."

We dodge in and out of the crowd, me pulling Henry along, and he groans. The smell of alcohol on everyone's breath is enough to make me nauseated. I almost feel sorry for him.

I barely get Henry behind the back wall of the pub before he loses it.

"Wow," I say. "This is almost as gross as the Sixth Grade Plague of Puke. Remember? I had to go to the hospital to get intravenous fluids."

"I gave you a stuffed bear." Henry leans against the building and swipes his mouth with the back of his hand.

I push his sweaty hair into his stupid hat so it's out of his face. "Come to think of it, its fur looked a lot like one of the Krampus impersonators."

I hear a noise and look over my shoulder. What if Belcher followed us?

If so, she is about to get eyeful or a shoe full.

Henry heaves again, and I pat his back in the dark while saying a silent prayer of thanks for a quick escape and my cast-iron stomach. Because no matter how you feel about someone, puking is gross.

"Thanks, Bex."

"Anytime, Henry."

We stay behind the building until Henry is empty and

the teachers are on their way back to the Edelweiss.

The whole time, my skin tingles with the sense that someone, somewhere, is watching us.

The next afternoon, Henry shovels in potatoes and sausage like last night was nothing but a nightmare. "We have to go buy masks."

"Why?"

"For tonight." He picks up his milk and chugs.

So gross.

We're the last people at the lunch buffet. Everyone else has already hit the slopes. Twice. "After last night, I'm perfectly happy to spend the afternoon in the lobby and drink hot chocolate."

"Fine." Henry leans back, rubbing his stomach. Frustratingly enough, after everything he's put away, it's still flat—even slightly rippled—under his shirt. "You drink hot chocolate; I'll hang out with the staff. I bet there's a storeroom around here that's empty for most of the day."

I stare at him. "Elke?"

"Do you have another suggestion?" He stares back.

"What's going on here?" I feel the need to clear the air. "Seems like last night, you were touching her just to piss me off."

"And *you* were doing the same thing with Kit." Henry bats his eyelashes and picks up another doughnut.

I wait until he takes a bite to answer. "Maybe we should touch each other instead of strangers."

He chokes. It's what I was aiming for, but I didn't expect him to turn blue. Once I'm sure his windpipe is clear, I sit back down.

"I tried touching you once, Bex. You remember how that turned out."

"So? You know I laugh when I'm nervous." I want to giggle now.

"I thought you were laughing at me."

"Maybe you thought wrong."

"Well"—Henry's tone reminds me of the one he used to use when I took the last red ice pop or piece of bubble gum—"you never asked me to try again."

I deadpan: "Oh, please, Henry. Lean over here and lay one on me. Wait, let me grab a change of unders first."

He blinks.

"Anyway, it's not like Cindy Evans wasn't ready to step in and play peekaboo with you once I was out of the romantic picture."

"Ahhh. Good old Cindy Evans."

I throw down my napkin, stand up, and push in my chair. Broaching the subject is obviously a bad idea or at least one we're not ready for yet. "Are you going with me?"

"Where?"

"To buy a mask." I turn on my heel. "I'll ask the concierge where we can find them."

Because whether I want to go back to the pub tonight or not, no way in hell am I leaving him alone with Elke.

The faint scent of gasoline and oil slips from between the door and the threshold of the woodworking shop. Through the window I see chain saws lined up carefully on a table, three rows of three across.

"That's a lot of chain saws."

"That's a pretty impressive display of knives, too." Henry nods to several on a table beside a half-carved mask.

"Don't worry," a deep voice says from behind us. The man it belongs to has a scruffy red beard and splinters of wood caught in the waffle weave of his thermal shirt. "I only use them to carve masks. Not to disassemble innocent American tourists."

"That's . . . reassuring." Henry's statement is more like a question.

"Can I help you?" The man has the definite accent of someone who's used to speaking English to tourists. Formal and precise.

"We were looking for masks. For the Krampus walk." Henry hitches his thumb in the direction of the main road. "The concierge at the Edelweiss told us to ask for Wilhelm."

"That's me, and I have plenty."

We step inside. Masks cover every wall.

Some have horns that extend three feet on each side. Others have teeth like industrial-sized needles, and long, curving tongues. Painted blood, so glossy it looks wet, drips from upturned lips.

Where did Elmo go?

There isn't one wall space in the entire room absent of a mask, and there isn't one mask that features anything resembling a smile.

"I wouldn't want to come in here at night," I say, breathing through the words. "This is enough to fuel a lifetime of bad dreams."

"Krampus masks," Wilhelm says, smiling, "are a specialty of our village."

"I thought Krampus was cute." I shiver, and try to avoid looking at the masks with the longest bloody tongues and biggest oversized horns. "These don't look anything like what we saw last night."

"Krampus is whatever you make him." Wilhelm picks up a finished mask. "This is carved from *windbuchen* beech from the Black Forest. Ram horns from one of the most fertile flocks our valley has known, and stained with his blood. Special order."

He puts it down when I shudder.

"What were you told about the Krampus?" he asks.

We give him the rundown of our convo and personal experience last night.

"No one mentioned that Krampus predates Christianity?" Wilhelm picks up a knife and a sharpening stone. "That some believe he's a demon who feeds on human souls?"

"Nope," Henry says, staring at the knife. I feel him tense beside me. "They left that part out."

"Good then." Wilhelm laughs. "It's not anything to worry about. Some people go too far. And it's bad for my business."

"Right." Henry nods. "Business."

"It's almost dark." Wilhelm looks through the open door in the direction of the market and begins running the edge of the knife against the stone. "The Krampus walk will begin soon. Last night's walk was mother's milk, for children. Tonight will be made of mead and meat."

"We're supposed to meet some people," Henry says, taking a step toward the door. "In the village. So. We should go."

"If you're going to play, did you want a mask?" Wilhelm asks, gesturing toward his morbid collection with the point of his newly sharpened knife.

"Thanks for the offer, sir," Henry says. "But I don't think so. Not one of these."

"**C**reepy mask seller is creepy." Henry's walking too fast for me to keep up.

"Your legs are longer than mine. Slow down." I catch him and tuck my hand in the crook of his arm.

"Did the concierge send us there as a joke? I feel like I'm in a horror movie." He tightens his arm around mine and imitates a movie trailer voice-over. "Innocent tourists led to the slaughter in a snowbound paradise. The demon must be fed! Rated R for sexual situations and nudity."

"You wish."

"Yes, I do."

I let go of his arm, and we crest the hill that leads to the pub just as the sun sinks behind the mountains.

We step into the warmth to find it more crowded than the night before. Several people have masks, but nothing like what we saw at the shop today. Less demon from hell, more Oscar the Grouch.

There's a girl behind the bar instead of Kit. I think he's bailed on me until he and Elke walk through the front door. Button Nose is missing.

"Hey! Where's your friend?" I ask.

"Hi." Kit slides his arm around my waist and pulls me close to his side. "She didn't want to be a tagalong."

I nod and put a half inch of space between us. Fifth wheel is always a bummer, but her absence has left us in the most awkward situation: an unintended double date.

We head toward the same table as the night before. Elke must be a regular, because even though the place is packed, the booth is empty. We're getting ready to sit when the murmur starts at the front of the pub.

The sounds are more menacing tonight. The crowd is a little slower to move toward the door, and some don't get up at all. Kit and Elke have an easy task as they lead us outside.

The masks we saw at Wilhelm's shop are baby toys compared to what we see now.

There are at least twenty Krampus trolling the crowd, wielding whips as well as switches. They have heavy chains, too, and they slam them repeatedly against the cobblestone streets.

A lone, piercing howl, full of malice, bounces off the sides of the dark stone exteriors of the buildings in the town center. I move closer to Kit. I really want to be close to Henry.

The crowd dances around the monsters in spite of the terrifying masks, laughing, flirting, even bending over to receive spankings from switches. I don't understand the lack of terror. The people in the street must be loaded.

"This looks nothing like the brochure," I yell to Kit over the crowd. "Nothing like last night at all."

"No," Kit yells back, holding on to my arm tightly as we move toward the street. "And this isn't even the real thing. Krampus uses the walk as a distraction to pick off one or two victims for his dinner."

"Stop messing around." I fight a full-body shiver. "It's not funny anymore."

He smiles.

As we get closer to the action, I see that the monster's skin colors range from moonlight to crimson to ebony. They all have glowing yellow eyes. They're adorned in clothing made of animal pelts, and claws extend from their fingers and toes.

Kit lets me go and I'm sucked into the center of the action. Their furs stink of death and rot. Most all of the figures have thick limbs and yellow nails in the beginning stages of curling into claws. If these are the fakes, I don't want to get anywhere near the real thing.

I'm losing my mind. Monsters aren't real.

They form a ring around me, and I lose track of Kit.

The slamming of the chains against the cobblestones becomes a song, and their movements become a dance. I can hear low grunts issuing from their throats. I am jostled and shaken and almost knocked down, and my heart beats with desperation. I want out. And I can't get out.

I'm halfway to a panic attack when I bounce off Henry's shoulder.

I grab the front of his coat. "Henry! What the hell is going on?"

Around us, the Krampus continue their dance. The circle closes, tighter and tighter.

"Elke disappeared." He takes my hand and holds it tightly, as if he's making sure he won't lose me. "I think they're playing a joke on the gullible tourists."

I take stock of our surroundings. The crowd has surged away from the pub, and I've been too busy looking for rescue to notice which direction. "Where are we?"

"Look!" Henry waves his free arm. "Over there."

Relief is sweet. Kit and Elke.

As we push through the crowd of monsters, I realize

how incredibly fast they move. Their horns are razor sharp, and every beast holds a wicked-looking stick in addition to the rusty chains.

I look toward Kit again and see that he and Elke have their arms wrapped around each other. And not in a friendly way.

"Henry."

We've fallen into a ridiculous trap. Whether the monsters we see are real or the plot of ill-intentioned humans, we're in trouble.

"I see them." He grunts in frustration. "We can switch dates and kick ass when we get out of here. But let's just concentrate on actually getting out."

Miraculously, he finds a way through the chaos.

We run hand in hand, and Henry jerks me into an alley. I try to catch my breath and figure out where we are. I don't think we're in the town center anymore.

"Why would they do that to us?" Henry looks up and down the street while I lean over to relace my boots. "Just for a sick joke? Is this how they treat tourists? Henry?"

I turn around.

Krampus.

What I would've thought was a mask five seconds ago has become skin. Strings of saliva pool around teeth attached to red gums. A long tongue leads to a wide-open mouth and gullet.

The smell is like being locked in a hot car with pounds

of rotted meat packed around you. And he's holding an empty sack.

"We're going to die," I say, grabbing Henry's arm and backing up. The monster does nothing. Just stares.

"Don't say that." I've never heard Henry so scared.

"You're my best friend."

"Don't do the whole last-words thing, Bex." Henry pulls me behind him, putting himself between the monster and me. "We could be hallucinating."

The monster roars so loud, it blows our hair back.

"Listen to me." Tears form, but I swipe them away before they roll down my cheeks. "I have to say this. I've played so many stupid games."

"We both have."

The monster is starting toward us now.

"I love you, Henry. I'm in love with you."

"I love you back. Even after you pee in your pants." He stumbles over a piece of trash. Krampus stills and tilts his head to the side.

I steady Henry. The end of the alley is so dark. Stacks of wooden crates lean perilously against the wall. No one can see us from the street. Krampus just has to knock us out, stuff us in his sack, and then blend in with the crowd until it's time to go home.

If a lair is considered a home, rather than a place to cook *people* for Christmas dinner.

"The next time we want to fight our feelings for each

other, let's do it in our own backyard instead of crossing several time zones and into the *Twilight Zone*?" Henry sounds hopeful.

"The next time?" I bark a harsh laugh. "In case you haven't noticed, we're about to be dinner."

Krampus takes two huge steps forward.

"Bex." Henry grabs my wrist so hard my fingers go numb. "Look."

There's a door in the building to our left, and a thin slit of light shines through. A tiny prickle of a memory of something I've read pulls at the corner of my brain.

"Get his sack," I say between my teeth.

Henry does a double take. "Say what?"

"Just do it."

Moving in tandem as only two people who've known each other for a lifetime can do, Henry jerks the sack out of the monster's hand. I jump behind the crates and push them over on Krampus just as Henry clears the space. Henry slams his hand against the door to open it, and we run inside the building.

The smell of rot is replaced by the smell of baked goods.

"Yes!" I slam the door behind us and fist pump. "Geek research for the win! If Krampus loses his sack, he loses his power. We did—"

Before I get the words out, Henry takes my face in his hands. His kiss is serious, scared, and full of all kinds of promises. When he pulls away, I'm dizzy.

There's a roar and a crash, and claws begin to scratch relentlessly at the closed door.

"If you want to do that again—"

"I do," I interrupt. "Many, many times."

"Then run."

When I was seventeen and he was eighteen, Henry Bishop and I went to Bavaria, stole a sack, escaped a monster, and fell in love.

Christine Johnson
Shadowed

he clash of swords rang across the field. The sound climbed the stone walls of the tower and danced through Esme's window, accompanied by a chorus of cheers. She pressed against the tapestries that lined the walls, the parchment window covering she'd ripped down clutched in her hands. Carefully, slowly, she peered through the narrow window like a thief.

Why did it have to be sunny on a Tournament day? After a week of gray skies, when she'd been able to stand at the window and watch the pages set up the benches and decorate them with standards, she'd been heartbroken to wake today to such shining weather. She'd harbored no hope of leaving her rooms, but it would have been nice to see the mock battle without the sweating fear that the light would shift and her shadow would spring to life behind her.

From the field below the tower, the chime of steel against steel came faster and the crowd roared. Two knights staggered to the edge of the field and into Esme's view. Their armor gleamed, still new enough to shine. The hair at the back of her neck stood on end as she watched them fight. One was significantly larger—a bear of a man with a stomach built to accommodate long nights of too much food and drink. He should have overpowered his opponent with little trouble. But the other knight, with a brass cap across each shoulder of his armor, ducked and danced as though the metal skin that he wore weighed nothing at all. His sword flickered through the air, the sun glinting off the blade as it swung.

The light hit the gleaming steel and shattered into a thousand rays. Esme caught her breath. She had never seen anything so bright. The mirrored flat of his sword turned the pollen-yellow glow into a white-hot beam that lanced painfully across her vision. After seventeen years of nothing but the dimmest and darkest, it was too much to bear. Her eyelids flew shut and she raised a hand to cover them, pitching forward as her knees turned weak beneath her.

Hers was not the only hand that brushed her skin, and the other was not so gentle. Her eyes sprang open, and in the mirror across the room, she saw her shadow pressed in close behind her. Panicked, Esme clawed at the inky hand that gripped her throat. She'd swayed too close to the window, too close to the sunlight.

With her voice crushed beneath the obsidian palm, she struggled toward the darkness in the room, but her shadow shoved her closer to the window. Stars exploded across her vision, a rainbow of lights that would have been beautiful if she weren't so terrified.

For one instant, her gaze fell on the field below her, and she saw the more nimble knight crouch and spin, avoiding the clumsy arc of his opponent's sword. Instinctively, Esme copied him, her skirts pooling on the floor as she bent her knees and swept in a half circle. The weight of her own shadow crashed against her back, its feet momentarily lifted from the floor. She fell, her knees cracking painfully against the cold, dark stone. But the crushing pressure disappeared from her neck.

She'd made it out of the sunlight.

Her shadow was gone and she was safe. For now.

Unsteadily, she got to her feet, stumbling over the hem of her skirt. As her breaths ripped through her battered throat, she realized that the only ringing she heard was in her own ears.

The tournament was over? Could that be?

Curiosity beat at her, forcing Esme closer to the window in spite of the patter of her heart. She gripped the edge of the nearest tapestry, ready to duck behind it if needed, and peered down. The two knights were still at the far edge of the field, but the larger one was on his hands and knees, his sword abandoned in the grass.

A cheer rose from the crowd, startling a few birds that rose in unison and flapped off into the distance. The smaller knight removed his helmet, revealing waves of auburn hair that nearly brushed his shoulders. From the horizon, a bank of clouds swept in, bringing with them the sort of rumble that promised a sudden storm. As the sunlight faded, Esme dared step directly in front of the window.

The knight turned and waved his helmet, acknowledging the crowd. Esme caught sight of his profile. A square jaw framed a smile that gleamed almost as brightly as his sword. Esme's heart galloped yet more unevenly. He was so handsome. It was as though his face had been shaped to satisfy the particular hunger of her gaze.

He started to step toward his opponent, but a trumpet sounded at the base of the tower, reminding the knight that he hadn't acknowledged her, and the knight stopped.

Slowly, he turned and faced the tower where she stood. His eyes scaled the walls and his smile faded as he stared at Esme. She didn't dare breathe. Behind him, the clouds roiled in the sky like a dark blessing.

She stood there, protected by nothing but the clouds.

The knight dipped his head to her, and she wondered if his acknowledgment was anything more than a nearly forgotten politeness.

But then he straightened. And the look he gave her glowed so brightly that, for a moment, she couldn't see anything else. Unbidden by custom, he dropped to one knee. The crowd murmured loudly enough for Esme to hear it. Their surprise mirrored her own.

Dizzy with the lingering effects of her own battle and the sweetness of this unexpected attention, Esme pulled out the wide blue ribbon that twined through the gold net that held her hair. She let one end flutter through the window, accepting his tribute. She was grateful that he couldn't see that it wasn't the breeze, but rather her trembling that shook the length of satin in her hand.

The crowd began to rustle and point, relishing a rare glimpse of the girl who terrified and entranced them at the same time. The gasp that came from behind Esme startled her so badly that she spun away from the window, half expecting to see her shadow reaching for her again.

"What are you doing?" Margaret came rushing in with her arms full of fresh linen sheets.

"Just—they were announcing the winner, and the clouds had come. I was only at the window for a moment, I swear." Esme started to cross the room, intending to pick up her needlework and stitch tiny red flowers until the blood quit galloping through her veins.

Margaret caught her by the sleeve. "A moment at a cloudy window doesn't leave marks like that on your neck." Her usually ruddy cheeks were nearly as pale as Esme's snow-white skin. "You got shadowed."

Though Margaret was supposed to be her lady's maid, she often seemed to Esme more like a jailer who was good with hairpins and small buttons.

With a sigh, Esme nodded. There was no use trying to pretend she hadn't been attacked. In a few hours, the marks on her neck would darken into ugly purple bruises that would be impossible to hide. "You're going to tell my father, aren't you?"

"I don't see how I can avoid it. Have you seen your neck?"

Esme walked over to the polished brass mirror. She'd expected to see red marks. Maybe the violet beginnings of a bruise. But the finger marks striped across her neck were black as tar.

Esme tried to hide her grimace. "You'll be in as much trouble as I will if you tell him. You were supposed to stay with me, remember?" She didn't want to put Margaret in a bad spot, but the last time she'd been shadowed, her father had ordered her to be removed to one of the interior rooms of the tower. A room with no windows at all. It had taken her half a year's begging to convince him to let her back into her room. She couldn't bear that again.

As it was, she hadn't been out of the tower since her

shadow had attacked her last. Not that she'd been out more than a scant handful of times before that—and always in the dark of the moon—but after that last incident, the tower felt less like a protection and more like a prison.

Margaret bit her lip. "Perhaps a wimple, instead of the gold net. If we wrapped it around your neck and pinned it . . . ?"

"We could leave my hair down," Esme suggested.

Margaret sighed. "We'll do both, I expect. I'll go see Old Anne. She may have something to lessen the marking."

The idea of Margaret walking through the feasting and revelry, walking so close to the knight—*her* knight— was more than Esme could bear. She tugged at Margaret's sleeves.

"Please," she begged, not caring that it was unbecoming, "wait until after dark. Let me go with you. Surely no one will notice one more body in the crowd on a night like tonight. I'll take my dinner in my room, say I have a headache. No one will know. It will be better if Anne can see the bruises for herself, anyway." The last was a lie. She neither knew nor cared whether Anne could serve her better after seeing the bruises.

She just wanted one taste of the revelry below. One sip.

It wasn't an outrageous request. Of the few times she'd been out of the tower, most of those had been to see Old Anne about her shadowy curse.

"That is an outrageous request!" Margaret announced,

her hand flying to her chest. "Anyone could recognize you. You could stumble into firelight or lamplight. Your father would have my head."

"Surely I could be well disguised," Esme argued. "And I'm not careless enough to wander close to a fire."

"The only thing we'll be disguising are those bruises on your neck. *I* will go see Old Anne. *You* will stay in your room until I get back. Now let me go get that wimple. You're lucky I don't tell your father what happened. Risking your life, just to watch a silly tournament." She clucked, putting down the sheets. Margaret walked through the archway into the adjoining dressing room and bent to rummage through the cupboard.

Esme turned back to the window, watching as the standards snapped and sagged beneath the howling storm.

"How much is this sort of life worth, anyway?"

The wind snatched her whispered words and swept them out the window. Behind her, oblivious, Margaret began to hum as she readied Esme's head covering.

After a lonely dinner, Esme lay across her bed, watching through the far window as the lingering clouds turned a crimson-tinged pink with the setting sun. The sounds of feasting—raucous laughter and ragged bits of music—rolled across the field.

The tightly pinned wimple chafed the fresh bruises on Esme's skin. But for those marks—but for the curse of her shadow—she could have at least been downstairs with her family. It would have been a more restrained gathering, of course. The thought of it didn't make her blood bubble the way the thought of skirting around the bonfires in the field did, but anything would be better than lying alone in her room, as far as she could get from the lamplight, embroidering flowers in the dark.

Margaret had disappeared shortly after dinner, looking at Esme severely as she went, making her promise to be good. If anyone could help, it would be Anne. With all her salves and poultices, her uncanny ability to see a person's problems in the dregs of their tea—she was better than any of the doctors. It was the only reason no one outright said the word *witch* around her. They'd all needed her in one way or another.

Esme tugged at her wimple. If Margaret hurried, if Anne was in a quick and giving mood, she might even be rid of the bruises by tomorrow. There would be a second feast. A second celebratory dinner. It wouldn't be as much, but at least she wouldn't miss everything.

She was so tired of missing everything.

The stars began winking in the purple sky, like eyes struggling to open after a long night's sleep. When no more light stained the floor beneath her window, Esme went to watch the celebration. The king had planned the tournament for a moonless night, which meant she could watch the revelers, at least. Even if her father would never allow her outside to join them.

Just because it was night, that didn't mean she was safe. There were a thousand ways to cast a shadow in the dark. Her father looked sad when he reminded her of the dangers, but not sad enough to relent.

From her tower vantage point, she could see the whole field. Fire dotted the grass. She watched the little gems of torches and lamps bobble in between the bonfires. Closing her eyes, she breathed as deeply as her bodice would allow.

Mostly, the cool, storm-washed air was all that she could smell. But faintly, just underneath it, was the scent of wood smoke and the mouthwatering tang of meat being roasted on a spit somewhere. Her stomach rumbled, complaining about the thin soup and airy bread that she'd eaten. It was a delicate dinner that had been sent up for her delicate constitution, but what she really wanted was a flagon of the small beer that filled the barrels, and a plate of the fire-blackened boar meat.

She sighed and tapped her foot in time to the music, watching as the dancers turned and bowed and spun, smiling in the firelight. While her feet beat out a jig on the floor, she pushed her head as far out the narrow window as she could, relishing every finger's width closer she could get to the beating heart of the celebration.

Something below her caught her eye—a sudden stillness in the seething motion of the party.

Esme's feet ceased their tapping and her hands curled

around the stone of the sill. The bonfire behind the knight turned his auburn hair into a flame all its own. Even without his armor, she recognized him. Even in the dark, she knew the twin lights of his sword and his smile.

The knight bowed to her, then put a hand on his chest. Esme hung from the windowsill, her toes barely touching the floor beneath her, suspended like a fly in amber. She wasn't allowed to go down there. She was unable to go down there. But she couldn't bring herself to turn away from him, either.

Margaret appeared next to her.

With a squeak, Esme let go of the windowsill and dropped to the floor.

"Hanging from the windowsill?" Margaret started. "Of all the—"

"Never mind that," Esme interrupted. "What about Anne?"

Margaret held up her empty hands. "She said you must come to her. That she'd read the tea leaves and they said, this time, she cannot treat your injuries without seeing them for herself. She said she would not cross the wisdom of the leaves." Her voice was quiet, but frustration poisoned her speech.

The jolt that went through Esme shook her so badly that she half leapt, half tumbled away from the window. She was leaving. She would go out of the tower and into the revel below. Her palms dampened at the thought, but her heart raced at the thought of seeing the knight, of tasting the dark air.

"When do we leave?"

Margaret shook her head. "We are not leaving. We will simply have to do without Anne. You will stay here and hope the wimple is enough. It is too dangerous. There are too many lights in the field."

"Margaret, look." Esme pulled the wimple aside, giving her maid full view of the horrible bruises on her neck.

Margaret bit her lip. Esme pounced.

"My father will want to see me tomorrow. If he becomes suspicious—if he notices the bruising—I don't know how I'll explain it. Please, Margaret. Taking this risk may be the only way to protect us both." Though she was creating arguments meant to convince her maid, the truth in her words made her shudder.

Margaret rubbed her forehead. "I can't think. . . ."

Esme stepped forward. "Anne knows more about what has happened to me than anyone else. It was her own daughter who wrought this curse. She knows the danger involved with leaving the tower. We've always trusted her before. I am inclined to trust her now. With or without you, I am going to see Anne."

Margaret nodded miserably. "I'll get you my spare cloak."

Esme turned back to the window. Her terror and excitement were so great that the night itself seemed to quiver. The fire-haired knight was gone, and she was surprised at the disappointment that lurched through her. Had she really been so hopeful of meeting him? She really should stop wishing for impossible things.

She was about to venture out of her tower for the first time in more than a year. After overcoming that impossibility, meeting a knight seemed trifling.

Margaret returned with her arms full of gray-dyed wool. While Esme ignored her heart, chattering in her chest like a set of teeth, Margaret draped the cloak around her and fastened it at the neck. Between the concealing wimple and the hood, she was well disguised.

"See? I might as well be invisible!" she crowed.

"You may be hidden, but you're not protected," Margaret warned. "We still have to get past the crowd, which won't be easy."

The truth in Margaret's words stole part of Esme's glee. Her tongue was too thick and pasty in her mouth to speak, so Esme nodded, but she wasn't sure Margaret could see the movement beneath the hood of the cloak.

"It isn't too late to change your mind," Margaret whispered.

The words unglued Esme's tongue. "Don't be silly." She hoped her bluffed confidence wasn't transparent. With a firm step, she strode toward her chamber door, telling herself that it was no different from going down to the dining hall for dinner. "Just—you go ahead and make sure there aren't torches lit. As long as there's no direct light, I'll be safe."

With her lip caught between her teeth, Margaret turned and scurried into the hall.

"No torches," she called softly.

Esme breathed a sigh of relief and followed the scurrying of Margaret's little mouse footsteps. There was a small door off to one side of the hall at the bottom of the stairs. A door that led outside.

"Is anyone there?" she whispered.

"It's likely to be guarded," Margaret whispered back. "There may be torches as well. Or lanterns. If we're lucky, it will be lanterns."

Margaret stepped around Esme and pushed open the door. The night was so close that Esme found herself rooted to the floor, temporarily more plant than person. After all, she did not move from her assigned place, the way the rest of the world did. But she wanted to. She wanted to.

The desire to be out was strong enough to unstick her feet and propel her forward, until she had nearly smacked into Margaret's back.

"Two ladies headed alone into that madness?" The guard's voice was thick with drinking, his words slumping against one another so that Esme could barely understand him. No one had ever spoken to her like this before, and it took her a moment to realize that—to him—she appeared to be nothing more than a well-hooded lady's maid. A lamp dangled limply from the guard's fingers, and Esme shied away from it. "You two need a chaperone, mebbe?"

"There's plenty of eyes out there without adding yours," Margaret answered in a flippant voice that Esme had never heard her use before. "Now let us pass."

"Only if you save me a dance," the guard wheedled.

"If your legs will still hold you up, it would be my pleasure," Margaret answered. She swept past him, reaching back to grab a fold of Esme's cloak and towing her along in her wake. Esme let herself be pulled forward, though she swung a wide berth around the flickering puddle of lamplight.

Once the black night air had settled around her, Esme had to resist the urge to laugh. Her terror had left with the lamplight, and all she saw spread out in front of her was the endless expanse of darkness beyond the fires in the field. It had been too long since she had wrapped her fingers around this much freedom. Out here, she could walk instead of pace—she could run, even.

At least until the sun came up.

Ahead of her, Margaret froze, swearing an oath the likes of which Esme had never heard pass her lips.

"What?" Esme spun around, certain that she'd wandered into some sort of light. She waited for the clawing hands of her shadow to latch themselves onto her neck— or worse. There were so many weapons nearby. The grass was littered with them and there was barely an arm or leg visible that didn't have some sort of blade strapped to it.

But the darkness was total. The shadow didn't come.

"Margaret!" A man, made somehow handsomer by the scar crossing his forehead, rushed forward and grabbed Margaret's arm. Esme ducked low into her cloak, and Margaret stepped away from her, putting enough distance between them that Esme at least had a hope of staying hidden.

"I've been waiting for you all night!" Margaret's suitor exclaimed—for it was obvious by the way his hand lingered at her waist that he was more than a passing acquaintance.

"I can't stay," Margaret said. "I'm with my . . . cousin. Rosalie."

Esme resisted the urge to sigh. She had never seen such a terrible liar.

"She'll be fine for a moment. Come on—one turn around the fire. You promised," he said, cheerfully dragging Margaret away by the arm.

Esme could see Margaret's face, terrified and confused, mirroring Esme's own feelings exactly. There was danger in being alone and danger in allowing Margaret's beau close enough to discover who she was. Esme shivered as the urge to run after Margaret crawled across her skin. Before she could take so much as a single calming breath, she felt a hand against her shoulder.

"Pardon me, miss—"

She glanced over her shoulder at the voice and found

herself standing a single step from the knight. Her knight.

"Y-yes?" she stammered. She knew there was only a moment before Margaret pulled herself from her sweetheart's grasp and came flying back to fetch her.

His eyes widened. "Is it you?" he whispered.

Panicked, Esme tugged the hood farther around her face, but it was too late. He had seen. He knew.

"It is you."

"Please. Please don't say anything."

"I won't. I swear it." He was a knight—his oath was binding. Esme tingled with relief.

"I thought you couldn't leave the tower," he said, keeping his voice low.

"I can—I mean, I don't. I haven't in so long, but it's— I'm . . ." Her stammering infuriated her. She sounded like a madwoman.

"You're cursed," he whispered. "That's what they say, at least."

She nodded.

"So it's true?" He shut his eyes. She could see him chastising himself. "I'm sorry to be so bold. Your companion looked reluctant to leave you."

"She was. I only have a moment. And yes, the rumors are true." Esme's voice came back to her, the words in her mouth as steady as the ground they stood on.

"They say you'll burn in the light, like one of the undead."

"If I were a revenant, wouldn't you be in terrible danger right now?" The frustration in her voice might have been impertinent, but she couldn't stop herself. Yes, she was cursed, but she was not evil. She didn't drink blood. She wasn't undead.

The corners of his mouth twitched. "I suppose I would. But for one thing, I don't believe a revenant would be so beautiful. And for another, I have a fairly remarkable sword." He tapped the hilt at his side.

"Remarkable enough to kill a revenant?" she asked, arching an eyebrow.

His answering smile was blinding. It was brighter than sunlight, but she could stand beneath it without fear. Something bloomed in her chest, so sudden and huge in the dark cage of her ribs that she thought she would burst.

"It has been in my family for many generations. Some say it was goblin-made. Another story says it sprang up in the middle of a faerie ring." He shrugged.

"Which do you believe?" she teased him.

His eyes blazed. "I don't need to believe either of them. The right weapon in the right hands is its own kind of magic," he said.

Unbidden, a vision of the hands that had cursed her awoke in her memory. "I know that to be true," she whispered. "And yet I do not even know your name."

His face softened. "Rylan Sedgewick." He offered a small bow. "And yours?"

"Surely you must know my name, Sir Rylan? Isn't it dragged out along with the rumors?"

"I would rather hear it from your own lips," he said.

"I am Esme. My father is the Duke of Lanford." She dipped her head, acknowledging his bow.

"I am better pleased than you know to make your acquaintance. And while I am being overly bold—what is it that makes those beautiful gray eyes of yours look so sad?"

"My own shadow," she whispered. "It hunts me."

Instead of being starred with disbelief or narrowing in horror, Rylan's eyes glittered with a warrior's hunger.

"Have you not found a way to make the hunter into the hunted?" he asked.

Esme shrugged. "When I am out of direct light, my shadow is powerless. I must avoid the sunlight. Moonlight. Fire. Then I am safe."

"But it still imprisons you," he protested. "A life without light is nothing but an enormous shackle."

"Indeed it is," she agreed. "But it's the best that can be done. Fire doesn't burn a shadow. Axes pass through it. I am the only one who can touch it."

Out of the corner of her eye, Esme saw Margaret hurrying toward them.

"My maid is coming," she said simply.

Rylan's face fell. "I must see you again. Please."

"It's impossible. I can't leave the tower," Esme said, the

words crushing her with the weight of their finality. "My father doesn't allow visitors."

"You left the tower this evening," he countered.

"It was a matter of utmost importance," she said.

"So is this," he assured her, and though there was jest in his voice, his eyes burned with a coal of truth that made her breath hot in her lungs.

Margaret was getting closer, her step quickening when she saw Esme was speaking to Rylan.

"I will wait," he assured her. "Every night, no matter how many it takes. I will be out here."

"I can't let you do that. Not when I have nothing to offer you." The words broke in her mouth, their new-made edges so sharp she swore her tongue was cut.

"Give me a token to remember you by, then," he bade her.

Esme swept her hands across the cloak—the pockets were empty. She had no handkerchief, she wore no brooch. Her panicked fumbling sent a wayward lock of hair tumbling out of the wimple that bound her neck.

She shoved it back and then froze as her hands brushed the ribbon that held the rest of her hair. The same ribbon she'd waved to acknowledge his victory.

How appropriate.

Hurrying, she yanked the ribbon free, and the length of blue satin, woven thickly with silver threads, slipped from beneath her wimple.

Rylan held out his hand and she pooled the ribbon into it. He curled his fingers over it as gently as if she'd laid a flower in his palm.

Esme turned, expecting to find Margaret at her back. Instead, she was startled to see her maid hurtling past them. Esme spun again, nearly as dizzy as the dancers. Her eyes found the head of untamed gray hair even before she spotted Margaret.

They didn't need to go to Anne after all.

Anne had come to them.

With her walking stick aiding her limping gait, she stomped to Esme and Rylan, who stood transfixed. Margaret raced over, breathless and unkempt.

"You've gotten yourself out of the tower. Good girl." Anne's voice creaked and cracked and she spoke—as usual—without preamble or politesse.

"I thought you commanded me to come."

Anne cackled, low and smoky. "I did. The dregs in my teacup said you were due for an escape. I suppose Margaret didn't mention that to you."

She had not. Esme looked at Margaret, who had set her jaw so tightly that her chin jutted. She turned her attention back to Anne.

"This is not exactly an escape, as you well know. A change of scenery, perhaps, but unless you come bearing a way to break this curse . . ." Esme let the unsaid end of her sentence hang in the air.

Anne sagged beneath the weight of it. "You know I cannot do that. When they killed my daughter, they took away the only person who could undo the hex."

Rylan jumped, his hand going to the hilt of his sword. "Your daughter was the one who cursed the Lady Esme?"

"Aye. Her own baby sickened and died on the day of Esme's christening. Blind with grief, my daughter twisted a bit of magic that should never have been done. She gave her baby Esme's name and then stole Esme's shadow. She thought if she bound her own baby's spirit into Esme's shadow, it would slip into Esme's body from the shadow, becoming flesh again."

Margaret stepped forward, her eyes narrowing at Rylan's obvious interest. "It didn't work that way. Which is why Esme must stay in the dark; why she is not . . . available, as other young ladies are."

Rylan looked unswayed by her attempt to put him off. "So the spirit—Lady Esme's shadow—why does it not have a body of its own? One that would allow it to walk in the light, as well as in the dark?"

"It could," Esme answered. "If it made space for itself first. If I am killed, and my spirit left my body, there would be room for it to come in."

"Which is why you must stay out of the light," Anne said sadly. "If Lady Esme is exposed to direct light from the sun, the moon, or a fire, it kindles her shadow."

Esme's palms pricked with nerves when she looked

over at Rylan, certain she would see him either backing
away in horror or else politely fighting the urge to do so. As
she read the expression on his face, she was stunned. Deep
lines had appeared at the sides of his mouth as his full lips
pursed in thought. His eyes were lit with a warrior's delight
in the challenge of strategy.

"If you would pardon my abruptness," he began, and
Margaret snorted.

Anne brought the end of her walking stick down on
Margaret's foot hard enough to make her yelp.

"My bones are telling me to be quiet and listen," Anne
growled at her. "They just told you the same thing." She
turned her withered face back to Rylan. "Go on."

Ignoring Margaret's muttered complaints, Rylan spoke,
his words measured and careful.

"I see how staying out of the light is a defense—a
necessary defense—but I do not think it much of a solution.
It seems to me that if a shadow is made of darkness, then
the way to battle it may be with light."

"That is the most painful bit of the curse," Anne agreed.
"I hear the truth in your words. But light also allows the
shadow to separate itself from the darkness at large. There
is no weapon that can be used against it. The time it would
take to discover one would be more than enough for Esme's
shadow to take her life. Speaking of which—"

Anne reached into the folds of her robe and pulled
out a small earthenware jar. "Margaret told me about your

neck. Rub this on it, three times a day, and take plenty of eggs with your meals. It will help."

Esme took the jar with a grateful nod. "Margaret has your payment."

Margaret handed the coin over grudgingly, with a pointed glance at her injured foot. Anne grinned, her smile more holes than teeth. "Enough for some food and something to drink. I think I may stay awhile. It has been so long since there was anything for me to celebrate. . . . Sir . . . ?"

"Rylan of Sedgewick." He bowed.

"Sir Rylan, then. Will you walk an old woman to the fire?"

Rylan glanced at Esme. His eyes were forlorn. She answered him with a determined stare.

Things would not end here. Not like this. She'd had a sip of the possible and she wasn't about to hand the glass back now.

"I will watch for you," he said.

"I hope so," she said.

"Oi!" The guard who had accosted them at the door let out a shout that cut through the din of the celebration as he lurched toward them, grabbing a torch that had been jammed into the ground. "Are ye ready to give me that dance?"

Margaret made a noise that was caught between a gasp and a retch.

Esme froze. She couldn't run past the guard and get

back to the safety of her tower. Behind her, the celebration raged, with torches and bonfires pockmarking the field. She was trapped.

"Douse that torch! At once!" Margaret commanded.

It did no good.

The guard was so drunk he couldn't halt his own momentum. He swayed so close to Esme that she was cuffed tight in the circle of torchlight. Before she could shut her eyes against the glare, Esme felt a set of hands jerk her head back and rip off the cloak hood and wimple that hid her bruised neck. She saw nothing but stars—she felt nothing but the night air on the exposed skin of her throat.

Margaret screamed. She grabbed Esme's arm and dragged her out of the light. Rylan wrapped his arms around the half-mast guard and tossed him back toward the castle.

But it was too late.

The commotion had attracted the crowd's attention, and before Esme's feet had moved, they were surrounded by a circle of people, each of them bearing some sort of light.

Esme's shadow leapt back into existence, solid as an anvil and just as black. It wrapped an arm around her neck, and her already tender windpipe folded like a bellows.

The gasping, shouting ring of spectators spread and deepened. In some places, it was nearly a solid wall of torch fire and lamplight. There was no way out. No way through.

A haze of sparkles appeared as Esme tried to draw breath and failed. Through the glitter, she saw Rylan draw his sword. The blade reflected the flames that surrounded them. Instead of gleaming metal, a column of fire leapt from the golden hilt. Hope rose in Esme. Maybe the light in his sword was enough to slay the shadow and break the curse.

Rylan slashed at the shadow, but the blade passed right through. The hope that had flared in her so suddenly dimmed, and her vision narrowed as death crept into her.

Words from the night danced through her head. Something Rylan had said . . . something besides fighting darkness with light . . . her knees buckled beneath her and Esme tumbled to the ground. Her shadow fell with her, loosening its hold on her neck just long enough for Esme to draw a single, burning breath.

The sweet heat of the air swept through her, and she remembered the thought she'd been seeking.

The right weapon in the right hands has its own kind of magic.

She looked up at Rylan, who stood with his sword pointed at the pressing crowd as he shouted at them to get back.

"Sir Rylan!" Esme croaked as the shadow's arm found its favored place against the soft flesh of her neck. In spite of the breathlessness of her voice, he heard her.

He spun away from the crowd, facing Esme with a look of powerless horror.

She could no longer speak, nor could she breathe. She held out a hand, staring hard at his sword.

If it was foolishness, so be it, but one way or another, the curse would be broken in the next moments.

Without hesitating, Rylan turned the point of the sword toward himself, offering Esme the hilt. With her arms weakened, the weapon was so heavy that she could barely lift it. The point dragged along the ground and, as the blade drew level with her eyes, Esme could see the shadow reflected in it, its features growing more distinct as her own life waned.

With the last of her strength, Esme lifted the sword's hilt above her head, moving the blade so that it would swing behind her like a pendulum. A susurration swept across her hearing, like a flock of startled birds taking flight. The sword slipped from Esme's grip and thudded to the ground.

A cloak of icy blackness settled over her, and as her vision waned, Esme glanced up at the distant stars and begged forgiveness as the last of the world slid from her view.

The darkness that followed was pure and limitless.

Vaguely, she heard Anne's voice. "Wake up, child."

Wake up?

Her throat tore and then tore again, as her breath hissed

in and out. Esme's eyes fluttered open and she mewled in surprise at the bedclothes that scratched against her skin.

She was back inside the tower.

Anne and Margaret huddled over her.

"Is it—is she?" Margaret's breath hitched so badly that she couldn't finish her questions.

Anne peered into Esme's eyes. Still too weak and stunned to move, Esme stared back. Anne glanced at Margaret.

"Lift her shoulders a bit and bring that torch just a bit closer. Carefully, now. Sir Rylan, be at the ready."

Esme winced as Margaret's arm slid beneath her, propping her up. Anne bent, studying the sheets beneath Esme, but Esme's attention was fixed elsewhere. Near the foot of the bed knelt Rylan, a mixture of pride and surprise written on his face. His sword was still unsheathed and his hand wrapped around the shimmering hilt.

Something was different. The blade—the shining, fiery blade was dull as the stone of the tower walls and just as dark.

"It's gone," Anne announced. "Look." She pointed beneath Esme, to the spot where the torchlight should have cast her shadow. "The torchlight casts my shadow. Sir Rylan has one. You do, too," she said to Margaret. "But Esme's is gone."

Margaret gasped.

The news shook her and Esme reached out her hands,

looking for something—anything—solid to hold on to. Rylan sheathed his sword in an instant and moved to Esme's side, scooping her weakened body into his arms. Margaret gasped, but Esme couldn't imagine that this scandal would outshine the breaking of her curse. Moreover, she didn't want him to put her down. The feel of his hands pressing against her through her clothes was delicious, even in her fragile state. No man had ever held her like this. Surreptitiously, as though he were adjusting her in his arms, he laid his cheek against her forehead, and his bright auburn hair swept against her skin, making her shiver gladly.

Margaret stepped closer, bringing the dancing light of the torch with her. Instinctively, Esme coiled, but then the sweetness of the glow against her skin reminded her that she had nothing to fear. She felt herself bubbling up—stretching and strengthening with the relief of finally, finally being illuminated.

"I'll go get the duke and bring him in to her." Margaret left, taking the torch with her. Without it, the feeble glow of the lamp near the door was the only light left in the room.

Esme was still cradled in Rylan's arms. Everything looked different. The stone walls looked softer, the tapestries more alive. She stretched out a trembling hand and caressed them, in love with everything, enamored of the very air.

Anne knelt next to Rylan, who laid Esme down gently.

"Are you feeling all right?" she asked.

Rylan stood and looked down at Esme, his shoulder brushing the bedpost. In the dim corner, surrounded by the dark bedclothes, panic clawed at Esme.

"Please bring a torch. Or a candle. Anything," Esme rasped. "I can't bear the darkness another second."

"Of course. At once." Rylan ducked into Margaret's quarters and returned with a candelabra that bore enough lit candles to make Esme's panic retreat.

Anne squinted at her. "So the curse is ended?" She handed Esme a cup of wine, which Esme sipped gratefully, though it burned her wounded throat.

"Yes. I mean, it must be. I'm here. There is light around me and on me and no one is attacking me." Her eyes filled with tears. "It's been so many years, locked in that prison. I never thought I would be free of it. I thought the darkness and sadness—dear God, the unbearable loneliness—I thought that was sure to be my destiny."

"But now it is not. And I am here to help you take your rightful place in the light," Rylan said, bending his knee.

"I am so grateful to you, Sir Rylan. And I am sorry to have seen your sword in such a damaged state. Though I must admit, I would be grateful not to have it used against me again."

"Against you?" The question dropped from his lips.

Anne's grip on her hand tightened.

"Indeed. If that monster's soul hadn't leapt from her the moment before she swung, I fear the outcome might have been different." She smiled up at Rylan. "I did think, if it was to be my end, that I would be happy to have my last vision be something filled with so much light. Dying in that brightness would have been better than being trapped endlessly in the dark."

Anne let out a strangled sound.

With great effort, Esme brought Anne's hand up to her face and rubbed her cheek against it, gently. "Oh, Grandmother. I thought I would never get to see you— to speak with you. I could hear them talking about my mother, sometimes, while I was in the dark. I never understood why she forced me into that black prison. It was worse than death. I fought so hard to come back into the light. Back to you."

Rylan gripped the bedpost. "You are . . . you are the shadow?"

Esme blinked. "I am myself. The shadow was my prison." She turned and smiled at them both, radiant. "And finally, I have escaped."

Saundra Mitchell
Now Bid Time Return

Dacey Shen had never won anything before. In fact, she hadn't even told her parents she'd entered the contest until the sponsors called to congratulate her.

"It would have been nice," her mother said as if they hadn't already had this conversation several times, "to know about this ahead of time. Daddy and I could have gotten time off work. We could have gone with you."

Clasping her hands, Dacey stood by and watched her mother rummage through her luggage. Again. "I know. I'm sorry."

"We're going to miss you." Producing an industrial

pack of crackers and cheese, her mom shoved it beneath the paperbacks. Just in case the plane crashed in Outer Mysteria, south of Nowherelandia—Dacey wouldn't have to eat the other passengers. She had mom rations.

Dacey watched, counting off the minutes until their cab arrived. "I'll miss you, too. But it's a once-in-a-lifetime thing. And it's going to look so good on my college apps."

"Extracurriculars are important," Mom agreed.

One week in Norway, to explore and discover and probably pose for a lot of brochure pictures. A student exchange program had sponsored the contest, and all it took to enter was an essay. Dacey had written hers in one afternoon.

If I could go anywhere in Europe, I'd choose Tromsø, Norway, so I could photograph the northern lights.

Like most essays written in one afternoon, it was fiction. She didn't know anything about photography. The aurora was pretty, but she'd never thought about it much. It was Tromsø that interested her or, more specifically, polar night.

Everybody had heard of white nights, when the sun never goes down. It was kind of a kick to find out there were polar nights, when the sun never came up. Weeks of dark, with just a little twilight at noon to stir things up.

So she wrote the essay, sent it off, and forgot about it.

Then she won, which meant dealing with her parents—they were cool with out-of-state camping trips, but across-the-ocean field trips? Not so much. But there were chaperones! Other juniors and seniors! A trip of a lifetime!

Finally, they gave in.

Well. Daddy gave in. Her mom was going to drag out the pain as much as possible.

Dacey shut up and endured the taxi ride to the airport, while her mother leaked anxiety everywhere: *If you get arrested, don't let them call the Chinese embassy! Make sure they call the American embassy!* Then there was the long walk to security: *Don't make any jokes about bombs.* It was good Mom couldn't go past the ropes, because Dacey had already heard the TSA lament: *Bare feet! Who knows what kind of diseases are on those floors?*

There were kisses and tears and finally Dacey was off. Alone. To Norway. For a second, uncertainty engulfed her. Maybe it was too much to do on her own. Maybe she should just stay home? Heart thrumming, Dacey looked back one more time. Her mother waved in the distance, then put both thumbs up.

Okay, maybe she *could* do this.

After boarding, Dacey settled into her seat and nursed a flicker of hope. She was in 2A, and in 2B a grandma with silvery hair and a kind smile. Grandmas loved to talk. Plus, bonus, they usually couldn't sleep, either. Which meant Dacey would have company on the long flight.

"Have you been to Norway before?" Dacey asked.

The woman smiled apologetically and answered in another language. No idea what it was, although Norwegian was a pretty good guess.

So much for a chatty granny, Dacey thought. Tightening her seat belt, she sighed. Eight hours wide-awake and trapped in her own head, while the other passengers slumbered around her. Whee.

The thing was, Dacey thought she should have gotten used to it—she barely slept anymore. It wasn't senioritis or SAT anxiety, it was insomnia. Hideous little pockets of it, leaving her marooned at three a.m. Sometimes she played on the computer; sometimes she went for walks.

Sometimes sleep came in a dozing chain, or restless dreams that were worse than being awake in the first place. She'd dreamed about lying awake in bed, studying the cracks on her ceiling. They stretched for the walls, and it wasn't until they touched the floor that Dacey realized they weren't real. And then, oh so cleverly, she woke up and couldn't get back to sleep.

Insomnia sucked.

She was sick of sleeping pills and warm milk, late-night television and endless exercise, caffeine, no caffeine, bizarre herbal supplements and well-meaning advice from people who thought insomnia meant it took twenty minutes to fall asleep instead of twenty seconds. She was tired of worrying her parents, who took her to the doctor over and over.

That's why she'd entered a contest to go anywhere in the world. That's why she'd chosen Tromsø in January. Polar night, long days of nothing but dark, just a hint of twilight spread across the midafternoon. Dacey had a new Nikon in her luggage and a photo-essay outline on her Mac.

One week of polar night—one week photographing the aurora borealis—she called the project *Winterglow*, but that would probably change. Maybe to something like *I Don't Know Much about Photography* or *I Just Thought I Might Get Some Sleep if the Sun Never Came Up.*

It was a work in progress.

The camera was busted.

Dacey glared at it, her only Christmas present just for this trip, all six hundred dollars' worth of it.

New images popped up on her computer screen. Unearthly greens and blues filled each shot, sinuous curves stretching the heavens. The software chugged away, piecing multiple pictures into one panorama—and it was almost breathtaking. Almost.

In the middle of each picture was a spot. A smudge. A pale something that repeated all the way across the panorama. She couldn't cut it out—she didn't know how to Photoshop it out. Her first set of pictures was ruined.

Dacey opened one and zoomed until the smudge filled

the entire screen. Tension burning between her shoulder blades, she leaned in to stare. A pale smear with dark streaks in it marred the shot. It was delicate, like a wisp of fog or an errant puff of cottonwood.

It looks like a face, her brain chirped.

"Shut up," she replied.

It seriously does, her brain replied. *A younger, cuter version of Thor.*

Sliding from her chair, Dacey closed the laptop and started for the bedroom. It was lack of sleep talking—when she was really low on *Z*s, she saw minotaurs on subways and phantoms during physics class. She felt rooms shaking when they totally weren't. And now, apparently, she saw handsome faces in the aurora borealis, in the middle of polar night.

Best to ignore it all; none of it was real. Maybe sleep deprivation made her crazy, but she didn't have to actively participate. She stripped off her jeans and collapsed into the turned-down bed.

Around her, the cottage cooled with a low, blue glow. Moonlight on the snow outside seemed to make the world quieter. There was a serenity to the long run of hills; they turned to stone mountains on the horizon. Dark water spread into the distance, still as glass. The world was a lullaby.

Sleep didn't come. Instead, her mind hopped on a hamster wheel. Tromsø wasn't what she'd expected at all. She'd thought there would be a hostel, tons of people everywhere. Instead, she had her own cottage, one of several tucked into the countryside.

The exchange counselor had given her a huge binder full of touristy things to do, and then left her alone to do them. Which was actually kind of nice, and something she would never, ever tell her mother.

Then she wondered what was wrong with the camera—if she could fix it here, or if her dad would have to return it. She couldn't go back to New York with *nothing*. It had a warranty, right? Of course it did—it was brand-new.

New camera, broken camera, face, not a face, what's that noise outside, maybe nothing, maybe wolves, until it finally settled into a soothing pattern of white noise.

Not once did she wonder who had turned down the bed.

Morning never came. When Dacey finally rolled out of bed, a dusky imitation of dawn greeted her—the sky still dark, sunrise colors at the horizon. Her travel clock insisted it was 9:00, but was that a.m. or p.m.?

Hunger ended the contemplation. Dacey stumbled to her feet and trudged toward the kitchen. Then she groaned when she realized the cupboard and the fridge were empty. Briefly, she glanced at the giant block of orange cheese crackers.

"Sorry," she told them. "I'm not that desperate yet."

A brisk hike and a ferry ride later, Dacey strode through the streets of Tromsø proper. Though the streets were narrow and the lights were on, it didn't feel like a village. It was very much a *city* on the edge of night, full of people, full of life. Everything glittered in purple and gold: the water, the buildings, even the mountains in the distance.

She followed the buzz into the heart of town and eventually found herself in a café that promised omelets and reindeer.

When her waiter greeted her in Norwegian, she managed to reply, then consulted her phrase book. *"Snakker de Engelsk?"*

"American?"

"Yes." She folded the menu and smiled up at him.

Ruddy cheeked and animated, the waiter could have been twenty or fifty—it was hard to say. His hair was so pale, it could have been gold or silver, but his smile seemed friendly. He leaned against the table comfortably. "Visiting family?"

"On vacation. Sort of." It sounded so weird to say that; to realize she was on vacation all by herself. Apparently, that thought showed in her expression, because the waiter laughed.

"Sort of?"

"I'm doing a photo-essay on the northern lights," she answered. "For my school newspaper."

"They *are* beautiful." He hummed his approval, then

leaned over to help her with the menu. After selecting a salmon-egg omelet and convincing her to try the *lefse* bread with currant jam, he stood and offered, "For the best view, you should try to get away from town. Just a hop on the ferry . . ."

Pleased for no real reason, Dacey gestured vaguely behind her. "Oh! I have that view. I'm in a little cottage across the bay. The harbor. The bay?"

"Harbor," he said.

"It's perfect; it's right on a hill. There are these huge windows. . . ."

Awareness lit his face. "Kristian's cottage."

"I didn't know it had a name."

The waiter tapped the edge of the table with his order book. "Let me get this started. I'll be back."

He disappeared for a moment, and Dacey reconsidered the whole conversation. He seemed nice enough, but she could just hear her mother now: *What were you doing, telling a stranger you're alone? And where to find you! That man could have been an ax murderer!*

Considering the number of people her mother thought were ax murderers and the number who actually were, Dacey relaxed. Besides, the guy was obviously on the clock. When would he have time to hack her to death, between courses?

When the waiter returned, he brought her a cup of black coffee and a tray of sugar and milk to sweeten it.

"Right, so," he said, leaning on the edge of the table. "It's an old cottage. Very romantic."

Dacey colored slightly. Was he hitting on her? "I'm just here to take pictures."

"No, no. Not for us. My Terje would have my head; you would be so disappointed. I mean, a romantic *story*." He laughed, a soothing sound that let Dacey settle again. Still leaning at the edge of the table, the waiter glanced up, like he was trying to remember something important.

Finally, he spoke again. "A hundred years ago, almost exactly, I think. A boy named Kristian arrived from the south. Couldn't have been much older than you. And he went to work, building a cottage for his sweetheart. He said she only came in the dark. He lived his whole life for the polar nights."

Leaning in, Dacey asked, "Regular night wasn't good enough for her?"

"He claimed she didn't belong to this world."

Starting to smile, Dacey shook her head. "Seriously?"

"The sunlight drove her away," the waiter said. He brushed his fingers together, holding back a laugh. "So she came when the nights were the longest. Maybe she was a vampire."

Dacey picked up her coffee. "*Let the Right One In*, right?"

"*Pfft*. That's Sweden." He spread his hands as he stood upright. "Do you want proof? He's buried on the hill behind the house. In the pine trees."

Wow, that wasn't creepy at all. Dacey tried to picture the land around the cottage. There were lots of trees and lots of snow. She definitely didn't remember a graveyard. A little uneasy, Dacey pointed out, "All that proves is that he existed."

"True." The waiter grinned, teasing. "But maybe his vampire is still out there, waiting. Polar nights, you know. Perfect for lurking in the dark."

"Now you're just trying to scare me."

Laughing, the waiter said, "If I were trying to scare you, I'd tell you that the cottage is haunted."

With a relieved smile, Dacey waved him off. He was *so* full of it. She didn't believe in ghosts, vampires, or quirky regional myths. The closest she got to encounters with the supernatural were the hallucinations when her insomnia got superbad.

But people loved legends, and there had to be more. If she couldn't get the camera to work, her editor would be just as happy with a local folklore and mysteries story.

She did a little dance in her seat and then dug into breakfast, recharged.

Striding through the cottage, Dacey held her phone in front of her as she talked. She'd gone through the camera manual page by page, spent a very tedious hour wiping all the lenses down in exactly the right way, and then shot another hundred pictures of the gold-edged dusk. Every single one of them was smudged.

"No, that's what I'm telling you," she said. "It doesn't matter where I go, the pictures are messed up. Right, I tried different locations. Yes."

She stopped to peer at one of the window frames. She hadn't realized it before, but someone—perhaps the legendary Kristian—had carved roses into the wood. They bore faint traces of paint, red and gold and blue.

Trailing her fingers over them, Dacey warmed at the detail. She could imagine masculine hands carving into the wood. Almost see them, paint smeared and rough, filling in the little details with so much care . . .

The tech on the phone interrupted the thought. "And you're using it outside?"

"Um, yeah. My dad bought it *because* it was recommended for outdoor stuff."

Dacey turned to grab the manual and stopped abruptly. It wasn't just that window—the room was full of rosemaling. Delicate curves and swirls framed all the doors and windows. The mantle matched, and so did the cupboard panels.

Suddenly, the cabin shifted. The distressed, faint streaks of paint turned vibrant. Gold poured into darkened outlines, glimmering in the light. The room swelled with color; thousands of hand-painted roses bloomed. Everything else faded—the furniture, even the light outside. A masculine scent hung in the air, musky and clean.

A cool touch raised the hair on Dacey's arms, and she distantly heard herself telling tech support that she didn't know *how* cold it was outside, just that it *was*.

"Are you wearing a scarf?" the tech asked.

The question broke the spell. Colors drained away, faded again. *Aged again*, her delirious brain insisted.

Rubbing a cold hand against her face, Dacey shook herself, catching up to the conversation she was trying to have. "I . . . no, what difference does it make?"

Gently, and surprisingly without condescension, the tech replied, "It's probably your breath. The flash reflects off the frost when you breathe. That's why you see it in *all* your photos."

A blush crawled up the back of her neck, heat to drive away the lingering chill that had touched her skin. "I don't know what to say."

"It's a common problem," the tech said. "Is there anything else I can help you with today?"

"No, that's all, thank you," she said, and hung up without waiting for a reply. She kept waiting for the colors to come back, or the cold. Prickles raced on her skin again when she realized that the scent of musk still hung in the air.

Patting her face sharply, Dacey started for the bedroom. The insomnia was getting to her, obviously. She didn't like to take sleeping pills because they didn't work very well. Sure, they left her dreamlessly unconscious for a few hours. Afterward, she'd wake with a hangover, aching and tired. But sometimes it reset her brain enough that the hallucinations faded. Better exhausted and gorked out than exhausted and loony tunes.

She dug out a prescription bottle and swallowed a half tablet without water. Sprawling across the neatly made bed, she waited for sleep to claim her. Her fingers ran restlessly over the patches that made up the top of the quilt.

And then cold came over her again, when it was too late to do anything about it.

She hadn't made the bed! She hadn't turned it down the night before. *Someone's been in here,* she thought. *That's why I smelled cologne. Someone's been in here!*

Panic swallowed her. Trying to claw back up from sleep, Dacey managed to pick up the card with the exchange counselor's phone number. But it fluttered to the floor when her woozy fingers refused to keep hold. She slumped onto the pillow and slept.

When she opened her eyes, Dacey felt like she was made of lead. She blinked, and confusion set in.

The world had an upside-down kind of dream logic, little stars and sparks drifting around her. The flowers on the headboard opened bright petals, and when Dacey sat up, she realized she wasn't alone.

A boy stood at the windows, cradling a cup in his hands. He was finely built, lean and tight, his shoulders tapering to a perfect triangle at the narrow straits of his waist. His close-cropped hair was so pale that it reflected the palette of blues outside.

Dacey tried to throw herself out of bed, but the molasses weight of dreaming held her down. So instead, she demanded, "What are you doing in here?"

Hesitating, he formed his lips, then stopped. After gathering his thoughts, he said in accent-tinged English, "This is my cottage. I'm supposed to be here."

Moonlight outlined his profile, glowing at the tuft of his brows and through the fine, silvery curve of his eyelashes. He had a strong nose, and a full mouth, and the slightest hint of transparency to him. Through the pale lavender part of his lips, Dacey could see the fence outside; the mountainous horizon traced a shadow on his cheek.

Relieved, Dacey fell back in bed.

"A dream. Oh, God. Thank God." She laughed, a bubbly, delirious sound that spilled out of her and didn't stop when he came to sit beside her. Instead, she clapped a hand on his knee, which seemed substantial enough. "You're a salmon-egg omelet and half an Ambien."

"What? You're talking out of your head," he said. He held out the bowl-shaped cup in his hands. "Tea?"

The clean scent of well-steeped tea flooded Dacey's senses. Struggling against the strange weight of dreams, she finally managed to sit up. She swayed into him, her cheek skimming his shoulder, her hand accidentally slipping down his chest.

His leanness was all muscle, tight and sculpted beneath the rough fabric of his clothes. Warmth radiated from him; it slipped into her and slowly spread. Tipping her face up, she smiled and asked, "Are you a *dirty* dream? I don't usually have those about white boys."

He pressed the cup into her hands. "You're the one; I've been waiting for you."

Swirling a finger in the air, Dacey spoke between swallows of tea. "Kristian, right?"

"Yes—" he started.

Leaving the cup on the bedside table, Dacey sat up quickly. With a lunge, she grabbed two handfuls of his shirt and pulled him back with her. The bed rocked slightly; the headboard whispered against the wall. Kristian felt remarkably real, deliciously real.

But despite his seeming solidness, and all his perfect details, she saw the roof timbers through him. Plainly, faintly—but most definitely there.

He blinked at her, a mixture of surprise and wonder playing across his face. "I must be imagining you."

"Fair enough—I'm dreaming you," Dacey replied.

And she kissed him, so crazy bold she couldn't even believe herself. Until now, all of her kisses had been a little bit shy, a lot awkward, with real-life noses bumping and real-life teeth cracking together. But this wasn't real life, was it? It was an eerily lucid dream.

Considering all the bizarre tricks her mind played on her, Dacey figured she had a right to enjoy this one. Why not let a myth she heard over breakfast come true?

His mouth skimmed hers. He captured her and chased her, all with a part of his lips. The stars and lights in the room surged, as if controlled by the rush of her breath. Kristian was gentle, but his hands were rough-hard from work—building a cottage, carving it full of roses. His fingers tangled in her hair; his thumb smeared the full curve of her lip.

Everything had a strange, giddy glow to it, and his kisses left a trace of honey on her tongue. Before she could steal one more kiss, he disappeared. It wasn't subtle at all. One moment, he wasn't there.

He's buried on the hill behind the house, the waiter's voice repeated. *In the pine trees.* Nothing but night air pressed against her. Breath shallow, she fell back on her pillow, staring at the ceiling.

"Kristian?" she called.

Of course, no one answered. Leave it to her stupid brain to come up with the perfect dream and the perfect way to destroy it. Nothing like a little bit of morbid reality to ruin the mood. Wrapping her arms around herself, Dacey sighed and sank into the pillows.

A cold trickle seeped through her hair. Jerking up, she slid back and stared. Kristian's cup had tipped onto the pillow, tea coursing through wrinkled bedding to get to her. It took just one thought—*I never could have imagined a detail like that*—to break the spell.

Actually, the dream.

"I'm awake," Dacey said. And she threw herself out of bed.

Wrapped tight in her hoodie, Dacey followed Herr Velten, the exchange counselor, through the cottage.

"Someone turned down the bed last night, then made it this morning. And they left . . ." She gestured at the cup, still overturned on the pillow. "That. I've smelled cologne!"

Herr Velten frowned, tugging his own ear as he considered the bedroom. "I have a key and you have the guest key. No one else should be in here."

"That's what I thought!" Dacey threw up a hand. "I didn't want to call the police but, you know, I don't feel very safe now."

"It's just so strange."

You're telling me, Dacey thought. *You didn't try to kick it with a ghost.*

But she kept the sarcasm to herself, especially when she glanced at the clock and realized it was approaching midnight. A taste of guilt ate at her, and she said, "I know it's late, and you probably want to get back to bed. Do you have another cottage available?"

Humming, Herr Velten knitted his snowy brows. He looked around, then hummed again, a thoughtful sound that lingered. Time seemed to slow as he considered this question, and Dacey found herself wanting to shake him.

Finally, he nodded. "Yes, but not until tomorrow night. There are boys in the other cottages."

It was all Dacey could do to keep from blurting out that there was a boy in this one, too. Clasping her hands together, she shifted her weight from foot to foot. "There's nowhere in town or . . . ?"

"I'll lend you my dog," he said.

Dacey stared at him. "Herr Velten, I don't want to be pushy or anything, but I just told you I thought somebody was in the cottage."

Gently, he put a hand on her shoulder and pointed to the floor-to-ceiling windows. No, to the nearly pristine snow outside. It gleamed in the dark, crystalline and clean. "Two sets of footprints. Mine. Yours. No one else could be here."

No one with a body, Dacey thought uselessly. Since she wasn't prepared to say that out loud, she went with "Oh."

"Is this your first time away from home?" Herr Velten asked. "Maybe you're a little nervous. A little jet-lagged."

"Maybe," she said.

With a smile, Herr Velten gestured for her to follow. "Take my dog. You'll like Skadi. She's very loyal. Very warm on the feet, too, if you enjoy that sort of thing. And she barks like mad when someone comes in the house. If there's an intruder, she'll scare him away."

Dacey wavered. She'd never had a pet before; her dad was allergic. It would be kind of cool to borrow a dog . . . but it really didn't fix the problem, and that was, this cottage was haunted. Or something. "There's really nowhere in town?"

"It's *Nordlysfestivalen*, and the film festival is starting, too. I doubt there's a room to be had."

Inwardly, Dacey groaned. She knew about the aurora celebration; actually, she knew about the film festival, too. She'd read about them in the binder. She was probably supposed to be enjoying them.

"Miss Shen?"

She looked around, her gaze falling on the camera. The only reason her parents had agreed to this was for the extracurricular value. Because she'd promised to create a photo-essay to add to her journalism portfolio. She had to go back with something—even if it *was* more travel legends.

Swallowing her nerves, Dacey nodded. "All right. I'll take the dog."

"And we'll get you moved tomorrow night," he agreed.

With a wave, he headed out the door—off to fetch a dog Dacey didn't know what to do with. Worse, leaving her alone in a cabin that had gone cold from the open doors and the unsettling sense that it wasn't entirely empty.

Outside, the northern lights began to shimmer. The otherworldly greens and blues were joined by streaks of pink, a stunning display. Threads of light hung in the dark, wavering as if strummed by an unseen hand. A faint crackling accompanied it tonight, as if the aurora sparked against the snowy horizon.

Awe pushed Dacey's anxiety away. It was hard to be scared when there was magic in the sky. Pulling her coat on, she stopped to carefully wind a scarf over her nose and mouth. Then she grabbed her camera and headed into the night to try again.

Maybe she'd made up the photo-essay thing because it sounded good. But as Dacey stood beneath the swirling lights, she had to admit they moved her. The ethereal twist of light drew her in, threads of blue and green hanging against the deepest black she'd ever seen.

Rationally, she knew it was just solar winds playing with the atmosphere. Logically, she knew that the high-pitched crackle when it was particularly quiet was just electricity confusing the fibers inside her ears. She wasn't really hearing a celestial event. She wasn't really seeing a Greek goddess spill out across the night.

Dacey took a few more shots, walking across the yard. The snow squeaked beneath her feet. Herr Velten was right: two sets of footprints, hers and his. Maybe the static that made the northern lights whisper also generated hallucinations. Or the insomnia. Or the jet lag. Or the whole lot of them had joined forces to drive her just a little crazy in an endless night.

Turning slowly, she searched for *the* hill with *the* trees.

And it was there, past the run of the fence. Cold air swept over her; her nose burned when she breathed. And she could feel the snow starting to work its way into her boots. She should have gone inside. Instead, she squared her shoulders and headed for the trees.

Some things had to be real. The iridescent gleam on the snow, that was real. The dark, spindling arms of the trees silhouetted against the sky, those were real, too. And they opened to a clearing, a rough stone standing in the center. It was dark, smooth at the base, but rough at the top.

It looked ancient, like Viking ancient. Like seriously olden times and Thor for really real ancient. A glint of silver caught her eye, and she moved closer. Smoothing a gloved hand down the surface, she wiped haze from a bit of glass. It was a locket—no, a picture frame set into the stone.

The boy from her dream-hallucination-whatever looked back in black and white.

The picture was damaged, water creeping around the edges. It ate the detail in the background and left just his shoulder and his face. But it was him, unmistakably. It wasn't like Norwegians all looked alike. Her brain hadn't summoned some stock Scandinavian to play the part of Overactive Imagination Boy.

Dacey sank to her knees, shivering at the cold that closed around her. She didn't need a phrase book to understand a gravestone. Kristian Dahl, born 1895, died . . . never. There was no final date. He was young in the photo, maybe eighteen? Maybe twenty?

Kristian Dahl, it said. Born and never died. Dacey clasped a hand to her chest, pressure against the tightness there. She didn't believe in ghosts or vampires, so what was left? The words had probably been cut deep and angular once. Years of elements had softened the stone and the shape of his name.

Someone had left the stone. The photo. Someone had remembered him.

A dog's barking broke the quiet, and Dacey pushed herself up. Maybe she wasn't the first girl to spend a night in Kristian's cottage, alone but not really. If parapsychology wasn't an option, maybe physics were.

She knew there was a third dimension, space. And a fourth dimension, which was time. And somehow, they got together and caused gravity. . . . If that could happen, could they bend the past toward the future? Or the future toward the past? Or was that completely crackheaded? Dacey sighed and wished she'd paid more attention in class.

Hurrying back to the cottage, Dacey barely noticed the green-blue glow that bathed her. The northern lights flickered on, shaping the permanent-impermanent sky above.

Bounding through the living room, Skadi—a Norwegian elkhound, according to Herr Velten—showed no sign of settling. She leapt and rolled, chasing a rubber ball with bells in it, and occasionally skidded past on the bare wood floors.

A streak of cream and black, she turned after every gambit, as if looking for Dacey's approval. When she got it, she started over again, filling the cottage with a rumble of motion. *Maybe Dad could start taking Zyrtec,* she mused, because having a dog *was* awesome.

As Dacey hooked the camera up to her computer, she smiled when Skadi dropped the ball by her chair.

"You want it?" Dacey asked. She shook the ball to make it jingle. With a cheery yip, Skadi rose on her hind legs, bouncing in excitement.

Considering that the hound was knee high and all muscle, Dacey hesitated to throw the toy very hard. She could only imagine the look on Herr Velten's face if she trashed his cabin playing with his dog. So she gave the ball a gentle toss, and Skadi lunged after it, curved tail wagging.

"Good girl," Dacey said, turning to watch the upload bar on her computer grind toward 100 percent.

Skadi carried the ball back, holding it expectantly until Dacey threw it again. Back and forth they went, but when the pictures finished uploading and thumbnails filled the screen, both of them stopped. Dacey cursed under her breath and enlarged one of the images.

The streak was still there.

Paging through the next few pictures, Dacey's heart

sank. It didn't make any sense. She'd cleaned the camera, she'd worn the scarf, she'd done everything she was supposed to do. Frustration washed over her in waves, tightening until it ached to sit there. Her head ached, too, and she wanted to cry. This trip was *not* going the way she planned and she was *so* tired.

When Skadi barked, it startled her. Dacey pushed her chair back and looked around as she buried a hand in Skadi's warm fur. "Shh, what's wrong, puppy?"

Skadi barked again and put her paws up on the table.

"It's just a computer," Dacey told her. She stroked the dog's head, trying to soothe her, but Skadi barked again and again. The sound echoed in the cottage, ringing in Dacey's ears.

Moving to close the laptop, Dacey jumped when Skadi pushed her head beneath her arm and barked again. With a frown, Dacey looked back at the screen. All her warmth drained away because Skadi wasn't barking at the computer. She was barking at the *pictures*.

The streak was gone, replaced with the lean, long shape of a boy in suspenders. The boy. Kristian Dahl, born 1895, died never.

"Okay, that's it!" Dacey clapped the laptop closed and threw herself at the couch. It was crazy. The whole trip was crazy. She hadn't slept enough to drive away the hallucinations. She must have seen Kristian's picture somewhere before. Online. In a catalog. Somewhere.

Or! Or the *camera* was bad. Kristian's face in the pictures was just pattern recognition. Brains liked to make pictures out of clouds and stars and haze on pictures. That's all it was. It had to be.

Pulling an afghan over herself, Dacey patted the cushion next to her until the dog hopped up. It would be morning soon. She just had to get to morning.

She wrapped her arms around Skadi's neck. "I'll go into town for the day. To the library! Or the festival! And tomorrow night, new cottage. Put this all behind me. You know what? It'll be fine. It's all good. We're so good, aren't we, Skadi?"

In response, Skadi barked at nothing. Leaping down from the couch, she barked again, then stopped. Her head tipped quizzically. Then, she moved—purposefully. Dacey shivered, because it was unmistakable. Skadi *saw* something. And whatever it was didn't scare her.

Curling her toes into the couch, Dacey watched Skadi pad after an unseen guest. The dog sniffed along the baseboards, then dropped to lie in front of the window seat. Whining, she pawed at the rosemaled panels, then nosed at them.

Suddenly, one of them popped open, which startled Dacey and Skadi both. The dog bounded away, then back, barking at the open panel.

"Shh," Dacey said. "It's not going to hurt you, shh."

But Skadi had hunting in her blood, and she'd flushed

out something for Dacey to claim. Slowly, Dacey lowered her feet to the floor, then crept to the window seat. It was a thankfully uneventful walk—no ghostly voices, no sudden cups of tea from the ether—which made it easier to kneel down and open a dark cubby. Skadi barked, bowing on her front paws before springing up again.

Inside the cubby was a small package, and she gingerly reached inside to claim it. Covered in thick dust, it was barely bigger than a deck of playing cards. The brown wrapping paper flecked away, aged and soft as ash. The twine was a little hardier, still tied tight, now around a small, leather-bound book.

Sitting back, Dacey carefully slid the string off and opened the first page. The sharp scent of paper turning acid assaulted her, but the pages still felt smooth beneath her fingers. Fading ink sloped across the page, but Dacey couldn't read it. Her Norwegian was pretty much limited to *"Snakker de Engelsk?"*

But she didn't have to speak another language to understand the drawings. Page after page showed ornate rose blossoms, the same designs that surrounded her now. There were building plans for the cupboard, for this window seat.

The cottage had started as careful ink drawings—the fence that surrounded it, the design laid into the hardwood floors. Even the bedroom, with its expensive glass wall, he'd planned it that way all along.

It wasn't a story told over breakfast anymore. And it wasn't a dream or a fantasy; emotion stirred in her chest and flooded her veins. She was right there, in that moment, with a real boy who'd selected the wood and hammered it together, piece by piece, to create this place. He'd loved every inch of the cottage, put thought, and sweat, and love into it.

Running her fingers over now-faded ink, Dacey stilled. Whatever the explanation, she definitely believed in Kristian. He'd pulled a dream into reality. He'd existed, and somehow, she'd seen him. Glimpses of the past come to life, right here in his cottage. When she turned the last page, she caught her breath. No more cottage plans or roses, the last page was a portrait.

Of her.

It captured the crooked bow of her mouth, and the way one of her eyebrows arched higher than the other. Kristian had spent a lot of time here, shading her dark hair and dark eyes with ink, shaping her round face with delicate care. It didn't just resemble her. It *was* her, down to the half-moon chicken pox scar on her chin.

Underneath, he'd scrawled a signature and a date: *25 Januar 1913.*

Dacey didn't have to check her phone to be sure. All the pictures she'd taken had time stamps—today was January 24. Tomorrow, she'd be gone. And now instead of anticipating it, she was dreading it. There was too much to figure out, too little she knew.

How could she pack up and go, now that she knew Kristian had disappeared into the polar night, waiting . . . for *her*?

Dropping her head in Dacey's lap, Skadi seemed to speak for both of them when she took a deep breath, then sighed.

Just as the midday twilight ended, Dacey woke up.

Smearing a hand across her face, she stretched, then apologized when Skadi leapt down at her sudden movement. It took a moment for her senses to sharpen. Suddenly, everything was crisp and new—she *woke up*! She'd fallen asleep!

Almost giddy, Dacey hopped out of bed, then dropped to bounce on it again. Slept, she'd slept! And now she moved in fast-forward. With a whimsical slide down the hallway toward the kitchen, she actually laughed. Skadi chased her the entire way, orbiting her with every step. She skidded to a stop at the kitchen door, clutching the frame.

The rest of the tea set, the one that matched the single cup Kristian had left behind, sat on the counter. Steam swirled from the pot's spout, and the air smelled fresh with loose-leaved tea. Skadi barked, then bounded past Dacey to sit and stare at an empty spot next to the stove.

Because it was still dark, on top of jet lag, on top of insomnia, time had lost all real meaning for Dacey. She could count breakfasts and pictures to try to sort it out, but the truth was she had no idea *when* she was. But the cool, tight prickle of awareness streamed across her body again.

She'd fallen asleep on the couch. She'd woken up in bed.

And now a century-old tea service sat on her counter, brand-new and full of water she hadn't boiled. Her borrowed dog sat happily, basking in unseen attention. None of it made sense, unless all of it did.

"Kristian?" she asked.

No one answered. Dacey walked toward the stove, ran her hand through the spot that held Skadi's attention so completely. It was cooler there. The hair stood up on the back of her neck, and her mouth tingled, like tasting the wind just before the lightning came.

Fixing herself in place, Dacey asked the air, "Can you see me?"

Still no answer. There was a connection, but she didn't know how to make it. She poured tea, two cups, and even took a sip. Nothing. She darted to the living room and returned with the camera. Shooting off a rapid succession of pictures, she checked the display. Nothing. Not a streak, not a face—just a handful of ordinary pictures of an ordinary kitchen.

"Look," Dacey said, putting the camera aside. "I'm not taking another sleeping pill so you can sneak up on me. Just say something. Do something. Anything."

Just then, she was struck by an idea. Reaching into her robe pocket, she pulled the small sketchbook out. It was his, and personal. She felt like she knew him, just a little, from the shape of the words she couldn't read, and the delicate precision of the sketches she couldn't stop looking at. This was her connection to him, not the ghost or the dream or the hallucination.

She held the book out—not sure what to expect.

The slightest spark filled the air, and the ink in the book darkened, sketches filling in until they looked freshly drawn. The leather cover grew brighter, until it shone. A sizzling sound raced around them, the rosemaling waking, repainting itself. The cabinets making themselves brand-new.

From nothing, Kristian reached out to take the book. His shape filled in, as if someone only had to pour details into him. Transparent, then translucent, he *became.* His gray woolen pants and cream linen shirt slowly took texture. His hair, which had seemed blue with snow and moonlight behind it, came in a pale gold. And his startlingly green eyes widened and swept over Dacey's shape.

She wondered if he saw her the same way she saw him, insubstantial, but slowly brightening to real.

"I put this away so long ago," he said, thumbing through the pages.

"About a hundred years," Dacey said. "Give or take."

Closing the book, Kristian put it aside and approached

her. "Something's not quite right, is it? I'm standing here, and everything looks old. All the paint is faded."

Dacey held out a hand. "Right now, it looks brand-new to me."

For a long moment, Kristian considered her. He took her hand and turned it in his. Trailing his fingers across her palm, he mapped every inch of it. There was no chill in his touch, and the last hints of transparency faded. "Are you a ghost?"

Laughter rang out, and Skadi jumped up in excitement. Shaking her head, Dacey murmured soothingly to the dog, then looked up at Kristian again. "No. And neither are you."

"Of course not." Kristian squeezed her hand before letting it slip out of his. "You came to me. You showed yourself to *me*, that's why I built this place. I thought if I did, you'd come, and you'd stay. . . ."

"I didn't. I couldn't have." It hurt Dacey to say it. "That's not how time works."

Lighting up, Kristian started for the living room. "I can show you."

Blood humming, Dacey followed. When she came around the corner, she saw Kristian kneel by the window-seat cubby. With a smile thrown over his shoulder, Kristian pulled out another leather-bound book.

This one was much larger than the sketchbook, and when he opened it, Dacey saw why. It was an old-fashioned photo album, each page lovingly squared with black-and-white portraits of a familiar landscape.

"I couldn't sleep," he explained, and let her take the book from his hands. "So I left my family and took a train north, as far as I could. And then a sledge until I got here. I thought the long nights would help me sleep. I brought my Seneca to take pictures, but look." He leaned over, turning the pages and then dropping his finger on a darkened landscape. "They came out wrong. I took more. And more, and on the last day, I saw you."

So did she. Though the photographs were grainy, the edges a little soft like most vintage pictures, her shape there was unmistakable. This was the picture he'd sketched from; this is what she'd looked like on her first night in Tromsø, scarfless and hatless, trying to capture the northern lights for her photo-essay.

Slowly, she lifted her head to meet his green eyes. "Kristian . . ."

"So I came back in the summer." He smiled and closed the book. "I bought the land and built this place. And I waited."

"For me."

Curling his fingers beneath her chin, he tipped her face up gently. "For us."

And this time when they kissed, the world came together instead of pulling apart. Everything matched again; Dacey's heart soared. Kristian's hands were warm and rough—and real. But she broke away, pulling her fingers over her lips.

She loved her life: her parents' cute apartment in Brooklyn, her job on the school paper, and every single one of her friends back home. She loved her anxious mother and her sweet father, and the way every single day was something new for her.

At the same time, she now loved walking into a cottage in Norway to find something magical. Something epic and legendary, waiting for *her*. How many girls got to say that? How many *people* ever did?

Skadi padded over, curling to lie against them. Snuffling her nose beneath Kristian's hand, she huffed and turned her eyes up to Dacey. Which wasn't fair at all; dogs weren't allowed to throw in their two cents when it came to completely life-altering decisions.

"What's the matter?" Kristian asked.

With a deep breath, Dacey gathered herself. Then she brushed Kristian's hair from his eyes and smiled. "You're just very complicated. This is complicated. And I'm going to have to call my mother."

Kristian blinked. "Call her what?"

"I'll explain later," Dacey answered, and tugged him into her arms. Just the thought of explaining Kristian, polar nights, and possibly time travel to her mother made her head hurt. So she kissed the non-stock Scandinavian. She could figure out the complications in time.

Sarah Ockler
The Moth and the Spider

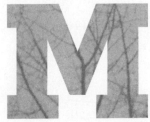oths sucked at dying.

Cali had read somewhere that a gypsy moth's whole purpose in life was to mate. That their entire life span was less than a week, and that as long as the female laid eggs, seven days was considered a good run. Way to go. Mission accomplished.

It didn't make sense to Cali, but then, at least the creature knew why she was put on this earth. Cheek pressed against the naked, dusty floorboards beneath her bed, Cali was eye level with a moth right now, one she'd seen flitting above her head the night before. Dried up, feet curled in toward its belly.

She hoped the thing had at least accomplished its purpose before it ended up under her bed, and as she mashed the carcass between her thumb and finger, she wondered if God would do the same to her. If at the end of her whole entire life, she'd leave nothing but a silky, silver-white stain on his fingertips.

Doctor Berg would call that a morbid and unhealthy thought, detrimental to the delicate recovery process, but it made Cali smile. That was something, anyway.

Cali blew the remains of the moth across the floor, and the stairs outside her bedroom door groaned. It was definitely her mother—the floorboards didn't protest otherwise. She never heard anyone else coming or going. Take the baby, for example. By the time she was aware of his presence, he was right there in front of her, messing with her things, chattering endlessly about Elmo or hot dogs or the black-and-white cats next door. This was normal for two-year-olds, Cali'd read, but it didn't make things any better for Cali.

Maybe if she lay still, she thought tonight, held her breath, her mother would think she'd gone out.

Cali almost smiled, twice in one day. That lying-still trick never worked on anyone.

Her mother knocked four times, hard-hard-soft-soft, then pushed open the door the rest of the way. Cali wasn't allowed to keep it totally closed, anyway, so the knocking part was just a courtesy her mother thought would show Cali they were starting to trust her again.

Her mother set the tray on Cali's desk with a clatter, pills hopping around in their opaque orange containers. Hundreds of them. Thousands, maybe millions even. She flicked on the big overhead light and gently tapped Cali's bedpost with her slippered foot.

"Calista. You'll catch cold under there."

"Not possible." Cali ran her thumb over the ropy half-bracelet scar on her wrist. The ridge was comforting and familiar against the pad of her thumb, as much a part of her now as her wavy brownish hair and naturally straight teeth and the smell of her armpits. "It's a virus."

"Out," her mother said quietly. It was almost a plea. Cali had read about colds and viruses and how germs attack your immune system, and she knew what she was talking about. But apparently her mother didn't read about that stuff, and now she stood in a cloud of silent disappointment and waited. *I could do this all night*, her mother would probably say next.

But Cali stayed put and still her mother didn't say it.

Fine. Cali didn't feel like playing the game tonight, anyway. She sighed and wormed her way along the floor until her upper body birthed its way out from beneath the footboard, bathed suddenly in harsh yellow light. She propped her head up, elbows on the floor, chin in hands, and watched her mother count three little white pills into a napkin. Under the bed, her legs stretched out behind her, limp. She wasn't ready to disturb them just yet.

"How are you feeling tonight?" her mother asked. She stirred soup in the plastic bowl, scraping the sides as she went. Steam curled and coiled from the rubber-coated baby spoon like twin serpents.

Cali closed her eyes. After being away for three months, it was easier to talk to her mother that way. "Fine. Better. Soup smells good."

"Carrot ginger," her mother said. "Your favorite."

Was it? Cali nodded, but she couldn't remember. Maybe her stomach remembered. Dinner was later than usual tonight, and Cali's insides growled impatiently as she crawled the rest of the way out from under the bed.

"Ready?" her mother said when Cali finally stood and they faced each other. Her mother had spent the last hour reading the baby one bedtime story after another; Cali'd heard it through the wall. She'd cooed about wolves and little pigs and then bears and monsters and fairies, and now she was standing in Cali's room, offering up the watery, reheated boxed soup and pills as if either could fix anything.

"Ready?" her mother said again.

Cali nodded. She'd been home almost two weeks now, and they were still tiptoeing around each other like strangers. Cali swore her mother sounded different before everything happened, but she couldn't for the life of her remember how. It was like the old voice had been replaced with this different version, tighter, less confident somehow, slipped in and changed like the locks while she was away. It was normal for everyone else who'd been here for the transition. Just not for Cali.

"Open up," her mother said after Cali had tossed the pills into her mouth. The part her mother didn't speak out loud was still there in the tone, just beneath the "I know what's best for you" surface. *Being back home is a privilege. It was granted. It can be taken away.*

Cali did as instructed, swallowing hard and then lifting her tongue so her mother could inspect the hidden regions of her mouth. Her mother was short—only reached Cali's collarbone—so she stretched and tilted her head and scoped out the situation.

"Good girl," her mother finally said.

The moths that circled Cali's room heard that a lot.

Cali closed her mouth. She tried to smile, but it felt like a grimace, so she just nodded again and hoped it was enough. Mercifully, her mother left the bowl of soup and a cup of water and waddled out of the bedroom, into the hall, back down the protesting stairs, the pill bottles rattling in her pocket. Cali shut her door as far as she was allowed and jammed her fingers down into her throat, probing the soft flesh until she located the chalky lumps. She'd read about this somewhere, too—maybe on the same encyclopedic site where she'd read about the poor gypsy moths. How to hide the pills behind the bend in her tongue, how to act mellow and even-keeled, to fake the intended results as if she'd been taking them all along.

Good girl.

She listened outside the door again. No one was there. She forced the damp pills through the tiny tear in her mattress into the hole with the others, a hidden cache tucked behind the handle they sewed on to help you flip it when one side started to sag.

*A*ttention-seeking *behavior.* That's what Doctor Berg had called this kind of thing after she'd been at the center for a month. *Not a real attempt,* he'd told her parents in their first family session, some kind of tough love, let's-all-face-the-facts-here-shall-we bullshit that was supposed to get Cali to admit her mistakes—because that's what they were, after all—and kick off the delicate recovery process. Cali had carved a ditch in the worn leather couch with her fingernail and nodded at his wise counsel. Her parents frowned and cocked their heads, watching her cautiously from behind the red rims of their eyes as if she were a poor, dumb animal.

The thing was, Cali wasn't dumb. She knew you were supposed to cut the long way if you *really* meant it, to follow the lifeline on your palm, press the blade in at the base of the wrist and slice down hard and deep toward the elbow. She'd gone crossways, though, hoping it would hurt less but still get the job done.

It didn't. And it didn't.

Now, again, she traced her silver souvenir with her moth-stained fingers.

Cali sucked at dying, too.

It was the note, see. That's where the whole problem started.

Dear Everyone I Know,
By the time you read this, I'll be . . .

It had occurred to Cali sometime last month, not long before she was released for good behavior and unexpected mental-health progress, that maybe Doctor Berg and her parents and everyone else would realize she'd meant it if she'd left a note. She'd skipped some of those vital steps last time. Skipped the note, skipped the part where you gave away your prized possessions while expressing a string of fatalistic thoughts to those around you. She hadn't known those were requirements, benchmarks, the things that separated the attention seekers from the real pros.

But now she knew. The living thought they deserved some sort of reasonable explanation for this very unreasonable action by the dead, and they needed to check off, in retrospect, all the warning signs they should've recognized.

So this time Cali had a book of Sylvia Plath poems her roommate at the center had given her and a list of the few nice things she still owned: her iPod with wireless speakers (wires were dangerous), some of her art supplies, the gift certificate to Macy's her aunt had sent to celebrate her return home. Next to each, she'd designated its new rightful owner.

The funny thing about the gift card was that she hated almost everything in Macy's, and she hated almost everything in her aunt, and it would probably take her an entire decade to cash the card in, one pair of nonoffensive socks or rubber-backed clip-on earrings at a time. And the funny thing about the poems was that reading them didn't make her feel morbid at all. They made her feel understood, less alone. Those words *got* her; they marched in and grabbed her and held on. But you couldn't walk through life with a book in front of your nose at every breath and turn, words tucked under your arm like the warm touch of a best friend, and whoever found the poems would jump to the right kinds of conclusions, and they'd see the note and the makeshift will and they'd nod somberly and say they should've known, they should've seen the signs. But at least they'd finally understand she wasn't screwing around, and maybe they would tell Doctor Berg, too, when they called for the medical files or whatever they were supposed to do in that kind of situation.

✦ ✦ ✦

Tonight was the night, and after her mother had left the soup and probed her mouth and looked at her once more with those sorrowful eyes, Cali was ready to sit down and write the all-important note.

There were no sharp things left in her bedroom. If her father could've sanded the corners of the walls into harm- less curves, he would've, but ultimately they concluded, over family dinner one night, that if Cali wanted to hurt herself using the corners of her walls, she couldn't possibly do it in silence. They'd be able to intervene. Still, her dangerous books were all paperbacks now, her dangerous glasses had been fitted with kid-friendly plastic lenses, her dangerous colored pencils had been confiscated. Cali had to settle for a new box of crayons, presented to her on her first night back home with a stack of soft, white stationery on which Cali had already written her list of valuable items. The crayons made Cali smile yet again, and she thought she should add those to the list as well. They were the most extravagant box of Crayolas she'd ever owned. She'd begged her mother for the ninety-six-color pack every year for a decade, back when things like crayons mattered. But her mother always said forty-eight was more than enough for any scenario a girl growing up in the great state of Maine might encounter.

Cali pulled a fresh sheet of stationery from her desk drawer and explored the color palette in the yellow-and- green box before her. Her fingers passed over the reds, which she felt were melodramatic and would detract from her message, and the blues, which were too overtly symbolic. Black was typical and uninspired and she hated the way it looked on her cloud-colored paper. She finally settled on a pink-orange one called Mango Tango and gripped the crayon between cold fingers, thinking. She didn't want to address the letter to her parents directly, even though they'd undoubtedly be the ones to find it. Her. It.

> To Whom It ~~Concerns~~
> May Concern . . .

Cali inspected the script, fat and slanty. Like the baby's attempt at writing his own name. She thought about his pudgy little hand holding on to a spoon or a crayon like this, drawing lopsided circles and stars with too many points. A weak pulse tingled at the bottom of her heart, a pressure, a squeeze she almost recognized, like a memory you didn't know whether you'd actually experienced or only seen in a photo. But it disappeared quickly and she underlined her words on the page twice, off to a good start.

The wind shifted and pressed itself against Cali's bedroom window. The black pines in the backyard swayed, their branches forced apart, then mashed together, and just inside the screen, a spider scurried across the sill. An orb weaver, Cali realized. She'd read about them somewhere, read that some of them didn't even make webs, despite their names. They didn't need anything so elaborate, that particular kind; they simply dangled a sticky substance from their front legs and enticed the unsuspecting little moths to approach. The moths got ensnared and the spider casually reeled them in, closer and closer. Then, predator devoured prey.

Cali appreciated that. Nature protected some, eliminated others, and left the rest to fend for themselves. Beautiful and terrible at once.

The spider explored a corner of the sill, and Cali thought this one was likely the kind that made webs, the kind that ate their own silky strands every twenty-four hours. They'd evolved from the Jurassic period, Cali remembered. A hundred and forty million years of doing the same thing every day: making a web, destroying it, making another, destroying it. The creature's bulbous body was orange and black like a tiger's, and now that Cali'd spotted it, she couldn't unsee it. The spider paced back to the other corner. The thing was trapped; she'd probably starve. Cali should do something, she thought. Open the window and the screen, maybe. Show her the way out.

Her phone buzzed against the desk and she jumped. She checked the caller ID after the vibrating stopped. Wrong number.

No one called her on purpose anymore.

Cali returned to her letter and scrawled out the next part.

by the time you read this I'll
I don't know how to
sorry I am so messed up
everything with the

Damn it. This was already the twenty-third draft, if you counted all the versions she'd written in her head. She'd probably have to start over. She had to get the words right. She had to get all of it right—nothing left to chance tonight, nothing misinterpreted by family, law enforcement, or medical professionals as anything less than the real thing.

Cali's eyes found the spider again. The creature dangled from the bottom of the upper sash now, suspended on a single, silky thread. Behind her, the sky was velvety purple and blue, smudged in places with hazy dark clouds. The summer sun must've set hours earlier, but Cali had no recollection of it. The whole day had been a blur, same as all the others, and now Cali tried to remember the last time she'd watched the sun go down. Really watched it, noticed the oranges and reds like fire in the sky.

Briefly, she wondered if she would miss it. She didn't think so.

Her phone buzzed again with that same stupid number. She hit IGNORE. The phone was kind of pointless, but Cali couldn't get rid of it. Memories, she guessed. Or maybe inertia. Her parents had kept the account for her while she was away, and after she'd returned, she'd checked an empty voice mail box, scrolled through a list of no missed calls from all the friends she used to have.

Crazy is contagious, didn't you hear?

The floorboards on the other side of the door moaned again, and Cali slipped her note into the desk drawer beneath a celebrity gossip magazine whose staples had been removed. She waited for her mother to pass, watched the shadow of her shrink and fade. Soon her mother would slip beneath the threadbare comforter in her own bedroom and watch Conan O'Brien until she passed out, keeping the television on low so she could still hear the baby monitor in Cali's room, just in case.

As if to remind her, the red light blinked from atop the squishy beanbag chair near the bed, and Cali sighed. She grabbed her water cup, downed what was left. Then she had to pee.

Cali slipped into the hall. She had to walk past her parents' bedroom to get to the bathroom, and her mother always kept the door open a crack.

Just in case.

"That you, Calista?" she said as Cali passed. Cali had mouthed the words right along with her.

"Yep." She rolled her eyes. It's not like she could do anything in there. Just like her bedroom, the bathroom had been carefully modified prior to her return home. No prescriptions. No nail polish remover or mouthwash or toilet bowl cleaner. No hair dryer cord or manicure scissors. No shower curtain rod from which something could hang. It was safe enough for the baby to toddle into unsupervised. In fact, there was another baby monitor on the shelf over the sink, and if Cali took longer than five minutes, her mother would barge in unannounced.

Just in case.

There was no lock on the door.

Just in case.

Cali did what she had to do, washed her hands, refilled her water cup, and quickly returned to her bedroom, pushing the door partway closed behind her. On the desk by the window, her phone glowed blue-green. MESSAGE, the screen said. 12 MISSED CALLS. Same number as before.

Cali pressed the button for voice mail and shoved the phone between her ear and her shoulder. As she waited for the message, she dug out her letter and picked up the Mango Tango crayon.

but I ~~don't~~ didn't know what else to do and

"You. Have. Twelve. New. Messages," the robotic voice mail system informed her.

~~then I realized maybe~~ it's best for everyone if I just

"You have a collect call from Eastport Juvenile Detention Facility," a disembodied recording on the other end said. "To accept the charges, press one. To decline the charges, hang up."

A thrill jolted Cali's heart and she almost screamed at the unfamiliar sensation, but the feeling was fast and fleeting. She held her breath, hoping to conjure that brief spark again, a pulse in her heart, but it didn't return. All twelve messages were the same. She set the phone back on the desk and watched it, waiting for another call, another thrill. None came.

go away. Vanish. You
can get back to your normal ~~life~~
lives and I will follow the

White light flooded the backyard that stretched beyond Cali's window. The trunks of the swaying pines were illuminated, two low spotlights cutting through the blue-black night. They blinked out and a car engine hummed and quieted and ticked itself down to silence. The car door opened. The car door closed. Footsteps on the path. Downstairs, keys jingled and jammed into the lock. The front door opened. The front door closed.

Her father's footsteps crossed the living room floor, heavy and full of purpose.

Cali pressed her hand to her chest, surprised as always

to feel her heart's drumbeat against her palm. Thinking of her father did that to her now. She'd tried to snuff out her life force that night, and as far as her father was concerned, she'd succeeded. He'd shown up for the family session with Dr. Berg, kept her cell phone up-to-date, allowed her to live in the house and eat his food. But he hadn't looked her in the eyes since. Hadn't spoken to her. Hadn't come home from work earlier than eleven or midnight, lest he risk crashing into her in the hallway or brushing his fingers against hers as they simultaneously reached for the television remote.

Like the natural cadence of her mother's voice, Cali had forgotten the warmth of her father's strong hand on her shoulder, his gentle stroke on her soft, brown hair.

Her phone started up again just as the air shifted in her bedroom and two long shadows slipped beneath the door, spreading across her room, darkening the hardwood floor like a spill. The skin on her arms prickled and her phone kept rattling. She felt her father's presence, saw the shape of him through the gap of the partially open door. He wasn't moving. The phone buzzed and whirred, its angry green-blue light blinking from the desk. She imagined his hand against the wood, his eyes closed, disappointment pinching his face. *Buzz buzz buzz.* If he had any words for her, they were lost, broken on the fortress of his anger, on his inability to understand or forgive. *Say something, goddamn you. Say something to me.* She willed it and wished *buzz buzz buzz* and crossed her heart and hoped to die *buzz buzz buzz* but the words never came. His shadow didn't move, his breath banging down the door with all the force of a feather. *Buzz buzz buzz* her father didn't speak, the phone didn't stop, and finally she answered, pressing number one to accept the charges and then speaking loud and clear into the receiver. Excited, as if she were receiving an expected but overdue call from an old friend.

The shadows outside her room disappeared and the moths circling her overhead light heaved a sigh of a relief.

"Mom?" a girl on the other end was saying.

Cali didn't respond at first. She'd expected a boy. A gruff, horny boy sneaking around the detention facility after lights-out, hoping to find a little company on the other end of a random phone number in the middle of the night.

"Ma?" the high voice came again. She sounded like a little kid, Cali thought. A scared little kid.

"Who is this?" Cali finally said.

"Don't hang up. Please don't hang up." The girl's words came out in a tinkling rush, like glass shattering against the floor. There was no sound after that, and Cali thought the girl must be holding her breath. The absence of voice and air jabbed at Cali's insides, sent a passing tingle from the base of her spine to her scalp.

"Who is this?" Cali asked again. In the background, there was a muffled echo, an intercom system of some sort. If the robot voice on the phone hadn't announced the caller's location first, Cali might wonder if she was in the hospital or maybe the airport. Coming or going. Staying or leaving. "Hello?"

"It's . . . Mom, it's me." The girl added that *me* part at the end, her voice cracking into a whisper. She said it like a question, like she wasn't even certain herself.

Cali lifted her crayon from the paper. She hadn't realized she'd been doodling. Beneath her pathetic scrawl and strikeouts was an asymmetrical spiderweb, a moth ensnared in its silky, Mango Tango threads.

Now she'd *definitely* have to start over. Once she figured out the rest of what she wanted to say. Absently, she went back to her words.

other path. disappear.
there are things you don't know and

"It's *me*," the girl was saying again, more forcefully now. "Your—"

"Wrong number." Cali didn't know why she'd accepted the charges. Desperate for a momentary connection, maybe. Curiosity, that was part of it, too. But her parents were in their room now and the baby was tucked away and the monitor's red light blinked from her beanbag chair and Cali had work to do. Solitary, important work.

She pulled the phone away from her ear to hang up, but the girl persisted, screeching across the wires. Her voice had somehow strengthened. Clarified.

"Fine. Okay," Cali told the girl. The letter stared up at her from the desk, messy and incomplete, littered with her absentminded drawing, and she didn't know what else to say. The girl was crying now, sniffling and trying to hide it and act tough or whatever you were supposed to do in those situations, which, like lots of things, Cali had read about somewhere but didn't actually know.

"Thank you," the girl said. She kept sniffling and Cali pictured her wiping her nose on the part of her hand where palm met wrist. She looked at her own wrist again, turned the silvery scar back and forth in the light.

"I don't know what else to do," the girl said quietly. "I need to find her."

"Your mother?"

"Do you know her?"

"I don't know."

"Her name is Laura Zelnick. Unless she got married again. Maybe she got married again." The girl's voice was giving out on her, the momentary strength of it spent. She couldn't have been more than fifteen or sixteen, Cali figured, and she sounded so broken, so lost. How could you not know if your own mother was married or what her phone number was, even?

Cali dragged the crayon across her letter, hovering in loops and swirls in the bottom left corner. Her hand wanted to draw a flower, a heart, a bird. She forced it into other shapes.

"I don't know," Cali said again. "I've had this number a few years. Sorry," she added at the end. And she kind of was.

There was a sigh on the other end. Then the squeaky, muffled sound of a receiver shifting from one ear to the other. "You were my one phone call."

The one phone call. Cali had read enough crime novels to know what that meant.

"It's the only number I have," the girl whispered. "I mean, it used to be . . . it's the one I remember."

things that maybe are
different in your memories.
memories always lie. there are
other things,
too, but

"What did you do, anyway?" Cali wanted to know. Her crayon pressed against the paper, still scribbling, alternating between her words and the drawing that crept along the bottom.

"Oh, you know. Whatever." The girl laughed, but not in a funny way. It was more like a dry cough. "What did *you* do?"

I ~~can't~~ ~~couldn't~~ didn't tell you. things
about that night and

"I cut my wrist." The response was automatic, Cali's lips and tongue conditioned to form the words after all those weeks in group. *My name is Calista. I'm here because I cut my wrist. I cut my wrist because I thought I wanted to die. I thought I wanted to die because—*

"I'm . . . shit. Sorry."

Cali sighed. They were both just *there*, connected by wires and waves, breathing into the phone and adding things at the end that you were supposed to say but didn't really mean.

> it's not your fault, so ~~please~~
> don't blame yourself.
> I need it not to
> hurt anymore and I know
> it ~~can be~~ could've been like that but I feel like
> everyone thinks

"It's fine," Cali said. The tip of her Mango Tango crayon had snapped on the last word, and she flipped the Crayola box around to the back. The built-in sharpener had been pried out, even though it was only a plastic one, too narrow for even her pinkie finger.

She selected another color at random. Outer Space, this one was called. She got back to work, scribbled messy words and long, wispy strokes like the trees outside her window, bending and blowing and almost black.

"What will you do?" Cali asked the girl. "About your mom, I mean." She wanted to ask again about how the girl had landed at the facility. She wondered what someone had to do to end up so alone, stuck in a messed-up place like Eastport with no one to call but a total stranger in the middle of the night. For a second she imagined what it might be like if the two traded places—if Cali could be left alone there, finally forgotten, and this girl could surround herself with parents and a baby and crayons and nosy next-door neighbors who liked cats and got involved in all the wrong things. Maybe their separate lives weren't so bad as far as lives went. Maybe they were just being lived by the wrong girls.

Anyway, whatever this girl did, Cali thought it must've been pretty bad. And now it was after midnight, and Cali had things to do. Soon she'd be somewhere else. Something else. Dust, maybe. Way to go. Mission accomplished. This girl and her mother and her sad story would go on without her and there was nothing she could do, even if she wanted to help. Which she really didn't.

Plus she still had to figure out her note.

"I don't know," the girl said after a while.

There was another long pause, dead air, the intercom beeping and echoing. It sounded like the girl was in a small room with the door open. Cali imagined the gray-green walls, the busy hallways, and file cabinets full of records. It probably looked a lot like the center. She wondered if

Dr. Berg visited Eastport. Talked to the girls about their mistakes, their attention-seeking behavior, their delicate recovery process.

"Do you know what's gonna happen to you after this?" Cali asked.

"No idea," the girl said. "But what about . . . I mean, do you know what *you're* gonna do?"

> I'm crazy. maybe I am, but all I can
> tell you
> is it's like
> I'm trapped and
> the walls are closing
> in. yeah, I know that sounds
> cliché, right?

Yes. The thing was, Cali *did* know. Like the gypsy moth, her destiny was short-lived, but she knew her purpose now. She'd decided when and how it would end.

> but the words
> don't always come
> out

Across the wires and waves, another voice shattered the quiet. An adult voice laced with impatience. Cali could practically *feel* the woman standing over this girl, arms crossed, giving directives with her eyes.

"I have to go," the girl whispered, mouth close to the receiver. The line cut out, and Cali shrugged and closed her eyes.

Cali lifted her head from the desk. Her cheek had been resting against the waxy crayon lines on her paper. She'd fallen asleep, drifted off in the midst of her work.

She checked her phone, confirmed what her stiff neck and sticky eyes already knew: three hours had passed. If Cali dreamed, she didn't remember it, and now she was behind schedule and her body was anxious to continue with the plan.

She listened at the crack in her door again, humid air from the hallway tickling her ear. It was quiet; her parents snored softly from the room down the hall, the baby kicked rhythmically in his big-boy bed as his *Sesame Street* CD reset itself. Cali knew all the words, but it was late, and she didn't feel like singing along.

She crossed the room, found the rubber spoon from her dinner, and fished out her collection of pills, transferring them two or three at a time from their tight little mattress cave into her palm. She slid open her desk drawer and tipped the pills inside the plastic cup that used to hold thumbtacks and paper clips, counting them twice to be sure. Nineteen. She'd accidentally swallowed them the first few times when she was still learning the trick. But nineteen was good.

More than enough. And Cali knew to take them with water. Alcohol, she'd learned from one of the guys in group, often induced vomiting, often expelled the pills. *Attention seeking,* the wise doctor would say. *Not a real attempt.*

The drawer whispered as Cali slid it shut. The spider in the window had started another web in the left corner, maybe a better one this time. It occurred to Cali that the moth under her bed, had it not ended up there, would've made a tasty meal for the orb weaver. The moths flitting around her ceiling light were too far away. Maybe too smart to go near the spider. Or maybe they'd get caught in the dish that covered the bulb and sizzle to death.

Cali picked up her Outer Space crayon.

right and original-like when you're
suffocating, burning up inside, when your
blood is

A memory floated into Cali's mind from earlier in the night. She'd almost forgotten about the phone call. The girl. And now her phone was buzzing again, screen lit up with same area code as Eastport, but a different number. Cali answered, but there was no recording asking her to accept the charges.

"Hello. My name is Regina Simmons."

Cali knew the woman was a social worker, probably the one who'd made the girl hang up before. It was the lilt in her voice, the strange combination of authoritarianism, compassion, and exhaustion. Cali drew another tree as she waited for Regina Simmons to continue, a sweeping trunk with feathery boughs. Some of the branches overlapped her words; she pulled out a different crayon and traced new ones over the treetops in Midnight Blue.

on fire, when your chest hurts and you
~~don't~~ can't
remember who you are. or if you even
exist at all. I'm

"Sorry to disturb you at this late hour. I'm a social worker for the state of Maine," Regina Simmons went on. "I work in the Eastport Juvenile Detention Facility. I understand you may be in contact with a woman named Laura Zelnick?"

"Yes," Cali said. Deceit was easy if you knew you wouldn't be around when the truth came out. Cali glanced at her bookshelf, scanned the author last names until she found one she liked. "My name is Wolff. Um, Gypsy Wolff."

sorry I ~~lie~~ lied
about
what happened last summer. ~~sometimes I think~~
maybe

"I have an unusual situation here, Gypsy," Regina Simmons said. Papers rustled in the background, and Cali imagined the woman sitting at a big industrial-looking desk, the cheap laminate kind with metal legs like the tables and chairs at school. There was probably a cup of cold, old coffee on the desk and a picture of two little kids in a dented gold frame and maybe an award for something, if they gave awards for social work things. Cali didn't know.

"What's going on?" Cali asked.

"How old are you?" the woman wanted to know.

I was born in the wrong time, to the wrong family.
And I do did this thing, and I pretended th I was

"Twenty-six," Cali said. It felt like a good age. She'd used it before. "Just turned."

Pen scratched paper. More shuffling. "Gypsy, do you think you can locate Laura Zelnick? Ask her to contact me at this number as soon as possible?"

"Possibly. Can I . . . May I speak with . . . the daughter again?"

"Theresa. That's her name, the daughter."

"I have a few questions for Theresa," Cali said. "The answers might help me locate her mother."

"Of course." Regina Simmons gave Cali the number to

her direct line again, made Cali promise she'd call with an update as soon as she heard from the mother. Then she was gone.

someone else, maybe.
I ~~make~~ made up these stories about

The girl, Theresa, breathed into the phone. She looked different in Cali's mind now that she had a name. Softer, somehow. Prettier. "Is your name really Gypsy?" she asked.

"No. I don't know your mom," Cali said. Shame crept up her neck, heat spread to her cheeks.

things. in my head, you know,
I made them up, someone from the
right time, the right place.
And for a little while, you know,

"Yeah. I know." The girl's voice broke again. "She left when I was . . . I don't know. A few years ago. I don't really remember."

Cali nodded, even though the girl couldn't see. The phone slipped a little, and Cali shifted it to her other ear. Her mouth opened and closed, opened and closed. Now that she had Theresa back on the line, she really didn't know what to say, didn't know why she was messing around with this girl and her messed-up situation.

~~it was almost like~~
they were real. But then they told me, or I don't know, not
them exactly, but ~~someone~~
something said

"I have to go," the girl said. "That social worker is giving me the signal."

"Yeah?"

"It's just that we're not supposed to be on the office phone like this," the girl said. "Not like this. Sorry."

"Okay," Cali said.

Cali, it said. Cali, it won't last. ~~And I knew.~~
But I forgot. I
forgot the parts
that happened, and the parts
that weren't real, and
I tried
to make the rest make sense, but

Outside the window, the orb weaver worked on the next strand of her intricate web. Cali turned her paper to a clean white spot in the corner and kept scribbling as Theresa sighed into the phone, waiting like there was anything left to say.

everything
that ~~matters~~ ~~mattered~~ matters
stopped.
And then

Cali set down her crayon. There was no more space. She couldn't even read the last three words she'd written. She needed a new piece of paper. She slid her drawer open and shuffled through the contents with her free hand, still holding the phone with the other. She couldn't find the rest of the paper. She went back to her letter, tried again.

"Okay. I really have to go," Theresa said. "The social worker keeps looking at me."

I stopped,
too. And
now

"I hope you find her," Cali said. She wanted to add something else about the girl's mother, but there was a murmur and muffled sounds and then the line cut out, and the phone blinked off. Cali set it on the desk. It was warm from her ear, moist from all those words and her skin and her breath. The battery icon blinked.

LOW LOW LOW.

Cali shoved the Midnight Blue crayon back into the cardboard sleeve, right between Razzle Dazzle Rose and

Tickle Me Pink, and folded the yellow-and-green hood over the box.

She flicked her phone into a backspin, watched it twirl over her letter. Beneath the blur of metal and graphite, colors scrawled across the paper, trees and clouds, stars, spiderwebs. Her words had been totally enveloped. The original orangey-pink Mango Tango letters were nearly lost, peeking out now in thin fingers behind the sky, like the sky outside her window. The sun would be up soon, on the drawing and on the outside. The darkness was slipping through her fingers.

Cali slid the window sash up, then the screen. The breeze tickled her cheeks, her eyes. She shivered. The orb weaver approached the edge cautiously and tested the surface, untrusting.

Cali could close the screen. Hard. End the creature's uncertainty, the aching and pointless need to survive. She curled her fingers over the edge, tips turning white as she held on and considered it. The spider stopped, perched on the ledge. It seemed to Cali that the creature was weighing her options. Stay, go. Hello, good-bye.

Suddenly, without warning or lead-in, pain flooded Cali's heart. It ripped through her flesh as though she'd pressed the blade to her chest instead of her wrist, as though this bright new hurt would be the death of her now, rather than the pills rattling in the cup in the desk drawer. Her lungs filled with warm liquid, a searing, sticky feeling she didn't recognize. Her insides burned, throat tightened. Her heart thudded and blood whooshed through veins, blue and taut beneath the scar on her wrist. Her ears rang and the room spun and she looked again at the spider, then her drawing, searching for a focal point. She found the only remaining clear words on the page and stared until they, too, swirled before her eyes, as unrecognizable in their simplicity as a foreign language.

matters
now

Cali's cheeks were wet but the dizziness finally passed. She relaxed her fingers, slid them off the lip of the window screen, the spider still in limbo on the ledge. She'd read somewhere that nature didn't like interruptions. Interference. But she raised the screen higher and blew a gentle breeze across the spider's tiger belly, anyway. The sun was rising now, its bright orange fingers reaching across the sky. Cali closed her eyes and let them warm her tear-streaked face and the orb weaver scampered out over the ledge, out into the unknown.

Cali opened her eyes. The spider was gone, the remnants of her web drifting lazily and unfinished in the window.

Cali's phone blinked off, finally spent. She'd have to get the charger from her mother later. Cali slipped it into her desk drawer on top of the magazine and pushed the drawer closed. She left the window open, though; closed her eyes again and inhaled the dawn breeze.

She hoped the spider would be okay.

Jackson Pearce
Where the Light Is

U nderground, it is cold.

The deeper you go, the colder it gets. In elementary school, I learned that if you go far enough, there's a layer of magma underneath the dirt, and beneath that the earth's core. It's hot—billions upon billions of degrees—and solid. Most people think it's made of iron. My teacher said some people think it's made of gold.

When I told my father that, he said it wasn't true—that it's the core of the *miners* that's gold. That they are brothers underground, protecting one another, using drills and shovels like wands and athames to uncover power for the world. A league of magicians working in the depths, in the secret places of the world where no one else has ever been.

I am in the league, but I am not like the other miners, who slap each other on the back and tell dirty jokes gleefully. When we go into the mine, all I can think is this—billions of degrees at the earth's core, yet it's cold. I think it's a sign, like the way people get a chill when they go into a haunted house. The earth is telling us we're not welcome.

But underground is where the money is, in the fat seams of coal, tall as me and ten times more valuable. We rumble into the mine on the cart, Roth's salt-and-pepper hair whipping back as he presses harder on the accelerator— he knows the track well enough to speed along with total confidence through the labyrinth. The headlights beam through the coal dust like we're driving through black snow; we turn our helmet lamps on as the sun vanishes behind us. I'm afraid of the dark in the mines. Afraid to be so, so far away from the world above.

I nod to a group of miners as we pass—most of them went to Middleview High with me. Just four months ago, we sat at graduation together. As the principal talked about bright futures, I entertained the idea that I would go on to something else—anything else. It was a silly fantasy, of course. The only Middleview boys who escape a life in the mines are the Runners, who slink away to colleges or the army, never to be seen till they return for their parents' funerals. The town doesn't welcome them back. They're deserters, traitors.

My father was a foreman, last out in an accident fifteen years ago. *The Middleview Mine Catastrophe*, the monument calls it. Four died; Dad kept a group of seven others alive, including Roth. My father gave them his lunch. He went hungry as three, four, five days passed until rescuers reached them. He is a local hero; he was a great miner. If I were a Runner, it would destroy my mother. It would destroy my father's memory.

I could never come back.

Roth drops me off, pats me on the shoulder as I walk away from the cart. Because I'm new, I get the boring jobs; because I don't talk, I get the solitary ones. Just like yesterday, I'm plastering an airflow wall, scooping white goo out of a bucket with my hand and rubbing it into the cracks of cinder blocks.

I pretend I'm a painter, drawing stick figures in the plaster. I pretend I'm a doctor and getting the plaster into all the cracks saves someone's life. I pretend that I'll keep my promise to myself this time around, that once this mine is dead, I'll consider leaving this town even if it means never returning. I'll escape, I'll be free, I'll be happy. I don't know how much time passes—it's hard to tell without the sun. If I check my watch I obsess over each second, so I just try not to look. I'm halfway into pretending I'm an archaeologist, making casts of something ancient, when I hear a sound.

A single knock.

No, not a single—there's another. And another. Knocks with just enough pattern to be intentional, louder than the grind of machines farther down the path. I lift my head, wipe my forearm across my mouth. *Knock, knock, knock;* before I know it I'm walking toward the noise. I pass a group of miners who look up at me, eyes of all ages lined with coal that's thick like a girl's eyeliner. Don't they hear it? We stare awkwardly at one another for a moment; I think of saying something—

Knock, knock, knock, knock.

Pause. The others stare blankly.

Knock, knock, knock, knock.

I hurry on—they don't hear it, and I don't want them to think I've lost it by saying something. Down another pathway, through an empty room . . . This is an old, old mine. The company reopened when they discovered the men from the 1800s hadn't entirely cleared out the coal. It's full of caverns, corners, tunnels that are easy to get lost in, dug with hand tools. Did someone get turned around, get sealed into an now-unused tunnel? I arrive at the retreat miners' area—a far corner of the mine, where they use mechanical drills to plant explosives. They'll take all the coal until the ceiling of earth above us is held up by a few precious pillars. Then they'll take the pillars and their coal, too, and the room will collapse. They're preoccupied with the machinery and don't notice me passing.

Knock, knock, knock, knock.

"Hello?" I call. The knocks answer. I run toward them, around the pillars—the retreaters' area looks like a big, empty ballroom. I reach the wall—is the knocking getting more desperate, or am I imagining things? I put my hands against the wall. I feel the knocking on the other side, the slight tremble that vibrates into my fingertips.

"Hello? Are you there?" I ask.

The knocking stops.

Silence. Long-drawn-out silence that makes me lean forward, wait for it, wait for it—

The knocking moves.

Along the wall, *knock, knock, knock.* I follow. The knocker and I move along the wall together to the corner of the ballroom, where he begins to knock swiftly, like he's keeping time with a song. It moves lower, to the bottom of the wall, to a crevice in the stone.

Voids in the earth aren't unheard of, but we usually don't drill this close to them. They're unpredictable, dangerous. The wall between the ballroom and the void could collapse, start a chain reaction that covers us all up. I glance back. The retreaters aren't in shouting distance—

A hand shoots out of the crevice, covered in coal dust. I leap back and scream like a girl—a *girl*. The hand grasps the edge of the crevice with white knuckles. It is not the grizzled, beaten hand of a miner. It's slender, a tiny wrist, white white white skin dusted with coal that looks like powdered makeup instead of soot.

There is a girl trapped down here.

My eyes widen and I yell for help. I duck down, shine my helmet light into the crevice. "Hang on!"

How did she get down here? I've heard about druggies wandering into mines, homeless people hoping for a place to stay, but these mines are so well guarded that I didn't know it was possible. I reach into the crevice, wait for her to take my hand, *Please, grab it, I'll help you.* Is she too strung out to know I'm here, to understand I want to help her? I wonder what she's on, I wonder how old she is, who she is, how long she's been here. *Take my hand, please.*

I hear her breathing; I pull myself farther through the crevice, and my body pitches forward on an incline. I start to slide away from the ballroom and into the void. It's only a short drop, the length of a child's slide, but my helmet falls away; the lamp flickers off. My stomach twists.

It is darker than it's ever been anywhere, ever.

I land on my back and gasp for air like a fish until oxygen rushes to my lungs. I breathe slow, wait for my eyes to adjust, but it's too dark in here without the lamp—I can't see anything, literally, not even my hand when I wave it in front of my face.

"Where are you?" I cough—the coal dust in here isn't blown away by fans, and it coats my throat. For the first time, I wish I wore my respirator.

I clamber to my feet and rub my eyes, then stand,

waiting to hear a sound in the darkness. She has to be in here somewhere—does she not want to be rescued? I reach my arms out until my fingertips brush against a wall, then begin to walk, shuffling along the edge of the room.

"You aren't in trouble," I whisper, because it seems strange to speak loudly in the dark. "If you sneaked in, it's okay. Come on, come to me. My name's Will; I'll help you. We have to leave—the air here isn't safe." *And the dark*, I want to add. *The dark is everywhere.*

Nothing. I walk farther. The room curves to the right, back toward the crevice that will lead me out, if I've got my bearings correct.

"I can help you. I can't stay in here, though." I pause, wait for any sort of response. My hands fall along a ridge— it's the crevice, it must be. I duck my head and can see into the ballroom and, on the far end, a speck of light from the retreaters. I have to go toward it. I want to help her, but I'll have to come back with a light, with help.

"Last chance," I whisper at the cavern.

Nothing.

I turn to climb out; the air from the ballroom is fresher, cleaner, and I welcome it into my lungs. I crawl forward and then, just as I'm about to put both hands on the outside of the cavern, I feel it.

Her hand slides onto my shoulder, so soft and gentle it feels like someone is pooling a silk scarf against my neck. I freeze as she dances her fingertips along my neck, to my jawbone. When she gets close to my lips, I turn my head toward her—no, toward the darkness where I know she is. She withdraws. I sit back on my feet, back in the dusty air of the cavern.

I don't speak, not this time. Instead I wait, eyes scanning the dark, longing to see. I force myself to stay still as she slides her palms over my cheeks, then down my shoulders, along my arms. She stops at my hands, not holding them, but touching them like she's a palm reader. I swallow hard.

My words slip out as a whisper. "Who are you? What are you doing here?"

Her fingers harden on mine, like she's fighting the urge to run.

Then her voice, the only sound and so much stronger than mine. When I hear it, I understand that she wasn't afraid of me earlier.

When I hear it, I wonder if I should be afraid of her.

"My name is Ennor. I live here."

"You can't live here," I say, shaking my head. I reach toward her, and she releases me and moves away.

"You don't understand," she says.

"You're right," I say slowly. "I don't understand. Tell me how—*why*—you live here." She must be crazy, or high, maybe that's it—no one would live here willingly.

She's moving, a rustling of fabrics I can't see. I tense, wondering if she'll touch me again, where I'll feel her fingers first, wishing there was light. Her breath is by my ear; strands of her hair tickle my collarbone.

"I'm a Knocker."

"A Knocker?" I say, and I can hear the doubt on my voice. The word is so silly, so stupid, that I feel the edges of my wonder crackling away into disbelief—I've heard the legends, all the miners have. Faeries who live underground, who help miners out or play little tricks. They were part of the bedtime stories my parents told me, the beings my mother promised would keep my father safe at work. I stopped believing when I saw the stretchers with the bodies of the four dead miners carried out of the ground.

"Yes. I called to you." She sweeps away from me, and I hear her knocking against the stone. The sound is so much louder than skin on stone should be, and it carries through the mine, all around me, passing into my bones until I feel shaken. I'm relieved when she stops, and I reach backward until my hands find the wall. I lean against it, shaking my head.

"Why me?"

She hesitates. Long hair touches my arm. She can see me, I realize—I'm blind here, but she isn't. She moves too deftly, too easily. "Knockers reward respectful miners. I'll lead you to a new seam, on the far side of this room." Something isn't right about her words, like this is a practiced answer instead of a real one. I'm sure if I could see her eyes, I'd know that for certain.

I chuckle nervously, trying to sound casual, hoping to coax the truth from her. "That's all? Because if that's it, you've picked the wrong miner then," I say. "I'm not respectful. My father was the miner; I hate this place—"

She makes a strange noise, one that sounds more catlike than human, one that sounds like she's hurt herself—I lunge forward, hoping to catch her arm, but there's nothing. I sit back and wait for her to speak again.

And wait.

And wait.

And realize that the sound of her breathing is gone, as is the rustle of her clothing.

The room suddenly fills with light, blinding me for a moment. It's from my helmet, lying on the ground nearby. The lamp has flickered on, and its tiny light is like the sun. My eyes adjust and I search the room for her, waiting to see her face, to connect eyes with the voice.

The room has smooth walls and a steep pitch, and the ceiling is high and cathedral-like. Thick seams of coal line it, like striped wallpaper. Behind me, I see the exit into the ballroom. But there's no other way out, not that I see, and there's no one else here.

Maybe she only exists in the dark.

She is the only thing I'm thinking of as we head underground the following day. I didn't mention her to anyone—as strange as she is, she is the only thing about the mines I've ever found intriguing. It's almost like the mine itself has changed—it's something exciting, something different than just mile after mile of darkness and coal. I don't want anyone, not even Roth, to take that away. I wonder who she is really—a homeless girl, a runaway? A lunatic? A traveler, a con artist?

A faery girl? I'd ignore the last prospect were it not for her so easily vanishing yesterday. I spent the night thinking about it, trying to imagine what a life in the dark would be like.

I wait till everyone is at work and go back to the ballroom. It's not easy—the retreaters are buzzing around, looking at pillars. I sneak around them, hold my breath when I see the tiny doorway into the cavern. Did I really plunge into that darkness so readily yesterday? I grit my teeth as I slide inside.

Nothing, no one. Not even the rustle of her clothes. I call her name softly, gently. I rap on the walls; I even resort to begging, but nothing.

Just as desperation is morphing to irritation, just as I'm about to leave, my helmet lamp flickers out.

"Why did you come back?" Her voice slices through the thick black. She sounds curious.

I lick my lips, turn my head to the sound of her voice. "I wanted to see you. Or, well, talk to you, since I can't see you."

"Why?"

I offer the simplest answer, the one I don't think I would give if I could see her eyes on mine. "I'm lonely."

Ennor waits to reply, but I can feel the words trying to escape the tip of her tongue. "I'm lonely, too."

We're both silent a long time. Finally, I sit down, leaning against the wall. Just as I reach the floor, I feel the tips of her fingers press into my palm. Her breath falls on the back of my hand, a thousand times warmer than the cool mine air.

I am afraid of Ennor.

I am afraid that talking to her means I am crazy. I'm afraid she isn't real, and I'm afraid she is.

And I am not afraid of her at all. She is the magic my father told me about. Talking to her makes me forget I am a miner, gives me a reason to look forward to going underground during the brightest part of the day.

Ennor herself is darkness to me—my helmet lamp flickers out whenever I step into the cavern. I'm left to imagine her face on every woman I see when I surface. I whisper confessions to Ennor, confessions a thousand times more honest than I've ever said in church, confessions that get deeper with each passing day. I can admit to anything—like not being able to see her means I also don't have to see myself.

She tells me about her life. About how she lives underground—I don't understand, really, but I listen. She tells me how the light would burn her skin, but how badly she wishes she could see things above the ground, like flowers and Ferris wheels. I describe them to her and she's enchanted, delighted when I explain that carnival rides glow.

When I'm with her, I'm not afraid of the dark.

Why do you hate the mine?" she asks one day, just as I step into the cavern and my helmet lamp goes out. I balance myself, dizzy from the sudden change in light.

"Because I don't want to be a miner."

"But you *are*."

I shake my head and reach for the wall for stability, then lower myself to the floor.

"Not because I want to be," I say. She sits next to me, her knee pressing against mine. She always touches me when we talk—a hand, her arm pressed against mine. It's not intimate, exactly, though it felt strange at first—now it's eye contact in the darkness. "It would be easier if I did. If I was like the rest of them and didn't care that I might spend most of my life underground. If I was more like my father."

"You don't like it here?" Ennor asks gently, and I pause, trying to work out if there is hurt in her tone.

"I'm afraid here, sometimes," I admit. "I'm afraid of suddenly being fifty years old and realizing that I haven't seen the sun in decades. I'm afraid of not living up to my father's reputation. And I'm afraid of getting covered up, of being trapped down here, where I don't even think I'm supposed to be to begin with."

"A cave-in," Ennor says. "Like the one that happened when I was young."

"Yes," I answer, raising my eyebrows. "My father was caught in it. You know about it?"

"It's my family's job," Ennor answers. "We protect the land and the mines, and if they're respectful, the miners."

"Your family's job?"

"Yes. Some of the miners weren't respectful like your father. He was a good man, my family says."

Wait. Does she mean what I think she means? I take a deep breath before speaking. "What happened to the ones who weren't respectful?"

Ennor sighs. "My family let the earth take them."

My stomach twists like someone is tightening a bow in it. Yes, she means what I think she means. Roth's face flashes through my head, my father's, and finally the four who died, whose faces are memorialized in bronze at the center of town. *My family let the earth take them.*

I lean away from her and stand up, steady myself on the wall; I'm not sure if it's the darkness or the knowledge that's making me dizzy.

"Will?" she says, and my name sounds exotic on her lips.

"Your family caused that cave-in?" I ask. My tongue feels thick.

"Yes. But *I* didn't do it," Ennor says quickly. "I had nothing to do with it. Are you angry?" She sounds almost desperate as I move to duck through the doorway. "Why are you angry?"

I'm trying not to yell, but my voice is loud, bounces off the walls. "Because people *died*, Ennor! My father could have died."

"My family protected him—"

"So I'm supposed to think it's okay? What did the other miners do that was so disrespectful they deserved to die?" My voice is high, almost panicked.

"They killed us!" Ennor says, and she *is* yelling—her voice echoes up, shoots through the rock the same way her knocking does. "They blew up the mountain, killed a thousand years in seconds. They murdered the earth that had given them so much with explosives and fire. My family had to fight back!"

I freeze. When the mine is dried up and dead, they blow the "overburden"—the mountain itself—so they can excavate the little bit that's left.

"They killed my father's brothers and sisters. Four of them. So he took four miners. But it wasn't me, Will," Ennor says. I wonder how she looks when she's sad. "It wasn't me any more than it was you who killed my people."

"It was still your kind."

"And it was still your kind."

"I'm not like them," I say, though I feel ashamed as I

say it. They're good people, they're my father's people. I should be so lucky, to be like them, to be like my father. "They aren't evil, Ennor."

"Maybe we're more like each other than them."

I press my lips together, start to agree, but I can't get over the image of my father walking out of the mine. Five days without food made him look gaunt, he was weak; Roth's head was covered in dried blood. They were the lucky ones. I think about the cry of relief and sadness and joy from my mother's lips as she ran to him. All because of the Knockers.

I can't escape the image just yet. I duck through the doorway and go back to my station.

Ennor is no more responsible for killing miners than I am for killing Knockers. I know that. It takes a few days for my surprise and horror to fade, though, for me to stop wondering what would happen if I made her terribly angry, for me to stop cringing when I see miners spit onto the mine floor—does that count as disrespectful? Is it only a life for a life, or are the Knockers less tolerant now? I feel like a child torn between two parents—the miners, yanking me in one direction, and Ennor, yanking me in the other. I'm not sure if I'm more like either. I'm not sure what I should do.

But I know this much, at least—I don't want Ennor to be mad at me. Not because she's a Knocker, not because

I'm a miner, but because she's my friend. I don't want to stop talking to her over something that happened more than a decade ago. So I buy her flowers.

It is very, very difficult to sneak a bouquet of roses, even a small one, into a coal mine. I shove them down my shirt and wince, wishing I'd purchased the de-thorned variety. I walk with a strange step as I try to keep the water dripping from the stems from running down my pant leg. The sound of the pink-and-white cellophane the grocery store wrapped the flowers in is thankfully masked by the fans in the retreaters' area. I snake around the pillars and finally duck into our cavern for the first time since we fought.

"I brought you something," I say as I enter, and am suddenly painfully aware of how ridiculous I sound. I feel like I did in high school, showing up to pick up my prom date: dressed strangely and like my tongue is too heavy for my mouth. I don't hear her, and my helmet light is still on—I don't like it; it feels like I'm exposing something sacred. I reach up and turn it off as I speak again. "Ennor? I'm sorry I left."

Silence. I sigh, look down. Maybe her temper takes longer to settle than mine. Maybe I should even be afraid that I've disrespected her, and the mine could close in on me. I'm not, though. I don't think Ennor would hurt me, any more than I would hurt her. I kneel to place the flowers on the ground, an offering that hopefully she'll find later—

Her hand slides down my forearm. I slowly rise. She

reaches for the bouquet in my hands; the cellophane wrapping crinkles in response.

"Flowers," she says as if it's a prayer. "Like you have above."

"Yes."

She takes the bouquet, and for a moment, only the quiet crackling of the cellophane tells me where she is.

"They're exactly like my mother told me about. Before she died."

"Your mother is gone?" I ask. I hear the delicate sound of her touching the rose petals one by one.

"I barely knew her. She wasn't like the rest of my family. She was like you."

"A miner?"

"A human." Ennor's voice drops to a whisper. "I think it's her blood that makes me sometimes wonder about the above." She says "above" like it's another world, and I suppose it is, just as much as the mine is another world to me.

There is a long silence.

"I'm sorry your father was trapped," Ennor says. "I'm sorry people died on both sides." She sounds tiny, fragile.

I exhale; it feels like someone has lifted something heavy off my chest. "I'm sorry, too. He's gone now. He died two years ago."

"How?"

"Black lung." The name of the sickness always sounded

like a pirate ship to me when I was little—back when I imagined the miners as magicians. The magicians and pirates battled over the coal, and in my games, the magicians always won. In real life, the pirates are the coal dust, years of it, building up and taking over until you can't breathe. An ally turned murderer that spent eleven long years killing my father. I slide down the cavern wall to sit.

The cellophane crinkles; she's growing closer—yet I still jump a little when she slides down next to me. She sighs, places her hand—wet from the bouquet—in mine. I feel her shifting and suddenly she's leaning against my shoulder. Her hair spills down; I can just barely feel it through my work clothes. I want to touch it, I want to touch her face and imagine what the curves of her cheeks look like. She'd do it to me—she's never afraid to touch me.

I wonder if it's because she can see here, where I'm blind.

For weeks, things are better. Things are wonderful, even. Ennor and I share secrets, but we also play games, we make up stories, we are ridiculous and happy and I miss her when I'm gone. I miss someone I've never even seen, and I don't care that that's strange. I finish work in record time; I get more done in a day than I used to get done in a week because I want to spend every extra moment with her.

And for the first time, I don't hate being a miner. Maybe being a miner is a fair price to pay for being with her.

"You seem to be in better spirits lately," Roth tells me one morning, slapping me on the back as I pull my work clothes out of my locker. Both of us are already covered in a fine layer of coal dust, even though we haven't been inside yet. It was the same way with my dad—I used to think it hid in his skin, coaxed out only with time, showers, and occasionally Vaseline to get it out of the corners of his eyes.

"I guess," I say, shrugging and trying not to smile—it'll only lead to more questions.

"Keep it up, whoever she is," Roth says, eyes sparkling like diamonds in the middle of his dusty face. "She's good for you. And she makes you a better miner, like your mama did for your daddy."

Ah, so that's why he's looking at me so closely—like he's trying to see underneath my skin. Trying to see if somewhere deep under there is the miner and the man my father was. The gold deep at the core. I still don't think it's there—in fact, spending time with Ennor has made me more certain than ever that my core is different. I look away, unable to take his eyes on mine any longer.

Roth sighs, then buckles his helmet. "It was a good mine. Took nice care of us. I always get a bit teary, seeing them go," he says.

"Go?" I ask, freezing with my helmet half latched.

"The retreaters are knocking out the last few pillars today. We start the new mine tomorrow. It's been on the calendar since the first of the month," Roth says, eyebrows raised. "Did you not see it?"

"I guess I wasn't paying attention," I say, trying to control the panic in my voice. I have to warn Ennor. She could die. I take a step away, and my foot feels heavy, weight suddenly compounds on my shoulders.

If I tell her, she'll tell her family. And they could bring the mine down on us. On me, on Roth, on the guys I graduated with. My hands shake as I inhale—there's no weighing the possibilities in my mind, there's only war, there's only helplessness. I close my eyes. There's no one who knows about her, no one who can tell me what to do, no one who can tell me which set of lives is more important.

Dad, I think as I listen to Roth humming an old mining tune. *Help. What would you do?*

As soon as I ask it, I know—so quickly that I wonder if the answer came from my father or my heart. Maybe it was both.

I grab for Ennor's hands when I enter the cavern—I know where they'll be, though I can't explain how.

"I came to warn you. They're going to blow the mountain."

Ennor doesn't move; I wait for the sound of her breath to quicken in the darkness.

But there is nothing, there's silence and the sound of her heart beating that I can somehow hear in the still. Or maybe it's my heart—I can't tell.

"Ennor? They're closing the mine. They're going to blow the mountain to get the rest of the coal. You and your family have to leave."

"I heard you. We already knew. My family heard other miners talking. I came to warn *you*. They're going to let the earth take them."

Her words are soft, gentle even. She slides her hands from my palms up my forearms. At first I think she's calm, but then I feel it—a slight, uneven tremble.

"How long do we have to get out?" I whisper.

"Not long."

I nod, and I mean to turn and run back to Roth. Instead I stand still—this time it isn't my feet weighing me down, it's something deeper, something that slinks around my heart and lungs. I inch my arms forward and then wrap them around Ennor, gently at first, then harder, till I realize I'm clutching her and, even more surprising, she's clutching me.

"Will I see you again?" I finally ask. I feel her chin tilt up and know she's looking at me, but it doesn't bother me anymore that I can't see her eyes.

"I don't know," she answers. "I can't stop being a Knocker, and you can't stop being a miner."

"You're only half a Knocker," I remind her. "Maybe you can leave."

"You're only half a miner," she answers. "The rest of

you belongs somewhere else."

She steps back and we release each other; I stand staring into the black, knowing she's watching me, certain that I see her despite the lack of light. "You've got to go," she says, inhaling.

I've got to save the other miners, my father's people. I focus on that, hold an image of my father in my head, think about him saving the others so long ago. I hope I'm like him.

I run out of the cavern, back toward Roth.

I fly through the ballroom—some of the retreaters see me and try to call out, but I ignore them. Roth, I have to find Roth. He and the other miners are almost done removing equipment when I reach them. I don't know what to say—I don't know what to think, even. When I reach Roth, I choke on air but force words out despite the burning in my lungs.

"We have to get out," I hack.

"What?" Roth asks, putting his hands on my shoulders and looking concerned.

"Now. There's going to be a cave-in—we'll get covered up."

"A cave-in? How do you know?" Roth asks, eyes focusing on me carefully, like he's trying to decide if I'm drunk.

What can I say? That a faery girl in a mine warned me?

"You have to trust me," I say, and even as I do, I suspect

he won't. He barely knows me. He knew my father. *Trust me like you would trust him, please, Roth.* I stand up straight, try my best to look like him, try to channel the intensity of my father's eyes into mine.

"All right," Roth says; I can tell he thinks I may be crazy, but he reaches for his radio.

In an instant, the mine changes. People abandon jobs, run, jump onto the carts and zip past us, supervisors driving like they're racing. No one jokes in mines, and no one would doubt Roth's word for a moment. People are running, running—

A blast, a sound that sends shock waves through the mine. The retreat miners would never do this while there are still miners in here. Words clutter Roth's radio—*accident, explosion, get out.*

Rumbling echoes through the walls, ceilings, floors; it's starting.

I have to be the last to go—if I'm here, maybe Ennor will make her family wait. She won't let me die, she won't let me get trapped in the dark, she knows I'm afraid of the dark—

No, I'm not, I argue with myself as I realize something: it's not the dark I'm afraid of anymore. It's failing the others. *It's failing my father by not being like him.*

I stiffen my knees, like doing so will keep the ground below and the earth above from touching, from crushing me.

"Get on!" Roth shouts at me, shoving my shoulder.

"I want to know everyone's out!" I shout back, but Roth isn't really listening—he's too preoccupied with yelling into the radio, watching carts fly past, counting people. He nods and leaps onto a cart; another miner grabs a passenger seat—everyone is ahead of us now, everyone is on their way out. I jump onto the back of the cart and we take off, speeding like never before.

Dust blinds me, settles in my throat until it feels like I'm breathing in sand. Just as we start to see light ahead, a rock hits the front of the cart; Roth slams the wheel to one side, lifting the wheels off the ground. It's only for a moment, but it's enough to throw me off balance—I hit the mine floor. I taste blood.

Rocks tumble down behind me, the tongue of the earth pressing me against the roof of its mouth, waiting to bite, to tear, to swallow me. I scramble to my feet and run toward the brake lights of Roth's cart; they look like glowing red eyes in the distance. I'm not going to make it. The world is getting smaller and my feet clumsier. *Am I running?* I can't tell—everything is hot and everything is getting blacker.

Maybe it's because it's getting darker that I feel her.

Her fingers slip over my wrist and for a moment, a fleeting moment, I see Ennor. Not her face, not her form, even, but her hair. It flicks behind her as she runs, over the stones like they're grass. She pulls me along, weaving around rocks that rain from the ceiling.

She halts; I stumble past her. Her hair spins around her face, obscuring it. I turn to her and she throws both hands out, slams them against my chest with strength like the earth itself. I fly backward, falling, tripping, sailing, until I slam onto my back at the cave's entrance. The air leaves my lungs, I'm choking, but I feel hands on me, strong hands, men's hands, the miners tugging me to safety.

The light burns my eyes, forcing me to close them. I feel dizzy, disoriented, I hear my name but don't understand where it's coming from or who is asking for me. The only phrase I pick up, a phrase I hold on to like it's a precious stone, is this:

Everyone's accounted for. Looks like we're okay.

They're out. Everyone is out.

But I feel like half of me is still trapped in the mine.

I am a hero.

They ask me questions: *How did you know? Are you psychic? Did you have a gut feeling?*

I tell them I can't explain it, because the truth is, I can't.

They decide it must be my father. That his spirit warned me, that he filled me, made my body warn the others. They toast him in my hospital room. Once I'm back home, I get cards from the wives and children of the men who would have been covered up if I hadn't warned them. They tell me my father would be proud. They tell me I'm more like him than I realize. They tell me I'm a miner to the core.

Then they start asking when I'll come back to work, they start saying I'm their lucky charm, that they need me there in the mine. And I wonder if things would change if I was part of it—if I'd be a miner through and through instead of a hero's boy pretending.

No. I'm not a miner. And I've lived up to my father, I've respected his work, I've helped his people. And now I'm moving on—maybe forever. But even if I never come back, I'll be free. I'll be happy.

I'm not afraid anymore.

When you're used to the inside of a mine, even the dead of night seems brightly lit—the moon, the stars, they all cast bright blue light on the world. I wonder if this sort of light would hurt Ennor.

The mine entrance is a wall of rock, and there are warning signs everywhere—in front of the entrance, on the rocks, by the guardhouse. I approach the entrance and put my hands on the stone. The dust curls like smoke at my touch.

I don't know what to say—talking to Ennor in the darkness was one thing. She felt real there. Out here, where everything is lit and my body aches, she seems imaginary again.

But she was not, she couldn't be, because if she weren't real, I wouldn't be certain that I am not a miner. I wouldn't be certain that I have to leave this place, that I have to stop being a coward about the world outside of Middleview. I wouldn't feel so certain that someone else knows what it's like to be trapped.

I ease myself to my knees.

"Ennor," I say; her name sounds loud in the night. I feel a little like I'm talking to a rock. No, I feel a *lot* like I'm talking to a rock. I suppose before I was talking to darkness, but I knew she was there. I could sense her, feel her.

And so I close my eyes.

"Ennor?" I say her name, and it feels more familiar on my tongue now that the world is gone.

There's a long pause, filled with crickets and stars.

"Will."

I don't know where her voice is coming from; it feels like it's from everywhere, like it's filling, warming my heart and lungs. I grin like a child, extend my hand just like I would have in the cavern, desperate for her to take it.

She doesn't.

"You're leaving," she says, voice low.

I inhale, drop my hand; the grin fades, but the longing for her touch intensifies. "Yes," I admit. I wait a long time to speak again, and it's only when the words leave my mouth that I realize how true they are. "I want you to come with me."

"But I'm a Knocker."

"Only half."

"Which half is it?" she asks, toying with the words.

"You're the only one who knows that," I answer. I feel her fingers, slight and smooth, brush the tips of mine.

She grows closer, and I squeeze my eyes shut to keep myself from opening them. I feel her breath on my cheeks, I feel her fingers wind around mine, and she presses against me. There are tears on her face, but she's nodding, nodding slowly. She pulls her face back and rises, pulls me up with her—I wince as I put weight on my bad leg. We're still, and I know that she's waiting for me to open my eyes. So I do.

She is perfect where the light is.

Tessa Gratton

This Was Ophelia

In the darkness, I go mad.

It isn't the heartrending, barefoot madness allowed to my sex, where I wander with bedraggled hair and dying flowers, wailing riddles of loss. My madness is the fierce melancholy of longing. It causes me to sigh through dinner parties and embroider hidden words onto bedclothes intended for part of my dowry. Mother offers excuses when I gaze out the window wishing to run past the horizon instead of making entertaining conversation; and when I don't demur over tea but laugh at Colonel Chapman's opinion, Daddy explains that my brother has always encouraged me too much.

But the sun sets. I strike a match and by candlelight don a tight suit of my brother's. My breasts are easy to bind and I've little in the way of hips, as is best for the high-waisted fashions of New York. The vest cuts a lovely line under my black jacket, and pressed slacks I've only had to mend once fall perfectly hemmed to the shine of my borrowed shoes. I've stuffed them with cut-up stockings. Atop it all is a hat to hide my curls, though they're short, anyway, to better show off choker necklaces and feathered headbands popular on women these days. And I wear gloves, of course, always gloves to disguise the delicate state of my fingers.

I sneak into Daddy's library for a pocketful of cigars and five dollars from the hollow *Book of Days*. Plenty of cash for a single night's escapades.

In the clubs nobody suspects who I am, because I'm tall enough, handsome enough, and my smoke is more expensive than theirs. I say that I'm a Polonius, let them guess I'm Lars or some visiting cousin. "Call me O," I say.

"As in Osric?" asks a young man with a scarlet tie.

"As in Oliver?" guesses another with a swirl of his brandy.

I bare my teeth at them around my slim black cigar. Slowly, I pull it from my mouth and let smoke trickle through my teeth. "As in . . ." I lean toward them. "Ohhh . . ." I moan in a low voice.

They laugh and swoon, and from then on at Club Rose I'm called "Oh," or "Oh, oh, oh!" or sometimes they buy me a drink and suggest other words the initial could represent.

I go once a week when I'm feeling mad, at midnight, to carouse with young gentlemen eager to ignore their home lives or futures or responsibilities, to dance with finely dressed but more common women and listen to the latest Rose. I wonder, sometimes, what it would be like to arrive in a dress with my curls slicked to my cheeks and red on my lips. But one of these dandies from uptown might someday be my husband, and wouldn't that crimp the engagement negotiations?

It's late autumn, one in the morning. I've been here for nearly two hours, because it is oh-so-much easier to escape as winter approaches and the sun sets earlier, when the cold wind from Canada blows into the city, chasing upright citizens inside to fires and family. I can tuck my hat lower, wear a heavier jacket, and no one wonders why I hide my face while I wait at the cabstand two blocks from my family's townhome.

I sit swiveling on a bar stool, my back to the liquor in order to watch Rose sing a song about steamy first kisses. A young man all in black, from his tie to his gloves, slides next to me and orders a bourbon and ice. He leans his elbows onto the bar, shoulder near mine, and opens a black-lacquered cigarette case. "Light?" he asks, and I lazily oblige without taking my eyes from Rose.

Her dress is the deep color of raw emeralds, with black fringe swaying as she twists her hips. I'm thinking how good she'd look with a tie around her neck when my neighbor asks, "What's her name?"

I give him a poisonous glance. "Rose."

He's beautiful, though, and instead of curling my mouth I'm caught in a stare. All that black makes his skin glow in a ghostly fashion and his wavy hair falls over his forehead without wax to make it shine or slick back. Worst of all, I know him. Halden King, the son of our glorious mayor who died only five months ago.

"I've not been here this semester," he says quietly, "and the last singer was Rose, only with darker skin and smaller tits."

I take a drag to hide my blush. "They're always Rose," I say too harshly. The Roses are my favorite thing about this place, why I picked it over the myriad other downtown nightclubs. The patrons understand some kind of anonymity.

"Why?" Hal takes the tumbler that Tio—the barkeeper—offers.

"They're here for the pleasure of money and art— names don't matter."

"I wish that were true." He downs half his drink, and the ice clinks hard against the glass.

Leaning nearer to him, I say, "I'll call you anything you want tonight."

He studies me, eyes lingering on my mouth as I smile around my cigar. So long I feel a jerk of panic that he sees through my disguise. "Sir," he murmurs, close enough I notice the strangely spicy smell of his dark cigarette. "You already know who I am."

"True." My heart pounds and I can't decide if I want him flirting with me because he knows what I am or because he doesn't. "I'm O."

"Oh," Hal King says, shaping his mouth around it. He pops his tongue so a ring of smoke escapes.

I laugh, forgetting to modulate my voice, but Hal doesn't seem to notice how girlish it is. As Rose and the piano pick up, I stand and weave my way toward the dance floor. A girl named Patrice holds out her hand and I catch it. I spin her into the crowd and we leap into the fast fox-trot. She grins and I mirror it, teasingly keeping our hips apart.

Every time I glance toward the bar, Hal is watching me.

At song's end, I kiss Patrice at the corner of her mouth, and Hal is there, standing beside the parquet dance floor with a tumbler in each hand. "Join me," he says, and I do, throwing my arm around his shoulders. His free hand snakes around my waist and blood rushes my ears.

I've never been so lost in laughing and alcohol and hot, delicious conversation! Hal and I take over a table, and he tells me stories about his late father, about his mother and uncle who married her a mere month past the elder Mr.

King's death. Hal laments into his drink, and I moan and cry protest at the right moments, leaning in to cuss a wild streak about his obviously treacherous uncle. I whisper to him that my father's said everyone expects Hal's uncle to run in the next year's election, and with Mrs. King's support he'll get in. Hissing, Hal slumps back into the booth. I gasp at his disheveled beauty and tell him I choose to come here because here I can be whoever I wish, not the person my parents expect.

"We can do anything here, Hal," I say, and he immediately looks at my mouth.

"Brother," he murmurs, "you make me believe it."

I can't breathe, but Tio yells out last call. Like Cinderella I leap up. "I've got to go!"

Hal catches my wrist. "Come back tomorrow."

Two nights in a row is a thing I've never done. It's too likely Daddy will notice I'm gone, too dangerous to think a cab driver would remember me.

But I say, "Tomorrow."

Our second night together is more lavish and desperate than the first. Hal arranges a private booth and our own bottle of sixteen-year-old whiskey. Between her sets, Rose joins us, purring lyrics into my ear to make me blush because Hal loves it so. "It makes you seem like a sixteen-year-old virgin," he says, caressing one long, bare finger down my jaw. "Do you even have a beard yet, O?"

I want to press my face to his and whisper my secret. "You've not so much beard yourself, my prince," I say.

He barks a laugh. "King," he corrects.

"But your father was the king, so. My prince."

Rose interrupts, "You're both such pups!" and she kisses us full on the mouths, one after the other.

As she kisses Hal, his knee presses into mine under the table. It thrills me into knocking my tumbler too hard against the wood as I suddenly set it down.

When Rose leaves for her next song, I slide along the round booth and say to Hal, whose eyes are bright and lips swollen, "Let's get out of here."

"And go where?" He shoots the last of his whiskey.

I only smile and hand him his soft black gloves.

Outside it's filthy dark and a wet, cold wind cuts under my collar. I dash across the street, loving how easy it is to run with no skirt to fight, no delicate slippers that will ruin in rain. Hal comes after, ducking with me between an old boardinghouse and a shut-down corner pub. The damp street cobbles glint like strings of black pearls in the moonlight. There's a slim public garden tucked on the other side of the block, which I discovered last month when I stumbled out of a cab that dropped me off in the wrong place.

I push through the creaky gate into layers of fallen leaves. A satyr fountain stands silent on the small lawn, spilling no water from its pursed mouth.

"O, this is gorgeous," Hal says in a hushed tone. "It's like the whole city vanished outside."

Emboldened by the moon, the full, madness-approving moon, I grab his hand and turn him under my arm into a waltz. It's no easy feat from my shorter stature, but he smiles and falls into the woman's steps, hand firm on my shoulder.

We dance around the satyr, to the music of the wind and the rhythm of the blood in my ears.

"O," he whispers as we slow.

I put my hands on his face and kiss him. At first it's only a hard press of lips, his cold nose shocking beside mine. Then Hal grabs the lapels of my jacket. He drags me onto my toes and opens his mouth under mine.

It is more than a kiss. I spill out of myself, and the garden spins in dizzy circles. I strip my gloves off and dig my fingers into his hair. As he kisses me, I can feel the muscles of his jaw stretch and contract beneath my thumbs.

A moan grows out of my throat as he runs his mouth down my neck, and his hands sink to my hips. One finger flips aside my jacket and hooks around the belt on my hips.

I tear away.

The violent shove trips me and I land on the cold, frosty grass, panting. I'm a girl! I cover my burning mouth. One more inch and he'd know it, too. Shaking, I stare up at him. Against the moon, Hal is a dark ghost.

"O?" he whispers, crouching before me.

"Hal." I reach out and touch his bottom lip with a bare finger. My gloves are discarded somewhere like so many dead leaves.

"You've never been kissed before," he guesses, his voice low and full of something I don't understand.

I snatch back my hand. "Was it so bad?"

But Hal smiles. "No, kitten, it made me feel like I'd never been kissed before, either."

My fingers hover over my own mouth, and as he watches me the garden opens up. I can see the entire galaxy of stars, of lives and loves, of families and cities and graveyards, of forests and foreign mountains, the oceans and plains.

And here is Halden King in the center of it all. My center.

No one but my brother notices the shift in my daylight melancholy. Instead of merely being distracted, I'm afflicted by smiles at inappropriate moments, prone to fewer snide observations, and given to sighing happily when Daddy plays a new ragtime record after supper Sunday night. The music is so delightful, my memories of Hal so consuming, I pull Lars to his feet to dance with me. My serious brother manages to enjoy himself, afterward chasing me to my bedroom. He follows me inside and bars the door with his body.

"Phe, what has gotten into you?"

I flit about, unclipping my hair and smiling over my shoulder, wishing I could tell him. Instead I say, "Life, brother! My life is wonderful."

He narrows his eyes, but I see the very moment he decides he'd rather have me happy even if I keep the reason for it a secret. The understanding lifts his eyebrows just a tick. My brother shakes his head, sits on my bed with his legs stretched out over the quilt, and asks me to read to him from whatever novel I've lately been enjoying most. It's a love story, of course, filled with passionate declarations and racing to stop boats from leaving the docks and tragic betrayal.

Lars falls asleep against the headboard before I'm through a single chapter.

Hours later, Hal escorts me home at the end of our third night. After drinking and dancing, after secret kisses in the satyr's garden. We avoid main thoroughfares, though at this time of morning no one's in our way but fellows as eager for shadows as we are—or the police.

I'm sober and cold by the time we're a block from my family's townhome, but my insides feel clean and light while my hand is in his. I walk as if my feet lift off the ground of their own accord and catch myself smiling too widely. When I pull Hal against a building, he smiles, too. The first hint of purple in the east reflects in his eyes. "I'm going back to school tomorrow."

In Ohio, I think. Wittenberg University, where his mother's father endowed several scholarships for farmers' sons as he himself had once been. "So far."

"You must be going to university soon. Apply to Wittenberg."

I smile bitterly. My brother goes next year, but me? "My father would never."

Hal kisses me softly. "I'll have to come home more often, then."

What are you doing? I want to cry—and I don't know if my desperate question should be addressed to him or to myself. Hal is the heir to an estate that might as well be a kingdom and that comes with responsibilities like marriage. How can he speak as though he and I have any future?

A tiny voice reminds me that he could marry me, but the thought pricks my eyes with tears. I don't want to be his dress-wearing, child-bearing hostess-wife. I want this! Suits and dark gardens, wild kisses that I can choose, that I can initiate. This mad power.

"Don't cry, O." Hal brushes my eyelashes.

If only I could explain the different ways men look at me when they believe I'm one of them.

Instead I say, "I've never felt this way. Don't go." I put force into my voice. I square my shoulders. I am strong.

"God," he breathes. "If anybody found us now, like this"—his fingers slide behind my ears—"they'd murder us."

I kiss him, jerk him against me. Into his ear, I order him, "Write to me, Hal King. Tell me everything there is to know about the man I'm in love with."

My head tingles with my own boldness, my sudden declaration.

"It's been a whole life in three nights," he says, putting his arms around me. I fold my own arms over my breasts, trapping them between us, hiding my truth.

It's mid-November, two weeks since my Hal has been back at school, when Mrs. Shay brings the post into the sitting room at teatime. She hands Daddy several letters, Mother her Parisian fashion magazine, and Lars two letters: one with the scrawling hand of his friend Markham, and the other smaller and blue. The address reads *Mr. Polonius, the Younger.* With a curious frown, he doesn't wait for the silver opener but slides his finger under the flap instead. It's one sheet, folded in half, and from the settee beside him I can't see enough to recognize the writing.

But Lars's frown only becomes more pronounced, so much so that Mother asks, "Whatever is the matter, dear?"

"'Doubt thou the stars are fire; doubt that the sun doth move; doubt truth to be a liar; but never doubt I love,'" my brother reads. "It's a love letter."

"Oh, God!" I snatch for it, but Lars tucks it against his chest.

"Ophelia?" Daddy stands up to tower over me.

I bite my bottom lip. "It's for me."

Mother sips her tea, lifting the china slowly and setting it back with just as much care. We all wait for her, though I suspect I'm the only one whose heart is melting down into her stomach. She says, "Who is it from, Lars?"

"There are only initials. H and K."

My hand trembles as I hold it out, palm up. I'll not beg.

"Wait." Daddy gently touches my hair. "Darling, we want your happiness. Tell us this boy is a suitor, tell us who and perhaps we'll let you write back."

The fire crackles behind me, the only sound but for my dying, rushing blood.

"H and K," Mother says. Her gaze scours me, appraising me as she would the wardrobe of her best friend and rival, Mrs. Tealy.

Lars unfolds the letter again, reads silently over it. "If he wrote it himself, he's educated. A poet, but no poor artist. 'Thine evermore, whilst this machine is to him, H.K.' That machine his body?" My brother pouts his mouth as he ponders the mystery of poetry, never his forte.

"Oh, please," I say, flapping my hand. "It's meant for me, not all my family!"

"Why would he send it to Lars?" Daddy asks.

My voice is too shrill. "Perhaps because he thought my brother could be trusted to secretly pass love notes between us."

Hurt jerks Lars's brow low, but I can't stand it any

longer. "Hal King. It's from Hal King," I say, balling my fists into my dress. I'm done for. Doomed. I shut my eyes and wish for the full moonlight to transform my face and body, for the sun to set forever.

But silence reigns in our cozy sitting room. I peel my eyes open and look at my family: Lars is surprised but still hurt, Daddy wears a slowly dawning expression of glee, and Mother is pensive, as if she's never seen me before.

I use their distraction to take the letter from Lars's limp fingers and flee to my bedroom.

There's never any doubt I'll be given permission to write back. He's too rich to ignore. My only requirement to my parents is that the letters be private. Anything they might've felt about propriety was ditched in favor of dreaming that their daughter might marry into the powerful King family. It isn't that we aren't well-off enough, for Daddy's father and grandfather both garnered huge wealth shipping along the first railroad out West, and our name has been a part of New York's rosters for nearly two hundred years. But even at that, Poloniuses are always second-in-command. A mayor's right hand or the clerk to the state's governor. Kings don't marry subordinates no matter how rich or well bred.

Until now, is the promise whispering in my parents' dreams.

I write to Hal. Oh, do I write to him. I tell him

everything there is to know about me, only edited to keep out details such as that the specific moment I realized I preferred Tennyson and the sharp wit of Mark Twain came when I happened to be embroidering. I write about my own dreams: traveling and studying, dancing in Paris and climbing the Pyramids in Egypt, that I'd even like to learn to read the ancient pictographs. Wouldn't it be lovely, H, to write these letters in complicated hieroglyphics? Perhaps we will make our own language, my prince.

He writes back with poetry: long, complicated poems about the nature of life and what comes after death, on mankind and fear and what makes us into cowards or brave men. I repeat them to myself over and again, until I can recite them from memory. I write, What will we do, my prince? How will we live and love? And Hal King replies, We love beyond all things, beyond material considerations.

Beyond our bodies and our sex? I ask.

I love you for your poetry, and for your mouth and your eyes. All these human bodies come with mouths and eyes. But few men I have known, no, nor women, neither, have had in them such poetry as you.

For my mouth and eyes, for my poetry.

And as weeks pass, I slowly begin to share some lines of our poetry with Lars, for he delights in puzzles and rambling philosophy. He knows I forgive him, though I can't quite say it in case he decides to pay too much attention to me when the sun sets.

For yes, I still go out. I put on my suit and shiny shoes, button up that tight vest, and knot the slim blue tie at my throat. I walk alone through the streets with a cigar, stopping sometimes at a club, but mostly roaming the darkness, my coat pulled to my chin, hat low. Ice and snow make barricades, but they are no more fierce than the barricades tightening around me as every night passes. As it grows nearer to Christmas, when I know Hal will come home, and what will happen when I see him again?

On December 13th, Daddy comes in to dinner with a letter in hand. The green wax seal is broken, and he waves it triumphantly. "I have heard from Charles King. He and his wife, Gertrude, will be joining us for the solstice night dinner to discuss the possible engagement between our daughter and their son."

My skin bursts into a rage of tingling, and my hands are frozen in my lap. I blink quickly, as if to make up for being unable to move the rest of my body, as Mother exclaims, "Wondrous!" in a rare show of enthusiasm.

Lars leans over to me, touching my elbow. "Phe? Aren't you happy?"

"Oh, yes," I whisper. In my evening dress I am soft and drooping, unable to stop the inevitable.

The night of my downfall, I take care as I put on the gown Mother commissioned in a whirlwind of fittings. The low ribbon waist suits my hipless body, and the overdress is beaded in a white-on-white floral pattern. White makes my skin shine and my dark eyes bright. I mold every curl precisely and put dark pink paint on my lips. In my mirror, I am unusually beautiful, but sad. Through my eastern-facing window, I see the half-moon rise behind the city, though the sun hasn't yet set.

Lars arrives to escort me into the formal dining room, tall and straight in a suit like I should be wearing. "Ophelia," he says, pausing just before we enter. He smiles his vague but reassuring smile. "Halden is come with his parents."

Horror makes my skin feel as though it's peeling away. I try to put my hands on my face, as if I could hide the femininity with only my fingers. But Lars catches my wrists gently, folding them together. "What's wrong?"

"I'm not—not prepared to see him! Why didn't I know?"

"Mother said he even surprised his parents by racing home early."

"God help me."

He frowns. "Don't do anything you don't wish to do. Only be true to yourself."

"Oh, Lars," I say, overwhelmed by the injustice in his words. There is no choice now.

Together we go in, and there he is. Hal King in a suit blacker than night, but a moon-silver tie hangs from his neck, tacked down with a pink-ruby pin. His mouth betrays his discomfort, and I can only imagine how strange it is for him—to have written to a son but be suddenly thrust upon a daughter. His chin lifts as we enter, as all the men stand from the table for me.

Mrs. King swirls around the table to catch my hands in hers, which are covered by long, silky white gloves up past her elbows. "My dear, we are so thrilled to have found such a beautiful cure to our son's melancholy."

I force a smile, but I see behind her that Hal glances back and forth between Lars and me, and his face falls by increments into a glower.

His uncle Charles is wide, with a sash of scarlet striping him from shoulder to hip. He says to Daddy, "Yes, yes, what an occasion!"

Hal bows coldly over one of my hands when his mother offers it. I refrain from speaking, hoping my horror will be taken for propriety, for shyness.

We sit, all seven of us, and it is easy to remain silent as the men, but for Hal, converse on the state of the city, and Mrs. King and Mother trade hair care secrets. Lars attempts to engage Hal twice, but my prince puts him off with quiet, convoluted answers that border on rudeness. I catch him watching me, but when I lift my chin he shakes his head, refusing to truly see.

And how can I blame him?

He came here expecting the agony of flirting with me, while longing for my brother. Instead, his is the agony of confusion, of not belonging. I recognize the madness hiding in his eyes, for it is a disease I know intimately.

Once near the end of the meal I say to him, "My father has excellent cigars, and I know you enjoy such things." As if I want to hint at our secret, as if I want him to understand.

He stares at me and sips his wine—his only glass, which he has nursed the last hour.

Daddy, who has somehow moved his chair nearer to Charles King's, says, "We'll retire to the study to taste them, straight from my cousin's in South Carolina. And I've some lovely brandy to match."

Hal's eyes are on Lars as my brother folds his napkin to stand. Lars dislikes smoking, but he puts his long hand onto Hal's shoulder with a polite smile, leading my prince out. Hal's face is tight, and I can guess he's panicking.

I am, too. I didn't mean to suggest they leave us.

Mother and Mrs. King lean back in their seats, glad to have the men gone, and I slouch, wanting to put my head on the table, to sigh out all my sorrow. "May I go outside, Mother?" I ask, interrupting her as she begins to discuss her longing for the springtime with its allowance for outrageous hats.

She waves her hand, and Mrs. King smiles with sympathy. "Poor dear, you must be overwhelmed. I know how strange my Hal can be, but he never lies, not with his poetry. He loves you."

I nearly choke on my thanks.

✦ ✦ ✦

Our garden is small and trapped between high stone walls. The hedges are trimmed and evergreen yew, with two iron benches facing each other across a centerpiece of brown rosebushes. There is a birdbath carved of marble, and the water is frozen at the edges. I come out here every morning to break the ice until it's too thick, so the cardinals can drink.

I arrive, and Hal is already there. His hands grip the birdbath and he hunches over it. I think, *We both fled to the garden. To the nighttime.* Looking up, I spot the half-moon between the roof of our house and the neighbors'. Its light shines purely in a cloudless sky.

Taking a long breath, I cross the frosted, dead grass in my thin slippers. They soak through, and I shiver from the freezing wind on my ankles. I've come out in a wool wrap, but this dress—this dress!

"Hal," I say in my low voice, and he spins around.

"O."

He peers through the darkness, but I know the moon is on my face. The face he knows, but painted like a woman's. My lips must be as dark as cherries. "What is going on?" he hisses.

Ignoring my cold toes and the layers of skirt around my calves, I stride forward. I grab his lapels in my fists and I drag myself up to kiss him before he can protest.

I open my mouth, I invite him in, and for one brief eternity Hal kisses me back. He tastes me, and I moan into him, I pull at him. His hands find my waist, silk against my ribs, the soft shape of me under that gown, and I am free. I'm kissing him hard, because I choose to, like a man, but his hands are on my own body, pressing into my hips, without thick layers binding me into a false shape, without a boundary between us, hiding me, disguising what I am.

I don't need my suit to be O, not when I'm kissing him.

The moment I realize it, Hal King tears away.

"Ophelia." My name is like a curse when he says it.

"Hal. Oh, God, Hal." I flicker my fingers in the cold air, wanting to bury them again in his jacket, in his hair. To touch him.

Laughing once, and then again, he covers his face. "You're a girl."

"A girl with a mouth, with eyes and—and poetry, Hal."

He spins away in an antic dance. "You'll throw my words back at me."

"All men and women have those things, you said. What you love transcends sex."

"God! I don't want—I'm not—" Hal shakes his head.

I go to him, to prove what I'm saying. To show him I'm O. He loves me.

The wool wrap is heavy on my shoulders, and I imagine it a coat, I take shallow breaths as though my chest were bound. Grabbing his head in both hands, I say as fiercely as I can, "Everything I was those nights, I can be again. I am. The moon is up and all I need is my jacket and hat, Hal."

He circles my wrists and pulls my hands away. For he is all man and stronger than me. "What of when the moon is down then? You're my wife?"

"Why not?"

"I don't want to love you only at night."

The words slap across my face. I am harsh in return. "It would be better if I were a boy and you couldn't love me at all? Except in dark alleys and illegal dance clubs? This is best." Now that we're here, together, all my doubts and uncertainties and fears are gone—I know what I want.

Hal pulls at his unwaxed hair. "I can't change my desires, or I'd have stopped kissing boys a long time ago, Ophelia."

"But you did! You kissed me and you loved it."

"Don't fool yourself. You're no girl. I don't know what you are. Girls don't do what you did. You're neither."

I want to be both, I think, but I can't say that. Hal abruptly releases my wrists and storms past me into the house, taking my heart with him.

Empty and numb, I sink to the spiky, frozen grass and lie back, staring up at the moon. At the spotlight of my madness.

And I remember how, just this evening as the sun still burned in the sky and I painted this color onto my lips, the moon was up, too, and visible. It rose before sunset, paler and blending gently into the darkening blue, but still there. Still the moon.

✦ ✦ ✦

In darkness and light, in the shadows between, I go mad.

I know who I want, but I also know who I am. I remember when Hal said to me if we were caught, we'd be murdered, and he didn't care when I kissed him. If he meant it, if it was true, he would love me still, in any clothes, in any body. Because my mouth and eyes and soul are the same.

But we need time. I can't go begging to him, for he broke off marriage talks. I can't play the girl only and win him that way, but neither can I arrive at Club Rose, hoping to see him, in my brother's suit.

All I can do is figure out how to live with this madness.

I never intended for anyone to think I died. Yet I stand, on an afternoon so gray with heavy clouds it's neither day nor night, in front of my family's town house where the memorial service for Miss Ophelia Polonius is beginning.

Ice slicks the pavement and I shiver into the long, fur-lined overcoat that I stole from Father's closet three days ago before disappearing near the train station. It slipped my mind that the river rushes on the other side of the meadow, and that when I was a little girl our nanny took both Lars and me there one day. I spent that afternoon telling my brother stories about mermaids who leave their undersea homes to get feet and walk on their own, and then I begged for weeks to go back. Mother forbade it because of the homeless wanderers to be found near the trains.

It's no wonder Lars thought of the river before the trains. And I did leave my favorite silk scarf in the meadow for them to find.

I was only running away from Ophelia, but my family believes I killed myself out of distress at my ruined engagement. Over a broken heart. I shouldn't have come back here, should have lost myself in the streets and clubs as I'd intended, or used Daddy's money for a ticket to California. Yet here I am, clutching my coat, hat low, eyes down as everyone my family has ever known walks slowly up the worn marble steps.

Seeing them grieve will undo me. I'll never be able to watch Lars stand stiff and pale, surrounded by flowers. They aren't at church because of my suicide. Ophelia has been rendered unholy.

The thought does make me smile, but only a little bit.

Just before I turn away, promising myself that I'll write to Lars as soon as I'm settled someplace, I see Hal.

The top hat suits him not at all, but the long coat swings around his ankles like a cape. All that black is muted and severe in the gray light, and his lips are pressed into a line. He sweeps through the crowd and inside, and I go after.

Everyone parts for him, and my prince's path is unobstructed until he reaches the sitting room. It is draped in the darkest violet and black cloths, the windows shut and lit by candles. A portrait of me as a fifteen-year-old girl rests on an easel beside a spray of hothouse lilies.

It's Lars who blocks his way.

"Devil take your soul," my brother cries. My stolid brother—cheeks flushed and fists clenched. "You cannot be here, Halden King."

"What is this?" Hal grasps Lars's shoulder, to push him back.

"It's for you that she's here—or rather that she isn't here, you animal."

Mother calls from the back of the room, "Part them!"

My hands are on my face, and I hit the door frame for backing away so fast.

Hal releases Lars, palms up, "You can't keep me from this."

"You denied her in life, so how could you have her in death?"

Oh, my brother. Tears blur the scene and I am awhirl with sorrow. I should reveal myself here, now, and they will all be well.

But I would be trapped again, stripped and put back in my dress and feathers, caged and prettied up for the feast. I dig my fingers into my mouth to keep myself from speaking.

My whole family stands as a wall against Hal, and all the crowd of mourners pushes nearer to hear. Hal touches Lars's face, and my brother flinches away. But Hal says, his voice raw and ugly, "I loved Ophelia."

I don't know if it's because I'm weak or because I'm strong, but I push forward through the crowd. "Stop!" I say, throwing off my hat and stripping the heavy coat from my shoulders. Beneath it is my suit, my tight vest and pressed pants, my jacket and tie. I am a slim young gentleman with the face of a dead girl.

"O." Hal rushes at me faster than Lars or Daddy or Mother, none of whom know me thus.

Whispers break out, and at least one feminine shriek, as Hal throws his arms around me and kisses me in front of them all.

We are the most incredible scandal to ever blaze through the city, they say.

I won't marry him, though I love him. So Hal takes me away to Paris with his inheritance and we rent a flat, the two of us friends from school we say, in the City of Light to experience the best life has to offer.

My family never contacts me until Lars shows up in the summer, hat in hand on the steps of our building. When I greet him in my favorite new suit, which is pin-striped and the vest curves against me smoothly without my bindings, Lars squares his jaw and says, "What should I call you?"

"I'll always be your sister," I say, grasping his hand and dragging him inside to supper with us. He's uncomfortable, but trying, hunting desperately for a way to understand this puzzle. That night, Hal goes out to the theater, where a friend of ours is singing, and Lars and I sit sipping brandy on the iron balcony. From there we can see the top lights of the Eiffel Tower, and all the hazy stars behind.

"This is dangerous, Phe," he says, quite drunk so that his cheeks are blotchy.

I've loosened my tie and slouch with my head against the low back of the chair. "Lars, anything else would be wrong."

"If you would marry him, you could come home."

I purse my lips.

"Halden told me he asks you every day."

"To be a wife would lock me into one thing, and I don't know what I am, yet."

Lars reaches across the little space between us and takes my hand. He flicks a finger over the topaz cuff link Hal gave me for my birthday last month. "You're mad, is what you are," he whispers.

I open my mouth and laugh at the sky.

About the Authors

Sarah Rees Brennan is the author of the Demon's Lexicon trilogy, a series about demons, magicians, and two very troubled brothers. The first book was an ALA Top Ten Best Book and received three starred reviews. Most recently she is the author of *Unspoken*, the first in the Lynburn Legacy trilogy, a Gothic mystery with imaginary friends who turn out not to be so imaginary, and coauthor with Justine Larbalestier of *Team Human*, about a girl who isn't very impressed by vampires. She lives in Dublin, Ireland, which she uses as a base for her adventures, and she blames Diana Wynne Jones for her incurable fantasy addiction. Visit her at www.sarahreesbrennan.com.

Kate Espey was born in Kansas and moved to San Antonio, Texas, in the sixth grade. She blames her mildly morbid and blunt writing style on this sudden relocation during her crucial formative years. Unfortunately, Kate is a high school student, but she likes to distract herself by making YouTube videos and writing stories in class. Kate has more experience with murder than boys (otherwise, she would have a date for prom).

Tessa Gratton has wanted to be a paleontologist or a wizard since she was seven. She was too impatient to hunt dinosaurs but is still searching for someone to teach her magic. After traveling the world with her military family, she acquired a BA (and the important parts of an MA) in gender studies, then settled down in Kansas with her partner, her cats, and her mutant dog. Visit her at www.tessagratton.com.

Rachel Hawkins is the author of the *New York Times* bestselling Hex Hall series and *Rebel Belle*. She was born in Virginia and raised in Alabama. This means she uses words like "y'all" and "fixin'" a lot, and considers anything under sixty degrees to be borderline arctic. Before deciding to write books about kissing and fire (and sometimes kissing while on fire), Rachel taught high school English for three years, and she is still capable of teaching you *The Canterbury Tales* if you're into that kind of thing. You can visit her online at www.readingwritingrachel.blogspot.com.

Christine Johnson grew up in, moved away from, and eventually came home to Indianapolis, Indiana. She lives there with her husband and two kids in a creaky old house that is disappointingly unhaunted. Christine is the author of *Claire de Lune*, *Nocturne*, and *The Gathering Dark*. You can visit her online at www.christinejohnsonbooks.com.

Valerie Kemp is an award-winning independent filmmaker from Michigan. She has been creating stories ever since she first learned how to write. After challenging herself to turn a too-complex screenplay idea into a novel, she fell head over heels in love with writing YA. Valerie loves to travel, and when not writing screenplays or novels, she can be found shooting music videos, reading voraciously, and possibly hanging out in foreign country. You can visit her online at www.valeriekemp.com.

Malinda Lo is the author of several young adult fantasy and science fiction novels, most recently *Adaptation*. Her debut novel, *Ash*, a retelling of Cinderella with a lesbian twist, was a finalist for the William C. Morris YA Debut Award, the Andre Norton Award for YA Fantasy and Science Fiction, and the Lambda Literary Award. She lives in Northern California with her partner and their dog. You can visit her online at www.malindalo.com.

Myra McEntire is the author of timeslip novels *Hourglass* and *Timepiece*. She lives in Nashville with her husband and two sons. She likes to make stuff up. You can visit her online at www.myramcentire.blogspot.com.

Saundra Mitchell has been a phone psychic, a car salesperson, a denture deliverer, and a layout waxer. She's dodged trains, endured basic training, and hitchhiked from Montana to California. She teaches herself languages, raises children, and makes paper for fun. She is the author of *Shadowed Summer*, *The Vespertine*, *The Springsweet*, and *The Elementals*. She always picks truth; dare is too easy. You can visit her online at www.saundramitchell.com.

Sarah Ockler is the bestselling author of the young adult novels *Twenty Boy Summer*, *Fixing Delilah*, and *Bittersweet*. She loves to defy the dark by staying up all night in her Colorado home writing, reading, and/or thinking about cupcakes. When she's not busy defying any darkness or licking chocolate batter from a spoon, she enjoys taking pictures, hugging trees, and road-tripping through the country with her husband, Alex. Sarah loves hearing from readers and invites you to connect with her online at www.sarahockler.com.

Jackson Pearce is the author of multiple books for teens, including *Sisters Red*, *Sweetly*, *Fathomless*, and *Purity*. She currently lives in Atlanta, Georgia, and—despite what she writes—admits she is sometimes afraid of the dark. You can visit her online at www.jacksonpearce.com.

Aprilynne Pike is a critically acclaimed, internationally bestselling author. She's been spinning tales since she was a child with a hyperactive imagination. At the age of twenty she received her BA in creative writing from Lewis-Clark State College in Lewiston, Idaho. When not writing, Aprilynne can usually be found out running; she also enjoys singing, acting, reading, and working with pregnant moms as a childbirth educator and doula. Aprilynne lives in Arizona with her husband and four kids; she is enjoying the sunshine. You can visit her online at www.aprilynnepike.com.

Dia Reeves, author of *Bleeding Violet* and *A Slice of Cherry*, is a librarian and lives in a suburb of Dallas, Texas. Her family, however, grew up in East Texas and has inspired her with many tales of the area. The fact that she writes gory, psychotic, romantic, surreal books about happily maladjusted teens who live in East Texas is in no way a reflection on her family. Or is it? You can visit her online at www.diareeves.com.

Beth Revis is the *New York Times* bestselling author of the young adult science fiction novels *Across the Universe* and *A Million Suns*, as well as several other short stories set on the spaceship *Godspeed*. A former high school English teacher, Beth drew inspiration for her novels from her students and their lives—although she took the claustrophobic feeling of being trapped in a small town and enclosed her characters on a spaceship instead. Beth currently lives in rural North Carolina with her husband and dogs, and she believes space is nowhere near the final frontier. You can visit her online at www.bethrevis.com.

Carrie Ryan is the *New York Times* bestselling author of the critically acclaimed The Forest of Hands and Teeth series as well as several short stories. Her first novel was chosen as a Best Book for Young Adults by the American Library Association, named to the 2010 New York Public Library Stuff for the Teen Age List, and selected as a Best of the Best Books by the Chicago Public Library. A former litigator, Carrie now writes full-time and lives with her husband, two fat cats, and one large dog in Charlotte, North Carolina. You can visit her online at www.carrieryan.com.

Jon Skovron is the author of *Struts & Frets* and *Misfit*. He lives with his two sons outside Washington, DC. You can visit him online at www.jonskovron.com.

Courtney Summers lives and writes in Canada. She is the author of *This Is Not a Test, Fall for Anything, Some Girls Are,* and *Cracked Up to Be.* You can visit her online at www.courtneysummers.ca.

Acknowledgments

More than most, this volume owes its existence to the hard work, dedication, and talents of many.

I have to sing the praises of my authors. Each answered a random email asking if she or he would write a story, if, theoretically, I could sell an anthology. Everyone who said yes is published in these pages, and I couldn't be more thrilled about their stories. These authors have been here since the beginning; their work is the heart, soul, and purpose of *Defy the Dark*.

I didn't tell my agent, Jim McCarthy, that I was writing an anthology proposal. I surprised him with it, and I'm grateful that he was excited, not gobsmacked. It made a lot of extra work for him, and it means a lot to me that he undertook it so enthusiastically. He found a perfect champion for *Defy the Dark* in my editor, Anne Hoppe.

By turns funny, insightful, and absolutely assured, Anne is exactly what she needs to be when she needs to be it: an anchor, a rock, a bulldozer. What's more, I don't think another editor would have allowed me so much input, latitude, and autonomy. It's been an exciting, eye-opening process with Anne at the helm; I'm so glad she's the captain of this ship.

I'm also wildly grateful to Estlin Feigley and Dreaming Tree Films. Estlin gave me a start when I was an aspiring screenwriter with nothing on my CV but cobwebs. In the fifteen years we worked together, Estlin never forgot his mission: bringing the art of filmmaking to teens who might not otherwise get the chance. Without Fresh Films, Girls in the Director's Chair, On the Road, Book of Stories, and Estlin Feigley, there would be no *Defy the Dark*.

There would be no brand-new author in *Defy the Dark* if it weren't for the incredible team at HarperCollins and the talents of a wonderful crew at Figment Fiction. It's not easy mounting a search for a new author on short notice, but they did it beautifully. Special thanks to Nina Rastogi, Lindsey Stanberry, Colleen O'Connell, Lauren Flower, Megan Sugrue, and Casey McIntyre. They worked incredibly hard behind the scenes to make this look easy.

For everyone named, and anyone I should have: thank you, thank you, thank you.